The

King's

Gold

Louis Lala

Louis Lala Publisher

Copyright Louis Lala

ISBN: 978-0-9979410-1-2

HIGHBALLS & PALLMALLS

The sun seemed to slow, hesitate at the morning horizon , unsure it wanted to ascend and see what absurd color the polluted atmosphere, the crazed makeup artist, driven mad by the dirt and grime thrown into it by the cars, factories and the metal chimneys of countless suburban homes, would paint it.

John Hamilton stood in the doorway of Pat's Corner Bar with his light cloth coat pulled up around his neck. He hated how seconds seemed to stretch out and crawl when he waited and he was forced to notice his surroundings to pass the time. He'd see things that would be complex, shaded and if he ever shared those observations, it would elicit nothing but unrelenting derisiveness about his masculinity. He did not like that particular kind of narrowness, death by a thousand gibes, in the people around him. It came up more often as he got older and he kept silent more often to conceal his distaste. No matter how he chose to think of it, it felt like time was creeping to a halt. He was cold and wanted the sun on him. He looked for the distraction available, browsing at eye level for anything to scrutinize. Simultaneously he realized he could switch it up by lifting his scans to the tops of the business buildings and homes that mixed uneasily in this area.

It was apparent that what had occurred, and had undoubtedly played out in neighborhoods like this all over the country was a battle between moneyed interests and the far more numerous but modestly settled residents. Homes would be built in groups in pristine bucolic settings. Taxes and fees would be levied on the new home owners to pay for the infrastructure to support the new community. Then, business men, anxious to use the newly installed water, power, roads and sewer facilities would swoop in not too long afterward and with a few palms greased, have the zoning altered and plop a monolithic dirt spewing factory adjacent to the residents. The drive to fill jobs would provide incentive to home builders to develop the area further so they built cheaper less expensive homes for more nomad like clients than the first group of owners and that offered further impetus for other business owners to increase their presence so there ended up a weird mixture of homes injured by the proximity of ugly utility and business degrading the well-being of the very people they relied on to work in their unsightly buildings. A union organizer had given him that history lesson. John recalled feeling like the man was living on another world, a better one than he, and that his observations were undoubtedly spot on but were beyond John's ability to care about or act on. He remembered their meeting making John feel as small as the times he would roll past the local University and wonder how anyone would ever know enough to go there and do something important.

As John thought about the uneasy coexistence of the two worlds he was shocked to note that Pat's Bar had a second story. He realized that he was usually so narrowly focused that despite having walked into the place hundreds of times over the past five years, he had never fully noted that the building that housed the bar was the ultimate in mixture of business and residence. The bar was fitted into what had once been a very sizeable, high quality home. It was a two story frame structure with the bar occupying the entire first floor and the second story mysteriously shut off, windows covered with a dark tint of some kind. John shook his head in amazement that he had never noticed.

His wandering eye, the idle observations, did the trick and picked up the pace. The sun was stoic, but to John's relief, it seemed to have finally accepted it's lot and crept up above the horizon.

The sun's powerful beams threw long morning shadows over the gray, washed out buildings and houses of the poor east side of town. The gray had a depth that matched the golden hue of the first light. John pictured a constant battle brewing for supremacy between the two. The gray teased at textures and hinted at depths while the golden light shown millions of colors and disclosed measures of bountiful intensity. He picked sides- he wanted to feel the golden light pour over and warm him. He felt a few of the frayed edges of his jacket tickling his skin. He was surprised that he was cold. It was early September and it seemed the colder part of autumn had come too soon. Winter and Christmas and the inevitable hustle to scrape his pennies together to get his kid decent gifts would have to begin immediately. Santa, the big load of bullshit, wouldn't be there to help.

He now decided the movement of time was always a clunky lopsided mixture; each day seeming interminable, a long grind, but the months, seasons, years accelerating at a dizzying pace, and he knew he was ill equipped to deal with the ramifications. His body was caught in the dichotomy. He had a baby face, but his youthful countenance had sprouted tiny crow's feet, and hints of lines in the forehead. His straight blond hair had, to his eye, bizarre arbitrary gray hairs popping up every few weeks, his bangs more ill suited to his age by the day. His knees hurt on and off in two to four hours shifts. He had a slight frame but it was covered in tight, mature, efficient muscles. He had just had his thirtieth birthday, and he looked it despite his "baby face."

He shook off the thoughts about his mortality and his miserably long days with a self-deprecating scold that he had no business complaining about his lot. If he wanted a better life, he need only get it, and he had better do it sooner than later. He looked at his watch every minute or so. It was ten minutes to nine and that meant he had been there less than half an hour. John tried to arrive just as Pat opened, which was usually a minute or two before the hour, but today he had awakened in the middle of the darkest early morning hours, around four, and he could not go back to sleep. The air had been strangely humid, and as it spent itself, felt like it conducted nervous energy and sent it crackling around him. He hadn't wanted to wake his girlfriend with his fidgeting and then his pacing so he left. She was unhappy enough with him.

He wondered why Ralph hadn't arrived. He liked talking to him because he was funny and always managed to say something to make him laugh. He couldn't trust him as far as he could throw him, which, considering the guy's diminutive size, he was five inches shorter than John's five feet eight

4

inches, might actually be a few feet, but the man knew how to tell a joke, and he never seemed to be in a bad mood, at least for more than a few minutes at a time so John knew he could count on Ralph for relief from the grind and the intensity of the world around him. John had seen Ralph in a foul mood a mere two times and he knew it was because he had been short on money and hadn't had anything to drink for a day or so. He was never sure how long Ralph could go without, because most times he came into Pat's already half looped, which meant that all of his drinking wasn't done there. Some was done at home, and some was done on the way there.

He knew that was accomplished by way of a silver hip flask he'd pull out during their wait in the morning. John had a gulp or two on occasions when it felt like it was the right thing to do, when the world seemed to have conspired to grate on his nerves. It was always filled with cheap wine that tasted like it might have some sort of cheaper whiskey mixed in with a third ingredient that was so bad he didn't have the guts to ask Ralph what he had just poured into his stomach, a stomach made of mere human flesh. He would silently apologize to his stomach while the foul mixture wracked his insides and soothed his nervous system.

The few times John felt crazy enough to knock down a swig or two from Ralph's grail, he could feel slight edges of flowery letters engraved on the bottom edge of the flask. It occurred to him that despite the four years he had known Ralph, he still didn't know what the engraving said. He felt asking would be prying, and knew that Ralph would not be forthcoming. He knew too that reading it would be offensive to his friend. Despite being hilariously blunt about other's personal foibles, Ralph had numerous subjects he did not want to talk about at all. John would begin talking about subjects like family and love in a very tentative way, sometimes aborting quickly when it seemed Ralph was getting roused.

It was still hard to figure out when he would be honing in on something taboo. Once Ralph pointed out Pat removed all of the trash bags from the cans at the end of each day whether they were full or not. He was incensed over the waste. John started to point out that letting anything stew overnight might create a smell that wouldn't be conducive to business but Ralph sat up straight in indignation before he could get it out. "When I grew up, we couldn't afford trash bags so we'd use old paper bags we'd got from behind the market. They'd get wet, you know with trash juice, and break and the trash cans in the house would stink to hell and don't ask me about pick up day. I was always the one who had to do it." He was pretty plowed so his next "S" was thick. "Suffice to say sometimes I'd wrestle, hand to hand, chunks of what I ate for dinner six freakin' days ago." John knew to shut up. Ralph sighed, "Terrible waste."

John quickly stuck a cigarette in his mouth and lit it, jamming his hands back into his pockets for whatever protection the threadbare material could offer, and scrunched his neck down as far as he could without making it sore. He had noticed that his knees hurt more the past four weeks than they ever had, and figured that his days laying carpet were numbered. He chuckled. He knew in a dark, partially hidden part of his head that he often relieved the feeling of his skin crawling by shoving carpet hard along the floor. His "therapy," the carpet installation, would have to end soon if he valued walking and he wondered how he would push off his creeping discomfort in the aftermath- a shrink? Blackly, he thought he'd have to lay carpet to have enough money to go to a shrink. He knew that the pain in different parts of his back, far more worrisome would probably keep him distracted. It was like the old joke about the guy who goes to a doctor and tells him "My arm hurts." The doctor stomps on his foot. "Ouch, that hurts like the devil," cries the patient. The doctor says, "forgot about the arm though, right?" He could not afford to have his back go out. He gingerly turned his head side to side a few times, trying to limber it up. The cool fall air had started to stiffen his neck.

A mixed feeling of good humor and puzzlement went through him as he spotted movement from the direction that Ralph invariably came. He lived about ten blocks away in a house that rented rooms. Five men rented the rooms on the second floor, and the woman who owned the house lived downstairs with her grandson. The men had to share one bathroom and Mrs. Weddington, the owner, cleaned it. She had decided long ago, when arguments kept erupting over who's turn it was to scrub, or who was the filthiest and the disagreements had became tiresome, she would charge a few dollars more a week and do it herself. The boarders had to fend for themselves for meals by using an approved hot plate, or buying dinner from her. She didn't charge much, but then, the men who rented from her didn't have much, so they rarely took advantage of her cooking, despite the fact that it usually smelled great, wafting out of the kitchen through the living room and up into the second floor- a wistful, aromatic sales pitch. Ralph had stated that he always tried to be out of the house by then so that he wasn't tempted to go down, and as he put it, "get ripped off by old lady Weddington." John figured it was because he didn't want to be tempted by hunger pangs to dip into his drinking money, so around six in the evening was a good time to be sure to catch Ralph at Pat's. Another time was now, first thing.

Pat was one of a few bar owner's in the neighborhood who closed at one AM weeknights and opened again at nine. The state allowed a bar to open at five thirty, and stay open until two thirty the next morning, but Pat had made it clear, despite a few complaints from the early birds, that he would not open until nine. He told them, over and over, that in order to open at nine, he had to be up at six thirty and that he might as well sleep there if he opened at five thirty, and his wife, unhappy enough with him under the current schedule, would divorce him and get the bar in the settlement and turn it into a woman's clothing store, and then where would they be? He invariably ended the story with the moral, nine o'clock is plenty early. Pat had confided to John that another big reason he wouldn't stay open the maximum hours was because he didn't want to encourage the "hard core guys." His view then was that he wasn't going to make money off of desperate alcoholics. It was a line Pat had drawn, a shaky line John felt, but he admired the fact that Pat was willing to forego money for a stand that was obviously a moral one. He put away from his thoughts that those who were drinking at 9 AM were probably not exactly in great shape either, including himself.

John had gotten so he could tell it was Ralph coming by the bouncing gait he had as he charged along. It looked like he was trying to make up for being short by walking off the heals, putting the emphasis on the balls of the feet desperately attempting to add an inch or two with each step he took, and with gravity rudely hauling him back to the ground, the process repeating, heals up, down. Although John never dared joke about it, it made Ralph look like he was pretending to wear high heals.

John had never exactly figured out the crux of Ralph's discomforts, the width and breadth of taboo subjects, but he had developed a sense of when he was approaching them. The pitch in Ralph's voice would rise a bit, and his words would come a little faster than his usual swift banter. John would then switch the conversation to something else, and the signs would disappear. This morning, as usual, he could make out the bounce before he could see the person, but it looked like there was someone with him, which had never happened, so John wasn't sure it was Ralph.

John stared down the street hard trying to make out what was going on. He couldn't afford glasses but he knew he needed them. It felt like he was trying to see the destination banner on the front of a bus, the slow disclosure of the street name as it approached titillating him with the possibilities of destinations unknown.

Finally, he could make out the baseball cap Ralph always wore. It was bright red, although dirt and hair oils had dulled it somewhat. At night, if a light hit it right, it looked like a neon beacon on his head. John found it hilarious that Ralph wore it to cover his baldness, but had picked a hat that drew a crowd's eyes to his head specifically because it was so bright, and then, of course, each person who saw it, would judge him to be hiding a bald head. John had seen Ralph's head one time when he and Ralph had gone to the restroom at the same time to relieve themselves, and Ralph, more drunk than usual had lost his footing on a wet part of the tile, and fell to one knee, his hat flipping off in front of him. For some reason, in spite of the ever-present hat, he had attempted a miserly comb over. Half a dozen unusually long slight strands were plastered over the bald area. They were matted to his head, looking like shakily drawn lines from a permanent marker. Despite how wobbly and looping Ralph's movements had been that night, he picked up his hat with lightning reflexes and put it back on his head in the exact spot it always was, like there was a groove along the ridge of his scalp that allowed him to place it correctly, no matter the extent of his impairment.

At the same time that he made out Ralph's hat, he could see that it wasn't a person with him but some sort of object that he was either carrying or pushing in front of him. John wondered what sort of goofy deal he had going. Ralph was always bargaining, whether it was trying to wheedle a few dollars out of someone for more beer, or attempting to raise money for rent. Ralph had a job at a factory in the neighborhood. It was a corn processing plant that made myriad raw products that became syrups, fibers, fuel and any number of strange products. John joked that he usually smelled like a potato cake. Whenever he'd say it, Ralph had an obligatory retort, "you love potato cakes, doncha big boy." John knew it was a slap at his masculinity. He had decided long ago that some men were jealous of his looks and the best way to deal with it was to ignore it. When he spent a few moments thinking about it, he figured that Ralph spent
his work money for drinking, and that would necessitate the wheeling and dealing, to pay rent and eat what little he did manage to eat. He didn't spend money on much else. He had worn one of two heavy felt plaid shirts for as long as he had known him, and the navy blue pants he wore, he knew were part of his uniform at the corn plant and undoubtedly supplied and replaced by his employer. His coat was beige. It reminded John of a railroad engineer. He'd spot them leaning out the window of the engine, going by at a crossing blowing the horn for all they were worth. It was beige, thick material with sewn edges on the outside making a visible seam, that, in Ralph's case, delineated where the darker dirty part would end and the creamier, lighter brown began. John could imagine one of the tall wide billed engineer caps on Ralph's head to complete the outfit.

Ralph was shabby. Most of the people John knew were dirty most of the time. John made
whatever effort it took to be clean and wear clean clothes. Sometime it would take an entire day

piecing together money for the Laundromat, using an
apartment machine at a friend's or
girlfriend's, walking around, hauling his entire meager
wardrobe with him oftentimes. Sometimes
when he was desperate, he would ask the one friend he had
who owned a house if he could use his
machine. He did it rarely so that he wouldn't alienate him, and
could rely on him at those tough moments. He had wondered
why he was so fussy about his cleanliness when it didn't seem
to bother the others, even Ralph with his odd version of vanity.
When John had been extremely depressed a few years back, he
had let himself go for a few weeks, but realized that it fed his
depression, and when he cleaned up, he started climbing out of
his morass. He tried to stay ahead of his laundry by washing a
few items any time the opportunity arouse, even if he'd just
managed to clean everything, so that on the days when he had
no money or options, he still had a modest stash of clean stuff
to wear.

As Ralph approached, John could see that it was a
vacuum cleaner he rolled along in front of him. When he
figured Ralph was within earshot John shouted "cleaning up at
the racetrack?"

Ralph shouted back in a gravelly voice "Gonna have
you blow me, Mincey Gaynor." John knew it was some sort of
movie reference and that it wasn't nice, but that was all. Ralph
loved watching old movies and war documentaries. It was all
he watched. John knew that if he had inadvertently wandered
into an irritating conversation with Ralph he could
immediately remedy it by literally asking, "Why did Germany
lose WW2?" and Ralph would hold forth in great detail for a
long while.

The typical morning at Pat's was John, Ralph and
Cary sitting at the bar, sipping beer and talking about
whatever. Cary worked the third shift, so this was his stop after
work to unwind. Four months ago, there was another man who
would come in at opening. He was a hard core alcoholic. He
would go to a bar several blocks down that opened at five
thirty, and migrate to Pat's around nine thirty, because, as he
explained, "the bastard down the street charges twenty cents a

shot more than Pat." John and his cohorts believed it was because he had worn out his welcome at the other bar by nine. He was desperately miserable, and drinking usually made him more so.

The three men were able to keep him from ruining their morning ritual by letting him moan and complain until there was a lull, which would come about fifteen or twenty minutes in, and without addressing anything the guy said, they would start or continue their conversation, avoiding eye contact with him. This seemed acceptable to the sour man, who would proceed to stare intensely at the wood on the bar, and drink steadily, sipping every five to ten seconds, as though trying to drown tiny petty little grudges one at a time, in hopes that at the end, the slate would be clean and he would be drunk.

The guy had a lot of physical problems. There were a number of times when he would go back to the restroom and vomit. Pat mentioned once, a bit subdued, that he'd spotted blood on the side of the bowl where the guy had puked. He seemed to be in pain when he'd get up on the stool, and seemed to move as little as possible while he sat there, wincing occasionally. The three wondered if he had cancer. He'd smoke the entire time even though he had a chronic, vigorous cough.

After three months or so of daily visits, he missed a day. The next day, when he came in he was pastier looking than usual. Pat asked him if he was ok. The guy looked insulted, and told him he was fine. When Pat persisted, saying that they'd missed him the previous day, he looked bewildered, and mumbled something about a cold, and said nothing more the entire time he was there, sipping and staring. When he stood to leave, he waved back at the three men, short and fast, but they all saw it happen because he had never done it before. He might as well have jumped up and down and howled his farewell, it was so out of the ordinary. He didn't come in the next day, or any day after. No one talked about the guy. Pat had seemed distressed at the man's presence, alternating between a barely discernable frown, to a vexed sideways look.

After three days, Ralph finally said something. "Where's Sippy?" The other three men laughed together. He'd given them permission to talk about him.

"Do you think Pat pissed him off, interrogating him?" John winked and nodded in Pat's direction.

Pat, working on some invoices he had spread out on the bar a few feet away looked up and groused, "I did not interrogate him. I just asked if he was sick. It's like asking about the weather, how's the family. You know- concern."

Cary ran his finger around the rim of his glass. He didn't like drinking his beer out of the bottle like Ralph and John. "I think he's dead."

Pat didn't go back to his paperwork, "Do we even know what his last name is?"

They looked at John. He was the go-to guy on personal information. They often joked that he was a good listener, which he was, but they said it about him as another attempt to undermine his manhood. "I have no idea. You guys heard everything that I did. He always talked like he was addressing the masses. He didn't talk one on one did he?"

"Who cares," Ralph waved it off, scooting around on his stool, as though he was looking for a higher spot. "He was a prick."

"He wasn't exactly a charmer, that's for sure." Pat turned around and picked up a phone he had on the back bar. It was an old dial phone. They regularly ribbed him that he needed to spend a few dollars and get a button phone, which was hopelessly out of date too, but less so- that was the second part of the joke. Pat always replied that the one he had worked fine. What he didn't say, (except to John),was that he didn't bring in a better phone because he knew no one liked the phone, so he figured it cut down on requests for personal calls. Pat usually obliged his regulars, it didn't cost him extra, but he didn't want the whole neighborhood walking in and lining up to use it. His fears weren't completely baseless. He'd told John that each morning, when he drove by the diner, which was cattycornered a few blocks away, he noted a pay phone outside of it was always in use, with one or two people in line behind the person using it. It was the only pay phone that worked in a several block area. When a pay phone was vandalized, it typically took six months to forever for the phone company to come out and replace the broken unit. John wondered why. By his figuring, they probably made more money on those machines in the crummier neighborhoods than a lot of other places. Cell phones had superseded the old public phones but Pat wasn't aware of it.

Pat dialed. "I'm gonna call Mike and see what he knows." He was referring to the man who owned the bar down the street that opened at five thirty. John pictured it. It was in a little prefab concrete block of a place- hard core for hard core- a concrete room for the stone cold drunks. "Hey Mike. It's Pat. Yeah, I'm good. Oh, I know, you can bet that they'll raise our fees. They don't call it a tax, but... yup, write a check anyway. It's as sure as the sun comin' up. Nah. Hey, they're all the same. Listen, I have a question. You know the fellow, uh, his first name's Bob, that, no, yeah, the grumpy one. He gets there at five thirty, yeah, wears the old black trench coat, well, that's what we were wondering. No, he hasn't been here for three, four days now. Really? Do you know his last name? You think it's what? Glass, Glazer? Something like that. Yeah, probably doesn't have a phone. What use would he have for it. No one would want to talk to him." Pat frowned without realizing it. "Yeah, well, I just wondered if you'd heard anything about him, because we thought maybe he might be more forthcoming at the crack of dawn. We guessed he's sick, some way. No, nada, zip. Yeah, ok. Take care. Talk to you soon. Bye now." He hung up, shrugging. "Nope. He's gonna be a mystery. If he comes in again, we've got to ask him his last name."

"If he comes in again, he's gonna be a zombie and we're gonna have to shove a long neck up his ass to kill him again" Ralph scooted around on his stool and looked at John with a mischievous grin. "Yup, most people think it's a bullet through the head to kill a zombie but its actually a bottle past the anus."

"What's a matter Ralph," Cary leaned back watching him, "you have hemorrhoids?"

John could tell that the joke wasn't Ralph's cup of tea. "You're the pain in my ass. I can feel your squeeter dick probing." John knew that he would have added more insult and disparagement to the remark if he hadn't been upset by it. The hemorrhoid guess was probably true. John felt he was in charge of changing the subject to keep Ralph from becoming dour. No one else seemed to see the pattern. He would ask about something different and the conversation could barrel off into safe territory. The mysterious fourth patron and Ralph's hemorrhoids would quickly be forgotten. John was glad that it had gone back to the three of them opening.

John wondered how his intellect compared to Ralph's. There were so many times when he would talk to Ralph, and explain something to him, only to have Ralph look at him with disappointment. "I'm not a butt wipe, John. I know that." There would be a bit of hurt in his reply. John wondered if it was Ralph's little boy traipse that made him underestimate his intelligence on a regular basis, or if he supposed that the alcohol had robbed him of it, he couldn't tell, but he continued to do it, luckily not often enough to permanently alienate Ralph.

Ralph had got rolling the vacuum cleaner down to a science, up and over curbs without banging it around. He rolled up to John and pulled the appliance to the side of the building like it was a riding horse, stopping it and then backing it to the wall. "Whoa Nelly. Good girl."

"John, what's up?" he smiled wide, knowing that John wanted the story behind the vacuum cleaner. John noted he was sober- he didn't have tell tale bags under his eyes.

"What's up with the vacuum cleaner?" John smiled, feeling lighter and happier already. He was anxious to be entertained. It was better than the movies. He couldn't afford the movies anyway. He took a deep drag on his cigarette waiting for an answer.

Ralph motioned with his arm, a sort of hand signal that had developed when he wanted to bum a cigarette from John, which was, by John's accounting, one of every two cigarettes that Ralph smoked. He never seemed to have any when John needed to bum one. John felt the cigarettes were a small price to pay for being able to hang around Ralph and enjoy himself. He gave him one. Ralph lit it with a silver lighter. It dawned on John that the flask and the lighter were a set. He wondered if there was an inscription on the lighter too.

Ralph always answered questions, even simple ones, like he was telling a story. He would begin with a prologue of sorts, an introduction to the tale unfolding and of the characters involved in the story, and often, a joke. "Blow jobs for sale, sailor." He looked at John for the obligatory smile before he proceeded. "Well, you know how dirty my place gets, since Mrs. Weddington only cleans the bathroom, and not our rooms, and she checks 'em all the time. She refuses to clean the floors, and she won't let us use her vacuum cleaner. She's afraid we'll break it, and she made it real clear that she couldn't afford to replace it if one of us broke it, and I tried using that hokey dokey deal. You remember that?"

John shook his head no.

"Well, it's a little black deal, I got it from work. It folds up pretty small, so I could take it out under my coat. I gotta clean the place, see, anyway, the damn thing didn't work worth a damn. The roller was worn out and the ass hole janitor at work apparently didn't see fit to replace it. He just moved the dirt around with it. Job security I guess he figured. So, I talk to my sister and she lets me have this vacuum cleaner that she had sitting in a back room. I cleaned my room and now I'm gonna sell it."

"What about the next time?"

"It's been two years since I vacuumed. I figure I've got another two years before she gripes again, and hell, we could all be dead in two years. Dust bunnies in heaven, man."

John laughed. He pulled the cigarette out of his mouth and looked at it. He needed to cut back. "I guess so. Who you gonna sell it to?"

"Hell, I don't know yet. But I'm gonna cut a good deal for whoever does. I'll throw in the hoker to sweeten the pot."

"But you said it doesn't work."

"Oh, I'll tell 'em they have to replace the roller. It ain't busted. Cheaper to buy a roller than the whole thing."

The two men heard Pat moving around inside. "Hey, Pat", Ralph jumped up and down, like it would help throw his voice through the wall, "let us in. We got money to spend, man!"

They could hear him reply but not what he said. They knew he wouldn't open the doors until he had completed all the tasks that he finished before he considered himself and his bar ready for business. "Hey, Pat, stop conkin' that red hair of yours- the Queen of England's out here and she's thirstin' for a Guinness!" He paused like he was listening to the Queen. "She says she'll take a Bud Light with dirt in it if that's all ya got!" Both men laughed.

The sound of the dead bolt and second lock being released surprised them both. It was five until nine and it was rare for Pat to open five minutes early. He opened the door wide, standing in the middle of the entryway. Ralph jumped back, holding his hand over his head, pretending to protect himself from blows. Pat looked up and down the block. "Don't spread it around that I opened early, or you guys will be standing out here 'til you're ninetieth birthdays before I let you in again."

Ralph moved ahead of John quickly, vacuum cleaner rolling up in front of him. "Your secret is safe with us b'wana."

After the two had walked in, Pat stood looking around outside. Ralph and John were puzzled. Pat turned to them. "Where's the Queen?"

John and Ralph looked at each other in disbelief. Pat was usually bad at jokes. They both laughed. "Nice job." Ralph mumbled. Pat grinned.

He looked back at Ralph, giving his vacuum cleaner the once over. "I'm not your b'wana
and what the hell are you bringing into my bar?"

Ralph got serious fast. "It's a fabulous vacuum cleaner, man. It has all the different settings, and a light on front and the bags are easy to get, and cheap, and it's really strong. It sucked up every little spec of dirt on my floor."

Pat kept moving toward the bar as he replied. "So why are you getting rid of it, if it's so great?"

"Oh I don't really need it. I just fell into it from my sister. She had it sittin' around and
gave it to me."

"How much you want for it?"

"You interested, Pat?"

"Yeah, actually, I might be. That old hunk of crap I have in the back works about half the time."

"Well, boss. I have what you need right here."

Ralph stood in the middle of the bar moving the cleaner back and forth, as if to illustrate how great a person would look at the controls of the fabulous cleaning device he offered. Pat stepped behind the bar and took two beers out. He put one in front of John, who had sat down on his usual stool, and put one where Ralph always sat. "Come sit down. I'll look at it in a minute."

"Where you want me to park it, chief?" He kept rolling it back and forth.

"Just stick it over there," he motioned to the corner near the door to his office. Ralph rolled it over quickly, removed his coat, draped it over his stool, that's what they all did, and took his seat. He took a long drink from his beer. John had noticed he always went through the first beer within a couple minutes and then slowed down drinking the innumerable bottles after that. John figured it was a constant tug of war between chintziness and alcoholism with Ralph.

"I have to call the a/c people today. This cooler isn't keeping this stuff cold like usual. Don't you guys think so?"

"It does seem like they been warmer the last couple of days." John noted.

"Why didn't you say something?"

John looked down at the bar, a sheepish expression on his face. "Well, we thought maybe you turned it down to save money, or something." It was easy to feel small and foolish in front of Pat. He was six foot four, red gray wiry hair that looked like it had been teased to add another inch to his already imposing height. He had a late middle age paunch, but his arms, shoulders and chest were as massive and strong as any young football player's. He always wore a white dress shirt with the sleeves unbuttoned and folded up his forearm, and even though he wore it with casual beige trousers, the white shirt added to the formal, authoritative aura he had. It was "civilized tough." Pat's cheeks were red, and a little rough , probably from a serious bout of teenage acne. John noted that Ralph had the same pits, but they were far worse, and on occasion, one would still erupt in a black head or small red pimple.

Pat looked at them surprised, "What in the world would possess you to think that I would do something as short sighted as serve warm beer to save a couple of dollars?" He shook his head.

John looked at Ralph. He didn't know if or how he should reply. Ralph, barely moving his head, looking straight ahead, shook his head no. They sat drinking quietly.

Ralph jumped up. "Hey, I could probably fix that for ya, Pat."

"And how could you do that?"

"I worked for Pretekin up there, " he motioned into the air, " the heating place for four
months."

"And that qualifies you?"

"Well, no it don't exactly, but I can see if I can spot what's wrong."

Pat looked at Ralph for a few seconds. "You can look at it, but do not, I repeat, do not do
anything until you show me."

"No problem, chief."

Ralph drank the rest of his first beer in one gulp, jumped up like he had a spring in his ass, and scurried behind the bar. "Where's the works, oh there." Pat stood over him watching. Once he was convinced that Ralph was not going to start fiddling with anything, that he was merely looking at it, he opened another beer, replacing Ralph's empty one, and then walked over to the vacuum cleaner. He took it to his office in the back and tried it out.

Ralph stood up just as Pat came out of his office. He had left the vacuum cleaner in his office. John knew it was negotiating time. "Find anything wrong?"

Ralph looked skeptical. "I'm not sure. You might have a leak. What do you usually keep the thermostat set at?"

"To be honest, I don't know. I never move it." Pat came over to where Ralph stood and they both stared into the little opening where the cooling unit's electrical and mechanical workings were.

"I think what you should do is turn the temperature down just a little, and see if that does anything. Maybe it got bumped. If there's a leak in the coolant, turning the temperature down isn't going to help. It'll just run a lot more."

"What if I freeze everything?"

"Oh, I don't think that you should turn it very much, just a degree or two."

"I could ask Stan what it should be set on."

Ralph nodded in agreement. "Yeah, you talkin' about the delivery guy?"

"Right." Pat put his hand on Ralph's shoulder. "Thanks for trying to help."

"Hey chief, I got your back."

Pat took his arm off of Ralph's shoulder and motioned for him to take his seat. "Go on and sit down." Ralph moved out from behind the bar. "I'll turn the temperature down two degrees and see if that changes anything." After he turned the knob, they heard the refrigeration unit kick on. "Hey, maybe you guessed it, Ralph." Pat proceeded to put the cover back on the cooler. He frowned. "Damn, am I losing it? It seems so simple."

Ralph leaned back on his seat a little, "That's what trained people do. Make things simple that are complicated for other people. Mighta saved you a hundred dollars." He winked at John.

Pat stood up. "We'll see what happens." He turned his head to the office and then back.
"Ok, fifty dollars."

"For the vacuum?"

"Yeah."

"Aw, come on Pat. It works ok, doesn't it?"

John wondered if Ralph actually used it before he brought it to the bar.

"Yeah, just like you said."

"Well, hell, an industrial cleaner would be hundreds, and you can tell that it's still got
plenty of life in it. My sister wanted a floor canister, and that's why she doesn't use that one
any more. It still works fine."

"I can buy a brand new vacuum cleaner for a hundred dollars Ralph."

"Not like this one. It's two hundred and fifty dollars if you bought it new. Those hundred
dollar ones are crap. They wouldn't last more than a couple months. My sister had this thing for a year and it never gave her a bit of trouble, like I said, she wanted..."

"Yeah, I know, a canister. Ok, sixty dollars. You wouldn't get more than twenty at a pawn
shop."

Ralph looked at John. John shrugged. "Don't get me in it."

Ralph stared at John for a second. John knew that stare. It was the witty come back stare. "You wouldn't fit in it. Go to Coney Island if you want a ride."

Pat picked up the telephone and started dialing a number. Ralph started fidgeting. John loved watching the two men dicker but he hated dickering himself. He couldn't fight for a bargain. He'd been with a girlfriend once who held up a line at a K Mart for ten minutes to get two dollars off an item that she had insisted was scanning at the wrong price. After two price checks, the manager refused to give her the reduction. She said then she didn't want anything they had then. She had four small items so John didn't think her threat would work. The manager said that it was her choice to buy it or not. She replied that she wanted to see the general manager of the store. The manager glanced at the line behind her and said between clenched teeth to the register clerk, "Give it to her. Use key twenty six."

As they headed out the door of the K Mart, John asked her why she was so adamant. She looked at John like he was crazy. "There was a sign right next to it and the price was two dollars less. They need to be honest."

What John understood was that since they had dared to put a sale sign on a different item adjacent to the item she wanted to buy, it opened the door for negotiation. He also realized that she knew that with people lining up behind her at the check out, her position was getting stronger with each minute that passed, and she wasn't about to back down. John quietly decided that in exchange for the ten minutes they stood there, he would have gladly paid the two extra dollars. He turned red thinking that he would have stolen it at some point earlier in his life rather than do what she did, but then, that's why he had spent a year in jail, and he had no intention of repeating that again. He did not like to barter, but he knew that with what little money he made, he should develop a taste for it. He wondered if he expected to soak it up just by hanging around Ralph. He hadn't so far. A penny on the ground was found treasure, but he couldn't dig down in himself to find a man who would dicker.

Pat stared at Ralph as he waited for his call to go through. "Hey, Janie." He had called his wife. "Do we have an old vacuum cleaner I can use here at the bar?" John thought Ralph would bounce up and down in his seat further and further until his head broke through the crumbly ceiling plaster, but instead he stopped and calmly drank his beer. John was excited by the back and forth and happy he had nothing to do with it. It was like the autumn wind he could hear blowing around the building outside. It was bracing with strong currents but it didn't have anything to do with him.

Ralph turned to John, speaking loud enough for Pat to hear. "He thinks he's yanking my chain, but I don't have to sell it to him. I'm doing him a favor selling it to him, and I think he'll figure it out." John knew that if it had been any one else but Pat, Ralph would have tacked on a rude remark about his heritage or sexual preferences, but because it was Pat he didn't add the disparaging color, at least, not to his face. Even if Pat was out of earshot, Ralph tended to pull his verbal punches regarding Pat. John supposed it was because he was worried that someone might pass the remark back to Pat. It was hard to keep secrets in the bar. Ralph was not about to bite the hand that "fed" him, so to speak. Plus, everyone liked or respected Pat, even, grudgingly, Ralph.

Pat smiled. "Ok, honey. That's fine. Thanks. No, about four, ok. Bye." Pat left for dinner at four. He had his nephew on his wife's side, Paul, tend the bar late and most weeknights. Pat tried not to live at the bar, but he had confided to John that when he wasn't he felt like he was missing something momentous, and even though he knew it was nonsense the feeling was strong and compelling and he tended not to fight it. He mentioned, in passing once, that his wife wanted to take a vacation, but Pat didn't feel comfortable taking two weeks off. That remark lead John to realize that no matter who came and went at the bar, who got drunk early, late or at all, who lie in bed at home sleeping off what they had overdone, Pat was almost certainly at the bar taking care of business.

It didn't snow much in their part of the Midwest, but when they did have a hellacious snowstorm two years ago, John remembered trudging to the bar through a few feet of snow, figuring he had lost his mind because there was no way Pat would open. The factory he worked at wasn't opening that day. He had walked there to find out. There was one harried secretary, still in her rubber boots, making and taking calls from employees and suppliers and anyone else who chose to continue doing business in the midst of a blizzard. He didn't have a phone, so the only way he could find out if they planned on opening was to walk there and check. He had proceeded to Pat's from there. There were a few cars sliding, spinning and stuck on the road and no one was out shoveling. It was coming down too hard to start digging out.

Sure enough, when he arrived at the bar around ten and leaned against the worn metal push plate, the door opened into a nice warm bar, with Pat sitting listening to the weather reports on a little radio he had brought out from his office. John had asked him what time he had managed to get there, and Pat replied, as if it was a foolish question, "same time as always. I just left about an hour earlier. I watched the weather report last night."

Seeing the radio he had pulled from his office into the bar told John it was an unusual day. Last year, about this time, Pat broke down and put an old color television up in the corner on a make shift stand he nailed in place. He had retired a radio five years earlier that had been on in perpetuity like the flame at Kennedy's grave. He had resisted putting anything new in, saying that he didn't want to have to deal with fights over channels, and he didn't want to interfere with anyone who wanted to chat, that most people came there to get away from television and radio, that human contact was better for everyone anyway. John had been surprised that Pat viewed the bar as a sort of social institution, a place where something nobler than drinking alcohol happened. John hadn't felt that way or thought that way, but figured maybe Pat was right, to a point. When Pat put a juke box in the past month, John wondered if he had changed his mind about the purpose of his bar, or if he wasn't making enough money and figured he needed another draw to stay afloat. Since he usually refused to plug the thing in before seven PM, John figured it was a mix of both his old philosophy and the reality that many of his customers couldn't afford a CD player, and this was where they could listen to music. Music was a social lubricant in some ways, too.

Pat hung up the phone. "Ok, ok. You made your point Ralph. I'll give you seventy dollars." Ralph raised his rear end ever so slightly off the stool. John figured the deal was done, but then he knew the negotiations always went further than he ever imagined.

"Give me a hundred and I'll throw in a great little hokey. It just needs a new roller."

"What do I need a hokey and a vacuum cleaner for?"

John thought Ralph had mis-stepped, but he didn't miss a beat. "The hokey is for when you want to clean up while you're open. The vacuum cleaner's for after you close or before you open. The hokey doesn't make noise, so it wouldn't piss off your customers who want to talk." John figured that Ralph had stored away Pat's little story about why he had held off on the TV for so long. It was the only revelation of Pat's that John had told Ralph. He felt himself break out in a sweat hoping that Pat wouldn't put the two together. He didn't.

Pat shook his head. "Jesus, Ralph. A hundred dollars?" He kept shaking his head while he opened John's second beer. With regular customers, Pat never asked if they wanted another drink, he would just bring the next one when they were nearly finished with the one in front of them, and he never asked them to pay until they were ready to leave. John had never seen Pat write anything down to keep track of who got how many of what. He figured he had a photographic memory, until one night when a fairly new regular had gotten belligerently drunk and questioned the amount Pat said he owed, Pat told him to come with him. John wondered if he was going to take the guy in the back and break his nose. Pat grabbed the guys arm, and yanked him up like he was a skinny forty pound child, took him over to a tray he put the empty bottles in and said "Those are your empty bottles. You count 'em." The guy looked at Pat with a puzzled expression. John guessed that he probably thought Pat was going to sock him one too. "Oh, I'm sorry. I'm sorry Pat." The guy had sobered up substantially during the walk from the table to the rack where the bottles were lined up. "Hey," he took money out of his pocket, "Here's for the beer I drank, and a tip, and I think that I could use one more on my stack there."

Pat refused his money. "You sit down, and when you are ready to leave, you can pay me. I'd suggest though, that this next beer is your last one tonight. If you're a mean drunk, I don't want you drunk in my bar. " Everyone understood that Pat was telling the guy that he would not be welcome if he ever pulled his nasty attitude out again. The guy was cowed, and had not dared pull the same stunt again.

"Ralph," Pat pronounced as he opened another beer, "I will give you eighty dollars if you
throw in the hokey, and I'll give you twenty dollars on your tab, and I'm only doing it because you
offered to look at the cooler, and I appreciate that."

Ralph wasn't happy that Pat had mentioned the cooler. He figured that would be a
bargaining chip at another time on another deal on another day. He didn't think it was fair to
include it now. John had watched Ralph enough to know that. He figured Pat did too.

Cary walked in. "Hey fellas, cold enough out there for ya?"

Pat looked up and smiled. "Hey Cary." He opened the cooler and pulled out Cary's
regular beer, putting it on the bar where Cary always sat, which was to the left of John. Ralph
was on John's right.

Cary picked up the bottle, giving it a mock inspection. "Hey, this ain't Coors."

Pat grinned. "We don't serve non union beers here."

This was a little dance that had played out before. Cary smiled. "But it tastes great."

"Less filling," Ralph mumbled.

Cary wondered why Pat would say things that seemed to be anti-union, yet he would not stock a beer that wasn't delivered or made by union workers. Cary always insinuated that it was just a show to please the customers, and Pat always insinuated that Cary didn't care one way or the other, he just made the remark to try to embarrass him, and that if he had ever been in a union, maybe Pat would take his question seriously. Ralph butted in, hoping to short circuit the normal course of the conversation. "Hey, Cary." Ralph grabbed his beer bottle and swung it back and forth by the neck, "This is a man's beer. Coors is fag piss."

John thought the joke was flat, but it succeeded in breaking the normal flow of the banter.
He leaned over to Cary. "Ralph and Pat are dickering. Better sit back and relax."

Cary looked at Pat, and back at Ralph. "A thought came to me, but I'm gonna keep quiet."

"Smart move, Einstein." Ralph returned his attention to Pat. "I'll tell you what. I really didn't expect anything from the cooler. I don't really know if I fixed your problem, and if I did, well fine, but I don't think I did anything you should give me credit for yet."

Ralph had essentially removed the cooler from the bargain through a show of false modesty. "I'll take eighty five, hokey thrown in, and the beer, which we both know doesn't cost you twenty dollars."

Pat laughed. "Yeah, I would say that if I didn't know that, I wouldn't have the bar." He shook his head. "Ok Ralph. You got a deal."

Ralph put out his hand. "Ok chief. It's a deal." Pat rolled his eyes. Ralph kept his hand thrust out. "Come on. Let's shake on it. It's official."

Pat shook his head, shook Ralph's hand, then pulled cash out of the till. "This is what makes it official, Ralph." He flipped the edge of a small stack of bills with his finger, then counted out the money into Ralph's hand. John noticed that there was a slight tremor in Ralph's hand as Pat counted the money into it. He stopped momentarily. "Where's the hokey?"

"I can run home and get it." Ralph started to jump off the stool . They were still negotiating.

"You don't have it here?" Pat grinned.

"I'm out the door chief, or I can bring it in tomorrow, when I come in to spend money in
your bar."

"Ok, Ralph." He motioned for him to sit back down.

Ralph hopped back on his stool. "I just need another fifty bucks and I can get my car." Ralph put his hand out for a high five. For the past few years, John knew that Ralph had been talking about trying to buy a car he had set his sights on. He had never mentioned a desire to have a car before that. He walked to his job, he walked to Pat's and when he wanted to visit his only relative in town, his sister, he would take the bus, and he never complained about it. It seemed to John, that it was a dream that Ralph probably felt comfortable with. He figured this guy wasn't thinking about climbing Mount Everest, or curing cancer. A car to drive around in would do. But he figured it was a pipe dream of sorts. He was floored that Ralph had announced that he had saved the money he needed to buy his dream.

"You, have, you've saved?...." John was known to be quiet, but not at a loss for words.

Ralph smiled wide. "I have been busting to tell you. I just worried about all the yahoo's around here gabbing about it, and it getting back to the wrong people."

John was hurt. "Jesus Ralph. You couldn't trust me?"

Ralph looked surprised. "No, no. I couldn't trust myself. I felt that if I told anyone, I'd tell everyone. Like a dam holdin' it back. One crack, and it's pissy pants time."

John hesitatingly accepted Ralph's explanation, although all the efforts he made to keep from prying into the parts of life Ralph was sensitive about, flowed through his mind, aggravating him that this little weasel had no idea how circumspect he was with everything he said to or disclosed about him. His secret would have been safer with him than Ralph himself. Now that the news was out, John wanted to oblige with the questions that would allow Ralph to brag, plus he was genuinely curious how this guy had secretly ascended to the place where his dream goal was in hand. "Fifty bucks is all you need? Wow! Does that include the plates and insurance and all that?"

"It doesn't include the insurance. I figure I can go without that for a little while."

"That's kinda risky."

"Oh, I won't let it go too long. I'll be careful."

John suddenly realized that his friend, who was regularly drunk, would be getting behind the wheel of a car soon. "Man, you aren't gonna drink and drive are you?"

"Nah, man." He looked away from John. "I'll be careful."

Cary had always had a car. He had a decent job and saved every dime he could. He didn't seem to drink heavily, and he currently had a girlfriend who worked and had a decent apartment, so he had moved in with her and wasn't paying rent. He was as good as rich in this neighborhood. "You need fifty bucks? That's all?"

"Yeah, that's all I need."

Cary looked wistful. He leaned over and pulled out his wallet. He pulled a fifty dollar
bill out of his pocket, and handed it to Ralph. "There ya go. Happy motoring."

John was tired. He didn't want to get up at four that morning, but his body had decided that he would. He wanted to have a nice light morning with Ralph and Cary, to counter the pain and tedium of work, but something seemed to be weighing Cary down, and Ralph was now more distracted than usual. John considered blowing off work for the day. His neighbor had told him about the job and he had been working it for a couple of weeks. He and his co-workers were alone and unsupervised in a huge building the majority of the time, so he felt he could get a little buzz before he went in, but today he felt like he needed something more than that. He knew he could get away with skipping. His boyish good looks would see him through. They seemed to affect men and women the same way, providing a seemingly endless supply of good will toward him. There was an occasional down side to being handsome. Because he wasn't tall and bulky, a lot of fat red necks would misjudge how strong he was, and in their jealousy figure he would be an easy target for teasing and challenges but it was a mistake. John had reluctantly knocked the crap out of guys twice his size.

His youthful appearance, everything from his blond hair, regularly falling into bangs, to the classic dimple in the chin, had made him a prime target for the tough guys in prison too. They also misjudged how strong he was, and quickly learned that he was not someone with which to mess. He didn't purposefully trade his looks for what he wanted, but it had a habit of falling in his lap, and he wouldn't refuse it. Today he felt like taking advantage of it. If the boss got mad at him for missing, he'd talk his way out of it, or he'd just get another job.

John knew that Cary was better off than most of the regulars there, but he had never offered to loan anyone money and for some reason, no one asked him. Now, all of a sudden, he had handed Ralph fifty dollars. Cary had a dark look, black

curly hair, a tall lanky body, big eyebrows, he almost looked like an Arab or a Jew, one of the middle easterners John would come into contact with every once in a blue moon. He had a beautiful girl friend who was obviously smitten with him, despite the fact that Cary really didn't have all that much on the ball. He worked at a freight handling service at the airport for the past year. They paid him a decent differential for working the third shift, but he had poor health insurance, and the work was grueling, and repetitive. John wondered how such a skinny guy could do such hard physical
work.

"Hit the lottery, Cary?", John knew something was out of place.

"No. Somebody oughta get their dream though. Might as well be Ralph."

"You betcha by golly, wow!" bellowed Ralph. "Thank you man, thanks so much. This is
freaking fabtabulous. Shit, I'm gonna go get the money and buy it right now." He stood up.

Cary waved him back to his seat. "Hey, that car has been there for years. It'll
wait a couple more hours. Sit with us and have a few."

Ralph literally turned in circles, jumping off the ground a few inches as he did, in a strange almost dance-like movement, looking for all the world like a gnome under a bridge who had tricked a traveler into giving him all his gold and silver. "Ok, man. Ok. It's definitely something to celebrate. A car. Damn. This is amazing."

Cary could see he wasn't going to calm down. "Sit down, sit down. Tell us what kind it is."

Ralph stopped jumping around and leaped onto his seat. "It's a Chevy Vega. I know, I know it's old and not such a hot car, but this thing has been sitting in a garage for twenty years."

"It hasn't been run in twenty years?"

"No, no. He turns it on to keep it running, and he has me change the oil regularly. He doesn't want it any more. It doesn't have any rust and it only has 45000 miles on it. He told me that if a collector would see it, they might give him thousands, but he likes me and he never did put an ad out for it, so he told me I could have it for a thousand dollars."

Cary crushed his spent cigarette in the ash tray in front of him. "A twenty five year old Vega? A thousand dollars? Man, I really don't know much about cars, but that seems like a rip off."

Ralph shook his head vigorously. "No, No man. He said I could turn around and sell it for at least ten times what I'm paying."

"He might be right." John recalled a conversation he had with a total car nut while he was in jail. He'd said that cars everyone thought were the uncoolest, junkiest cars in the seventies were now collector's items. The guy explained that part of the reason was because they were bombs so they didn't make a lot of them. That meant there weren't that many to find any more- the holy grail of collecting. He mentioned how much someone could get for a Corvair, the model that Ralph Nadar made his name trashing because of it's tendency to roll. John recounted this.

"Yeah", Ralph jumped up and down, "they had aluminum in the body or frame or somethin' and the engine made it too heavy on one end so it would flip."

Cary shrugged, losing interest, "To each his own. Enjoy your car."

"You can bet I will, and then maybe I'll sell it for a profit and get me a nicer, newer car."

John looked at Ralph suspiciously. "Do you have a driver's license?"

"No, but I can get one."

"You don't have insurance, and you don't have a driver's license."

Ralph drank his beer in big gulps. Since Pat had given him the tab, John noticed that
he began to drink faster. "I'll get that stuff mommy. Jesus, I'm not stupid. I just don't have
any money after I pay for the car."

"You gonna drive to the license bureau without a license? That's not such a good idea."
John was thinking about Ralph behind the wheel of the car, wrecked into a tree, bleeding and
unconscious.

"Hey, don't be a spoil sport. Let's be happy for Ralph." Cary was sullen.

"What's wrong? You are one sullen son of a bitch I have to say," John asked it point blank.

Cary had lit another cigarette and was taking a long leisurely drag on it. "Well, Deb's
pregnant." He let the smoke trail out of his mouth and nose like an indifferent dragon. "She told me last night."

John had a sinking feeling. A baby meant a whole different world. He could see that Cary had already thought a lot about what was coming. Sleepless nights, doctor bills, clothes, diapers, school, marriage, or a ruined relationship and on and on. John had gotten a girl pregnant when he was seventeen. She was sixteen, and her parents were furious. John's father had left his mother when he was three, as John grew up, his mother had descended into alcoholism. They were always in financial straits and his mother tended to close herself up as failed jobs and relationships mounted, leaving John to guess about what was going on, how life was supposed to work, what school was for, everything that surrounded him every day. He thought that it was probably then that he had developed his habit of staying quiet, and watching everything around him. It felt the safest. He didn't realize that he could get the girl pregnant when he started having sex with her. His daughter was thirteen now. Her name was Darlene, the mother's choice, and from what John could see, she seemed to be doing ok.

He attributed that to the mother's parents. His girlfriend had no idea what to do, being little more than a child herself, so her parent's essentially sat John down a few days after they found out she was pregnant and told him that not only did they expect nothing from him, they preferred that he not come around, that he not be involved in the child's rearing. They would take care of the baby and their daughter and John could and should go on his merry way. John had no job at the time, and no idea what he could do, so he had reluctantly agreed, although he immediately went out and got a job, and started buying baby clothes and furniture from second hand shops. He worked at a warehouse, so he would pay a few dollars to have them ship the stuff to the grandparents house. He always put a little note in the box thanking the girl's parents for helping make right a wrong he had done. He never heard from them despite putting the address and phone number of his mother's apartment on the note and the cartons. He found out a few months after the baby was born that they had called, but his mother had neglected to tell him. He was never sure if it was the alcohol that made her forget, or she preferred he not have anything to do with his new, estranged family. He had been sitting in his bedroom one night when he heard her answer the phone, and mention that he was not home. He ran into the living room and waved his arms in front of her. She hesitated, haltingly corrected herself and handed the phone to him. His girlfriend started yelling at him as soon as he spoke. She asked why he had blown off her parents and their attempts to contact him, and he replied, flabbergasted, that he hadn't known that they had called. His mother had wandered off into the kitchen where he saw her sit at the table, reading a tattered novel and clutching an ever present beer. She had become fairly heavy, and he had to occasionally delicately nudge her into taking baths and keeping her clothes clean. Sometimes John felt he over compensated because he always kept his clothes sparkling clean. He used an old iron and board that he found under the bed to remove every single wrinkle on every square inch of his trousers and shirts, no matter how old or worn the clothes. He learned hard lessons about hot water, bleach, and starch, but he always looked neat and sharp. He had continued that habit to the present. Ralph once insinuated that he always looked proper because of an oversized ego, and John, quickly and without humor, let him know that he was wrong and to let it go. Ralph wasn't intimidated, but felt that he had hurt John some way, and changed the subject immediately. He figured that if John had the ego he accused him of having, he wouldn't look hurt. He never said anything about John's ego after that.

After John's girlfriend heard the explanation that he hadn't received the messages, she calmed down and told him that her parents had had a change of heart about his involvement in the baby's life. The gifts he had been sending had softened them and made them reconsider their judgement of him as nothing but a reckless pack of trouble. She told him that he was welcome to come and meet the little girl she had given birth to, and visit on occasion. She also said that he should probably continue to send the gifts and notes and offer to help out any way he could. He agreed and when he did go to their house, he started his visit by promising to send money, to save money for her to have when she grew up and to do anything they wanted him to do besides that. They accepted his offerings like the King and Queen of a small, poor country, hesitant to trust the outsider, but willing to take the risk in exchange for the benefit to the child. When John had finished prostrating himself before the grandparents, he was allowed to see his daughter.

When he held the baby in his arms, he felt nothing but grief and an overwhelming dread that he had made a horrible mistake that this tiny little person was going to pay for longer than John himself would be alive. He cried quietly for several minutes while he held the sleeping infant. He looked at her gentle, sweet features the entire time, his head down in shame. He watched his tears fall on the tender pink skin and wondered that it didn't wake her from her steady, deep sleep. Finally, when he felt as though he had cried every drop of moisture from his body, she awakened and smiled briefly. Effortlessly and suddenly all of his darkness lifted and changed into hope and certainty that everything would be ok. He laughed to himself now that gas pains had probably caused the smile that profoundly changed his perspective. Her gastrointestinal pain had removed his emotional pain. He ended up at one point baby sitting when the mother started college and the grandparents were unable to watch Darlene every time she had a class. He enjoyed those hours he spent with his daughter more than anything he had done in his life. When the mother had finished school and started working as a nurse, both grandparents had retired, and his job as back up baby sitter was diminished. He still was allowed to visit whenever he could, but they lived about seventy miles away so it was difficult for him to get there very often and he knew that money spent going to her could be better saved and used for her needs. He sent money every week, whether he had a job or not. Years back, because he knew how hard it was to keep a job and stay ahead of bills, he had started putting aside money but sending only part of it. In the event that he would be out of work or broke he could continue to dip into the little pool and send money. He felt the consistency was at least as important as the money itself. A few times he had only been able to send five dollars.

John had it tough for as long as he could remember, so the burden of the added responsibility felt like just another one of those hardships that he knew he would deal with some way. From what he'd learned about Cary over time, he'd had stretches where his life had been, if not a cake walk, then at least fairly trouble free, if not care free. This would strip that away. That is, unless he decided to abandon the child and mother- it happened, a lot. He wondered how Cary would react in the long run. His tenuous financial well being would be sorely tested many times over the next eighteen years.

"How far along is she?," Pat had over heard Cary's confession.

"Three months."

"Only three months?" Ralph tried to tamp down his jubilation about the car. He knew it was appropriate to be concerned about Cary, especially since he had just solved a money problem for him, but his attempt turned him into a fidgety wreck. He hummed between his words, like he was trying to take the wind out of an uproarious laugh anxious to break free. He was beside himself. His two years of scrimping had finally paid off. He had gone through another beer, and his speech was thickening around the edges.

"What do you mean, only three months?" Cary was perturbed. "She's not gonna have an abortion. We already talked about that. She's had a couple already and she's afraid she won't be able to have kids if she keeps getting 'em."

"Is that true, though?" John thought it sounded like a myth.

Pat had a stool like the ones on the customer's side of the bar. Even though the floor behind the bar was lower than the serving floor, Pat's height still allowed him to tower over his patrons when he sat down to chat with them. He laid his arms on the bar with his hands open, palms up. He did this often, and it seemed to John that it was a way to make him seem more open, accessible, and his size less imposing. "It is true. My wife always had female problems. That's why we don't have kids. Her gynecologist actually told her that the scarring in her uterus looked like the type caused by sloppy abortions. Of course, it wasn't from that, but I guess there are scars if it's not done just right."

Cary nodded in agreement, but looked grimmer as he spoke. "Yeah, there's no way she's gonna have an abortion." The three men understood then, that Cary wouldn't have minded her having one, but she wouldn't do it. "I never said the word, but she did, and accused me of thinking it, and that I didn't care, and didn't love her and all that stuff."

"That's tough." Ralph had calmed down. John noticed that Ralph's tolerance for alcohol would go up and down, or possibly, he drank dramatically different amounts before he arrived. He'd gone through five beers and was mildly plastered. Normally, it wouldn't phase him.

Ralph had never mentioned a woman in his life, other than his sister. John, Cary and Pat never asked or addressed the fact that he had never been involved, that they knew, with a woman, at least as long as they had known him. Once when Ralph mentioned that he had never hugged or kissed his sister, a remark that was something of a non sequitur during the conversation they were having at the time, John had a fleeting thought that maybe Ralph's sister was actually a girl friend or hooker, that he was deeply ashamed of, but just as quickly knew that he was wrong. Another thought flew through his consciousness and was discarded as quickly that maybe Ralph had done some things with his sister that were not proper. John questioned his own normalcy after the thoughts had occurred to him, but wondered why he had never thought about them before in regard to any one else. The whole sequence had nauseated him and he shoved it out of his mind quickly.

John patted Cary on the back. "We're behind ya man."

Cary's sour expression softened a little. "Thanks. It's a bitch."

"Hey," Pat put a fresh beer in front of John. "Don't you have to go to work pretty soon?"

John grinned, looking ornery, "I'm sick."

Pat looked like he smelled something ripe. "You are gonna get fired."

John was uncomfortable. "Hey, Pat. They don't care if I show up. I'm nothing to them. You know I give as much loyalty as I get, otherwise it's a waste." Pat's expression altered slightly, changing from disappointment to skepticism, then acceptance.

John sipped his new beer. His face brightened "Hey, it's cold!"

Ralph put his hand on the bottle Pat had just placed in front of him. "Hot damn, it is cold!"

Pat opened the cooler and stuck his hand inside. "Sure enough!" He pulled another
bottle out, opened it and put it in front of him. "This calls for a celebration." Pat rarely drank alcohol, let alone in the morning. He raised his cold bottle to Ralph. "Ralph, today is a good day for you. You got another twenty dollars on your tab."

Ralph looked embarrassed. His laugh came from deep within his chest. "Thanks, chief."
John felt bad for Ralph. The man was embarrassed by his own success, not pleased or satisfied. He hadn't experienced it enough to be comfortable with it, or, undoubtedly, believe he deserved it.

SMOKE 'EM IF YOU GOT 'EM

"Boys and, girls, uh, boys and boys!" Cheryl Patterson stepped into the bar bellowing her greeting. Her salutations were as big as she was. While she was not obese, she was full figured, her curves straining to keep supple tapers under a build up of fat. Long ago, she became aware of the changes and had started wearing clothes that cloaked her shape, clothes she felt comfortable in, usually a man's shirt, whether a blue jean shirt, or an oxford with the tail out and navy blue jogging pants. She kept her brown hair short. John figured she felt that it was a way to control the appearance of her weight since changing her actual weight seemed to be out of her hands. Her tennis shoes were always bright white. John wondered if she laundered them all of the time or bought new pairs constantly. He knew that she had worked at a sign company for a number of years, where inks and solvents were everywhere, yet, whether she came from work or home, her tennis shoes were always sparkling white. He knew she worked in the printing plant, not the office, and despite whatever tales she told about her hard working ways, her shoes told the real story. John admitted his judgment was also colored by a couple of drunken half confessions she made while snuggling up to him at a back table one evening. She told him that she was pursuing a workman's compensation disability claim because she hurt her back. She said she was about ninety percent sure she injured it falling down some steps at home one night or when she was dry humping a guy in the bathroom against a sink here one night. She limped into work the following day, and when she picked up a couple of sign boards it hurt even worse, so she complained about the pain at that point. She figured they owed it to her since they didn't provide health insurance.

She had been getting pain pills from a couple of doctors who were more than happy to treat her under the worker compensation program because it paid a large portion of the fees they wanted. The pills and alcohol made her far chattier about personal issues than usual. Her normal conversation was littered with jokes and small talk, all delivered in a booming voice. This confession was delivered in a slurred, secretive hush. She obviously had a crush on John but wouldn't pursue it further than flirtations. Any one who dared speak of her attraction would say, for the benefit of anyone within earshot that he was too young for her, that she would be robbing the cradle. He decided that on a subconscious level she figured he would have nothing to do with her because of her weight, but John kept his emotional distance from her because he believed she was a pathological liar and big trouble waiting to happen. He never knew when she was making something up wholesale, or telling part of the truth, and he had caught her in enough lies and distortions that he wanted to keep his emotions checked when it came to buying into Cheryl. Others at the bar focused on her overwrought warmth and upbeat humor, and seemed to miss or ignore her avoidance of the truth.

"Four guys and me. Ooohhh." She howled, laughing. She was light on her feet, and John noted, didn't seem to have any problem with her back, although it seemed apparent that she had medicated herself pretty thoroughly with pain pills already.

Pat smiled when he spotted Cheryl. He didn't give a damn about her lies or pill problems.
John got a whiff of an attraction to her from Pat whenever she was around. John had met Pat's wife one time when one of their cars were in the shop and she had stopped by to pick him up for dinner. John happened to be outside smoking a cigarette and chatting with Ralph. He was shocked at how much she looked like Cheryl. Her clothes were very nice and she spoke gently and with a feminine quality that Cheryl rarely hinted at. John only saw this feminine side in Cheryl a couple of times when she was out of it, and pawing him. John didn't know how to put her off without making her mad, but his usual quiet and expressionless demeanor kept her wondering how far to go, so he ultimately avoided having to fend off anything more serious than heavy duty flirting and the occasional hand on the leg or peck on the cheek. He could ignore the rest. She regularly mentioned that he was the strong silent type, so she forgave him his standoffishness. At those moments, she would be a

high school girl smitten with him, and speak in a higher pitched girlish voice, that was, John noted, pretty and lilting, and very incongruous with the big tough woman swaying next to him.

Pat slapped his hand down at the bar next to Cary and matching Cheryl's gusto said, "Sit here girl, and I'll set you up!"

"It is a deal boyfriend!" She sprinted over to the stool next to Cary, glancing at John as she passed, and then stopped. She looked at Pat with mock shyness, holding her hands together in front of her and pushing her shoulders up, like she had just entered a musical and was going to sing a little song about love and happiness. She walked over to the jukebox instead, and did what no one else in the bar was allowed to do; plug it in before 7 PM.

Pat looked put upon. "Ah, come on darlin'. Not this early. We have things to talk about."

Cheryl dug into her pocket, pulling a hand full of change out, and started picking the quarters out. "Pat, I've got a big mouth. You'll be able to hear me over the music." She cackled like the wicked witch of the west.

Pat looked at the three men at the bar with pleading eyes. John didn't know if it meant that he was hoping for help in discouraging her, or that he was asking their forgiveness for being weak, and letting her have her way.

Pat didn't know music at all. He had let the guy from the Juke Box distributor program the machine the first time and his regulars quickly let him know what they wanted him to get rid of and what should replace the stuff they hated. He'd write it all down in a little ledger book so between them and the service guy, the music was a diverse mix of rock and country heavy on old songs with a sprinkling of new. "Honky Tonk Woman" by The Rolling Stones started playing. Cheryl, limber beyond her weight and supposed injury, got down on her knees and reached around behind the unit and turned the volume up.

"Oh yeah, baby!" She was ecstatic. Pat smiled and patted the bar in front of her drink again. She ignored him, and fed a number of quarters into the machine. "John, get your ass over here and help me pick some stuff before Pat figures out he's actually in charge." She said it teasingly, but there was a little bit of a serious edge to it. The effect was funny, and they all laughed.

John didn't want to get up. "Put a Hank Williams Sr. song on. I'll be happy."

Cheryl wasn't letting him off the hook. "You push the buttons boy. I'm not your DJ. Choose or you'll get Hank Williams Jr."

Cary, seemingly oblivious to the dynamic, got up and walked over to the jukebox. Cheryl looked at him, a little pissed that he had butted in, and then, noticing his melancholy air, put her arm around him and said, "Darlin' looks like you need to pick a couple good songs too."

Cary and Cheryl took turns pushing buttons and laughing. Ralph had started getting worked up again. He had passed his quiet, slightly smashed stage to a manic one which would spill into a slobbering, hilarious one a number of beers down the line. "I gots me a car, and I'm gonna go far," he started singing in no particular melody or rhythm.

"And Pat's gonna throw you out on the tar, if you don't stop that." Pat said, half serious.
Now that Cheryl had decided that they would listen to music, Pat wanted it to be the only other distraction. He sat another beer next to Ralph's nearly empty one. "You better slow down Ralph or you won't have a tab left and you won't be fit to go get that car today, if that's your plan."

It was Thursday and John was happy that he had decided to take the day off. He knew that it meant that he would take Friday off too, and if he would get yelled at for one day, two was no bigger a deal. He would fake illness. They would drop him when this job was done anyway, so he didn't feel that he owed them allegiance. Jobs were doled out grudgingly, so he'd attend to it grudgingly. He noticed that the difference between him and Cheryl was that he let it be known to everyone there that he was faking, and he'd essentially let his employers know it too, in so many words, but Cheryl could and would easily spin a story about how she had been laid off, or told to stay home, or had worked sixty hours that week and needed to take a break.

John turned on his stool so he could be heard over the music. "Hey, Cheryl, why aren't you at work?"

She turned to him, poker faced, "I have to work this weekend so I got today off. They didn't want to pay me over time, so I said ok."

John wasn't sure if she had forgotten that he told her she was going to a workman's compensation hearing that morning, and had no intention of going to work any more if she could help it, or she was trying to implicate him in her fiction. He felt uncomfortable but didn't want to confront her on the two versions so he replied, "How'd your hearing go?"

"Oh, yeah," she said, without a change in expression, "the preliminary finding, they call it, is that I'll get 100% disability."

Cary, Ralph and Pat had heard nothing about this and they all responded with questions. Cheryl fanned their barrage down like a small fire, and sitting down on her designated stool, told them about half the truth, as John knew it, that she had been hurt at work and despite her injury had continued to work until the doctors had decided how bad she had been hurt. She proceeded to complain that the owner of the shop was mad at her when he found out about her pursuit of disability and had made her job impossible, despite her valiant efforts, so, as of her worker's compensation hearing, which she still didn't admit had been that morning, she had decided she wouldn't go back to work. She explained that her general practitioner had strongly suggested that she stop working, because she could further injure herself if she didn't.

She looked at John a few times as she told the tale, and John didn't see any indication in her expression, like a wink or a raised eyebrow, that she felt she was conspiring with him to keep the full truth from the rest, so John figured she had blacked out the fact that she had spilled the majority of the beans to him. He figured the combination of the pills and the booze were probably making it easy for Cheryl to believe her own fibs.

During her drunken confessional, she had mentioned that worker's compensation had decided that any days she had missed since she had been injured were "compensatory" and by her estimation, with the reduction they had built in, she would get a check for thousand of dollars within a few weeks. John had been surprised that in her state at that point, she could say the word "compensatory" or even recall it, but then, it was money in her pocket, so she had locked the term in, and could, hampered as she was still regurgitate it. The part about the money didn't make it in to the story told to Pat, Cary or Ralph. John knew that Cheryl lived with her sister and brother in law in a room at the back of their house, so she paid little or no rent, and that even with the crummy wages she made, by virtue of her living arrangements, she had been able to afford a car and even a vacation six months ago on a cruise ship, and John suspected that while her injury and the damper it would put on her money making potential would be fully disclosed to her sister and husband, the first check would probably be a secret kept from them. John felt tempted to take advantage of her by getting her alone and mentioning that he could use some money, and then getting chummier with her than usual, but something in him welled up and scolded him for considering it.

Cheryl started singing along with the second song, "Her Strut" by Bob Seger. John mumbled to Ralph that he liked "Ramblin' Gamblin' Man" by Seger, otherwise, he didn't much care for him. Ralph replied that he thought he remembered the song, but didn't know one song from another. When he heard them, he knew what they were, otherwise, he didn't give a shit.

He liked Jethro Tull and Alice Cooper. That's all he could say about music.

John really cared about what songs he listened to, and he was glad that Cheryl, on the whole, played stuff that he either liked, or didn't mind. He had never had the money or inclination to pick the songs himself, so he was beholden to whatever someone else chose.

The door to the bar opened again. A small young man with a blonde page boy hair cut leaped in, like Superman on vacation. "Yo!"

Pat looked over at the man and yelled. "Hey, is anybody working today?" Two older men came in behind the younger one and sat down at a corner table. The room they were in was fairly small. There was a larger room connected by a passageway. The floors were hardwood, worn, but still handsome in the way that good solid wood flooring is, scars and all. There was heavy wood framing around the front door, and the trim at the base of the walls was the same dark wood found around the rest of the room. Despite there being no decorative touches attempted by Pat, the wood gave the room a substantial feel. Pat's office and the restrooms were the rooms that broke the bar into two halves. It was apparent to anyone who chose to sort it out that the two areas had been completely separate in the past and the wall had been broken through in two places. An absence of the heavy wooden trim in the throughway was the biggest clue.

Pat owned the building. One morning when Ralph was running late because he was suffering from a hangover, and Cary was doing over time , John and Pat had sat by themselves for a few hours. After Pat had made a phone call to an electrician about some repairs, he had confessed that he owned a couple apartment buildings, and that while it was a hassle finding good tenants and good repairmen, he didn't mind being a landlord. So John discovered that Pat owned the bar and a couple other buildings. He wondered how hard it would be to have to pay mortgages on them by depending on unreliable renters.

Pat had also revealed that he bought the bar when, after fifteen years, he had grown tired of working in the food service industry for an eccentric fellow, whom he politely refused to identify. He said that even though they had paid him a nice salary, he didn't enjoy going in to work and wanted to leave soon after arriving. He said he knew that most people supposed that it was the way of the world, but Pat had decided that it was not going to be the case for him. During his work at the company, he was required to visit clients, some of which were bars, and as time passed, he started developing the idea of getting one of his own. John wondered again why he seemed to be the person who found out all these things about the people around him. He was the dirty little secret repository. Part of it, he knew, was because the secrets were safe with him. He never gossiped. He never sought out gossip, even though it was what made up the bulk of the entertainment in the bar. Everyone talked about what everyone else was doing, true or not.

For example, the rumor mills had drawn a complete picture of the kid with the page boy. His name was Joey. He was as wiry as John, but shorter. He wasn't more than five foot three. He had turned twenty one a few months back, and by the way he had been behaving, wouldn't see twenty two. He took every drug he could get a hold of, drank everything that was in front of him, had sex with every woman he could sweet talk, and there had been plenty. It was rumored he had already fathered at least one baby, possibly two- the rumor mill would have that sorted out or embellished soon enough. He quit jobs every three or four weeks. He had been in jail for drunk and disorderly so many times, no one kept track any more. He was a walking disaster, and every one knew it. John's friend Daryl, the one friend John knew who owned his own home, (his father had given him the down payment) had been trying to get Joey to clean up. He had decided to take him under his wing and attempt to help the kid get his priorities straightened out. John noted that Joey had charmed the otherwise fairly savvy Daryl. When he would have a heart to heart with him, Joey responded with what seemed to be complete sincerity, but would turn around and do the opposite of whatever it was to which they had supposedly agreed. He did this over and over, yet Daryl didn't seem to understand that either Joey wasn't capable of straightening out, wasn't willing to, wasn't convinced that he had problems, whatever it was, all Joey had to do was put on his sincere act, and Daryl was good to be set up for another disappointment.

When Joey threw open the door to the bar, John could see his big black Camaro parked across the street, cockeyed to the curb. He got the car after his brother had died, from alcohol poisoning. The night his brother died was legendary. It hadn't happened in any of the bars in the neighborhood, but at a drug dealer's house. There was a huge party and it had spilled into the front yard and street, but no one on the block dared call the police from fear of retribution from the drug dealer, so there were people everywhere drinking, yelling, urinating, and dancing. Joey's brother had gotten into a spontaneous drinking contest with another guy and after he won, he had walked out of the house into the street. He bummed a celebratory cigarette from a woman and immediately after he lit it, he laughed and said, "Damn I am so fucking drunk!" He fell on the ground. The cigarette was still clenched in his mouth, broken in half near his
face. In fact, when someone noticed that it had actually burned his face and he hadn't responded, he was flipped over on his back, and as soon as it had been discerned that he wasn't breathing, his body was pushed on the other side of the street between cars at the curb, and the party dissolved like thick smoke in a room with all the windows thrown open at once.

Joey and his brother's parents weren't very well off, but had, through the father's work, been able to afford to secure a small life insurance policy that paid for the funeral. The car had been paid for with cash. His parents didn't want it, and planned to sell it, but Joey raised a huge ruckus, saying it would be a reminder to him of his older brother, that it would honor his memory to drive it, and wore the grief stricken couple down until, against their better judgement, he ended up with it. Everyone had been surprised when Joey was careful with the car, had taken care of it, and never drove it when he was badly loaded.

It was always nerve wracking when Joey was around because he was in constant movement. John was never sure whether the boy was that way, or if it was stimulants. John thought it was a combination of both. When Joey was nasty, he felt that it was when he was on the pills, otherwise, his nervous energy seemed, although aggravating and distracting, benign. Today Joey seemed fine. He sought out John. Daryl was John's friend too, and so Joey knew John better than anyone else who frequented the bar.. "Hey John, John! What's up!"

"Not much, buddy."

Joey noted that Ralph sat to the right of John and Cary the left. " Hey, Cary. How's about moving so I can sit with John boy?" Joey and Ralph didn't get along. Both were prone to overreact and when they talked to each other it usually didn't take much for one of them to get angry at the other, so they tended to avoid all but cursory acknowledge of the other's existence.

Cary shrugged and moved to the other side of Cheryl. Pat had gone to serve the two older regulars who were at one of the corner tables. Joey slapped the bar, "Hey, where's my beer?"

Pat ignored Joey. He served the two men and began chatting with them. Joey jumped up-he never just got up-zipped behind the bar, got a beer from the cooler and returned to his seat before Pat realized that he had done it. He gave Joey the evil eye when he sorted out that he had got his own beer. "Hey, Pat, I'm paying for it. No problem." Now he looked like a little kid who was asking permission. Pat furrowed his brow, and let it go.

"Hey John, I'm looking at this motorcycle. Think I'm gonna get it."

"A motorcycle?.." The tone of Joey's remark had a touch of the confessional in it.

"Yeah, it's small. More like a scooter. It's a Honda."

"Why do you want a scooter? You have the Camaro."

"I'm selling it. He's gonna pay me in cash."

"What about driving in the winter?" John knew that wasn't the right argument.

"I'll dress warm."

"What about women. All the women, Joey. They aren't going to sit on the back of the bike."

Joey's grin oozed with confidence. "They'll do whatever I tell 'em."

"Did you talk to Daryl about this?"

"Yeah, man, he thinks it's a bad idea, that I'll regret it."

"So, then...?"

"I'm lovin' it. I dream about it. I can see the color. I can see me drivin' it. I'll have money left over by the buttload."

John believed too that Joey would regret his choice. He didn't want to bring it up, but nothing else seemed to affect him. "What about the car? Your brother?"

Joey's expression was, as usual, a mixture of anticipation and hard core detachment. "Fuck that. He's dead. I'm alive."

"Why the change of heart?"

"Hey, man. I thought you'd get it. Fuck this." In one lightning motion, Joey was off his stool, out the door and roaring away in his car.

"I'll cover his beer, Pat." John could sense that Pat was within a second of being on his way to beating the money out of Joey, and he wanted to defuse the situation. Relief seemed to flood the room after Joey left.

"Put it on my stack." John smiled at Pat. Pat was angry, but John's remark about his tab system cajoled a little grin out of him. He went back to chatting with the two older regulars. John could hear them expounding on the stupid kids of today, that because they didn't have to serve their country, they were ignorant of responsibility in that and all other areas of their lives. Ready-made traitors.

John pictured Joey and Pat in a fight, and it played out in his head with Pat as victor. Joey would get a few punishing punches in early, and Pat would swiftly deliver a debilitating blow, partly because that's the sort of blow he would invariably deliver, and partly because he would know that if he didn't put the little wire of a boy down immediately, that he'd find himself on his back, bloody and barely conscious. John could tell that Pat always sized up the men who came into his bar, to work out how he'd get the best of them, in the event that it came to violence for any one of a million ridiculous reasons. John had done the same sort of sizing up while he was in prison. He knew he had to get good at it fast. Anyone who had any kind of will to control the slivers of life they had in prison developed the skill of viewing every other inmate as an opponent first, with all the inherent weaknesses and strengths and then, if in the coldest harshest judgement, they were neutralized or disinterested, or irrelevant, they could then be viewed as an uneasy ally, or in Pat's case, John amused himself to think, a paying customer.

Even though Cheryl and Cary seemed intent on what the other was saying, Cheryl noticed the empty seat next to John, and got up to sit down between him and Cary. Cary had to move one chair. He looked slightly aggrieved. "Now I got my boys on both sides of me." She placated Cary for breaking into his story of woe by gesturing to Pat that his next beer was on her.

Ralph leaned very close to John's ear. John could smell the slightest hint of a strong sour smell. "Careful there buddy. Look's like Orca's comin' in for the kill." John didn't respond directly to the remark, another reason, he guessed, that people trusted him-he took no pleasure from unkind or cruel remarks about others, and there were always plenty of them floating around in the alcohol haze that most of them moved in.

He wondered what it took to view heavy people, cripples, retarded people as human beings. He recalled in grade school that there was only one class for children with severe mental or physical challenges. It was a small group. The rest who were mildly or moderately disadvantaged were thrown in with the rest of the kids in classes with populations of forty and up per room. They had to sink or swim with the other kids and the limited attention they could be given. Most of them sank. The "Eddys" as the special education class was called by many of the kids, were butts of practical jokes, rude comments, and outright ridicule. John recalled being confused why so many kids thought it was funny. He wondered if his outlook toward the kids was informed by his uncle. He had visited once when John was six. When he was introduced, his uncle spoke to him in burps and rasps. He had a hole in his throat that he pressed on when he spoke. John laughed and his mother scolded him. John's uncle knelt down and said, "your mom thinks you're disrepectin' me, but I know you think it's cool that I have two mouths." He took a lit cigarette from John's mother and put it at the hole and puffed away. In one moment, John saw differences as strengths, to be accepted, admired and respected.

He acknowledged Ralph had made the disparaging remark about Cheryl to him by asking a question. "Why don't you like Joey?"

Ralph's expression flipped from conspiratorial to quizzical. "Yuh, know, it's not that I don't like him. I don't like that he makes me nervous. It's all that jerkin' around. Jesus, it's distracting. Ya just wanna pick his little wiggly bug of a body up and plant him into the dart board, head first, and see if that stops him from moving around. Bulls eye, godamn it."

"He can't help that he's like that."

"I can't help that I'm like what I'm like. If you prick him does he not a prick?"

52

It was one of those attempts at a joke that collapsed under the burden of the booze that was pretty quickly soaking into Ralph's brain. John was surprised that Ralph seemed to be quoting Shakespeare, or at least bastardizing it for a non sequitur of a joke. He couldn't get over the seeming fact that Ralph's appearance in some unfathomable way, exuded naivete, stupidity, something, that continually encouraged John to underestimate his intelligence. He grinned, thinking that he was at *his* stupidest when he underestimated Ralph and that the lesson his uncle had taught was sometimes lost on him. It stank of the Eddy branding and John was disappointed in himself.

Ralph took his grin to mean that he had said something witty. "Hey, hey. John. A doctor walks into a bank, grabs a deposit ticket, and pulls a rectal thermometer out of his shirt pocket. He looks at it and says to the clerk, 'Damn, some asshole's got my pen.'"

John grinned again. "Why don't you get some new jokes?"

"Hey, you laugh. Why should I?" Ralph laughed this time. "Ok, a couple of hillbillies are out in a puddle of mud, fucking. The guy says, "hey baby, is my dick in the mud or in you?" The girl hillbilly says, "yer screwin' mud", so he says, "well, stick it inside you", so she does and a little bit later the guy asks again, "hey baby, is my dick in the mud or in you?" She says, "you're in me", and he says, "put it back in the mud."

Cheryl mock laughed. "That joke sucks."

"Ya got somethin better Cheryl Apparel?" Ralph was amused by the challenge.

Cheryl didn't hesitate. "Guy goes to a costume party, and knocks on the door. Host opens the door and sees this guy's not wearing a shirt, socks or shoes. The host says, "what the hell are you supposed to be?" The guy says," I'm a premature ejaculation. I just came in my pants.""

Everyone laughed. Ralph sat up straighter on his stool. "Guy goes into an elevator and stands next to this woman. He turns to her and says "Can I smell your pussy?", she freaks and says "Hell, no." The guy looks her up and down and says, "Must be your feet then."

Cheryl nodded her head between snorts. "Ok, ok. I guess I had to challenge you to get something decent out of you."

One of the old men in the back chimed in. "Have ya seen the new Clinton Highway in Arkansas?" He waited a beat and then said "It's a little crooked and has a yellow streak going down the middle."

"Hey," Cheryl hollered, "leave him alone. Why do people still pick on that man?"

The regular responded, "because he's still a bum!"

Pat spoke up. "Here, here."

John sat quietly while things started heating up. Cheryl continued. "You men are all the same. I swear to God, I think you hate Clinton because he's the first cool guy to be President since Kennedy, and you're all jealous jerks."

"He's a liar, and so is that wife of his." Pat retorted.

Cheryl softened as she turned to Pat. "That wife is more proof that you guys are insecure. Why is this poor woman such a threat?"

Sam, one of the old men sitting at the table piped up. "She wanted to be President, but we didn't elect her."

"Ha", Cheryl threw her head back, like she was an actress in a play and had to exaggerate her movements so the folks in the cheap seats could see her disdain for Sam's remark. "like this asshole in office was elected?"

The two old men became indignant. "He's tough, and we need that, in these times."

Ralph stepped in. "Know how to clear out a bingo game in Baghdad? Yell B-52!"

Cheryl whipped her head around to Ralph. "Shut up, pip squeak. We're having a serious discussion."

Ralph's dander was up. "Clinton was a liar and a crook."

Cheryl shook her head. "Jesus Christ. It's a good thing you people don't vote. Bill Clinton cared about people. These bastards in there now would eat us for lunch and pick their teeth with our bones, if they could pay attention to us long enough to do it."

Sam stood up. "He's a traitor!" His red face made his graying hair look whiter.

Cheryl rolled her eyes. "Bush? You mean Bush, right?" She knew he didn't.

"No godamn it. He had people killed, he sold missiles to China, he let the fags run things, he had sex in the White House."

Cheryl butted in, "Oh that's true. God, we all know Nixon, and the Bushs never had sex in the White House ..."

Pat broke in with a mumbled piece of advice. "Better take it down a notch, hon. We don't want Sam to explode into little bits. I don't want to clean it up. It'll use all my sawdust."

Cheryl turned quickly to Pat. "Screw that. You people don't know what the hell you're talking about. You listen to that Shamu, Rush Limbaugh on your fuckin' Wal-Mart radios lying

through his teeth about anything he lays his tongue to, and you believe it's gospel. Jesus, Tokyo
Rose hasn't got a thing on Rush Limbaugh."

"Tokyo Rose," Pat could see he wasn't going to stop them, so he figured he'd try to
move the discussion to less volatile territory. He looked at the men at the table. "Did you guys
ever hear her? I actually did once. It was a tape though, after the war."

Sam answered first. "No, I didn't."

"Me either."

Cheryl jumped back in. "She was forced to do what she did. Rush Limbaugh makes millions of dollars a year destroying this country. That fucking bastard should be slit open for his blubber, and we'll light fires with it and burn all the tapes of his show."

Cary spoke finally. "He's just a radio personality. He's not a news reporter."

Cheryl turned to Cary. "Right, that's what he says when someone confronts him with his
lies. He can't defend them, so he says "Oh I'm just an entertainer.", but the bastard doesn't act like
he's joking. His show sounds like a news show."

"He's a patriot." Sam spoke, still standing.

"Well, he's not funny, that's one thing he isn't." Cary said it, sighing, tired of the
conversation.

Cheryl jumped off her stool and walked over and got nose to nose with Sam. "He's a petty
piece of shit laughing all the way to the bank at stupid fuckers like you. He's a multi-millionaire. He doesn't give a shit about you or me. He's evil and..."

Pat spoke up again, gently but firmly. "Hon, we're all talkin'. Let's keep it civil."

Cheryl stepped back, quieter, but still angry. "None of us here are rich. You all act like you belong to a country club when you side with these assholes, but you don't. They despise all of us."

"Boy, girl." It was Pat continuing to try to turn the conversation. "You oughta run for office."

Cheryl sat back down, sullen. "Why should I? You assholes wouldn't vote for me." She took a drink. "Don't even read. They use the newspaper for lottery numbers and coupons." She was mumbling now.

Ralph looked at her. "Hey, I'm not an asshole."

Cheryl rolled her eyes. "Oh, I stand corrected, asshole."

Ralph looked at Pat. "Hey, chief. Come on. Make her behave."

Pat smiled, a helpless look on his face again.

Cheryl took a drink of her beer. "You don't listen to Limbaugh, do you Cary?" Cary looked embarrassed. "I don't listen to him. I listen to the music." This crap makes me tired any way. Let's talk about something else."

"Achy Breaky Heart" by Billy Ray Cyrus came on the jukebox. Ralph let his head slump forward. "God I thought I'd never hear that song again."

"And then I got 'em to put it on here!" Cheryl jumped up, taking John's hand. "Come on, dance with me buck!"

John got up because he knew it was futile to turn Cheryl down. He'd dance one song to appease her. Cheryl used the dancing as an excuse to touch John in a number of places that she normally wouldn't be able to without being overt. John quietly moved. He was a decent dancer. One of his girlfriends had made a point of teaching him to dance. She loved dancing. She would have gone dancing every night if she could have convinced John to, but because he was intent on staying home, she consoled herself with teaching him to dance a number of different steps. He tried to be as subtle in his moves as possible, because he didn't want to see Cheryl stoked on pills and alcohol getting excited by his body. He didn't feel he was bragging about himself, he just knew that she was loose enough, that she might make a scene.

John heard the old guys grumbling at the table about the music. Two more older men who were regulars came in. They sat down at the table with Sam and the other man. Their conversation became more animated, compensating for the loudness of the music. John noted that the older fellows usually controlled the bar between one and six o'clock. They were being fairly gracious today because the juke box and Cheryl dancing around were treading very heavily on their "quality time". She continued dancing by herself after John gently extricated himself from her grasp at the end of the country song. He sat down with the old timers, figuring he'd chat a little, and take the edge off the confrontation that had just occurred.

Sam, the obvious ring leader spoke. "So I heard Joey's gonna trade that car in for a scooter?"

John sighed and nodded. "Yeah, it looks like it."

Sam shook his head. "My nephew was one of them water heads" he waved his hand at his head for a few seconds, "couldn't do a thing for himself. Well he was in a nursing home. It was mostly old people."

"Like you Sam?" one of the old guys, Ben, taunted. John wondered if Sam was insinuating that Joey was mentally retarded.

58

Sam looked at Ben, dismissive. "Well, my nephew was there, and there was only one other young person there. It was a girl, about twenty two. She had some kinda spine thing. She was in a wheel chair and all shaky, but she could talk and all. Well she made friends with my nephew. They kept each other company. The only young ones there. She always talked about getting out and being on her own. She hated being in the nursing home. They set up a program where you get a place, and they pay for you to live on your own, and nurses visit,"

Another of the older men interrupted. "Wouldn't that cost more?"

Sam shrugged. "Supposed not to, any way she gets out and six weeks later, she's dead. She had these so called friends to look after her, and wires got crossed and she starved to death in her bed. We never told the nephew."

"What's that got to do with Joe?" Ben puzzled. He seemed to resent his lower status in the pecking order at the table.

Sam looked at him like he had sprouted a second head. "Well, wheels can be your enemy, or they can be your friend."

Ben was exasperated. "The wheels were her friend all the way. If she had been in her wheel chair she could have wheeled out for help."

Sam, disgusted with Ben, looked at John. John stood up and laughed. "I understand what you're sayin' Sam. Ben needs a little clarification, I guess." He took his seat at the bar while the men continued arguing at the table.

John looked at Ralph. He had become fairly drunk, but was still functional. Ralph could be badly wasted but still talk without slurring much. Walking was different. He became unsteady on his feet when he'd drank too much. The aroma of fresh coffee came wafting out from under the bar, where Pat kept the maker. John thought it was funny that it was as if he was hiding it from view, while all the booze was proudly displayed on the mirrored wall at the back of the bar, along with a couple of neon signs blinking beer names over and over. It must have been around one o'clock because that was normally when Pat made a fresh pot, and one old fellow who came in drank coffee. He had been a hard drinker for most of his adult life, but his doctor had told him three months earlier that he would be dead within a year if he didn't stop immediately. He still came in every day, but didn't drink anything but the coffee. Pat charged him a dollar for the first cup, with all the refills he wanted for free. Some times between what the customer drank and what Pat drank, he'd have to brew a second pot. Pat ate his lunch around this time. John was fascinated by the way he did it. He always had it in a paper bag. It was always a sandwich and a cup of Jell-O or pudding and he'd lay it out under the bar on the paper bag, which he reused until it was worn out. He would transfer the sandwich to a small glass plate he kept there. Each time he wanted to take a bite, he would lift the plate with one hand and pick up the sandwich to complete the short trip to his mouth. To John, it looked like a child trying to keep a sloppy ice cream sundae off the floor because his mother was watching. He looked almost dainty. John supposed that he ate a huge meal when he got home later in the evening because there was no way a big man like Pat could eat tiny little meals like the one he ate at the bar, and still be a big red bear of a man.

"Hey Pat, can I get a cup of that coffee?" Ralph asked evenly.

Pat looked surprised. "Sure. I guess you must be serious about getting that car today after all."

"Yup." He accepted the cup from Pat, and turned to John. "Why don't you come along with me?"

"I guess I might."

Cheryl overheard them talking about leaving. "Hey boys, you aren't gonna leave me, are ya?"

John spoke quickly, to keep Ralph from saying something rude. "Yeah, we're gonna pick up Ralph's new car. We'll come back." He looked at Ralph to verify this.

"Yeah. *We'll* be back," He had a sarcastic tone, knowing full well it was John she was hoping would return, "in my car."

"How did you manage to get a car?" She looked at everyone, like someone would crack a smile and say it was all a joke.

Pat was heading to the table with the coffee, "he saved the money."

Cheryl looked at Ralph like two different puzzles had been thrown out on a table, and she had to decide how many pictures she had, and which picture she could assemble.

THE STARS HAVE ALIGNED & THE VEGA'S IN THE GARAGE

Ralph hopped off his stool. "Man I gotta take a beauty break, then I really would like to go get my car. You comin' with me?" He semi-jumped around waiting for John's answer.

John was, despite the beers he had downed, restless. It felt like his early morning wakefulness revisiting. The idea of going with Ralph on his dream mission was satisfying. It looked like the coffee had straightened Ralph up just as quickly as the beer had made him sloppy. "I'll go."

"Good. Starsky and Fuckhead." Ralph trotted off toward the restroom. John wasn't sure who Starsky was and who Fuckhead was, but it didn't matter. The walk was the attraction and he was up for it.

Pat looked at John as he pulled another beer from the cooler. "Are you going to leave with Ralph?"

John nodded. "Yeah, he's really hot to get it. I figure I'll tag along and make sure he doesn't kill himself."

Pat puffed out a half laugh. "You'll save him today, but a car and Ralph equal doom."

John stood, started to put his coat on, "Pat, I hope you're wrong."

Pat shrugged, "I don't want to be right, John."

"Yeah, me either. Tell Ralph I'm outside having a cigarette." He paid Pat what he owed him.

Cheryl had been in a spirited exchange with Cary about his imminent fatherhood, but she wasn't engaged deeply enough that she missed John putting his coat on. "How long you gonna be gone, love?"

John smiled. "It shouldn't take too long."

Cheryl was obviously displeased. "That little pip squeak doesn't need you to hold his hand. Let him go get it himself."

John moved his head in a gentle roll, like he was dodging the meaning of the words Cheryl had shot out. "Actually, I'm kinda curious. This car could be a collectible. It's a seventy.."

Cheryl interrupted. "Fine, fine. It's a car. You're a guy. You don't have to explain any more." She seemed to be satisfied with comforting Cary, at least for the moment. John pictured Cheryl looking at the top shelf of booze at a bar, and while she would give lip service to the various whiskeys and liqueurs up there, she would drink the cheap stuff and occasionally make a show of drinking a few middle rung mixtures. The bulk of the time, she would guzzle the cheap stuff. John was embarrassed to realize that within the analogy, he was considering himself to be the top shelf stuff. He told himself that he would have to examine how often he thought that way and take a hard look at how often his decisions were colored by that outlook, because ultimately, his looks weren't always gonna be with him. He knew his body looked pretty good, but his knees were giving him loads of trouble, he had a couple of ugly scars from scuffles he'd been cornered into while he was in prison, and his back, there was something going wrong with his back. He gauged that he wouldn't look so attractive in a neck brace, a wheel chair or a walker, like the guy he regularly saw at the grocery store in his neighborhood, who used two big metal canes of sorts, that had handles on them that allowed the guy to tumble first to his left, then his right, then back again, in a jerking, awkward, even painful combination of walking, staggering and lurching. There was, despite the clunky movements, a solid sure footed dignity in his each step. It was so palpable that John would feel dignified being in the room as he crossed past him. John figured he had some sort of birth defect because the man's back didn't seem to be able to play a part in his mobility, having a curve in it, that if it had been at the proper angle from his back, would have been a great hump, but was more like a wing that had never been able to completely breech the skin and shake loose into a working singular sign of evolution. John did believe that people would have wings some day in the dim future. He had never breathed a word to any one about it.

When he was ten, and his mother had left the apartment late one afternoon, and, as her usual behavior dictated ,wouldn't return until the middle of the night, John was forced to fend for himself. He decided that instead of hiding in his room, not answering the phone, not answering the door, per his mother's instructions, he would rebel and walk to the park to see if any of his play mates were there at this unusual time in the late afternoon. He had always come home at dinner time, not because it would be ready, his mother usually had him open a can of something to eat, but because the rest of the kids went home at that time, and he would have felt left out if he didn't go home for the reasons they did. Going to the park after five would be an adventure, and safety didn't seem important that day. He didn't know why. He suspected that part of his motivation had been that there was nothing to eat, and while he figured his mother hadn't known, his feelings were a bit hurt that she hadn't been sober enough to notice. As an adult, he knew that she probably hadn't had any money, and he also knew that she still had enough of her looks at that time that men would pay for her booze the entire evening, and that she either had noticed that there was nothing there to eat, but was driven by her alcoholism to ignore it, or she was distracted enough by it to leave him without something to eat and be completely oblivious to it. Either way, he had known, as a child and an adult, that it wasn't a reflection on him. He knew that a little adventure, putting aside the rebellious nature of it, would help him forget that he had grown very hungry.

When he arrived at the park, twilight was rapidly approaching, and that unnerved him enough to excite him, but not enough to send him running back home to his television or well-worn wrestling magazines. There were a number of older kids playing basketball at the court on the far end of the park. He didn't recognize any of them. None of his friends were there. He was mulling the idea of going and watching the big kids play ball when, out of the corner of his eye, he saw movement near one of the few bushes for which the park designers had made accommodations by way of a small round hole in the asphalt. As he approached it, he saw a tiny bird lying on it's side, flapping it's wings. It's feathers were new, almost bushy, unlike the sleek and shining feathers on the adult birds. The young bird would flap its wings in a frenzy for a few seconds then it would lie quietly, like it was regaining it's strength from the Herculean effort it had just made. At one point he heard a strange squawk from a nearby tree. It immediately occurred to him, that it was probably the mother. He had never seen a baby bird, he had never seen a mother bird tending to it's children, but the squawk was intense and urgent, similar in tone to the call he had heard when mothers called children who had stayed too late at the park. He looked toward the tree where he thought he had heard the noise, and wasn't sure, but was half convinced that he saw a bird extending it's neck and shaking it's head, a grayish brown nest directly behind it on a branch that was camouflaged by two big branches crossing in front of it. When he returned his attention to the small bird, it was on it's way into the air, wavering and swerving away from the dangers and vulnerability on the ground. It seemed perfectly logical to John that if people could do that, then life would be better for everyone. It would be easy to see the big picture, swooping and looping around towns, forests, oceans. Removing themselves from bad neighborhoods, situations and danger would be easier. The criminals wouldn't evolve. They'd be stuck in the dirt.

He had been taught in school that people, in the dim distant past, were fish that could
not come out of the water and then were apes who couldn't walk upright. Why wouldn't they move on to flying from the mundane ability to put one foot in front of the other? He remembered seeing a local television show about weather one night. They had done an aerial shot of town, and despite the fact that their TV antenna was broken and the picture was snowy, he could see that they went over the apartment complex where he lived, and he could still recall the thrill at how cool it all looked from that point of view. He didn't tell any one about his theory, because it seemed as though it was a secret that people would be better off finding out about on the day that they were ready for it, ready to fly, and John was ok with hanging on to the information until then.

Ralph driving a car, though, felt like a perversion of the inevitable forward development of man, and John had decided that it would be best if he tagged along to intercede if it got out of hand. He hadn't got aside to smoke when Ralph came out of the restroom, quickly, too fast to wash his hands, John noted. The two headed toward the door. "Put mine on my tab, chief." Ralph called back as they exited.

Cary and Cheryl looked at Pat in disbelief. Pat held up his hand like a traffic cop. "I owed him money for a trade, and he took it out in beer. He paid for the beer ahead of time, not the other way around." He wanted to quash any rumor that he was a softie and would let someone drink on credit. He wanted to kick Ralph's scrawny ass. He would make it very clear that he should never mention a "tab" again, but Ralph had already left. The warning would have to wait.

Ralph bummed a cigarette from John as they headed toward the house where Ralph had his room. John figured that he would bum even more often now since Ralph would be paying for gas and oil and whatever else his new car would require of him but maybe he could get a ride from Ralph every once in a while. The bus was a huge hassle and he didn't like walking every where he needed or wanted to go.

"I figure you got a chick car Ralph." John watched steam puff out of his mouth. It was past lunch and the sun had been up in a clear sky, but it hadn't taken the cold out of the breeze that blew steadily from the north.

Ralph looked at him suspiciously. "You bein' a smart ass?"

John showed his surprise. "No, I'm not. Shit, Ralph, in this neighborhood, you're gonna be big time with this car." They walked for a few more minutes.

Ralph drew his breath in deeply, like he was preparing to yell at the top of his lungs, and needed to get as much air behind it as possible to make it loud enough to count. He used the extra air instead to rattle on at length. "Man, I've been thinking of all the things I can get done with this car. I can take aluminum cans to the recycling center over on Beckett, and I can sell stuff to a whole hell of a lot more people than now, get better prices, and if I want to work somewhere else, I can actually drive there and put in an application. Most of these places don't want to have anything to do with you if you don't have a car. If I want to, I can pick up and take a drive. I don't have to go anywhere in particular, I can just drive."

"It'll be sweet." John blew out smoke mixed with the steam. "How the hell did you manage to scrape together a thousand dollars? Jesus, that might as well be a million dollars!"

Ralph looked embarrassed again. "To tell you the truth, I didn't think I'd do it. I put a jar near my bed one day and started putting my change in it. I got tired of having it all rolling on the floor whenever I took my pants off, and I'd have to go around and dig under everything to find it all, so I stuck this jar there. It was kinda weird because I always spent every dime I had. You've seen me put a pile of change on the bar before. Anyway, I just put it in there every time and ignored it. I finally filled it up and sat down and counted it, and it was over a hundred dollars. I figured right then, that if I could ignore a hundred dollars, even when I was really broke, I could ignore enough to get the car. I think maybe that started me on it really. I saw that car a couple of months before that. I was helping an old guy stack stuff in his basement and reorganize his garage. He never was gonna get rid of it, but he liked me. I told him it would take me a long time to get the money together. I think maybe that's why he agreed to sell it to me."

"Because he liked you?"

"Yeah, but because he knew it would take me forever to put the money together and he got to let it sit in his garage like an oversize good luck charm for another year or two."

John knew Ralph had been in on a scam where all of the window air conditioners had been stolen from a new low income apartment building. He heard through the grapevine that Ralph had sold three of the units. That certainly would have added some money to the stash fast.

"Have you talked to the car guy lately? Maybe he changed his mind."

"I stopped over there about three weeks ago. He seemed pretty surprised that I had put the money together, and he hemmed and hawed around a little, but he said the deal was still good."

"Great. Where's the money?"

"Man, I tell ya. That was tough. I thought about giving it to Mrs. Weddington, but then I figured if she got hard up, or her worthless daughter found out about it, I could kiss it goodbye. I didn't want to hide it in the bathroom because everybody goes through there, so I had to come up with someplace safe in my room."

"Where, and why not a bank?"

Ralph flicked the ash off his spent cigarette, and motioned for a fresh one. John popped one out of the pack. He was stalling, thinking about telling him his hiding place. His expression changed as he smiled wide, having decided that he'd trust John. "Man, I hid it in a pair of my dirtiest underwear. I wore a pair for a couple of months and got skid marks on it and everything, I know I know," he was half talking, half laughing, "but I knew that if Mrs. W ever nosed around in there, and I don't really think she did, well, she sure the hell wouldn't touch that pair of underwear."

"So you stuck it in your dirty laundry."

"It wasn't just my dirty laundry. It was *the* pair of underwear. It's nine hundred dollars, plus the money I got today."

"That's over a thousand- and the bank?"

"Damn," he grinned. "It is." He stood straight. "How would I get to a bank? There aren't any near here, plus what if they get robbed?"

John didn't want to tell Ralph that it was all insured and he wasn't sure if he was smiling because Cary had given him more than he needed and he knew it, or because he had miscounted and had just been made aware of his windfall. He felt the underwear was a stroke of brilliance, because he could imagine that Ralph's dirty underwear was very, very dirty. He knew that Ralph had to use a laundry to wash his clothes, and that he didn't want to spend the money, so he usually waited until one of his sporadic trips to his sister. That meant that Ralph's dirty clothes were filthy. He had complained once that his boss at work had mentioned that because they worked around a food substance, everyone was expected to be cleaner than usual and that Ralph really needed to keep this in mind. Pat and John had looked at each other that day because they had had a conversation a few days before when Pat asked John what he thought would be the best way to broach the subject of Ralph's sour smell. John had said that the best thing to do would be to get him alone early one day and just flat out tell him. Pat admitted that he didn't relish
discussing it, but that he was afraid it was starting to put customers off, and he couldn't let that happen so he intended to go ahead and lay it out to him. Ralph came in with his work story the day before Pat had chosen to talk to him about his hygiene. While he continued to look fairly dirty, he didn't smell after that. They could tell that it had hurt his feelings, but that he had taken the observation his boss had made to heart, and Pat and John had been relieved. The worst aroma coming off Ralph after that was the corn from the refinery, which smelled like greasy pancakes, but it wasn't strong or repulsive. The air in the area smelled worse sometimes. The corn plant spewed fumes constantly, and depending on which way the wind blew, how hot it was, or stagnant the air was in the summer, it could be overpowering. There was a foundry nearby too, and people living in the area were always up in arms because there was a lot of soot and a strong acrid pollution that seemed to be very heavy at night, indicating that they were probably blowing off the sediments they were supposed to filter out when no one from OSHA or the health department were around to measure

or check it. A soap factory added to the outrageous mixture of noxious fumes that flowed through the air.

John recalled that just prior to the discussion Ralph had at work, they had been walking somewhere, and it had been pretty cold. They had their coats pulled up around their necks. John could smell a sour odor coming off Ralph and was bothered that the smell was strong enough that the cold didn't tamp it down. He often gauged how cold it was by how much or how little smell was coming off the dumpster near the apartment he shared with his girlfriend at the time. During the bitter cold part of winter, there was almost no stink coming from the big green container, and it bugged him that Ralph smelled despite the cold. Not to worry now, though. Ralph was fine.

His thoughts returned to the reason for their walk. "Hey," what's the interior like?"

"It's cherry, like they never used it."

"I wouldn't go messing it up hauling a lot of dirty cans around, or old greasy car parts."

"I'll put something in the trunk and use that."

"I'm just saying, if the car really is worth something, it'd be dumb to mess it up for a few bucks worth of junk."

"Oh, I'm gonna be sure it stays clean."

John was skeptical.

Ralph opened his coat and dug something out of his shirt pocket. It was the money that he got from Pat for the vacuum cleaner. He re-counted it. He pulled the fifty that Cary had given him from his pants pocket and put it all together in his shirt pocket, and buttoned it shut. He pulled his flask out, and offered it to John, who turned it down. He took a quick swig and tucked it back in his pants. "Hey, why'd god invent alcohol?"

John never replied to jokes. He would just smile.

"So fat women can get laid too"

"So you think you might sell it for the extra money? Get a cheaper car and pocket the rest?" John thought about Joey when he asked.

"Nah, I figure as long as I take care of it, it's like money in the bank, so I'll hang on to it no matter who offers what for it."

"Unless they give you twenty thousand dollars, right?"

"Crazy people's money's good too," he cackled.

When they arrived at the house where Ralph lived, John was curious as to whether he would invite him up. Despite Ralph's considering John his closest friend, he had let John see his room one time, and that was on an evening when he was incredibly drunk and needed John's help getting home without passing out in some unlucky person's yard. He had helped Ralph up the stairs and directly to his bed. Ralph collapsed on the bed, and mumbled "Thanks, man. You can leave," which was a clear sign that he didn't want him lingering.

John wondered if he was ashamed. The place was dirty, thick with dust, but in impeccable order. The sum total of his furniture was a metal framed bed, an old, cheap veneered chest of drawers, the veneer falling off at will in little pieces, making it look like a damaged advent calendar and a little card table with a folding chair. Since table top space was at a premium, there were books and papers neatly stacked on the floor, the top of his chest of drawers was loaded with toiletries, little stacks of odd boxes, old books and papers. It was all arranged, tightly packed. There were a few very old photos of a woman and a young man on top of one of the stacks. A third picture had the same two people and a child maybe five years old, running, smiling in the background, arms extended like he was an airplane. John thought he saw Ralph's face in the boy's looks. Maybe this was his mother and father. He wanted to know who they were, but Ralph was too wasted to talk and he felt like he was invading Ralph's privacy. The majority of the clutter had a coating of dust on it, indicating it had sat untouched for a long time. John could see the edges of ragged boxes peaking out from the underside of his bed, so he figured it was a major storage area. There wasn't a closet in the room, so he supposed what little clothes he had were stuffed in the chest of drawers. John thought for a moment that maybe Ralph's secret money stash had been the reason he hadn't been allowed up, but quickly retreated to the original idea that Ralph was very private and felt uncomfortable having anyone visit in such close quarters. It was an extension of one of his many taboos.

As they walked up the steps to the front door, Ralph motioned to the seats on the large porch. "I'll just be a minute. Gotta go wipe out my underwear, if you know what I mean."

John sat and looked at the leaves on the large maple tree in the front yard. There were bright and dark shades of leaves sticking out amongst the dark green leaves. Mrs. Weddington had threatened to have the tree cut down many times because, she had explained, she was sick of paying someone to clear the leaves out of the gutters and rake them during the autumn. John couldn't understand how someone could cut down something so beautiful just to eliminate a fairly easy task. Luckily, he guessed, she had not come up with a cheap safe way to have the massive sugar maple cut down. A number of the neighbors had volunteered to come over and, for the wood, remove it, but she was worried that the would-be lumberjacks would make a mistake, and her house would end up crushed under the heavy trunk. So the beautiful old tree would continue to bless the house with it's shade in the summer, it's elegant shape in the winter, it's brilliant colors and shifting, flowing, rustling movements in the fall and it's yellow-green freshness in the
spring. John mentioned the cutting of the power bill, but she waved off that aspect by saying that the tenants rent money paid for her utilities, so it didn't affect her decision one way or the other. John had never come right out and said that she shouldn't cut the tree down, but whenever he spoke to her, he would try to construct remarks that would discourage her from

the idea. John had watched so many trees come down in the neighborhood that he was perplexed and frustrated. What did these people have against trees? Utility bills did continue to climb every year. Maybe that was the unspoken reason. Free fire wood. Like the poverty stricken in Africa chipping away at the rain forests, slowly killing us all so they could barely survive.

When Ralph emerged seven minutes later, John was irritated. He had become cold. The porch and tree had shaded him from any warmth the early afternoon sun could provide and the breeze was nippy. He felt Ralph was being idiotically cautious. "What the hell took so long? It's cold out here."

Ralph had his hand in his pocket while they walked. "I'm sorry. I had to talk to Mrs. W. to be sure of where I could park the car. I can pull up here in the driveway on the right because she puts her car in the left side of the garage. John knew Ralph had his hand on his wallet, which he put in his front pants pockets, not his rear. He stared at his arm, in it's awkward position. Ralph noticed and laughed. "Shit I got my hand on my wallet like the money's gonna fly out of it and fall down a sewer grate or something." He pulled his hand from his pocket.

"How far is this guy with the car?" John blew his breath on his hands to warm them.

"Three blocks."

"Good."

As the men approached the house, Ralph did not have to point it out. John figured it was the one with an old hand crank washing machine on the front porch. He came to the conclusion that if someone had a fifty or sixty year old washing machine on their front porch, then it was likely that they had a thirty year old car in the garage.

He was right. "This is the place." Ralph pointed as he turned, with a bit of a slick pivot, toward the front porch. He knocked. As they waited, they noticed that there was an old toaster oven and some nondescript parts for a car, lying on the porch keeping the ancient washing machine company. There were many years of leaves drifted and rotting around all of the items.

"This guy gets pack rat of the century award." John remarked quickly.

"Shush!" The front door opened. An elderly man wearing gray polyester pants with a stretch waist, a white T-shirt, sloppily tucked in, and combat boots stood before them. The boots looked substantial enough that they could have been the only thing holding up the frail looking man- that and his suspenders.

"Hi, Ralph. Hey I got some leaves that need to come out of the gutters. It rained the other day and man there was water everywhere." He looked back and forth from Ralph to John, like he was watching a tennis match. John was just glad that apparently hoarding extended to hanging on to trees.

Ralph looked at John. "Sure we can take care of that for you, Mr. Emery, but I actually came to buy the car today."

"Oh, Oh. Why, you got the money?" The man had shown no indication that he had trouble seeing, but now he squinted.

"Yes, sir. I do. One thousand dollars." Ralph put one foot forward.

"You do. I see. I see. Well, uh," he looked at John.

"This is my friend, John, Mr. Emery. He's a good guy. I vouch for him." Ralph didn't smile during his introduction.

John wondered if Ralph had brought him along to intimidate the old man, in case he was thinking about changing his mind. John didn't like being recruited as muscle without his knowledge. "I can go on back, if I'm not needed."

Ralph opened his eyes wide as a signal to John that it was not what he desired. "I had John come along for his car knowledge, in case we have a hard time getting it home."

"Nothing wrong with the car. It starts fine." The old man was adamant.

"Oh I know, sir." Ralph pulled his wallet out.

The old man scanned the block. "Come inside, first. Put that away." He gestured with his head to the wallet.

He turned and went inside, John and Ralph following close behind. The room was stuffy, hot and dark. The slant autumn sun was all the light in the room, and it was impeded by stack after stack of newspapers, magazines, and numerous boxes and plastic storage tubs that filled the living room. The men had to maneuver down a pathway that had been left in the midst of it. John could see that soon, using the front door would not be an option, that the back door, probably in the kitchen, would be the only way to get in and out.

John felt claustrophobia creeping up on him. He had never known what it felt like, thought it was nonsense, but he repented. It was real and it was unpleasant.

They approached a hallway that looked nearly filled. His nervousness grew. He wanted to breath deeper, so he talked. "That old washing machine on the porch. Did they really wash things by hand with it?"

The old man answered without breaking stride. "Sure. That one's got an electric wringer not a hand crank though." He laughed. "Modern version."

The hallway was narrowed by stacks of old metal boxes that housed some sort of obsolete radio equipment. It looked like military surplus, various shades of green, drab with the dials and knobs sticking out in an ugly but practical way.

"Ham radio?" John ventured.

The old man, intent on getting them through quickly, nodded his head, but kept moving. "Old short wave ."

John looked down the pathways leading upstairs and other rooms. It dawned on him that they were probably walking around under literal tons of junk upstairs. All of the rooms, including upstairs he figured, were crammed tight with boxes, stacks of books, clothes, appliances. He could see the edge of an old guitar amp sticking out from behind a huge unsteady stack of vinyl records. "You play guitar?"

The old man stopped and turned. "Hell no. What made you ask me that?" He sounded suspicious.

John was flummoxed. "I didn't mean any offense Mr. Emery, sir. I just saw that guitar amp, there," he pointed, "and figured you played."

Mr. Emery looked puzzled. He moved past Ralph and next to John. It was so close, they were all against each other, full body. The old man smelled like musty paper. He peered in the direction John pointed. His expression changed to surprise and then amusement. "Oh hell's bells. I forgot I had that. No, son. I don't play a guitar. That was my boy's. He musta left it when he moved out." John pictured a younger pack rat with new suspenders out there somewhere filling another house with newer radios, newspapers, books and other ephemera of his generation. Mr. Emery was four inches taller than John. He looked down at him, "you wanna buy it?"

"Oh, no sir. It looks pretty old. You would probably get a lot of money for it." John had seen a show on public television during one of his rare short stints watching. It was a discussion of vintage rock and roll instruments and equipment. The amp looked similar to the stuff he saw on the show.

Suspicion flashed on the old man's face again, and then disappeared in a smile. "Well, about the time I sold it, my son would come looking for it. I'll tell him what you said though."

John didn't like the old fellow's suspicions about him. He was used to people trusting him quickly and completely. He knew that he was intrigued by the accidental museum that had been created here and that his newfound claustrophobia had made him more talkative than usual. He wondered if that was why he wasn't trusted in this instance. He rarely asked as many questions as he had in the last few minutes. It disturbed him to think that the trust he so easily gained might be a simple side effect of quietness, and not because he was imminently trustworthy. His mood darkened.

The men entered a kitchen that was jarringly clutter free. It was a big room, large enough for a full size dinner table and chairs. Everything was white, from the Formica top on the dinner table, to the work stations below the cabinets, and the cabinets themselves. Mr. Emery started rummaging through a drawer. John felt his spirits lifting. He knew relief from the tinge of claustrophobia was part of it, and the rest was probably from the brightness of the room. He remembered being told by Garlene, Daryl's wife, that Daryl's moods were vulnerable to the amount of light in a room and in this moment, John decided that maybe it wasn't quite as big a load of bullshit as he had thought it was at the time.

Mr. Emery turned with a set of keys in his hands. "Now, I started it and let it run earlier today and it turned over fine. You shouldn't have any trouble with it. I always took care of it. When my wife passed, I bought a new car. I couldn't get her out of my mind when I'd drive it. Darndest thing. Seeing her clothes, looking at her stuff in the medicine cabinet, none of it affected me as much as sitting in that car."

John laughed to himself. Ralph looked scared, like someone had told a horror story at a camp in the night. "You mean your car is haunted?"

Emery looked at Ralph like he had lost his mind. "Haunted? Good God boy. I'm just saying she liked that car, and it reminded me of her. We went everywhere in that thing. That's all." He waved his hand across the room. "She loved being in the kitchen too. See her here, boy?" He was sarcastic now.

Ralph masked his fear with a laugh. "I remember a show about a car that..." He thought better of what he was going to say. "Well, here's my money."

The old man raised a brow. "You mean my money?"

Ralph was embarrassed. "Oh, yes, sir, uh, your money." He handed the bills over, folded in half.

Mr. Emery sat down at the table, licked his large rough, chapped thumb and counted the money out on to the white surface, firmly pressing each bill on the table as he went. "It's a thousand dollars all right." He stood and shook Ralph's hand. "You own yourself a Chevrolet Vega. Let me get the title and sign it over to ya." He rummaged further in the kitchen drawers and pulled the paper out. He dug a pen out of another drawer. It seemed that if there was paperwork or items he wanted to avoid losing, he kept them in the relatively empty kitchen. He signed the sheet, had John sign on the witness line and handed it to Ralph, along with the registration and extraneous other paperwork. Ralph folded it carefully and put it in his wallet. John enjoyed signing his name. It always felt like a momentous occasion, that he placed his stamp of legitimacy on whatever document he signed. He also knew he was in a minority- many of the people in his neighborhood could not write their names or anything else for that matter. Mr. Emery motioned toward the back door. "Come on. Let's go get it out for ya."

Ralph looked stunned. Mr. Emery looked down at him and smiled. "Having a hard time believing you got it? I know you been working a while for it now."

Ralph, the confused look still on his face replied "Uh, it's hard to believe you gave me such a good deal."

Mr. Emery put his arm on Ralph's shoulders. "Now son, you don't think I would cheat you? I let you keep it running this last year just so you could see that it was working fine. I didn't want you to think I'd put sawdust in the transmission, or additives to make it run better for a little while. It's as solid as the day I bought it." His voice betrayed a trace of hurt.

Ralph heard it. He shook his head vigorously, "Oh, gee, Mr. Emery. No, I know it's a good
running car. I appreciate it." His expression changed to one of embarrassment. "Are you sure you want to part with something that reminds you of..."

"My wife?" Emery looked thoughtful. "It's a sadder feeling than a happy one. I can get a
nicer feeling from looking at a picture or a home movie, or just imagining her. It's going to waste here."

Ralph looked pale. "Yes sir. I do thank you very much."

Mr. Emery had to move various lawn mowers, junk and other pieces that were piled between the garage door and the car. John helped him, moving the bigger, heavier items. He had difficulty undoing the latch that kept the door secured in the down position. After some WD-40 and a rubber mallet tapped on the handle, it broke free, allowing him to, with John's help, haul the door through the rusted track and up beyond the top of the car. "Let's not let the door go all the way up. I don't trust those old stops up there to keep that door from headin' right on through the other side of the garage." He pointed up at two old rubber and steel bolt pieces sticking out at the end of the track.

"Good idea." John didn't relish the idea of having to get up on ladders and retrieve a heavy weathered wooden garage door from a stuck position in the ceiling of the garage.

They pushed the door, inch by inch, a little further past the height of the car roof and Emery signaled to Ralph, who had already got in the car and had it running, warming up, to go ahead and pull it out. Ralph put the car in gear and it lurched and stalled. He turned the ignition again and it cranked several turns, making everyone nervous that it wasn't going to start again. "I smell gasoline." Emery stated, crinkling his nose. "Easy on the gas, Ralph." He yelled over the whirring starter and engine. With that bit of advice taken to heart, the engine turned over and ran smoothly and relatively quiet.

Ralph turned the window down. "Thank you sir. I gotta get the hang of driving again."

Emery look disturbed.. "How long has it been since you drove?"

"Six years. But I drove all the time sir. I'm a good driver. Just a little rusty." He had driven a cab for six months. He couldn't handle the wide variety of people so he quit but he logged thousands of miles behind the wheel. Ralph still looked upset. John wondered if it had been a lot more than six years. He had a license, but he wouldn't be any better driving than Ralph. He hadn't driven since before prison, and he rarely had opportunities to drive through out most of his adult life. He knew he wasn't so hot.

Emery seemed satisfied. "Well, pull her out son. She sounds ready to go."

Ralph engaged the drive gear and the car pushed against the brakes that Ralph had firmly pressed. He let the brakes off slowly and the car crept out and into the alley, gravel churning, crackling under the wheels. It cleared the door and with a glance from Emery, he and John closed the garage door. As they headed back to the car, Emery leaned in to John and mumbled "Be sure he doesn't go drinking and driving that thing. We don't want to see him kill himself."

John pushed his shoulders back, working the stiff muscles. He was aware now that he had been stiffened the entire time he was inside the crowded house. "Count on me, Mr. Emery." He
answered quietly. They walked around the corner of the garage, John climbing into the passenger
seat and put his seat belt on. The shiny tough fabric was stiff. Emery stood at the driver's window.

"You be careful now Ralph. I don't want you to go hot rodding and hurtin' yourself. I
would blame myself if you came to harm."

Ralph still looked nervous and scared. "I will be very careful. I can't afford not to, Mr.
Emery. Thanks, again."

"Well," he tapped the top of the car, "good luck boys. I'll expect you in a few days to deal with the leaves in the gutters. Bye." He waved them off and quickly walked to the house, head down.

John looked at Ralph who still looked very uncomfortable. "Man, don't worry. It's an automatic. You'll remember how."

As if in answer to the remark, Ralph accelerated and, braking, signaling properly he pulled into the street smoothly and confidently. He nearly whispered, "The driving isn't what worries me. I think he sold me a ghost car and he didn't want to admit it."

John became aggravated. He knew that Ralph had a superstitious bent, like a lot of his friends and family, and he had no patience for it. "That's an old TV show, Ralph. Jesus, not reality."

Ralph's dis-ease was quickly replaced by indignation. "I'm not saying that the damn radio is gonna talk to me about world affairs, I just think that for an old guy who seems to hold on to every damn thing he ever owned, he sure seemed ok with letting go of one of the biggest things, barring his house, that he's ever owned. Why? Because his wife is haunting it. That's why." John could see that they weren't heading back to Pat's, but toward Daryl's house. Daryl was John's friend and didn't care much for Ralph. While Daryl didn't make a point of letting Ralph know it, he let John know it in various conversations. He had no use for him. Daryl did love cars and motorcycles, though, and he knew a lot about them, so John figured he was going to get Daryl's assessment of his purchase. No one knew or could afford a mechanic. The car would be the salve between the two on this visit.

John could not let Ralph's continued superstitious ramble go unchallenged. "Did you think maybe he's been eyeing that floor space to pile more stuff up? He sure seems to like doing that." Ralph scrunched his face for a second or two, saying nothing. John continued. "He was going to sell that guitar to me. He's retired, probably needs the money and this was a way to get some without going back out into the world." He stopped. Ralph would not be dissuaded.

They pulled up in front of the house. The garage door was open and Daryl's car was gone.
He was probably at work. Through an unspoken agreement, while Ralph waited, John got out of the car and walked up to the porch to see if he was home. His wife took the car for errands sometimes. He knocked on the screen door. The inner door was open. John could smell latex wall paint. Daryl's wife, Garlene came to the door, paint brush in hand. "Hey John." She smiled, looking down at the floor. John was never sure if she flirted with him. If she did, it was far too subtle for him to pick up, so she did it for her own entertainment if she was doing it at all. He would never do anything untoward with her even if he did figure out that it was what she was about. Daryl was his friend, and he had a hell of a temper. Even John's hardened life didn't allow him to feel that he would successfully win in a fight with Daryl with a full head of steam on, and he valued his friendship too much.

The house had to be cold, because the autumn air, despite the afternoon sun, was still brisk, and blowing constantly though mildly. "Shit," she exclaimed spotting the car and Ralph. "Daryl doesn't like him."

"Oh I know. He just wants Daryl to tell him what the car's worth. We think he got a really good deal and he knows Daryl would know."

Garlene was in her early thirties and in good shape. She wore a flannel shirt, unbuttoned. She wore a T-shirt without a bra under that. The flannel shirt was old and large, so it hung far around her sides. The cold air made her nipples stand out against the white threadbare fabric of the T-shirt. They were large and stuck out noticeably. John noticed and made a point of looking her in the eye. "Is he home?"

"He's at work. I'm painting the damn dining room. Jesus, I don't know what I was thinking. It's so fucking cold, I don't know why I didn't do this in the summer."

"It's too hot in the summer." John smiled. "Mind if we stop by later, just long enough for him to look it over?"

Even if she had noticed her exposure, she hadn't done anything to cover it. "Sure. He doesn't like Ralph, but he loves cars, so he'll be ok." She shivered and pulled her shirt around her. "We'll be done with dinner at six."

"Cool, thanks Garlene. We'll be by then." John looked away quickly, not daring to look down to give her an indication that he had been looking at her breasts. He remembered a girlfriend telling him that men were idiots if they thought that women didn't know they looked at their breasts at all times under all circumstances from morning to night, and no attempts to hide it worked. He always hoped he was better at it than that.

He waved back as he rambled down the steps of the porch. "See ya then." Garlene closed the door behind her.

John got to the car and then snapped his fingers. "Hey wait a sec." He ran back up to the house and rang the bell. Garlene looked out the curtain and smiled. "It's not six yet."

She opened the door. John laughed, "What's the big hand supposed to be on?" He was mortified that he said something about a hand being on something as he involuntarily looked at her chest. Garlene smirked, pulling her shirt around her again. "I, uh, wondered if you want the garage door closed? He's got all those tools in there, and it's wide open."

83

"Shit". She looked frightened. "I left the fuckin' thing open when I got the paint out. Jesus, yeah, close it will ya? He'd kill me if he knew I forgot."

"No problem. I'll check and make sure that everything's there."

She smiled sweetly, "Thanks, hon. I owe ya one. See you at six."

"Bye."

"Bye-bye." She waved a little goodbye. It was uncharacteristic. Her typical demeanor was the tough chick.

John pushed the garage door button in the garage and rushed out before it shut. He thought it amusing that he'd been in two dramatically different garages in the last hour. During his brief stint as a thief, he worked garages. They were usually easy targets, without alarms, and they were usually where people kept their tools, which were easy to resell. The chance of coming across a person while ripping off a garage was almost nil, another reason he preferred them. He knew that if he had ever stumbled across or had been confronted by a person, he would have given himself up immediately. In fact, he had. It was how he was caught. He had turned himself in when confronted by a home owner. He felt good that he'd been trusted in two garages that day. He was glad that time put more and more distance between him and his past mistakes. Part of the torture of his imprisonment was keeping it from the mother of his child, and her parents. He knew that they had suspected something, but because he continued sending little sums of money regularly, they were willing to ignore their vague misgivings.

Ralph still looked very unsettled. John resented having to talk enough to explain to Ralph how ridiculous his fears were. "Even if she were a ghost, which she isn't, she would haunt him, nota car."

84

They pulled away from the curb. Ralph shook his head. "He said he felt her presence in the car. He specifically said that she didn't come to him anywhere else."

"Jesus, Ralph. You're smarter than that."

Ralph lit a cigarette, and pulled the ashtray open. It was sparkling clean. "She must not have let him smoke in here. This thing was never used. Sorry, ma'am." He tilted his head up slightly as he offered his apology.

"You're gonna ruin it, man. You worked all this time for this car and now you blow it, can't enjoy it because of some bullshit your imagination made up."

"Hey life fucks things up, not me."

John tried to think of a different angle to come from. He felt un-moored while he tried to figure out how to win an argument when what they argued was complete nonsense. "Why, would, she be evil, even if she existed? Maybe she'd watch out for you."

Ralph took a long drag on his cigarette. They were heading back to Pat's. "Ghosts are unhappy. They don't want to be here. You're talking about angels."

John gave up. He looked around the car. The dashboard was loaded with chrome. He had forgotten how much of the silver coating there was in older cars, even cheaper ones. What year had they stopped using it? Late seventies? He couldn't recall. He crinkled his nose. "I smell exhaust."

Ralph blew smoke out of his nose, and sniffed. "I don't smell anything."

John sniffed around. "It's not much. Did you have your window open when you were waiting for me?"

"No. It's cold."

"We need to check for a leak. The muffler sounds fine, but I swear I got a whiff of exhaust fumes."

"Could be her... Plasma, or whatever."

John rolled his eyes. "You call Ghostbusters if you want. I think we need to call Muffler King." It dawned on him that Ralph hadn't bummed the cigarette he was smoking. He patted his shirt pocket. His pack wasn't there. He checked his coat pockets. Nothing. He looked on his left. He had thrown his cigarettes on the seat. Ralph had taken one of his cigarettes. He didn't care. He had already resigned himself. If they jacked up the price again with more taxes though, that could all change. The extra dollar per pack they tagged on in the past year had hit a lot of people hard. The price for a pack of cigarettes in some gas stations and quick stores was just over five dollars, although you could still find off brand cartons for twenty five dollars. John had tried different generic cigarettes until he found one that tasted close enough to the Camels he was used to, and switched back and forth. He picked up the pack. It was light several cigarettes. Ralph had taken more than one. Fine. He better not bum anymore today, although, he could ask John for the rest of the pack and he'd give it to him. Pat sold his brand of cigarettes. He'd get more. They pulled up to Pat's. Ralph parked the car across the street in front of an abandoned house. It was
boarded up. The first few times it had been sealed up, crack addicts had found ways in and it quickly became a crack house. Pat had no tolerance for the dealing, the rough characters that hung around, the prostitution. He knew it would destroy his business. After several calls to police and some friends he had at the station, plus a discrete show of his sawed off shot gun at the right time, the house had been sealed up again by the city. John vaguely recalled hearing someone at another bar say that Pat had bought the house for almost nothing at auction, for back taxes, and he planned on turning it into parking.

"Let's get a drink." Ralph still looked shaken.

TOASTED & GHOSTED

John and Ralph stepped into Pat's. He noticed that Ralph lingered at the door, keeping it open so that his car was noticeable from the doorway. He half called out to Pat. "Chief." He rolled his head toward the door.

Pat took the hint immediately. He looked at the car. "Hey, Ralph's got a car!" One of the couples who were regulars on the weekend were there, and Mike the Poor Fuck, as they called him, was there. Cheryl was slow dancing with Cary. Both of them were plastered.

Every person in the bar, including the old guys who were now playing checkers while they sipped their beers and coffee, looked at Ralph and stood. They all walked outside as they asked Ralph various questions. The couple, William and Charmain, weren't usually there this early. William asked a question that John heard. "Wow. How'd you afford it?"

Ralph, truly modest, replied "Been saving my change and stray money for two years."

"How much?" Everyone knew that the answer wouldn't be the truth, but that the truth would leak out later. This was the opening salvo.

"Couple thousand."

William was in his early sixties. His hair was thin and stringy, his comb over so insubstantial it was nearly invisible. He was skinny, probably as thin as he was when he was a teenager. His worn clothes hung on him. On the other hand, his wife, Charmain, was morbidly obese. She always wore the same sort of badly worn clothes. Her clothes did not hang. She barely fit in the top she usually wore. Her pants were only less of an embarrassment because the shirt came down over part of her rear end and the front roll of fat. She had two outfits, one, dull pink sweats and the other a white blouse with fatigue pants. She joked that it was her patriotic outfit. John always thought of them as Mr. & Mrs. Sprat. The couple was a constant source of jokes and scorn for Ralph.

William looked at Ralph with disbelief. "You saved two thousand dollars?"

Charmain charged forward. "We coulda done that." She looked at John, sweating. Any exertion made her sweat like she had run a marathon. "We got laid off again." The couple worked at a factory where the work was up and down like a roller coaster, so they were unemployed as much as they were working. They would collect their tiny unemployment checks and wait to be called back, spending the bulk of their time at Pat's. Even if they hadn't mentioned being laid off, all John had to do was see the check Pat cashed for them. He could tell the difference between the larger blue checks they received at the factory and the smaller green checks the state issued, not that he really cared. He had simply noticed.

A lot of the customers there used Pat as a bank, of sorts. No one there, to a person, had a checking account. He would cash their checks from work, or the government, all for one dollar, unlike the check cashing stores that soaked a person upward of ten percent of the amount. The only thing Pat required in return was that the person was drinking there, that way he didn't end up taking care of half the neighborhood, and he was steadfast about that. He wouldn't let someone manipulate him either, say, have them come in with some strange check, and tell him to take the price of a beer out of the check and give 'em the change. They had to be regulars, or they had to be square dealing, in his tough estimation. He didn't have to do it, he would say. John understood it was another way to nurture loyalty in his regulars and it was worth it to risk having some extra money in the bar to cover it, plus he knew at some level, he figured, Pat wanted to be helpful.

Ralph seemed to be reconsidering his car through the eyes of everyone around him. He started to puff up as the compliments and well wishing washed over him.

William seemed the most pleased. "Damn I had one of these when they came out!"

Charmain looked at her husband suspiciously. "When?"

William took the question innocently, not as a judgement on his honesty. He did that a lot with Charmain. She seemed to wonder if he told the truth most of the time, yet John had never heard anything untrue or exaggerated come out of his mouth. "I had one for my job at Mollor's, the candy company. I was a salesman. They let me use it to make my calls."

Ralph laughed. "You're kidding, right. Molar? Candy? Sweet tooth?"

William thought for a moment. "Well, no. That was the guy's name what's owned it, pretty sure."

Charmain did it again. "You worked at a candy factory?" John wished she had known William then. Maybe then she wouldn't be so jealous about the stone cold fact that he actually walked and drew breath before he met her. He wanted to leave the fat and candy jokes to Ralph and his karma. He never said the word karma around them, only thought it.

"I was a salesman. I sold candy, cigars, trinkets to bars and little mom and pop stores."
He took his glasses off and started wiping the lenses with a tattered handkerchief he had in his shirt pocket. He usually left an edge of the handkerchief hanging out of his pocket, making him look like a dandy that had been sand blasted out of his finery. "I wonder if they're even in business any more. They laid me off when things went sour for 'em. I think the owner got divorced and things got all mucked up."

Ralph looked at John. He mumbled, loudly, "Things went sour at the candy store."

Charmain grinned and grabbed William's arm, leaning him over to her shoulder. "What else don't I know about you boy?"

"Plenty." He said it without humor. He turned his attention to Ralph again. "How's it run? Can I sit at the wheel?"

Ralph was downright embarrassed by the attention now, even though he had welcomed it
with his tease at the bar door. "Sure, go ahead. You wanna drive it?"

William looked surprised. "Well, boy. That's generous of you, but maybe you should ask
how long it's been seen I drove a car."

Charmain butted in again. "Probably the car at the candy joint."

William looked at her. "You sure are smart-alecky today. Go have another beer, woman."
Everyone whistled. William rarely stood up to Charmain.

Charmain was thrown off. Her brow angled, expressing hurt, unusual for her. She regained her cocky attitude immediately though. "I will, and it'll be on your bill, mister." She stayed beside him though.

William continued his story. "My brother just bought a Riviera. It was a massive hunk of car. He gave me his old Skylark. Lasted me 'til a couple of years before I met you kitten." He looked at Charmain. "I bought a bus pass after that and haven't been behind a wheel since then." He looked at Ralph and smiled, "so I'll be happy to just sit at the wheel." Ralph motioned and tipped his body toward the door, inviting him to get in.

William jumped in like he was late for a date in high school. He sat with his hand on the wheels. "I had my files down on the floor there. Wintertime they'd be hot as hell because the heater really blasted out the air." He looked at Ralph. "You'll love the heater. I loved getting' out of the car because I was so warm, and them files were like a hot water bottle up against me, it didn't matter how cold the air was. It was like a heat cocoon. I liked my job too. Shame it went kaflooey." He sat looking out the windshield, seeing the past ahead. He looked in the rear view mirror, and turned his head. "Thought someone was back there." He adjusted the mirror. "It's got one of them night filter things on it." He sighed and got out of the car. Ralph looked disturbed. "Did you say you saw something in the rear view mirror?"

William pointed at the mirror. "It's one of them night time, day time things. If you angle it, it filters for bright sun, but the angles are off. You can see people off to the side, upside down, if it's not lined up."

"And you saw somebody."

"Son, relax. I adjusted it. You're a little shorter 'en me but just move it a little more and it'll work for you."

John intervened, hoping to get Ralph off his ghost kick, which he was obviously back on. "Let me buy you a beer Ralph. A congratulation beer." He wanted to be sure Ralph knew it was for a special reason, or he was certain he'd permanently be taking care of Ralph's beer as well as his cigarettes.

It worked. Ralph looked at him with the expression of a child distracted by too many toys. He enjoyed the attention, the new car, but he wanted a beer. "That's a deal." He headed back into the bar. Pat strode fast, getting ahead of him. "Keeping tabs, chief?" Ralph seemed aggravated.

"Ready to pour you one." He replied, nonplused. He stepped behind the bar, and opened a beer for Ralph, placing it at his spot at the bar.

Ralph sat down, and drank deeply from the bottle, his Adam's apple rolling as the beer flowed down his throat. "This sucks."

Pat stood in front of him, like he had waited for Ralph to take a drink and tell him what he thought of his beer. This wasn't wine tasting, though. "What sucks?"

He whispered. "My car is haunted." Ralph was like a lot of superstitious people John knew. They typically kept their superstitions to themselves, because of the concern that they'd be confronted with the illogic of their beliefs, or were concerned about another superstition that led them to believe that talking about the first taboo subject would bring more bad mojo on their heads, so his public admission did not bode well. It meant he was pretty sure of his ghost.

Pat stood quietly, continuing to look at Ralph. "Ghosts? You mean niggers been riding in your car?" John got the reference to spooks, and knew Ralph would.

Ralph laughed. "Chief. I didn't think you had a joke like that in ya." It seemed to cheer him up.

Pat was proud of himself. He rarely made a sly reference. His clowning was normally reserved for the stilted retelling of jokes he had heard from other customers. John was vexed one of his few attempts were so utterly racist. It depressed him. "You're kiddin' right, Ralph?"

Ralph hesitated. "Yeah." He said it flatly.

John didn't understand the intense hatred the people in the neighborhood had for black people. He didn't care about blacks, he certainly didn't hate them. Despite being surrounded by prejudice all his life, John could never quite figure out the sense in it. When he was eight, he had been introduced to an aunt. She was the only red-haired person in his family. The first thing he noticed about her was that she was wearing a white cotton dress with a low cut front. There were hundreds and hundreds of freckles on her chest and arms. John thought that she was becoming black in degrees, like a leopard slowly changing from black spots to solid black. No one in her family seemed to dislike her at all because of her freckles. John had stared at her skin when introduced and his mother had said, "John, what's the problem, boy. Don't stare at her tits. Where's yer manners?"

His aunt, Ruby, laughed. "He's lookin' at my freckles, Janet." She pushed her chest toward John. "I do have a lot of freckles, don't I, hon'?"

"Looks like stars." He replied. Both women laughed and went about their business. John didn't get skin differences being an issue from then on. His aunt had been an inadvertent educator regarding skin color and his uncle had clued him in on disabilities. John laughed to himself that he wished he'd had more aunts and uncles while growing up. He knew the few black kids that were in his school stayed away from the white kids, but wasn't sure for a long time if it was because they didn't like the white kids, or spoke a foreign language. The blind hatred of blacks he witnessed more and more as he got older explained their staying to themselves. They were afraid for their safety. He figured they were better off on their own.

Ralph had finished off his beer in a few gulps, a morning style attack on it. While he waited for Pat to set up a fresh one, he leaned over to John. "How'd you like somma that wench?" He pointed, wavering, directly at Charmain. John chuckled into his beer as he sipped. His laugh encouraged Ralph to continue. "William won't mind. Hey, he'd like you to take a little pressure off him, if you know what I mean." John kept the neck of his beer poised on his lip as Ralph talked his trash. It allowed him to smile without it being obvious. "I said pressure but I think it's called shear strain. Machine shop lingo. Learned it from the Corn Colonel, ya know." He extended the word lingo like he was Latin American. John did do a little spit take, some of his beer going back into his bottle. Ralph could see he was getting to John, so he tried to keep it going. "Hell, if ya fuck her from like the right side," he motioned to his side, "William wouldn't even see ya." John laughed quietly. "He'd think you were one of her moles vibratin'."

John was amused and a bit peeved that he had ruined his nearly full beer. He waved it off. "Pat, I just spit into my beer. I need a new one."

Ralph laughed, nearly uncontrollably. "Bladder control, John." He sat up straight, seeing a half ass play on words swimming in front of him. "Goin to the john 'cause I don't have bladder control. Everybody knew it was the end... for Big John."

John hated toilet jokes about his name. He looked at Ralph with an expression that let him know that he had better not go further down that road. Ralph got it, swallowing deeply. He leaned again, in a swerve, toward John. "I'm gonna get me some of it." He poked his thumb at himself in mock confidence, "I'm so short, she'll think I'm a yeast infection."

John laughed out loud. A number of people looked over at him. His voice, loud, was a rare occurrence. "Godamn it Ralph. You son of a bitch." In one oddly sputtered sentence, John voiced his displeasure over Ralph's rank manners, and admiration for his ability to make him laugh even though he didn't like the meanness in the jokes.

Cheryl, in her inebriated state, was slow to turn her attention from Cary and back to John, where it usually focused.

Cary had made a vague mention that he better get home soon, although everyone knew he was less than enthused about confronting the mess he had created at home, so he would probably stay. They all knew that his girlfriend worked the first shift and wouldn't be home for another hour or two. He'd stay at least that long, but Cheryl realized that he would, undoubtedly, go sooner than later if she didn't change his mind. John, on the other hand, was not at work, and not going. That meant that it was time for her to refocus her attention. John had worked this out before she did, and it allowed him to judge himself to be less than enthused, tired, beer fatigued, to some extent, to put up with her shit. He knew he would have to, though, if he wanted to hang out here and enjoy himself, so he figured a few more quick beers would get him in a more receptive mood. He downed the next two pretty quickly.

He hatched a plan. He turned to Ralph. "Hey wanna get something to eat over at Eta's?"

Ralph, forlorn, and getting drunk fast, shook his head, no.

"You won't be able to drive home ya know."

"Told Pat. He says it's ok to leave it here." It was a public street but Ralph let Pat decide if the car stayed there or not.

John could see that Ralph would be getting scraped up later that evening. He became more aggravated by the superstitions that were confounding Ralph's moment of triumph. He figured he needed to go ahead and eat because he'd be the one hauling Ralph's dead weight home later that night. Paul, the night bartender did it once, but let it be known to anyone who cared, that if he had to do it again, Ralph would end up in the alley sleeping it off.

He waved to get Pat's attention. "I'm getting something to eat. What do I owe you?" He spoke quietly, hoping Cheryl wouldn't hear.

Pat was oblivious to John's attempts to keep things quiet. "Hey, going to Eta's? Can you pick something up for me? Paul's running really late, so I'll be here for a while."

Cheryl perked up. "You going to Eta's? I'm there, baby doll."

John was glad he had downed the extra two beers. His worry about her pawing him had subsided in the golden blur that pushed forward in his thoughts. He was fine joking around with her over a meal. Alcohol was a social lubricant. The first time he heard the term it sounded gay but now he began to not only understand, but agree. She knew how to enjoy food too, and it was catching. He always ate more when he ate with her, and he had a good appetite. He was glad his metabolism still allowed him to eat and drink like he did and not balloon his gut like he knew it would some time in the near future. Laying carpet, incredibly rigorous work, helped, he was sure. The thought of his knees aching came to him again. He had downed enough beer, his aches had disappeared, but he knew they would be back in full force in the morning.

"What do you want Pat?" He knew what Pat would order before he asked. It was part of his regimen, his food. "Pork Tenderloin Sandwich, lettuce, tomato, and extra mayo. Two large orders of home fries.

John had to admit, the sandwich was a magnificent thing to behold. The tenderloins were huge, sticking out on all sides of the oversize sesame seed bun. John laughed to think that if people knew how good and cheap the food at the shabby little restaurant down the street was, it would be overrun every day, and end up being on the other side of town, five times the size, five times the prices, but that was not the situation, so the owner, Vic, and his wife Vivian, would continue to offer kindness and incredible food to the unwashed masses here in their lousy neighborhood. Most of the couple's customers were older retired men, who, for any number of reasons from divorce to death, were on their own, and ate all of their meals at the restaurant. It wasn't as cheap as a can of soup, but it wasn't much more. John didn't understand why they didn't charge more. He had a feeling that they were thinking of the

men being able to afford it. The women who survived their spouses stayed at home and cooked for themselves, or so John thought. The husband and wife team were retired truck drivers themselves, and owning and running a restaurant had been their dream, so they bought Eta's from a man who had let it run down to the point that it had been closed for six months before they got it. They didn't pay much
for it, and they didn't need money, so John figured they'd decided they would charge what people could afford, not what it was worth, almost like a food shelter, although he was sure that they would be unhappy with that description, and he'd have to say, when sitting with a beautiful mound of food in front of him, steaming and delicious, the low end no frills way a soup kitchen ran was not a fair comparison. He was glad they were cheap though, because he ate there a lot too.

He wondered why they hadn't changed the name of the restaurant to Vic and Viv's. It seemed perfect. He loved alliteration and would never speak the word in front of any of his friends or acquaintances. He couldn't remember how he knew the word. Eta's had actually been a drunken sign painters mistake, or at least it was rumored so, because no one knew of an Eta or heard of someone who knew of one. Vic said that Vivian liked the name, and didn't want her name up on the sign, so it stayed. John figured Vic would be ok with that because it didn't cost money. If there was ever talk of charging more money, it had been Vic. He would occasionally complain, usually when sorting through food service invoices in the little back room that was clearly visible to the patrons. He'd grouse that they weren't doing this for their health. Vivian would nod her head and smile at him, saying something in the vein that they did indeed do it for their health and he would shut up, knowing that she loved what she did, and that he loved her being happy, so as long as they weren't losing money, everything would remain the way it was.

John paid his tab. Pat handed him a ten dollar bill for his food. Cheryl had hugged and squeezed Carey so much it looked like he had run out of air and was swooning. John knew better. He had been drinking steadily. He now had a cup of coffee in front of him, and a pack of cupcakes that Pat sold from a little metal rack at the back of the bar. John thought it was funny that he set them up near the liqueurs, like he had lined up the items for sale by sugar content.

Cheryl bounded up to John, and holding his arm in what could almost be considered a vice grip, headed toward the door with him. "Whoa, hon. You forgot your tab." It was Pat, chiding her for heading out without paying. John felt she knew what she was doing.

"Oh darlin'. I'm sorry. I get so light headed around this boy." She let go of John and returned to the bar to pay her bill.

John decided he would make a break. "I'm gonna have a cigarette." He walked out the door quickly and started toward the restaurant through an open field. The gaping hole in the block was created when five houses, all of which were owned by the same shady people out of state, were condemned, and despite back taxes owed, were torn down to make way for low income housing. That was nine years ago. The project was held up by lack of funding, bureaucrats, and people like Pat, who believed it would harm his business, lower property values, and bring in the wrong element. John figured that meant blacks. He figured with racism behind it, the field would be a tribute to the barren devastation of that hatred.

The air was still cold, and as the autumn sun abandoned the area earlier every day, it was getting colder. The wind, unfettered, blew strong against John's back. He imagined how much more uncomfortable it would be on the way back. He'd get a coffee to-go to warm him up. He wondered why he felt warmer when he lit a cigarette. It certainly wasn't the tiny little fire at the end, or the smoke. It must be the nicotine, or maybe the ritual, the comfort from performing it. He wanted to stop smoking, but he didn't seriously consider it. He'd smoked since he was fourteen and while he knew it wasn't good for him, he didn't feel like enough things in his life were lined up to be able to put any real effective measure of will power behind the effort, so quitting was an occasional flitting thought.

His daughter was going to high school the next few years and he wanted her to go to a private school. Her grandparents had planted that thought in his head the last time he visited. John felt that they brought it up as an insinuation that it wasn't going to happen because he hadn't bothered to do any better than he had. The child's mother went to nursing school, and John knew for a fact that she borrowed a lot of the money in student loans to do it because her parents couldn't foot the bill. She said they planned on helping her pay the loans, but it seemed unlikely that on the father's pension and their social security, that it would happen, so their guilt trip didn't motivate him as much as his own desire to see her get a good education and live in a better class of the world than he had.

Maybe the fact that John's knees were giving out was a serendipitous event that would force him to get a better job and make things better for himself and his daughter. His current job paid him decent money per hour, but it didn't include travel time, which could often be two hours per day, and it didn't include any insurance or vacation or personal days. He didn't get a paid lunch. His hours each week varied wildly. Two weeks ago, he had worked ninety hours, the next he worked forty five, and this week they insinuated he would work sixteen to twenty hours per week for the next several weeks. It was part of the reason he decided to blow off two days of work in a row. He'd save them hours on his schedule, not theirs.

He heard Cheryl running behind him. "Hold up. You that hungry?" John slowed down.

"Yeah, I'm hungry."

"Me too." She rubbed her hands together.

He figured she was always hungry. She was pretty smashed too. Vic and Viv tried not to turn anyone away at their place except trouble makers. That could include someone, who was loud, or who gave Viv a hard time or who was so drunk, it made others uncomfortable. They were usually very generous, Viv more so than Vic. "Better behave over here."

"Oh, I don't know." She cackled.

"Cheryl. I want to eat, ok."

She looked at him in mock seriousness. "You think I'm gonna screw up getting' to eat ?" She cackled again. "You don't know me very well."

"Why aren't you at work today?" Cheryl kept tabs of his schedule.

"I didn't want to go." He tried to avoid frowning. He was not interested in having her pry.

"Well, I can dig that." She wasn't going to pursue it.

They stepped into the restaurant. Cheryl bowed. "Thank you. Thank you. Yes, I'm here to eat." It was nearly four o'clock so it wasn't yet busy with dinner customers. The half dozen people there turned to look at her. John noticed that Vic was behind the counter, frowning.

John gave a quick smile and wave. "Hey Vic." He grabbed Cheryl's arm and whispered "Behave."

Cheryl calmed down. "Hey, just gotta keep the fans happy."

John pushed her gently into a booth, whispering, "Vic is not a fan."

She raised her eyebrows, and giggled. "I'm not so hot on ol' Vic myself." Cheryl hung on most men, and was very deferential and complimentary, but not with Vic. John noted that if a man rebuffed or misspoke to her a certain number of times John had not yet counted off, she very obviously put them in a different column, and those men got nothing but observations dripping in acid. She would ignore the fact that her snubs would often go unnoticed. She would over-snub them.

The fixtures in the restaurant were installed in the sixties and worn, from the cut and taped leather on the booth benches, to the turquoise and maroon color scheme in the trim and chairs, but it was very clean, courtesy of Vic's younger brother, who worked part time as their janitor. The clean smell, combined with the aroma from the cooking was intoxicating. John closed his eyes and drew a deep breath. John always came to the same conclusion after the first moments in the place. Vivian had decided, that despite the problems it might cause with the majority of the customers, her restaurant would be a no smoking restaurant. Vic was very concerned, because he knew that they couldn't afford to alienate the majority of their customers, but he also knew that Vivian was not going to change her mind. She felt that the smell of the food, the cleanliness were tantamount to anyone being able to indulge their nicotine habit. Vic smoked, and Viv didn't. Vic figured it was a backhanded attack on him, but he had explained a number of times to crabby customers that she lived with a smoker and knew better than all of those who smoked, what it did to the non-smokers. He got a rap down that essentially said, "I'm a smoker, I don't like it, I'm on your side, my wife doesn't smoke, she lives with a smoker, she knows better than we do how it affects non-smokers, and I love her and you all love her and she gets her way because of that and because she's right, now, you want coffee?" Occasionally he'd just say "Let's not piss off the cook." John knew states were all slowly banning smoking everywhere so in a matter of time, it would be a non-issue.

Vic was worried enough about the ban that he built a small cage like area with nine foot wire fencing off of an old delivery exit near the restrooms. When people asked about the fence, he said it kept people from using it as a second entrance, but everyone knew it was to make sure people didn't eat and then sneak out without paying. No one considered doing that. Vic had let it be known through many casual conversations and a show and tell of numerous guns, that he loved guns, was good with guns, had guns and would have no problem using guns if someone tried to rob him. That included stiffing them. One old guy with less sense than money told Vic that he'd go to jail if he shot someone for stiffing him. Vic calmly replied that the stiff would be dead. Jail was a much better deal for him. The old guy canceled his food order and drank coffee. John wondered if he didn't have the money. Vic and Vivian occasionally reclaimed a tab from a customer. They were very quiet and subtle about it. They didn't want to be overwhelmed with charity cases, but the regulars who came up short once in a while were forgiven. Viv felt it was the right thing to do, Vic looked at it as good business; The customer would be faithful, and spend their money there when they did have it to spend. They were both right as far as John was concerned.

The cage assuaged most of the heavy smokers. They seemed happy standing in the snow or rain or cold wind, like today, to be able to have a smoke. Their tables were not cleared while they were in the cage. It was as if they were at the table while they were outside. The balance of the smokers weren't so badly addicted that they couldn't wait until after they left to smoke. It wasn't unusual to have half a dozen or more people standing out in the cage waiting for their food. Viv would knock on the window and point to the person who's food she had and head toward the table.

The couple had gone through a lot of trouble to make the place pleasant. Another way they made it nice was not an effort but a happy circumstance . They were a handsome couple, good to look at. Vic looked a little like Burt Lancaster in late middle age. He was ruddy, well built, the ravages of age beating at the edges of his body, but not winning the battle yet. He had a tight stomach, broad shoulders and bulging biceps that set the ladies to smiling and blushing. His hair was dyed jet black. It was obvious, but because he was so good looking, everyone could understand, overlook, even give the thumbs up to this obvious surrender to narcissism in the battle against old age. Viv looked like Bo Derrick at age fifty five with black hair. There wasn't a man, crude, stupid, or sophisticated who couldn't appreciate her looks. It was a pleasant part of the experience to have a peek at the couple who ran the place while you soaked in the good food and clean comfortably worn surroundings.

Vivian came out and took their order. Cheryl ordered roast beef, double gravy, double mashed potatoes, green beans, corn, ice cream, pie, and Coke. Everyone ordered their dessert when they ordered their meal. No one wanted to put Viv out to have her take a second order. John ordered a super bacon cheese burger with home fries and a chocolate malt. They had two sizes of hamburger, a generous regular size a third of a pound of meat, and a super size which was a half pound of meat. The bun was bigger, making it look cartoon huge, but it was a favorite. He ordered coffee. He decided that he didn't want to be blasted so early in the day. He always regretted it the next day.

Cheryl immediately started talking about her hearing at the worker compensation meeting that morning. "They poked me, stared at me and asked me about a thousand questions. It was ridiculous."

"Well, they don't want to pay fakers."

Cheryl looked hurt. "I'm not faking."

"I didn't say you were. I said they need to sort the fakes out if they can. They can't afford to pay everyone who walks in the door."

"They damn near can. Tax a few of these rich guys more than a dollar a year"

John shrugged. "Maybe." He didn't want her to go off on her rich people tirade, even though he agreed with her, it was a useless exercise to talk about it because what could they do about it? He knew that she read the newspaper and a couple magazines every week and he was certain that she could run rings around him on facts and figures and he didn't care.

"The funny thing is, I didn't see an actual doctor for more than a minute or two. The rest of the time it was nurses and nurse's aids."

"They make more money seeing a lot of people."

"I'm not sure how it works with the worker comp doctors but I'd guess that you're right."

"I wonder if I could get worker's comp?" John puzzled out loud.

"What's wrong hon?" She looked genuinely concerned.

John was surprised that he had thought about worker's comp and even more surprised that he had given voice to it. "I, well, my knees are really starting to give me problems."

Her brows flattened out and she leaned forward. "Do you work as an employee for Jack and those guys, or do you get money under the table?"

"I got it under the table until this last job. They said they'd put me back on it after this job. That way I don't have to pay taxes on it."

"Right, hon, and they don't have to pay unemployment, workers comp, vacation, sick days, on and on. You need to be on a payroll. Whose name's on your paycheck?"

"Right now? It's JBE. Something like that."

"Well, now we're getting somewhere. You could get comped, easy. You've been hurt working. They keep eliminating stuff from coverage, like repetitive motion injury, but they haven't been able to dump 'em all yet. You should go see a doctor. I've got a name."

"I can't afford it."

"You tell 'em that it's workers compensation. They don't take any money then."

"I don't know." John absentmindedly lit a cigarette and then immediately snuffed it out on his jeans. He looked around to see if Vic noticed. He was busy chatting with someone at the counter.

"John, why didn't you tell me about this before? I'm hurt."

"Well, it really hasn't been a problem until recently."

"Let's have a cigarette outside." Cheryl stood. Viv brought John's coffee and Cheryl's Coke.

"I need coffee." John raised his cup, indicating she should wait until he'd drank a little.

"Hey, bring it with you." Viv smiled, John got weak kneed. She was one older woman he could see himself with, but the fantasy always got muddled with a smiling Vic appearing over her shoulder.

John heard two women's voices behind him. He turned to see his girlfriend from a little over a year ago with another woman whom he'd never met. He suspected that it was Susan, a friend Annie had talked of a number of times. She seemed reticent when talking about her, and now he understood that she have felt that he would be attracted to her. Annie's fear was accurate. John wasn't sure that he wanted to talk to Annie, but he liked the look of her friend. He waved.

Annie spotted him, smiled and walked over. "Hey John. How are you." She ignored Cheryl. John stood and met her halfway. Annie hated Cheryl and never made a secret of it. She felt she was disrespecting her when she hung all over John. John wanted to keep a little distance between the two.

"I'm ok." He wasn't very convincing. "Gonna introduce me?" He motioned to Annie's companion with his eyes.

Annie looked angry. "I'm fine too, and she," she motioned behind her with a movement of the eyes as well, "has a boyfriend."

"I'm trying to be polite."

"Right, John." She walked over to her companion. "Susan, this is John, my old boyfriend." She said it like it was a consumer's warning. The goods are faulty. Don't try them.

Susan, didn't look at all like Annie. Annie was a thin woman, her brunette hair dyed blonde. Susan was curvy and had black hair. He seemed to recall Annie saying she was twenty one like herself. "Hello, John. Nice to meet you." Her voice was sultry. She turned to Annie with a look of knowing, "So how come you never told me about him?"

Annie, as she had often done with John, involuntarily stood slightly off the heals of her feet and leaned in toward Susan, "LISTEN, bitch. My boyfriend is Billy. I talk about Billy. If you think I'm trying to keep you from THIS," she gestured at John with a fling of an unlit cigarette, "you are more fucked up than I thought!"

Vic was out from behind the counter. "Keep it down." He was furious, and it showed. One of his fists were balled up, as if he would punch someone any second. Annie and Susan ignored him. Susan yelled. "You talk about everybody, but not him. Maybe you still want him?

Vic took two steps closer. John put his arms around the girls, and in his usual quiet voice said, "If you don't shut up, I'm gonna act like I don't know either one of you and Vic is gonna put you on the menu as dead meat."

Both girls looked at Vic. They scowled. Annie spat. "I don't need his fucking pop."

Vic charged up within an inch of her. "Get out, and don't come back until you can act like a civilized woman." He looked at John. "If they are your friends, John, you need a better class of friends."

"I'm sorry Vic. This is my fault. Don't take it out on them." John knew that he had shut Annie out. He was doing it with his current girlfriend, Diane. Despite the fact that he had essentially moved in with her, told her he really cared for her, he wouldn't say he loved her. That would be a lie. He let her feed him, do his laundry and drive him around in her car, which her father had given to her, all the while knowing that these efforts were an attempt to get him to say "I love you."

He wondered about her relationship with her father. It made him uncomfortable. Even though he'd never heard anything from her concrete enough for him to have the suspicion, he distanced himself from her partly because of some vague gut feeling that she might have had a sexual relationship with her father, and, he had to admit when he was honest with himself, more probably because he didn't feel comfortable that close to anyone. He knew that he had no right to take advantage of her, but he hadn't forced her to do anything she was doing, and he'd hoped that maybe his suspicions or the feelings that he always needed lots of space would change by simple exposure to her loving disposition. It didn't happen fast enough. Their relationship was failing. He felt guilty, and here in front of him was the last woman he had cold shouldered out of his life.

"Let me get your pops for you." He looked at Vic, pleading.

Vic liked John, so he knew he had the edge, but only if he could get the girls under control. "They still have to go." He had now included Susan in the banishment.

John saw Annie moving off the heals of her feet again. He took hold of her hand and while holding it firmly, caressed the back of it with his thumb. "Let me do this for you." He had turned it into something about him instead of about her defending herself and her friend against Vic, so he figured she would relent, and she did. "I'll take a super Coke."

John continued to hold Annie's hand. He glanced at Cheryl, who was steaming. He could see that she was on the verge of getting up when Vivian brought their food out. She was always fast. It was always hot. Cheryl sat down again. That situation was under control for the moment. He looked at Susan. He wanted her. He pictured her body under the layers of clothes. He knew there were at least a couple tattoos somewhere in there and he wanted to see where. He'd check every inch of her to find them. He let her know that when he looked in her eyes. He made sure that Annie didn't see it. He felt bad about Annie, but it was over, whether his fault or not, it was over. She had a new boyfriend. "What do you want to drink?" He smiled politely.

" Mountain Dew, large" She liked caffeine. He would give her a jolt. She smiled. He could see that her teeth were slightly skewed. They weren't perfectly straight, and one just behind the edge of her lips had been broken, and was half black. She had the slightest overbite, but he liked that. It made her lips fuller and juicer. He'd forget about the black tooth. He suddenly noticed a bruise below her left ear. She had actually covered it with makeup, which he thought was odd. He wondered who hit her.

"Who hit you?" He pointed directly at the spot.

Both women looked embarrassed. Annie spoke up. "He was drunk."

John looked at them with a puzzled expression. "Who was?"

Annie looked like she had been called on the carpet. Vic quickly put the pops in a carryout tray and handed them to the women. "Put 'em on my bill, Vic." John looked at him, thanking him with his expression. He still held Annie's hand. "Who was drunk?"

Annie spoke very quietly. John was surprised to realize that like Cheryl, here was another person he knew who either yelled or whispered, nothing seemingly, in between. "Billy did it."

"Your boyfriend hit her?" He was confused.

"We were hanging out. We were all blitzed. She told him he was a dumbass, and he kinda poked her."

Susan's look of embarrassment turned to one of indignation. "He is a stupid fuck."

John had no doubt about it. He'd heard about Billy. He was dangerously stupid. It seemed like Annie had gotten involved with him just to let John know that she was done with him and any man vaguely like him. "Does he hit you?" He had heard rumors but ignored them.

Annie grasped his hand harder. "No."

He looked at Susan. She shook her head slightly, letting him know that she was lying.

John pulled her hand up a little to get her to look at him. "If he hits you again, ever, the
first thing I want you to do is get out. The second thing I want you to do is call me because he'll need a fucking head transplant when I'm done with him. I'll do him a favor." He was frustrated. He felt incredibly guilty and it was deflating the sexual tension he felt with Susan.

Annie looked at the floor again. Her tough façade had dissolved. He hated it when she was this vulnerable. He knew though, that she would dig around inside and bolster her bravado in a few moments. She always managed to. He looked at Cheryl. She was eating through her heaping plate with anger, so she'd be done in a matter of minutes. He had to break away. He looked at Susan. She looked at him with admiration, then with desire. He returned the look. He broke the spell by letting go of Annie's hand. She breathed deeply. He took her shoulders. "I mean it, Annie."

She looked at him seriously. "How do I find you?"

John realized he could not give Annie his girlfriend's number. "Make sure you two come by Pat's and we'll come up with something." He jerked his head toward the table. "I gotta eat. You guys goin' to a party?" He knew they usually went to the numerous parties a group of them unofficially held nearly every day.

Susan spoke up. "No. Annie has to get shoes. We're goin' shopping. Where you going?"

He hesitated. "I'm going to Pat's."

Annie had recovered. "With the sow?"

John could see the uneasy peace falling apart if Cheryl caught what she said, but she had taken some pills when they sat down, and they apparently were kicking in because her angry expression was melting into a blank stare. She continued shoveling the food in her mouth, but more mechanically now. She hadn't heard what was said. "Jesus, Annie. Keep it cool. She's tagging along for something to eat."

"Yeah. She'd do that."

John smiled. "Ok. You know there's nothing going on there." He felt bad making an allusion that Cheryl was too unattractive to be of interest to him, but he was getting tired of trying to keep a lid on things and was running out of ideas.

It worked. Annie and Susan both laughed. Annie blew her cheeks up. For a moment, John was grateful that Cheryl was eating the pills like candy. Susan spoke. "Well maybe we'll see you at Pat's later." He knew they'd be there, if Susan had anything to do with it.

Annie nodded. "Yeah." She smiled. John noticed that a dimple miraculously appeared when Annie smiled a particular way. It showed up about one in four times, and he knew on some level that it was a smile tied to him in some way, but he couldn't figure out how that could be, or why. It softened him, and then the guilt welled up.

"Ok," he turned to go back to the table. "See ya." A chill went down his spine. He had waved like grouchy Bob the day he had disappeared from the face of the earth, or at least the earth as they knew it.

GREASE MONKEY SEE

Cheryl was shoveling mashed potatoes into her mouth as he sat back down. "Food's cold", she said it evenly, and quietly.

"I know. I wanted to say hi. See how she was doing." He figured that was close enough to the truth to get by.

"She's not doin' so great. Not with that fucker she's with. He hits her." She said it without emotion.

"Man," he thought, "those pills must be good." He sat up straight. "You mean, you heard about this guy hitting her?"

Cheryl rolled her eyes. "You knew it too. You act like you didn't hear it."

He knew that she was probably right. He hadn't wanted to know. He smelled the onions on the side for his burger. He picked them up and put them on the sandwich, and took a big bite out of it. "I feel bad."

"About her?" She was coming out of her calm state, but slurring her speech a bit. If she went back to Pat's and drank more, she'd be a mess. "Why should you feel bad? You aren't the one hitting her. It's not your fault she hooked up with a loser." She was getting worked up. "You don't control every move that every woman makes John Hamilton."

John was surprised at the venom with which she said it. He resented it. "Fuck this." He dumped his burger on his plate upside down and stood up.

Cheryl laughed. "Sit down." She motioned with one hand to sit. "Jesus Christ you're touchy. I'm sorry. I want to eat with you. That's getting all fucked up. Sit down, hon."

John was still angry. "Apologize."

Cheryl looked surprised, and laughed. "For what?"

John wondered what for too. She had said something that angered him, but he couldn't put his finger on it. Was he upset that he didn't control Annie, or didn't care if he did, or that he was capable of such passive cruelty with his current girlfriend? He realized that Cheryl would be the one to tell him, and that there were few if any others who could tell him. He sat back down. "You really tick me off sometimes."

She attacked her pie, washing it down with big gulps of Coke. John reassembled his burger and ate. "You, John, can't commit. You don't connect, and then you feel guilty because you don't like what it does to people who try to hook up with you. You don't want to hurt their feelings, but then, the women you choose are hurt by it."

He ate and chewed on what she said. She sat looking at him while she finished her pie. She motioned to Vivian. "Hey Viv, we need to get a pork tenderloin with double mayo, onion, no, no onion, lettuce and tomato and two large home fries to go, please."

John was amazed that he had forgotten Pat's sandwich. "Shit, I forgot."

Cheryl cackled. "I don't forget food, baby, you can count on me."

John also figured it was because it was Pat's. She knew he was interested in her and she liked him.

John sipped his coffee. He had decided it was too cold to drink the malt. "Want my malt?"

Cheryl looked at it for a minute. "Nah. It's too cold."

"Why don't you eat less? It's healthy."

Cheryl looked injured. "I don't need to lose weight. I'm a fat chick and I'm sexy." She took the malt and began sipping it absentmindedly. "My sister told me I should go to AA."

"AA?" John had been to one meeting in prison. It seemed like a religious cult of some kind, and the men there had some serious problems with alcohol and drugs that he had never had. He didn't feel it was relevant to him. "I went to a meeting once."

"What was it?"

"I'm not sure really. It didn't seem to have anything to do with me so I didn't go back." He had known that if he went to the meetings while in prison, there was a possibility that he'd get out earlier, but he didn't like the emotional way some of the people there behaved.

"What do they do?"

He shrugged. "They talk about their problems, get kinda sappy. It's a little weird. I don't think you'd like it."

"That's what I thought. I told my sister she was wrong. She didn't press it, but I think that's because hubby told her not to push it too hard. She seems sold on it. I think one of her girlfriends went there and started getting things together. I still get the impression that it's real hit and miss."

"Yeah. I wouldn't waste my time."

"I don't have a problem any way. I just drink a lot because I like to. I can take it or leave it."

John wondered. "Yeah." He stood. "Let's have a smoke."

They both stood and walked toward the door into the smoking cage. "I have to go to the little girl's room."

John nodded. He knew that Ralph would have had a field day with "little girl's room". He went outside. The air was biting. He huddled against a dirty wall as he lit a cigarette. There was an older man standing there smoking. He looked to be in his fifties. He had straight black hair with specks of gray in it. He was ruddy, and had a couple of scars on his face. They both looked like they came from knife cuts. The cold didn't seem to bother him. John nodded without looking him in the eyes. It was acknowledging his existence without getting involved. It worked well for him in prison, and it served him well outside too.

The wind whipped up, rattling the chain link that made the cage. John shivered. The man stood staring out at the field. "No houses." He had a heavy foreign accent. John didn't know enough about other countries to be able to figure what sort of accent.

John supposed his observation about the field required a response. "They tore 'em down years ago."

The man continued looking at the green grass and weeds. "So many nice houses in this country. So big."

John was extremely curious. "Where are you from?"

The man didn't turn. "Romania."

John was impressed. He had met so few people from other countries. There were a couple of foreigners in prison, but he had never had contact with them. He wasn't sure if he should ask, but his curiosity got the best of him. "How'd you end up here?"

The man remained still, but John thought he could see a bit of a smile form. "This weather is nothing. Where I lived, this is summer." He looked around quickly. "The fence is the same though." John had no idea what that meant.

Cheryl walked out. "Damn, it's cold out here!" The man glanced in her direction.

John motioned to the Romanian. "Not for him."

She eyed the stranger. "Don't know to come in from the rain, either?" She smiled hesitatingly. The Romanian continued looking at the field. "Rain is a shower. That's a good thing."

Cheryl tried to refocus her attention on John, but seemed unable to let go of the remarks she was making and getting from the stranger. "So I need a shower?"

The Romanian gave her a quick look up and down and a smirk. "You look clean to me." He pulled his cigarettes out. They were a strange brand.

He hit the pack and one cigarette popped out of the top. She looked at the pack "Gauloise?"

The Romanian shrugged. "French." He offered one to Cheryl.

She put the cigarette in her mouth and the Romanian lit it. He slipped the package and lighter back into his coat with smooth, fluid movements. "Are you from Russia?"

"We were part of Soviet Union for as long as they could handle it." He turned from the fence toward Cheryl.

"So where," she asked, flippant.

He shrugged and smiled a little. "Romania, near Ukraine."

"Jesus Christ. What are you doing here?"

He laughed heartily. "It's not so great in Romania."

Cheryl looked at the cigarette after she had taken a couple of drags off of it. "Damn this tastes good!"

She pointed it at John. He waved it away. "I've got one lit."

"Yeah, but honey, this is good!"

"I'll pass." John didn't want to talk.

"Suit yourself."

Cheryl turned back to the Romanian. "So what do you do?"

He looked Cheryl in the eyes. "Importing, groceries. I work for a man who owns a Distrib... a distribator."

"Distributor." Cheryl corrected.

"Yes." He nodded ever so slightly.

John looked at him. He knew the place he was talking about was the small building over on Philmore Street. One full wall of the clean brick building had an elaborately painted mural of fruit and ornate foreign letters at the bottom, along with "Delicious!" in English in a chunky oddly angled font that was incongruous. The bright ad was out of place in the dull trashy residential neighborhood, hard to miss or forget. He rarely saw any activity in the place. He figured it was empty. He didn't want the guy to know he'd figured out where he worked. John was becoming very uncomfortable. He'd seen guys like this in prison. They were hard core. John considered them psychopaths. They didn't seem to be phased by anything regular people were phased by like hunger, fear, morals, and on.

He felt like he had inadvertently stepped into a cage with a man eating tiger in it and now he was trying to figure out how to get out with his skin. The Romanian knew too, John figured, but he was distracted somewhat by Cheryl, who was oblivious to the undercurrents developing, or she was aware of some stirrings but had mistaken them for sexual tension between she and the stranger.

He was willing to let him go in exchange for Cheryl. John knew it. "Cheryl, we're due
back at Pat's."

She looked at John perplexed, then aggravated. "You go baby sit Ralph. I'll be along."

John shrugged. He looked at the Romanian. He would acknowledge in an obtuse way, his superior strength. "Glad we met." He stepped back inside the restaurant and shivered. He wondered why he felt no guilt over leaving Cheryl in his clutches. Maybe he had misjudged the situation. He seemed to like Cheryl. Maybe he dug big girls. They needed the fat to keep warm in Romania, right? He paid his bill and started back to Pat's. The warm restaurant was very comfortable and the cold seemed that much more bitter in contrast. He scrunched his neck down into his wisp of a jacket, and while it didn't keep him warmer, he at least felt like he was doing something and that stopped the shivering briefly. He glanced back and saw that Cheryl and the Romanian were still standing in the cage where he had left them, Cheryl laughing and talking loudly, and his responses if any, were indiscernible. John shivered again.

He stepped back into the bar. Ralph was weaving slowly but regularly on his stool. Pat had gone and been replaced by his nephew. It was a good thing, because John had forgotten the take out order Cheryl had placed for Pat.

Pat's nephew, Paul nodded toward John. "Hey, John. Pat told me that you thought he'd be here."

John pulled his wallet out. "Yeah. I ordered his food, but forgot to bring it back. Here's the ten dollars"

Paul took it. "You forgot the food?"

"Yeah. I screwed up. He gave me ten, so I'm giving you ten."

Paul looked confused. "Ok. Did he take it out of his pocket or the register?"

"I think the register." Paul nodded and popped the drawer and replaced the ten. John noted Cary was still there, and that it was late enough that he was courting big trouble with his newly pregnant girlfriend. He also noticed that Cary had stopped drinking coffee and was drinking beer again. Charmain's husband William was sitting next to him. Charmain had her head down on the table, sleeping.

John sat on the other side of Cary. William was talking. "So you gotta get you some more if'n she's pregnant. She can't get any more pregnant!" he laughed like he had just learned how to, a surprised look on his face. "She's a hot girl, boy."

John frowned at William and addressed Cary. "I thought you were going home."

Cary looked at John. He was teary eyed. "What am I gonna do when I get there?"

"Do you know for sure that it's yours?" John knew it was a blunt, maybe even rude question, but he was flustered from his meeting with the Romanian. His weakness shocked him. Was his toughness a mirage? He didn't think the feelings and attitudes he had developed during his stint in prison would ever dissipate, but, good or bad news that it was, some of them seemed to be fading.

Cary stared at John with a coldness that told him he was close to being hit. As he looked at John, unblinkingly, Cary drank deeply from his bottle, a boozy equivalent of counting to ten. He took another long drink. He had abandoned drinking from a glass .

Cary blinked. A tear formed at the bottom lid of one eye. It transformed his hard, cold expression to a bleary melancholy. He had realized that John's question was not all that foolish. His girlfriend had been a dancer at a club for a year, and had been known to be willing to make money on the side when things had gotten tough. "It's mine. We've been exclusive for a long time. She makes decent money at the store. She loves me." He said the last sentence with his eyes downcast, as if ashamed that the woman would feel something as foolish as love.

John felt weak and foolish all over again. Here he was, picking on a guy with a huge life changing event hanging over him, and all he had wanted to do was prove he was a man by being blunt.

Cary smiled. A few tears fell as he quickly wiped his face. "I wondered if it was mine the minute she told me. It was just my sad fucking way of trying to get out of dealing with it. I knew she was faithful." He chuckled. "The way I looked must not have been what she hoped for. As soon as she told me, I know I looked horrified, because she got really hurt and started crying, yelling she wasn't getting an abortion, and all that. I told her that I was glad, but I wasn't selling it so good. I was just shocked, surprised, had no idea. She was on the pill."

John took a beer from Paul. "She was on the pill? Did she miss one?"

"No, she's good about it. She told me that the clinic nurse warned her that they're really good but they're not foolproof." He paused. "We fuck *a lot*." Both he and John laughed together.

"Well," John looked at himself in the mirror at the back of the bar, "you are thoroughly fucked now."

"I'd say so." Cary looked in the mirror.

Cheryl burst through the door, talking a mile a minute. John could tell that what she had been taking at the restaurant, or something she had taken since had her higher than a kite. She had a Styrofoam box of food. Pat's order. She rushed up to John when she didn't immediately spot Pat. She didn't seem to see his nephew Paul. "Here Johnny," she thrust the box at John. "I got me a date and I can't be late."

John was appalled. "Not that Romanian guy?"

Cheryl leaned in on him, a mischievous grin on her face. She had a smell of chemicals, something she must have smoked, and John couldn't put his finger on it. "I'm gonna put my foot on foreign soil."

John looked away from her. "He's bad news, Cheryl."

She moved closer to him. "Jealous, baby?" John wondered why a woman who was obviously smart was such a bad judge of men. In her defense she was under the influence of alcohol or drugs when she made the poorer choices.

John averted her eyes. "Just be careful Cheryl"

"Ha" she shouted, "Where's the fun in that?" She turned and nearly twirled as she headed to the door. She was still light on her feet.

"Crank." Cary croaked over the neck of his beer bottle.

"What?" John wasn't sure he'd heard him correctly.

"She smelled like it. My cousin's a crankhead. She's a fucking mess."

"The Romanian must have it."

"What are you talking about."

John felt uneasy talking about the guy who had unnerved him. "We were having a cigarette with this dude from Romania over at the restaurant. I could tell he was bad news the second I laid eyes on him, but not dumbass Cheryl."

"Romania? What the hell is he doing around here? He'd stick out like a sore thumb."

"I have a feeling he hasn't been around long, at least here. His English is so-so."

"Weird." Cary's voice trailed off. He perked up again. His speech had a thick edge.
"You have a kid. What's it like?"

John was tired of feeling uncertain, almost foolish. The Romanian, the estranged daughter, abandoning Cheryl, all conspired to conjure up feelings of inadequacy. He knew that he could point to his persistence in sending gifts and money to his daughter, that Cheryl was a grown woman, and he didn't really want to stay in the mindset he had while he was in prison, so feeling uneasy around the Romanian was normal, but he felt he should be further along dealing with these issues emotionally., and not just logically. He wanted to answer Cary. "I really didn't raise her. I mean I was around, but I never had to deal with the day to day stuff, and the money, her grandparents did all that." John knew this wasn't going to be information that cheered Cary, so he tried to spin it, "but, you know, I didn't have a decent job like you do, and the mother was too young to work, and I was young. You two have a much better set up than I did."

Cary nodded quietly. "I feel crazy. I mean there's this little kid that's part of me coming into the world. He'll be middle age when I'm dead. It's like bad time travel."

"It's pretty weird to see them looking like little bitty versions of yourself, I'll admit. I mean, I have a girl, but I can see my face in hers."

"Poor girl," Cary grinned.

"Yeah," John laughed quietly. "I mean it's inescapable. You can't get around someone who is part of you."

"You mean it's like, wherever you go, there you are?"

John had to think. Was that what he meant? "Maybe, more like whoever you do, there you are."

They both laughed gently. Cary looked down at the bar. "I'm not sure I can get her out of this hell hole we're all in."

John looked at the mirror behind the bar. He saw a middle age man in a bar, half looped. He tried to conjure up an answer for Cary. "You do the best you can, and it's the end of it." He felt that his gifts and presents let his daughter know that she was always on his mind, always a concern of his. " I think you gotta let 'em know you love 'em all the time. That'll make up for the lack of limos."

Cary looked at the mirror now too. "I hope I can even pull that off."

John shrugged, trying not to sound too indifferent, "Most fathers don't give a shit, don't care what people they brought into the world. It's all some macho bullshit for them and fuck them, the bastards."

Ralph was in the process of standing up. He had drunk enough that the process of hopping off the stool without falling on the floor was step wise. First, he'd turn slowly so that his back was to the bar, eliminating the need to maneuver around the lip of the bar as he got up, then he'd focus on the first foot, which, as the toe touched the floor, and the heal descended , would be supported by the second foot coming down on the toes, and leveraging slowly to a standing position. As he concentrated on the way his feet would be spaced and set as he stood, trying to line up against the swaying it reminded John of setting up a shot in a pool game while there was an earthquake. Ralph would stand for a few minutes getting synchronized with his dizziness so that his attempt to go to the door or the restroom wouldn't end in a spill and a bloody nose. Ralph had broken his nose a couple of times from being flat out, fall down drunk, and while he usually didn't feel much, he didn't think it was, as he put it, " A good look on him." So he walked toward John, his hands out at his sides, palms down like he was positioning them so that if he fell backward, they would be in the right place to save his ass from too big of a jolt. Of course, his wrists would probably snap.

As he shifted past John, he mumbled, "let's go to Daryl's, wan you to dribe."

John looked at him in mock concern. "Think we should? You seem a little, uh, drunk."

Ralph motioned like he was underwater, that he'd continue the conversation after he returned from the restroom. John smelled urine. He wondered if Ralph had actually already pissed himself, although, his pants looked dry.

Many minutes later Ralph came back. He wavered next to John. "C'mon. Let's go to Daryl's."

John knew that Ralph was not a hard headed drunk. When he was blasted, he was more easily persuaded than when he was sober and cranky. "You are too drunk. Go have some coffee, or drink some more beer and we'll go over tomorrow."

"No," He shook his head in an exaggerated back and forth motion. "We are gone to Daryl's."

John was surprised that the old stand by of "go drink more", didn't work the first time like it usually did. He put his hand on Ralph's shoulder. "Man you are too wasted to go there. Daryl would be furious."

Ralph stood swaying. It looked like his feet were glued to the floor so that he wouldn't tumble over. "Let's get something to eat and I'll have some coffee."

He was intent on going to Daryl's, that was for sure. John hadn't seen him try to bring himself back from a drunken stupor before. He knew he seemed to be holding his booze pretty effectively today. Maybe he could sober up. He had an idea. He handed Ralph the Styrofoam box Cheryl had foisted on him. The food was paid for, so why not give it to Ralph? "Here, have Paul give you some coffee, and eat this. It'll help sober you up."

Ralph looked at the box like it was a puzzle. "K" He took it and wavered over to his stool. John waved Paul over. "Give Ralph a cup of coffee will ya?"

Paul nodded and even though he was busy assembling an order for a table, the bar had gotten fairly busy, he broke from his tasks and poured a cup in front of Ralph. Paul was a young guy who seemed to be ill at ease in the bar most of the time. He was very methodical, very watchful, and no one waited for a drink when Paul was on duty, but it seemed like his mind was split and the other half was far, far away from the bar. John knew little of him, except that Pat had talked briefly about him working his way through college. He seemed to be too old to be going to school, but then, it was common for people to go back to school and get new degrees, or finish degrees never completed. He thought about the fact that most of the people in the room had not finished high school. He hadn't. It didn't seem important. He didn't like the people at school. He never had much to say to them. They wouldn't miss him if he quit. He also remembered looking through a science textbook and it was so old, Pluto hadn't been discovered. He had spoken to enough people whom he knew had college degrees and most of them didn't seem any smarter than him, so what was the point? He understood as he got older that it was all about specific knowledge for specific careers that a person would get in college, but it seemed like an unnecessary burden to think about ever going back and getting a degree. He didn't seem to be able to conjure up any inspiration on what he'd do once he went back. The final nail was that he was pretty sure he couldn't afford even the cheapest college and he had no idea how to get a GED.

John thought it puzzling that Paul seemed to respect him. He always seemed to be deferential when he spoke, and he seemed to hear everything that John said, no matter what he was busy doing, like he hung on every word. John didn't understand it, but it made him feel good, so he didn't question it further. He didn't want to sort out that the guy might actually be condescending, but subtler about it than John would ever hope to be able to discern. The admiration, or fear, whatever it was that Paul displayed was positive in John's eyes.

Ralph ate and drank two cups of coffee in thirty minutes. It did the trick and sobered him up substantially. He still slurred, but his waver had subsided, and his nervous energy had resurfaced enough to make him seem a little more alert and less addled than he had been.

John overheard Ralph tell Paul to put his drinks on his tab. He turned on his stool, and stood with a lot less effort than he had a little over a half an hour earlier. "Ok. Let's go." He waved to John. He didn't want to waste energy walking over to him. He stood where he had got up, waiting. John paid his tab. Ashe put his coat on, Ralph, in the loud voice of alcohol impairment, told Paul he wanted a coffee to go. John quickly added one for himself. Paul quickly obliged, making a point of being sure the lids were sealed tight on the Styrofoam cups before he handed them over the bar to John. Ralph stayed put in his spot near his stool. When John handed his coffee to him, he clumsily stuck his thumb in the top to pop out the plastic piece that sealed the drink hole. He dented the top, but managed to get it open and he slurped the hot coffee. "Shit that's hot," he exclaimed, wavering a bit.

As Ralph turned to head out the door, it opened. A small man in a black T-shirt, jeans and cowboy boots came in. Despite the cold air, the bomber jacket he had with him was hanging from his hand. He smiled and waved almost singing "Hello all," as he entered. Ralph staggered back a step, as if the wind and the man's presence had blown him off his shaky balance. The majority of customers looked up and in varying degrees of enthusiasm returned the cheerful man's greeting. Ralph mumbled. "Pin head." The man had to have heard Ralph, but acted like he didn't.

John shushed Ralph. "Don't be cute. Let's not get sidetracked by you having your ass beat."

As they went out the door, Ralph snorted, and replied. "Shit, probably fit his dick in his bowling ball."

Often times, John saw flashes of jealousy in Ralph's remarks. This was definitely one of those times. The man he had directed his bile at was a minor celebrity in the neighborhood. He worked at the crummy little bowling alley on Clymer St. It was ten lanes and it's glory days had passed years ago when the huge, shiny multi lane alleys had cropped up all over the place in the sixties and seventies.

The guy who owned it had complained as long as John could remember that he never made any money, yet the place was still open and the owner, who was a beefy guy with a bright red face and thick fingers that probably wouldn't fit in ninety nine percent of the chipped and dull "house balls" that had been there for nearly as long as the lanes, did not seem to be starving.

Hardy, as the young bowler was known, had been the pin boy since he was fourteen. He was paid very little but was allowed to bowl free as much as he wanted in his off hours. Over the years, he had become very good, averaging an amazing two fifty by the time he was eighteen. He was plied with favors and gifts, like new bowling shoes, and beautiful new accessories to persuade him to be on various teams for leagues, where his presence always assured the lucky team the number one position at the end of the season.

In the past year he had started entering tournaments around the state and in a few of the Nationals. As his star rose, the little lane that had sponsored him received some of the "juice" from his association with it. The owner was thrilled and constantly bragged loudly and publicly about their local star. The grapevine spread this throughout the neighborhood, and everyone started feeling like they had been given the blessing of a local star. Needless to say, Hardy was a very popular fellow.

John had never felt any jealousy when he saw or spoke to Hardy. He admired the fact that the man had figured out what he liked to do early on, and did it to death, becoming someone of stature by virtue of this single minded exertion in his vocation. He was as dirt poor as any of them and he was making good for himself, and by extension for a lot of them. John was impressed.

He was also impressed with Ralph's efforts to sober up in early evening. He rarely turned away from a good drunk this late in the day. Ralph pulled his car keys from his pocket like he had been doing it for years. "Here, you drive."

John was worried. Emery had kept the plates on the car up to date, but he could imagine his unsteady driving catching the eye of a cop, figuring he had himself a DUI bust and a jail cell for John. He also knew that Ralph was too drunk to drive. He took the keys. It wasn't that far to Daryl's and he knew all the back streets by heart. He'd cross his fingers. This was one night he hoped the cops were as scarce as they usually were. As they settled in, John looked over the various controls. The drizzle that had started was turning into sleet, which made John more nervous. "Maybe this should wait until better driving weather."

"Baby's goin' in the water, better swim." Ralph spoke with garbled finality. He sank down in the passenger's seat looking up and over the dash board.

John sighed and put the key in the ignition. He turned it and the engine fired up. He was amused that the ritual of getting the seat and mirrors adjusted, checking gauges and turning the engine on felt so foreign to him. He liked the feeling of power being behind the wheel though. It felt similar to holding a gun. Despite his rough path in life, he'd only briefly held a gun in his hands twice in his life. Once, a man he had met at a bar was bragging about a piece he had, and pulled it out to show it to John. The bar owner saw it while John was turning it over in his hands, and even though the owner confessed it was his, the barkeep threw them both out and banned them permanently, telling them that he wasn't going to have his license pulled because of a couple of assholes. The other time was when John had been talking to a gay friend of one of his girlfriends. He had finished cutting his hair for free, a favor to John's girlfriend, and the two of them had been talking about crime, and the hairdresser mentioned that he had a gun. John figured that he was attracted to him and trying to impress him. He had pulled the gun out to show it to John, unsolicited, and put it in John's hands with both of his hands, like he was passing a delicate porcelain figurine for his perusal.

The first gun he had seen had barely been in his hands before the barkeeper had his fit. This time, John had the opportunity to hold the gun, point it, cock it, which is when the hairdresser told him to be careful, that it was loaded. John accidentally pulled the trigger and shot a hole into the floor a few feet ahead of him. The hairdresser was beside himself. He told John to go fuck himself and to get out. John felt like beating the guy, but figured that would really piss his girl friend off. The shop was empty when he shot the gun, so no one saw what happened and the hole was in a corner of the shop where it wasn't visible. John laughed at the guy, and said that he thought that he had given it to him so he could shoot it. The hairdresser calmed down a little, realizing that he had done a foolish thing, and more gently, but very firmly told him to leave, that he had to compose himself before he drove home. John knew the guy had not intended for him to shoot the gun, but John would get angry when gay men hit on him and he wondered if he wanted to upset this one since he felt insulted by what John was sure was a come on. Was the accident an accident? It bothered him that he was uncomfortable when gays hit on him. He figured it was an unintentional challenge to his persuasion and he'd had enough of that from the homophobes in this neighborhood. He couldn't understand why he was immune to all sorts of direct challenges to his manhood yet this benign one twisted him. He always summed up with the idea that maybe he wasn't as secure in his masculinity as he had supposed, but was unclear what he'd have to do to remedy that. He wasn't clear at all. A lot of gays he was aware of were very masculine, so was that the issue for him at all or was he getting a glimpse of what women went through being objects of sexualization and he hated that he was one of the men that did it?

The hairdresser told John's girlfriend that he had upset him, but not how. John had complained that his girlfriend could have warned him that the guy was gay. She replied angrily that it hadn't crossed her mind, and that it sure the hell shouldn't have crossed his. They broke up not too long after that, not so much because of that incident, but because of John's usual hesitance to talk, interact, display emotion and her dashed expectations that he should and would and that she'd be the one to make him change.

Ironically, John had been sexually turned on by the power of the gun, but decided that he didn't need the weapon to feel sexual. It held no interest to him after that. He had always relied on his wits to protect him, and a gun wasn't going to seduce him with it's sleek metal sheen and perfume like gun powder.

He felt more secure and sure of himself when he had a few dollars in his pocket, which admittedly, wasn't often enough. Right now, he had to convince himself that driving the car was no big deal. He didn't want to be too nervous. He would over react if he was too edgy. He looked for the familiarity in the wheel that he had his hands wrapped around, and noted the gauges that told him battery status, engine temperature, and gasoline level. It seemed to help. He gently put the car in drive, his foot firmly on the brake, and let go in a smooth action that allowed him to pull into the street and toward an alley he wanted to use to head toward Daryl's house. Ralph half slept as they headed down the narrow way. He seemed to sense John's growing comfort driving the car, and relaxed.

John had forgotten how much of the road you could feel through the steering wheel. He could feel the bricks and stones under them as he navigated through a series of narrow alleys and side streets. It made it seem like the car was part of him, and the width of the car as he saw it out the front windshield was an enhancement and extension of his shoulders. He felt strong and sure as small movements of his hands became big turns and jigs of the jet black tires underneath them. The air space in the tires was like an echo chamber and the bumps and curves of the road rolled into his hands through the rigid plastic and steel construct of the wheel.

John was exhilarated. Not only were his movements magnified through the car, it seemed his eye sight had sharpened and his sense of smell was intensified. He could smell gasoline, oil, the vinyl in the car seats, and on and off, he could smell a thick odor. He became alarmed when he thought he recognized it as exhaust, yet it smelled rather sweet. He became disoriented for a moment. He looked out the side mirror, the windshield and the rearview mirror to reorient

himself. He thought, shocked, that he saw the gray outline of a woman sitting in the back seat. A chill infused him and snapped him into a hyper alert state where he could quickly look behind to the back and forward again without turning the wheel or losing track of the road. He noticed that there was a lot of fogging on the windows on the sides and back. He felt relief
flow through him as he tied the vague image of the woman sitting in back to the color and shapes of the fog in the windows. He cranked up the defroster and as it blasted the glass windshield it eliminated parts of the gray fog unevenly, making Rorschach type images in the cold surface. John decided he had been more affected by Ralph's fear of ghosts than he had known. He was angry that he seemed to have been cowering again, this time, instead of a menacing man from Romania, it was the misty outline of a woman's upper torso in a car window. Was a kitten going to scare him next?

Every light in Daryl's house was on at night. He loved lights and kept them on in every room. Garlene said she had seen an article in a magazine about people who suffered from light deprivation, and that winter usually plunged these people into deep depression. She figured that Daryl might be prone to it and decided the few extra dollars on the electric bill every month was well worth it if it helped to keep Daryl from being unhappy. John had known Daryl long enough to have witnessed this usually confident, talkative, cheerful man become weepy, unsure and deeply blue for brief but startling periods of a few days. It would happen every six months or so. Garlene would alternate between trying to comfort him and avoiding him, wondering what was going on, as unsure and confounded by the bouts as everyone else. It usually took him a good part of a day to realize he had descended into one of these funks, and then he'd go home and stay in bed for the next few days, as though he were fighting a bad flu. He'd then emerge in the buoyant, self assured mood everyone expected.

John pulled the car into their driveway. He figured if Daryl did decide to come out and look at the car, there was no point in the three of them walking too far in the cold drizzle.

Ralph was quiet. John thought he'd have to rouse him, but when they stopped he sat straight up in his seat, quickly unbuckled his seat belt and popped the door open. "Come on. We're at Gramma's." John followed. They strode up the front steps. John noticed that the screen in the outer door had been replaced with a storm window. It was shut tight, and the inner door was open. It was completely fogged. John rapped on the glass. He didn't like ringing the bell. It seemed impersonal.

He could see the curves of Garlene back lit against the thick fog on the glass as the latch was undone. As the door opened, they could hear a thumping bass from somewhere else in the house. The volume increased dramatically as they stepped in and Garlene greeted them. "Hi. He's listening to music. He got a new whopper sub, or whatever it's called." John thought he could see a glimmer of disdain from Garlene as she glanced at Ralph. "You guys want a beer?"

Ralph spoke first. "Sure, thanks ma'am."

Garlene rolled her eyes. "Don't call me ma'am. I am not a ma'am."

Ralph blushed. "Ok."

Garlene raised her eyebrow as she looked John in the eye, as if to say. "This one is easy to put in his place."

The two followed their hostess through the living room, dining room and kitchen toward the basement steps. The music was so loud here that Garlene had to yell to be heard. It was one of the dozens of heavy metal bands Daryl liked listening to that blasted up from below. John could never remember one from the other, despite Daryl's numerous attempts to school him on who was who. "What beer do you want? Lite or regular?"

"Regular." John shouted. Ralph nodded his head.

"I see you finished painting the room. It looks good!" John hollered as she handed the beers to them.

"What?" she pointed to her ear.

"I said I see you finished painting! It looks good! Is that two coats?!"

She shook her head again. Without hesitation, she moved in very close to John on his right, her left breast pressing up against his chest. She put her head next to his, which enabled her to talk without yelling. "I couldn't hear a word you said."

"I'm not so good at yelling." John stated as a matter of fact.

He thought he heard her laugh. "What did you say?"

John wanted to finish fast. Her breast was firmly pressed against him. "I just said you did a great job on the painting. No biggie." He started pulling away.

He took one step back which still had them nearly touching. "I take it he's expecting us."

She didn't seem to be thinking of anything other than whatever was necessary to be able to talk. She leaned in again. "What?"

John felt his penis stirring. "Can we go on down?"

She leaned away so he could see her face. She smiled and nodded yes.

He gave a thumbs up. He was grateful it was over. He had never seen concrete evidence that she was flirting, and this wasn't any different than any other time. He knew that Daryl cheated on her every few years, but the affairs were always one night stands. Daryl insinuated that she knew about the affairs, and as long as he didn't get serious, she didn't really care that much. John had supposed that she felt that way only because she had been unfaithful to him at one point or another, although nothing had ever come down the grapevine to suggest it. Maybe she didn't have a clue about his infidelities and Daryl was just trying to minimize it all.

The music blasted all of those thoughts out of his mind. He descended the steep wooden steps ahead of Ralph. The basement was partially finished. The area they were in at the bottom of the steps was unfinished. The furnace, hot water heater, washer and dryer were all here along with boxes of the sort of things people collect and put in the basement never to be seen or heard of again. They turned and headed through a doorway to the right of the furnace. There were a number of halogen lamps in the room. The light was brilliant and white and almost as overwhelming as the music, which was now loud enough, John could feel it in his teeth. Both Daryl and Joey were standing on a weight bench playing air guitar. Daryl had the pained look a lot of the flashier guitarists put on their faces during long excruciating solos. He opened his eyes briefly, and upon seeing John and Ralph, jumped off the bench and ran up to within a hair of John. He knew how loud the music was, so he yelled loud enough to be heard the first time. "It's Man O' War's new album! I got it on vinyl!" Daryl's kid might not always get the fanciest clothes for school, but Daryl had a very nice stereo set up. John didn't know much about stereos, but Daryl was always happy to explain to him how upscale his system was, and describe in detail why it was. Daryl never actually bragged. He was excited about these things, and talked about them exuberantly.

John had to admit that it was sort of exciting to hear music this loud. It was crystal clear, sounding like the band was putting on a live show there in the basement. He tired of it pretty quickly though once the adrenaline rush of the volume had worn off. He knew that when Daryl listened to this stuff, he would listen for hours, while Garlene sat in their second floor bedroom with the door shut watching television. Their little girl would watch with her, unable to concentrate on anything else.

John pointed back at Ralph with his thumb, and trying as hard as he could to yell, said, "Ralph wondered if you'd check out his new car."

Daryl couldn't make out what he said. Joey had continued his air guitar performance. When he saw John and Ralph, he jumped up and down more, whipping around on the bench, making it tilt and lean to the point that John was sure he would tumble off.

Daryl went to the stereo and turned it down. John was amazed that his ears were already ringing. "Hey, I didn't mean to interrupt. I wonder if you'd check out Ralph's car. He got it today. He wanted to know what the pro thinks."

Daryl looked at Ralph, his dislike thinly disguised in a tight smile. "Sure, I'll look at it."
He stepped back over to the stereo and turned it off. Joey opened his eyes and let loose a blood
curdling scream. "Why'd you turn it off?" He was wild eyed. John could see that he was nearly out of it on stimulants. He imagined that he saw a bit of foam at the corner of his mouth. "Nah, nah, fuck this man. Turn it back on!" Joey leaped to the stereo and turned the volume up beyond where Daryl had it. It started distorting and rumbling. Daryl charged over, knocking Joey aside, and turned it down and off.

He grabbed Joey by his shirt, nearly lifting his body off the floor. "What the fuck do you think you're doing? Did I EVER say that you could touch my stereo you little fucking asshole?"

He dropped Joey to the floor. Joey looked like a mentally deranged child. He looked around the corners of the room, his eyes darting, seeming to overshoot everywhere they were trying to go, and then trying desperately to go back in the direction they had intended and then overshooting again. "Fuck you, man. I just wanted to listen to music. This is fuck shit!"

Joey bolted up the stairs. Daryl ran quickly and grabbed him three quarters of the way up the stairs. He held Joey like he was a python that wanted to strike. His grip was firm and restricting. Daryl whispered in Joey's ear for a minute. Joey didn't say a word the entire time. It was like Daryl was squeezing his lungs so that he couldn't get enough air movement to voice his protests. Ralph had stayed a step or so behind John. He leaned forward, whispering, "This is fuggin' weird."

John turned quickly and whispered fiercely, "shut the fuck up." Daryl's restraining embrace of Joey, his attempts to keep Joey in line reminded him off Cheryl. He thought of her foolish decision to hang with the Romanian and his allowing it. He could have been more forceful about extricating her. He knew he turned women's heads, yet Cheryl dumped him immediately when some stranger with an accent offered her a fancy foreign cigarette. He had to admit, the cigarette smoke smelled damn good. Maybe she'd get a good screw out of it, and that would be that. He hoped that was all that would happen.

Daryl released his grip of Joey. Joey relaxed on the steps, like the little spring wound up in him had been undone. It was almost as if Daryl had hypnotized him. "Go get a beer and meet us in the front." Daryl came back down the stairs, while Joey walked up the remaining steps.

Daryl looked behind him to be sure that Joey had gone on. "Man the kid is in some kind of state today. I thought he was excited about the bike, but it's more than that. He's fucking flipped or something. I don't know what to do about him, I swear." He talked like Joey was his errant child. He usually did. He talked like a proud father when he'd do something halfway sane too, recounting it for whoever was around. It didn't happen often. Joey came by his poor behavior honestly. His brother had committed suicide by alcohol, his mother was a drunk, and his father was a drunk with a horrible temper. His father had worked as a janitor in the county and retired for a pittance at age fifty. He drank so heavily he looked like he was seventy. They were still paying for the tiny house they had bought years ago. His mother worked at different menial jobs, but usually had to quit them or lost them when she got fired for missing too much or being late too often. She would call in "sick". Ironically, these were times Joey liked, because she would be home when he got home from school, on the days he did go to school. Sometimes, when the father was there, she would want to get away, so under the guise of entertaining Joey, she and he would walk to the park and then the corner grocery, where she would give him a dollar and he could buy one hundred pieces of penny candy. It would take him an hour to sort through the various kinds, and he'd be buzzed on sugar by the time they got home. He rarely ate much dinner those nights. Dinner usually consisted of canned soup and one TV dinner split two ways to supplement it. Joey's father rarely ate with them. He'd make a sandwich and go off to the living room and eat and watch television.

In the past year Joey's father was slipping into dementia. A doctor told his mom it was the alcohol, that he was suffering from Wernicke-Korsakoff syndrome or wet brain, and that if he stopped and was treated he might be able to recover most of his facilities. They never talked about it, and he hadn't stopped drinking. At one point Joey had told Daryl that he felt that his mother prayed for his father's dementia, because he would become docile, and she could continue to get his pension. It wouldn't be long before he would be helpless and she could finally have peace.

Daryl knew all of this and had tried, for reasons inexplicable to every one he knew, to be a surrogate father. It was puzzling in that Daryl had his own child, which, while he regularly professed his love for her, didn't interact with her much. Pat had put forth the hypothesis that Daryl had wanted a son, and he had been given a daughter. This was his way of correcting the wrong he had been dealt. Those who were at the bar that day to consider it, agreed it sounded plausible.

John didn't want to deal with Joey. He also didn't want to deal with the uneasiness between Ralph and Daryl. "If you have a minute, we just want to see what you think about his car?"

Daryl seemed put out that they had changed the subject from Joey. "What's in it for me?" He wasn't laughing.

Ralph spoke up. "I'll give you twenty dollars to tell me what I could get for it."

John put his hand up. "How about you get to kiss my ass Daryl?"

Daryl looked at John expressionless for three seconds, then burst out laughing. "I'd rather have the twenty, but you don't have to give me any money. We'll check out Joey's new motorcycle too. I've got the heat cranked in the garage." Daryl did a lot of puttering on his car in the garage year around, so he put in a large closed system space heater that took a while to heat the large garage, but kept it fairly comfortable once it did.

They went up the stairs and into the living room. Daryl called up the stairs. "Hey Garlene, where'd you put my coat?"

They heard her open a door. "In the same closet I put it in every single time."

Daryl nodded. He opened the closet near the front door and yanked his coat out. He had Joey's coat too. "The fool goes out without it all the time."

OLD FLAMES & NEW FRYING PANS

John, Ralph and Daryl walked out on the front porch. Joey stood in his T-shirt, smoking a cigarette and drinking a beer. He seemed much calmer, even happy.

He pointed at Ralph's car. "That's a nice car. It's antique?"

Ralph stepped forward, his chest out a bit. "Yeah. I wanted Daryl to tell me what it's worth."

John laughed to himself. For a second, Ralph seemed like Barney Fife bragging about his cruiser.

Joey flipped his cigarette into the yard. He walked out into the rain to get a closer look. Daryl followed behind and cajoled him into putting on his coat. "Man it doesn't have any rust."

"Well," Ralph sounded unusually modest, "there is a little on the underside."

Daryl looked at it carefully, circling around it. "Turn it on."

John got in and turned the key. Daryl hopped in on the passenger's side. "How much did he pay for this?"

"Thousand."

"He got a good deal. I'm impressed. How'd the weasel manage it?"

"He did a lot of favors for this old guy who owned it."

"Drove it to church on Sundays, right?"

"Pretty close."

Daryl looked around the cab. "He could get five thousand for it today."

"He'll be happy to hear that."

Daryl scrunched his face. "Is there a hole in the exhaust?"

John nodded. "It smells like it, but I don't hear any noise, and it doesn't smell exactly like exhaust." He grimaced too.

Daryl reached for the door handle, "It's not much, whatever it is. I'm not interested in sniffing around a car that Ralph sits his dirty ass in."

John shook his head. Daryl did not like Ralph, and that was not going to change. Daryl got out. John turned the car off and followed. "You might have a couple of leaks in your exhaust, and it sounds like you need to have a tune up, but other than that, it sounds pretty good. I'd say you could get at least four to five thousand dollars for it."

Ralph puffed again. "Man, that's cool."

Joey jogged over to the garage door. "Come look at my new bike." He stepped into the garage, and closed the door.

Daryl looked at John. "I wish he hadn't got this damn thing, but since I couldn't stop him, I'm trying to be positive."

Ralph looked at John and Daryl. "Why's it a bad idea?"

Daryl gave Ralph the evil eye. John leaned over to Ralph. "He sold his brother's car for it. That car had a lot of meaning to him. He'll regret it when he realizes what he's done."

The three men followed Joey into the garage. It was pleasantly warm. Joey was crouched at the side of his bike. He looked up at them and smiled like a child. "It's really cool. We've been tuning it up."

Ralph walked around to where Joey was crouching. Joey didn't seem to have a problem with Ralph. Joey didn't have a problem with anyone. "Tuning it up? Why do you have to tune up a new machine?"

Daryl walked around to the side they were on. "They don't really set the engines so that they go all that fast."

"Why?"

"It's sort of a lame safety issue. It's like making a car go twenty miles an hour so that you can't crash it as bad, if you crash. It's fucking stupid."

Ralph pointed to the spot on the exhaust Joey was messing with. "What are you doing there?"

"He's smoothing a piece that we hacked off. It's part of how they slow it down."

Joey finished the filing motion and stood up. "I want to see what it can do now."

Daryl looked at Joey like he was crazy. "It's raining and it's colder than a motherfucker right now."

"I'm not talking about going eighty miles an hour Daryl."

"It's too slippery out there Joey."

"Aw come on." He was agitated.

"Try it tomorrow."

"Ok." Joey calmed down. John knew it was silly, but it did seem like Daryl had some sort of hypnotic control over Joey.

John looked around the garage. "Did you get a new tool box?" Most of the time John spent with Daryl was either in the basement or the garage, the two of them chatting while Daryl puttered with his Plymouth Superbird or blasted something like *Accept* from the stereo. John was convinced that the cartoonists for the Jetsons had based a couple of things on the car but he'd never tell his friend that his car looked like a cartoon.

Daryl looked where John stared. "Yeah. Got a Sears card. They had some great shit. I had to hold back. They have this massive tool area now. My dad says it's like it used to be when he went to Sears thirty years ago. They had a huge tool section back then too. Somewhere along the line, they screwed up and got rid of it."

Ralph looked at the massive tool box. "Looks like somebody remembered."

It dawned on John that Daryl didn't trust Ralph not to rip him off, so the focus on his tools was probably a bad idea. John knew that Daryl would settle in and start digging at Ralph any minute, so he decided that they had better leave. He looked at Ralph. "We have beer calling us over at Pat's."

Joey perked up. "Hey, I'm going too."

Daryl behaved like he hadn't heard any of it. He pointed to a wire running along the ceiling of the garage. "That's the burglar alarm. I set it every night."

John wanted to rush Ralph out before Daryl started verbally connecting him to the reason he brought the alarm up, because he knew he would. He gently grabbed Ralph's arm and headed toward the door. "We'll see you guys around."

Joey moved toward the door with them. "Bye guys." Apparently Joey knew he wasn't going.

Daryl rousted Joey out of the garage, closing the door behind him. Ralph and John were heading toward Ralph's car. John turned and waved. "Tell Garlene thanks for having us in."

Joey turned back toward the garage. "I think I'll head home too."

John heard Daryl tell him that he would stay there tonight. He wondered if Joey had slept with Garlene. As Ralph and John settled in the car, John behind the wheel again, Ralph giggled. "Five thousand dollars. Shit. Thank you Mr. Emery." He seemed to have forgotten about the ghost. Maybe Daryl mentioning the leak in the exhaust had settled it for Ralph.

They drove without talking. As they approached Pat's, Ralph spoke up. "I think I'll go home and turn in."

John was glad he wouldn't drive the car in his condition. He didn't relish the idea of walking back to Pat's in the rain, but then, he'd done it many times before. "Ok. Where did you say they'd let you park?"

"Mrs. W said I can pull it in the driveway as long as I pull all the way to the right and near the garage." They drove past Pat's. John saw William and Charmain walking home. It was dark, cold and wet, so they were up against each other, heads down, going as quickly as they could. William held what looked like a newspaper over Charmain. Ralph harrumphed. "Only Christo could keep her dry."

John didn't understand but scolded any way. "Crisco, Jesus Ralph."

Ralph sputtered a laugh. "Cristo, not Crisco." He shook his head laughing gently.

John pulled the car into the driveway as Ralph specified. He pulled it in perfectly. He was happy with how quickly he had recouped his driving skills and comfort level behind the wheel. He slipped the keys out of the ignition and held them up in front of Ralph, indicating he'd drop them into his hand, when he opened it. Ralph's eyes were half closed, but he opened them enough to see John's hand in front of him and opened his hand below them. John dropped the compact little set of keys, glad that he had done a good job, and that Ralph would utilize him in the future and let him borrow the car as well. He knew it without talking about it. John would be the designated driver and that would allow him to use the car sometimes without Ralph.

They got out of the car. Ralph headed toward the door in the back of the house where the boarders entered at night. "See ya tomorrow."

John started toward the sidewalk and back toward Pat's. "You gonna open Pat's with me?"

"Yabet."

John walked quickly, thinking about whether he should go home. It was a long way. His girlfriend would be pissed off by now. It had to be seven or eight o'clock. She didn't care normally whether he got home at a certain time, except that this time she had mentioned that she wanted to make dinner. John had been living there, essentially like a visitor, for two months. He rented his apartment month to month and had abandoned it three weeks ago, just in time to avoid the next month's rent. When he was putting the few possessions he had in his girlfriend's car, the apartment manager had spotted him and asked him what he was doing. John told him that he didn't intend to rent the apartment any more. The manager, a fat guy who always smelled like stale cheese, complained that he had to give thirty days' notice, therefore he owed for another month. John told him to go fuck himself. The manager yelled that he would have him arrested.

John recalled, with a little embarrassment and pride mixed together, that he had pushed the guy against a wall and said, "I know you're lying and that if I tell your boss you charge notice, he'll wonder where his money is."

The fat manager didn't seem to be concerned about being pinned against the wall, like it was a regular occurrence for him. He calmly replied that the owner did indeed want the thirty days, but that he'd do John a favor and over look it if he'd give him fifty bucks. John laughed. He replied that he wasn't worried about the owner. When he let the guy go, he straightened up and, as if no confrontation had happened, he asked where John was moving. John was calculating that he would have to go into the apartment twice more to get the rest of his stuff, so he'd string the guy along for a few minutes. "I'm going to move closer to work. It's too far to go right now, and I'm going to be working on the job for three months at least. I'm doing the art center." He lied about all of it.

The manager's greasy wheels were turning. "You gonna stay at Manor Arms, then?"

"Yeah." He could tell the moron had taken the bait.

"That's not a bad place. The manager over there isn't as nice as me, though."

"You're a real prince, yourself right?" He tried to keep it light. He had one more load of stuff to get.

"I stay out of your hair." He followed John around as he gathered his last batch of stuff. "What's the guy's name over at Manor? I can't remember."

John looked at the manager with his best threatening look. "I don't remember."

The manager was nonplussed. "What's he look like."

John didn't think the guy was smart enough to figure he was going to live with his girlfriend, but now he wasn't so sure. "Who?"

"The manager at Manor."

John had the last of his stuff in his arms. He had to divert the guy. "You know, I told you where I was going because I don't care if you know. I don't care because if you hassle me, or your boss hassles me, I will come over here and put your fat ass in the hospital. That's a promise. I don't owe you any money. I will tell your boss that you take bribes to let people out of their rent, and you won't have a place to stay when your sad sack gets out of the hospital six months after I put you in." He turned away from the guy. He continued to follow John as he walked to his girlfriends car. When he had first spotted the manager, John had told her to be behind the steering wheel, ready to go, and she was there waiting.

John turned, and in a dramatic gesture, dropped his stuff on the sidewalk in front of the building. He stepped up to the manager. "Go back inside now, or I'll save myself a trip and put you in the hospital now."

The manager stared at him blankly. John breathed his words out as a hiss. "I'll break that filthy nose first. Ever had your nose broken? It doesn't hurt for a few minutes, then, Jesus Christ, is it painful." He looked around. "I don't see any witnesses either."

The manager stood as though in a trance. John lowered his voice further. "I'll count to three."

The manager seemed to snap out of it. "You can't make me leave. I run this place."

John could see that the guy was calling his bluff or was an imbecile. Either way, he'd have to follow through. He decided he didn't want to break the guy's nose, or actually put him in the hospital. He noticed the guys filthy feet because he wore sandals. He knew how to break his foot, and the reverse, by virtue of that, how not to break it. He stomped on the fat guy's foot to cause pain but not critical injury. He pushed him as he stomped. The top heavy man fell backward, tumbling into the grass. Oddly, he didn't cry out or yell. He tried to reach over his stomach and hold his aching foot, making no sounds or complaints. The silence was so incongruous, John thought for a flash that he had lost his hearing. He scraped up his stuff quickly, hopped in the car and they drove off. He looked back and the guy was still rolling around. As they turned the corner, it looked like he was attempting to sit up.

He was glad he had moved in with Diane but, had hoped that her attitude about him wouldn't change too quickly. He supposed that she would start to become, at least in his view, possessive and controlling. It wasn't that he didn't like being around her, he just didn't want her telling him what to do. He figured, invariably, when he told her this, she would cry and say that she wasn't trying to control anyone, she just wanted consideration. He felt exclusive sex, the fact that he wanted to be with her, not someone else, the money he would contribute to rent and utilities was consideration. Emotional outpourings were unnecessary, not part of the deal, even if he did feel guilty. It was never part of the deal. If emotional displays came from him, it would come later. He wondered why women liked him quiet when they met him, but then complained about it when they couldn't get him to talk. He recalled Annie and her friend Susan at the restaurant and how he had admitted to himself that his relationship with Diane would
probably end up going the way it had with Annie, and with Barb before that, and Cindy. John felt he was getting better at being close but that everyone seemed to want it on their schedule, not his. It angered him that he had to worry that an

argument probably waited for him at her place. He recalled what Cheryl said about picking the same sort of women all of the time. His gut told him she was right, and it told him at the same time that Susan was different.

He decided he probably needed to be fortified before he faced Diane, and he recalled that Annie and Susan would probably stop by the bar. He ran to the bar, two blocks off yet and barged in. Everyone turned to look at him because he came in so quickly and loudly. He looked at everyone. "It's colder than hell out there."

A few people laughed, the rest went back to what they were doing. The bar was packed. Paul was very busy. Annie and Susan came, it seemed, out of thin air walking slowly toward John, who stood in the door, shaking the rain off his wisp of a coat. Both of the women were drinking Coke. The two women had been wearing their coats when they were at the restaurant. They had removed them here. Annie was wearing what she usually wore when she had been with John, a white blouse with a few well placed ruffles, bright tight new jeans, and boots, usually black.

John knew she had beautiful breasts and a perfect rear end, but her blouses were usually loose and long enough to obscure her shape. He felt it was because she didn't have large breasts, and was ashamed of it. He had told her over and over how absolutely perfect they were, but he also knew that she didn't believe him, that in one turn she figured he was being kind, and in another turn he was telling a tainted truth because he had access to them and was biased by being turned on, despite their size.

Susan on the other hand wore jeans that were very ragged, and a T-shirt that left absolutely nothing to the imagination. John wondered if she had a boob job because her breasts were something that most men dreamed of, and most women would pay for with hard earned money. He figured she couldn't have afforded a boob job, and Annie would undoubtedly have told him about it as soon as she could, but hadn't. They were large yet stood up and out. She had full hips, and in John's estimation, could have been a model. Two of her teeth weren't in such great shape though. They were off to the side so she had to be laughing out loud before one could glimpse them.

John knew that he normally didn't size a woman's attributes up so consciously, but Susan, with tattoos of some sort of an animal he couldn't identify on one arm and a foreign language of some kind on the other, and her tight clothes, begged to be put in the front of anyone's mind who stood before her.

Annie grabbed one of his arms and laughed as she whispered. "This old dude is hitting on us. Paul's too busy to save us so save us!"

Susan grabbed the other arm, and rubbed up and down the inside of it. "Yeah, save us."

Annie seemed more relaxed than earlier. John worried about Billy. She couldn't stay with the lunatic.

John could see the guy, a strange looking man, in that he was obviously in his mid-fifties but wore bell bottom pants, a psychedelic print shirt, and a red velour jacket. His shoes were a black industrial type with steel toes, like Red Wings, and as with each item in his outfit, they didn't belong. His hair was long and stringy, a mix of mostly gray with spots of brown. John was surprised that the guy hadn't dyed his hair.

The man looked longingly at the women who had swarmed John. He showed his yearning unabashedly, and it embarrassed John. John spotted a table near the door, on the opposite side of the bar from the would-be playboy. He directed the girls there. "I can't believe we got this table."

Annie kept her arm on John, as did Susan. Annie spoke closely and quietly near John's ear even though nothing she said this time required discretion. "William and Charmain left a little bit ago. It was their table."

"I saw 'em going home." John explained as he sat down. As soon as the girls sat down on either side of him, he stood again, draping his coat on his chair. "I'll get your coats." He had spotted them on stools at the bar next to the hippie from outer space.

Susan pouted. "Get me a drink too, baby. Tequila on the rocks."

John looked at Annie. "I'll take a beer."

John was always amazed that she could drink one or two beers, then pop, then a beer, going back and forth between alcohol and non-alcoholic drinks. He went to Paul, and placed the order while he scooped up the girls coats. Playboy spoke to him. John had tried to avoid eye contact. "Those are some beautiful girls you're with my friend." John acted like he hadn't heard him. He waved and said hello to an acquaintance he saw in the middle of the bar as an excuse to stay distracted.

The playboy wouldn't be ignored so easily. He spoke louder. "Hey buddy, those girls with you sure are beautiful." The guy was an inch or two taller than John, but he had a protruding beer gut and looked soft like butter in summer.

John ignored him. The guy started mumbling out loud. "I'm just trying to compliment him." He mumbled and then, barely audible. "Don't need 'em both."

John didn't understand how saying they were beautiful was a compliment to him. He didn't like this guy's persistence. He obviously had no chance with the girls in the first place, but because he had spoken at them for a few minutes, he had now become a little braver and in some hair brained way, thought that he was a familiar of John's. John took the coats to the girls. Susan laughed out loud, scooting around in her chair, John thought, just to show off her hips, "Is he *still* going on?"

John didn't want to destroy him, but he was getting aggravated. "I swear, now he's trying to hit on me."

Susan laughed again, and blurted out "Fag!" at the man, without looking at him.

John put his finger to his lips. "Behave."

He went back to get their drinks. He grabbed the two beers in one hand, and the tequila in the other. The playboy would not be deterred. "Hey buddy, I was just trying to compliment you on your taste in women."

John noticed as the day had gone on, his patience had slowly dissipated. He held his tongue. As he choked back a nasty retort, a thought popped into his head that the guy had given up and was merely trying to keep himself in the imaginary game by identifying with John's tastes. He put on a smile and turned to playboy. "They are beautiful." He choked out, "Good eye. Gotta go now."

Playboy raised his drink in the air. "Right on." John noticed that he had a ponytail that had come half apart because his hair wasn't long enough. Some of his hair near the ends was dyed red. Now he realized why the guy hadn't dyed his hair to a natural color. He was trying to dye it like the kids. John could taste the beer in his mouth and feel the buzz in his head. It wasn't enough. He put the drinks on their table. The girls laughed and thanked him like he had just dropped off punch to two teenage girls at the prom. He hadn't graduated from high school, but he crashed the senior prom with a couple of friends to see if they could score with the girls. They had shunned them. They scored with girls out for a smoke between classes, not the tight asses that went to the prom.

He went to the bar, near playboy and ordered another tequila for himself. When he sat down, Annie looked at his second drink and frowned. "Don't get drunk John. I wanted to have fun and talk."

John took a big gulp of the tequila. "I can be drunk, talk and have fun at the same time."

Annie shrugged and smiled.

John looked in Susan's eyes with intense desire, surprising himself, but apparently not Susan, who smiled and sipped her drink. He tried to shake his lustful thoughts, or at least put them in their place. Annie would pick up on them. She would have already if it hadn't been for playboy distracting her. "So you girls find something at the store?" He didn't care. He just wanted to talk about something removed from his desires.

Annie spoke up. " I got a really cool coat. It..."

John interrupted. "That's not it." he pointed at the coat she had with her.

She frowned. "No, Susan and I were in such a hurry after we got back, that I had to leave it home."

John averted his eyes from Susan. "What was the hurry?"

The girls looked at each other, and laughed. "Girl stuff." Annie mumbled.

"Oh." John wanted to get off that subject. "Ralph got a car today."

Annie scrunched up her face. "I know. What'd he steal?"

John frowned and shrugged. "Saved his pennies. Literally saved his pennies."

Susan drawled, "and stole everything he could get his hands on." John wondered for the first time that day, whether Ralph was telling the truth about the vacuum cleaner he had that morning. He took another big drink.

John wanted to find out more about the situation with Billy, but his mind kept filling up with images of Susan's scraggly pants and the girl under them.

"Annie." He had gulped the tequila down. It started to relax him immediately. He started on his beer. "I wasn't kidding today about this fucking Billy. In fact, what the fuck are you doing with a lunatic like that?"

He knew it was the wrong thing to say because she became rigid. "You don't have any fucking right to tell me who to see." John's guilt welled up in him again.

He was glad the tequila had started to affect him. It diluted the guilt . "Annie, I'm just saying that you could do a lot better than him."

Susan looked anxious. She spoke up. "That's right. That's right. I told her she doesn't have to deal with this loser. He was trying to get us to do a three way the night he hit me."

John was thrown. He knew that sort of thing would be repulsive to Annie. "Annie, Jesus." She started to cry quietly. Susan looked at him imploring him to continue the conversation along the lines they had started. "Annie, if you don't believe me, because I was your boyfriend, why wouldn't you believe Susan. She's your friend. *I'm* still your friend."

Annie tried to choke back her tears. She screwed her face up and then relaxed, as if she had resigned herself to something. "Susan's beautiful. Of course, she'd think I could get somebody else. If I looked like her, I might have a chance." She grabbed a drink napkin and dabbed her tear filled eyes.

Susan looked at John. John didn't know why he should tell her how beautiful she was again. He had told her a million times. "I've told her ..."

Susan interrupted. "John knows you're gorgeous. He's seen you. Girl, we've tried clothes on together. You turn *me* on!" she laughed, "and I don't like girls."

Annie glanced away from the table. Playboy walked up to the table. "Night to all of you." He bowed. He had put an army jacket on over his red jacket. John wondered if people

151

who wore military surplus thought they were tough or patriotic. Maybe it was cheap. He hated the stuff.

Susan grimaced. "We're having a private conversation."

Playboy saw Annie had been crying. He looked discomfited. "I'll be going." He walked out the bar door staggering slightly.

Susan spat with more venom than the occasion seemed to require. "He'll go home now and yank it 'til it falls off."

John understood why Ralph made jokes all the time. They took the edge off of almost everything. "He'd be better off if it fell off."

The girls laughed. Annie was quickly regaining her composure. She looked down at the table while she wiped the trailing tears away. Susan took the opportunity to look John in the eye and lick her top lip in a single darting movement. She was apparently juggling her concern for Annie with her attraction to him, like he was with her. He now knew that he would have her that night. He was happy to realize that it meant that he could concentrate on the problem with Annie now.

He spoke more gently and in a lower tone than usual. He'd been told many times that when he spoke in his deeper voice it looked like a ventriloquist spoke for him. The resonance didn't seem like it should be able to come from his slim frame. "Annie, can't you stay with someone?" He didn't want to mention Susan. He wanted her and her bedroom to himself.

His question made her tear up again. "I'm not going to leave him."

John sighed. "Promise me that you'll leave him if he ever threatens you again."

She started pulling and kneading her drink napkin. "Ok, I promise I'll do that."

A thought came back to him. He couldn't have her call him at Diane's. "I'll get a cell phone. What's your number? I'll call you with it."

Susan broke in. "Don't call her. Call me. If Billy gets the call from you..."

John interrupted. "Ok, Ok. That makes sense."

"Then I'll call her and let her know."

"Right. There's a cell store on Court Place, right?"

Susan nodded. "Yeah. They have pay as you go too."

John didn't understand. "What's that?"

"It's like a calling card, but it's a phone. You buy so many minutes with the phone included. When the minutes run out, you get recharged, or get another phone. It's not cheap per minute, but you can get one for like twenty bucks."

"I'll do that." John pointed at Susan, looking at Annie, who looked in John's eyes with fondness. He felt guilt pangs again. He looked at the table. "I'm sorry Annie."

Annie sighed heavily. "I know." She looked across the bar and was startled. "Where's the hippy?"

Susan and John looked at each other. Susan laughed. "Hon, he came over here to the table and bid adieu."

John shrugged. Annie was perplexed. "He came over here and said goodbye? You are screwing with me."

John made a cross on his chest. "Swear to God, he did."

Annie laughed, in a sort of gasp. "Jesus. I'm sure having a good time. I don't even know what's going on."

"Darling," Susan said looking at John, grinning mischievously, "I wish I could remember all the fun I had. I keep having to have more to try to remember again."

DEAD BROKE

John, Annie and Susan shifted gears. It was as if Annie's having confessed that she didn't know if she was having fun or not had given them an order to put the past ten minutes aside and have a good time. Susan started things by saying how stupid Billy was, first for treating Annie badly, but also because he was just plain dumb. Annie nodded, grinning. She sipped her beer as Susan talked. "Ok, so Annie told me that she was watching a show on the space shuttle, and they were talking about the one that crashed," she looked at Annie for a sign that she was telling the story right so far, and Annie nodded her approval. "She starts getting choked up when they show the thing blowing up, and he walks in and sees the tears in her eyes, and asks her what's wrong. When she tells him that it upset her to see the space ship blow up he looks at her like she's nuts. She defends herself, saying that it's sad, that there was a school teacher with them and they had families and worked real hard and they all died. He stares at her for a minute," Susan looked at Annie for acknowledgement that she's still getting it right, and Annie nodded giggling a little now, "and he says "None of that's real. They do it all with special effects. They never went to the moon either. It's all make believe." All three of them laughed.

Annie jumped in. "I asked him if he was kidding and he said everybody knows that it's all fake. I didn't know what to say, so with him, I decided, it wasn't worth it."

John was glad the story didn't get her upset again. He wanted to change the subject. "So how'd you guys meet playboy over there?" He gestured toward the empty chair where he had been sitting.

Annie took up that story. "We came in looking for you and the only seats were at the end of the bar. So we went and sat down to talk to Paul." Annie looked over at Susan.

Susan jumped in "I *told* her that he looked weird as soon as I saw him."

Annie laughed. "You didn't say he'd try to pick us up."

"Well, that's what I meant when I said he was weird. I didn't say he would sing to us either."

John stifled a laugh. He thought he misunderstood. "What?"

Annie laughed heartily. She could see that John wasn't catching on. "He sang to us, John."

John drank his beer. The tequila was strong. He knew he hadn't had much. He bet Susan could hold her liquor. He shook his head, trying to eliminate the image of the guy singing.

"He didn't sing loud. He said something like, oh you girls are a song in my heart, or some crap like that, then he sang some song I never heard of."

Annie had just taken a sip of her beer. She waved her hand to stop so she could swallow and add something. "If we knew the song, how could we know that he was singing it. He was so far off key."

"I didn't know any of the words he sang."

"It was embarrassing." Annie was excited. "Then, right before you came in he did this thing. I don't know what it meant."

"Trying to get our attention."

"Well, yeah, but he was trying to do something with drama I think. He acted like he was on stage the whole time, like their was people watching..."

"Besides us..."

John looked over at Paul. He was coming around the tables to take orders, so John stayed put. "What was this guy doing?"

Susan put her leg next to John's and pressed the side of it into the side of his. "He asked Paul for a phone book. He didn't want to give it to him at first, because he knew that Pat would be mad if the guy lost it or messed it up, but he was too busy to be bothered so he gave it to him."

Annie interjected. "He paged through it with big arm movements and kept pointing his finger at spots on different pages."

Paul came to their table. John ordered tequila for him and Susan, and another beer for Annie. "Did he say why he was doing it?"

Susan stopped rubbing his leg while Paul was there, but she started again after he left. "No, he didn't tell us. He'd just point real exaggerated and say, "no" and then finally he circled something on a page and threw it on the bar. Paul picked it back up and put it away."

"That's it?"

"He said something. I didn't understand what it was. It sounded like "we shaft"

Paul had returned with the drinks.

Annie jumped a bit in her seat. Susan's leg disappeared from John's. "Maybe he said "we and man"".

Paul looked at her with a puzzled expression. "What are you talking about?"

Annie was excited about trying to sort out what Playboy had said. "We couldn't tell what that weird guy said after he marked up your phone book."

Paul put the last drink on the table. He collected the money. He did not use Pat's bottle counting methods. He couldn't keep track that way. "He said "wheat from the chaff." The three at the table looked at him, surprised.

Susan put her leg back against John's. "Wheat from the chaff?"

"Yeah. It's an old saying about sorting out the winners from the losers."

"The bastard." Susan spat.

Paul turned to go. "I don't think he was insulting you. He liked you. I'm not sure what he was talking about."

"Weird." Susan slouched down and put her leg more firmly against John's and started rubbing slowly and steadily.

John knew he would get an erection soon. He pushed her leg away and turned his eyes toward Annie trying to wordlessly explain that he didn't want to get caught doing anything that would upset her all over again. Susan seemed to get the message and sat up straighter.

Annie smiled. "That was fun. A mystery solved."

Susan leaned in. "But we still don't know what it meant."

John gulped his half empty drink down to make room for his new one. He was at the stage when the tequila made him giddy. It usually didn't give him a hang over. He hoped that would be the case again. John knew that Annie would be sure to call him if she got in a jam with Billy again. Short of him beating her to death, she would leave him at some point in the near future. He felt that his mind was free to think of Susan. He didn't want to think about Diane. It depressed him. "How'd you two get here?"

Susan smiled. "I drove. Billy has Annie's car."

"When you guys go home, can you drop me off too?"

Annie smiled. "Sure John. It is getting colder than hell out there isn't it?"

"I was up at four this morning" It seemed like days ago to him. "I could feel the cold blowing in right on top of the warmer air. I guess that's why it's raining and sleeting."

Annie chuckled. "You were up at four in the morning? You never got up that early when we were together. You could sleep through a bomb."

"I don't know what got me up. I couldn't go back to sleep."

Susan smiled mischievously again. "Busy in bed?"

John didn't appreciate Susan bringing Diane up. "No. I was staring at the ceiling in the dark and then I sat in the kitchen, staring at the walls." He said it with a touch of anger.

Annie patted his hand. "It's ok, baby. You'll catch up on your sleep soon.."

"Maybe", Susan muttered into her glass.

John wanted to get out of the bar. He wanted to have sex with Susan and he didn't want to have to dance around anything else that night. He felt like he'd danced all day on and off. "Let's go. Mentioning this morning made me sleepy."

He stood. The girls protested in unison. "Aw, c'mon. Let's at least finish our drinks."

John sat back down. If he wasn't getting what he wanted right now, he would at least control the conversation so that someone else would do the dancing. "So, Susan, what's your
boyfriend like?"

Annie laughed and answered for Susan "He's a truck mechanic. He's a nice guy, but Susan treats him like he's her younger brother."

Susan blushed. She knew John was getting back at her for mentioning Diane. "He's an ok guy. He makes good money, but Jesus he smells like grease all the time. He's dirty even after he scrubs himself for half an hour in the shower."

John smiled. "A grease monkey."

"And you lay what, John, rugs?" Susan smirked.

John laughed. He imagined Ralph pulling the old joke about hair piece/herpes out at that point. "Ok. My mistake, but I am good at it." he said the last part quietly.

Her comeback was fast, and not subtle. "That's because carpet just lies there. You wouldn't know what to do with some action." She laughed to cover her come on.

Annie was in too good a mood to take notice. The beer had loosened her up and her jealousy radar had been switched off. "Carpet burns," She blurted out. She laughed uproariously.

"Shag" giggled Susan.

"Great." John's mood was unnaturally elevated by the tequila. He actually felt talkative. "Carpet jokes." He looked down, holding his chest, in mock pain. "I'm gonna go into wigs. Hair pieces to the stars. It's gonna be top notch." Ralph would say something about "hair plugs" guessed John. He couldn't figure out how to work it in.

Susan started laughing hard and delivering a rejoinder at the same time. "Are you gonna cut a notch in their heads?" Her laughter dissolved into near hysterics.

It was contagious. Annie sputtered out another one liner. "Parting is such sweet sorrow!"

John was impressed that she knew the quote. He tried to recall what it was from. He noticed it was hard to focus. The booze was working fast. As he tried to remember where the quote came from, he had a blank expression on his face.

Susan started laughing to near breathless again. "He's wondering if he can make wigs out of rugs."

"Lotta flat tops." Annie spit out.

Across the room, a patron none of the three knew pushed himself away from a table, and putting his head between his knees, started to vomit. Paul was out from behind the bar with towels and cleaners in seconds. Pat had made a little clean up kit that could be toted out quickly. He said, like it was a pronouncement that should be engraved in granite somewhere, that "Puke in the middle of the bar can put a damper on sales."

John figured that Pat was also worried about a chain reaction. Lots of boozy, gassy people seeing vomit might be inclined to go the same route, causing a domino cascade of puke that would drive them all out into the night, never to return.

He stood. "That's our cue to go." He was still talking through his laugh, like the girls. This time they didn't protest but stood up, Susan far more unsteadily than Annie, and started putting their coats on. John slipped his on quickly.

He nearly got an erection thinking about what he hoped would transpire in the next hour. He turned to where

Paul was cleaning up the patron and the floor. "Bye, Paul. Bye Spewy."

They laughed and headed toward the door. Susan started driving toward Annie's apartment without saying anything. By the time they were at Annie's door, she had come to her senses enough to realize John was still in the car. "Why didn't we drop John off first? He's closer." She seemed to sober up quickly.

Susan was on top of it. "I don't know where he lives, hon. I know where you live. Where does he live?"

"Oh, that's easy he lives on…. Oh shit John, where do you live?" Annie had realized that she wasn't sure.

He put his best nonchalant voice on. "I'm not too far from here. I live at my girlfriend's place. It's over on Blue Ash."

Annie started to settle back. "Well, let's get him home."

Susan was right on the situation. "Baby doll. I'm going straight home after my taxi services are over. Can I get rid of you now, so I can go home after I drop John off?"

Annie was oblivious. She leaned over and in baby talk said, "You po ittle fing. Shoe you can." She laughed heartily. "I'm kinda drunk." For Annie, John thought, she was.

She got out of the car, and opened the back door where John was slumped. He put his feet out on the ground, surrounding her legs and holding her around the back. She leaned down and he tipped his head up and they kissed, for the first time in nearly a year. Annie stood back up, blushing. John could see it in the street light. He thought maybe it could be the cold air too. "Annie, I'm getting one of those cell phones tomorrow. I want you to have my number by the end of the day tomorrow. If someone, you or Susan or Pat haven't caught up with me so I can give it to you, I'm gonna come over to your place and give it to you there. Billy better not be home."

Annie moved her legs between his in a trusting sexual way. "Ok. Thanks John."

He didn't want to say anything else lest she start to cry or laugh. "Good night." He pulled back in and slumped in the seat.

Susan turned around. "Hey, sit up front. I'm not driving Miss fuckin' Daisy."

John looked at Annie. "She's a cab driver, not a limo driver." He smiled, and waved unsteadily. "Home, James."

He thought it best that he sit in back in the event that something of the fishy situation did start soaking into Annie's head, but Susan was adamant. "No godamn it. I'm not gonna have you in the back. Fuck that. Get up here!"

Annie shrugged. "Bye." She turned and headed toward the front door of the building. She turned again as John piled into the front passenger seat. They both waved back.

"I didn't want her to see us sitting together alone in the car."

"She hasn't got a clue. Jesus, don't worry." They watched her go in. She pulled the car away from the curb.

The heat in the car had raised the temperature to uncomfortably warm. It made John a little queasy. He started rolling down the window. Susan put her hand on his left hand. "Hey don't open that. It's nasty out there."

"It's hot in here."

An earthy laugh rolled up from deep in her chest. "You bet it is." She put her hand on his crotch. His sexual desire began to stir. She drove a few blocks, pulled over where there were no street lamps and turned the car off. They embraced, their hands moving all over each other. After all the noise and laughing, the quiet was enticing. It allowed John to hear the movement of their hands over the material of their

162

clothes, their heaving sighs and sharp intakes of air as they kissed. It seemed to magnify the rain hitting the car, or maybe it was raining harder. It might be turning to sleet again. He was fully erect now, and Susan had him hard in her grip through his pants. She started to fumble with the button at the top of his jeans. He started trying to reciprocate when it seemed like his hyper hearing swerved away from inside the car and out into the night to a strange noise. It was a sound that was not out of the ordinary for the neighborhood, but it caught his attention, none the less. There were several sirens crying out. All of them were converging on one spot somewhere not too far away. Susan seemed to hear it at the same time, or she sensed his change as he turned his attention to the sounds.

"What the fuck is going on?" she stared out the window. She looked at him and laughed when she realized how ridiculous it was to suppose she could see something blocks away from their dark little hiding spot.

John looked too. "I don't know. Maybe it's fire."

Susan's tone indicated that she was not pleased with the ease with which John seemed to be able to stop focusing all of his attention on undressing and making love to her to something vague out in the evening streets. " I don't see any lights. Who the fuck cares? Let's get it on."

John spotted a man walking down the street toward the car. He wore a long coat. As he approached, he could make out that it was a trench coat. He had his head down and walked quickly, obviously trying to get to where ever he was going so that he could dry off and warm up. He pointed at the man. "We have company. Can't we go to your place?"

Susan looked up at the man as he neared the car. She tapped the door lock involuntarily.He must have heard the click because his head jerked up as he passed the car. He was looking in the direction of the click, so he was staring directly into the window at Susan and John.

He had a startled look on his face. John pushed back in his seat like they were going to hit a brick wall. "Jesus!" he gasped.

Susan gave the man the finger. "He's just looking for a show."

Susan and John turned their heads and watched him retreating into the watery blackness.

"That's so fucking weird." John was incredulous.

Susan realized that John hadn't simply been taken by surprise, but that he was upset for some other reason. "What's wrong?"

John didn't want to seem idiotic, but his reaction had been severe enough, he knew he wasn't going to minimize it with a simple lie. "Well, I think I know that guy. I thought he was, uh, dead."

Susan's frown twisted into a perplexed expression. "Dead?"

John tried to compose himself. He sat up straight. "Christ that Tequila is good." He pushed outta little laugh.

Susan seemed to be relieved by his forced laugh. "So either the guy isn't dead, or that's not the same guy."

"I don't think it was him."

"Who is he, I mean who'd you think he was""

"His name is Bob. He came in to Pat's every day for three months and then just disappeared. He didn't look so good, so we figured he died."

"He disappeared, as in he didn't come around any more?"

John knew it sounded ridiculous. He felt ridiculous. He recalled how hard he had been on Ralph for sounding like a superstitious moron. "I know. I just got spooked. Fuck it. Hey, you didn't answer me. Can we go to your place?"

"Sure, Sam doesn't stay over unless I bless it, and I don't bless it tonight."

"He doesn't have a key does he?"

"No one has ever got my key darlin'." She took John's hand and put it on her crotch, "but you got this."

The sirens had multiplied as they sat. They both looked out the window again, half expecting to see the orange flickering lights of a fire pulsating in the dark, but there was nothing.

Susan started the car.. "Let's go to my place, but,"

John finished for her. "let's drive by over there and see what happened."

She turned the car around. "Right, we have all night, and all day if you can handle it."

He laughed quietly. As they approached the block where the sirens had converged, a police car was pulled across the street they were driving down. Susan turned a block away and moved further down the street. Each street was restricted by a police car for six blocks. She pulled in at the sixth blocked street and parked at the curb. They got out of the car and started walking toward the lights where a couple of ambulances were parked. There were firemen and paramedics everywhere, standing, waiting, talking. Neighbors were standing in the rain looking at one spot, craning their necks, and then talking, animatedly.

As John and Susan walked toward the crowd, they could see that there were barricades holding the spectators back. They walked up to the back of the crowd. Susan tapped a woman on the shoulder. "What happened here?" The woman said she didn't know, that she had just got there too. She was in night clothes and slippers with a bomber jacket over it. She shivered almost uncontrollably.

John looked around to see if someone else might know what had happened. When the sea of heads parted at just the right time, he could see police detectives checking various cars along the way. There were dents and scratches in some that he could see from his vantage point. It must have been an accident.

He pulled Susan next to him, partly to tell her his theory, and partly to feel her warmth against his body. "Probably some drunk screwed up. Let's go."

Susan giggled and moved in close to him. "You're the one that wanted to see what it was all about. Now I want to know." She took him by the hand and pulled him toward a break in the crowd. There were half a dozen guys, big guys who were smoking and talking loudly to each other. The others had moved away from them a bit, leaving gaps in the circle. Susan was in her element. She walked up to the men who towered above her and John. "Hey guys," she thrust her hip out a little, "what happened." The men took one look at Susan and fell silent. They weren't quiet for long.

"Jesus Christ, what are you doing with this shrimp honey. I got what it takes." The first one started. John could tell that the rest of them would start trying to out brag each other in the loudest possible way.

Susan stepped forward a bit more. "You boys behave. I'm not in a mood for any shit." She stood with her feet spread slightly, flat and steady, her hands on her hips, like she was braced for a strong wind. "I just want to know what happened."

John realized what she had already figured. These guys were lightweights in over size packaging. She could wrap them around her little finger. "Damn," he thought, "she could handle prison easy."

The six men were stunned. They looked at each other. One of them felt that he couldn't let this woman order him around in front of the others because he stepped forward and demanded. "I'll tell you if you suck my cock."

Susan focused a stern look on him. "If I suck your cock you fucking , moron, it would kill you. Let's see who's gonna suck who's dick." She stepped forward one step. The other men looked at the giant whom had dared challenge her and then laughed simultaneously at his defeat.

A small group of people within earshot sniggered. They started closing in around the guys everyone had thought were bullies, but had been shown up as lummoxes. Susan sensed the switch and moved forward past the six and near the front of the barricade before they lost their positions. John held her hand and followed her forward. He didn't mind her taking charge. He didn't understand why. It wasn't the usual for him.

She saw a woman who seemed to have a bird's eye view of the goings on. "Hey, can you tell us what happened?"

The woman turned and looked Susan over, and it seemed that from the expression on her face that she wasn't going to tell them anything, but when a man next to her began to speak, she spoke over him. "Motorcycle. Guy's deader than a door nail, smeared all over the place."

John finally realized that he wasn't that far from Daryl's house. He was a person who took the same route to a destination every time. He could pass a street two blocks off from his usual route and not know it from a street two thousand miles away. He didn't remember street names. He used landmarks. He spotted an angular house on a corner a few blocks away that he used as a visual cue coming in from a different direction to get to Daryl's. He started shivering uncontrollably. Daryl's motorcycle was powerful and he was something of a daredevil.

He tried to talk to distract himself from his shivering. "What kind of motorcycle.."

A man behind them said one word. "Scooter."

Another concurred and added. "It was a motor scooter, but it's not much of anything now." John felt frantic. He started pushing by and to the front of the barricade. The street had a thick swath of a blood smear that looked like it had bits of flesh throughout it. It disappeared under a car that had a huge dent in the door and side. The wrecked vehicle was under a tarp next to the car. There were two fireman and a policeman under the car talking and moving uncomfortably on the cold damp ground.

John looked at the ambulance. The doors were open and it was empty. Another ambulance was parked further away and its doors were shut but it wasn't moving. John watched the doors to the second ambulance open and three people pile out of it. There were others that remained as the doors shut. The three people walked briskly toward the first ambulance. They all jumped into the open door and two of the people sat down as the other opened drawers, and looked back at the two. John saw that it was a woman sitting near the back. He recognized the short black leather jacket. When he looked at the hair, he realized that it was Garlene. He immediately recognized Daryl who was sitting next to her, his head in his hands. It looked like he was sobbing. John released his hand from Susan's and jumped the barricade. An officer ran forward yelling "you can't come in here. Get back."

John was fully prepared to deck the cop, and the cop seemed to sense it, because he stopped and started to put his hand down toward his gun. John gave him as threatening a stare as he thought he would ever dare give a policeman, considering his intense desire to not see the inside of a cell again. He barked. "These are my friends." He gestured broadly toward the ambulance. The cop seemed relieved to avoid the confrontation and waved him on. Susan had no problem following him. The cop didn't say a word to her. He stared at her rear end as she followed John to the ambulance.

John crouched down in front of Garlene and Daryl. Daryl was crying hard, hysterically. The third person was a paramedic and he had rolled up Daryl's coat and shirt sleeve and was giving him an injection. John whispered to Garlene. "This couldn't be Joey."

Garlene's grim expression and nod told him that it was indeed Joey who had died.

John looked at Susan. She didn't know any of these people, but she could see the look on John's face. He thought for a second that he might become hysterical. He looked at Garlene again as he asked another question. "But how?"

She looked at Daryl. His crying was starting to subside. The paramedic spoke gently to him, asking him to lie on the stretcher. Daryl didn't seem to hear him. He said it again. This time Daryl stood, one hand still firmly placed over his eyes and he allowed himself to be placed on the cot. Garlene looked at him as she answered John in a hushed, hoarse voice. "He fucking was racing that godamn bike around."

"But how could he kill himself. I thought it didn't go that fast?"

Garlene continued to watch Daryl as she answered. "Daryl and him changed stuff on it." She stopped talking for a moment as she concentrated on Daryl. "He was going like sixty, seventy. Showing off."

Daryl sat straight up, like he was rising from a coffin, back from the dead. "He killed himself. I'm sure of it. He wanted to go out like his brother." His face was so contorted with grief that John barely recognized him. His face red, swollen and clinched was drenched in tears.

Garlene leaned toward him. "You don't know that for sure, honey."

Daryl slammed the metal frame with his hand. "It doesn't fucking matter. He's DEAD."

The paramedic moved next to him quickly and whispered in Daryl's ear. John thought it odd that it resembled the way that Daryl had spoken to Joey hours earlier, and it had the same calming effect on Daryl that it had on Joey at the time. Daryl choked some indecipherable words out. Garlene looked at the paramedic. He spoke clearly in a measured tone to her. "We can take him in and keep an eye on him if you like."

Daryl's words were thick, his lips looked like they had been injected with fluid to the point of bursting. John noticed for the first time that he had blood all over the front of his coat and shirt. " I want to go home."

The paramedic spoke in his calming voice. "Ok Mr. Watson. That'll work." He looked at Garlene. "I'll get him to the house for you."

Garlene looked like she might break down now. "Thank you." The paramedic helped Daryl stand, he walked him out of the ambulance toward his home several blocks away. He draped a blanket around him as they walked away.

As Daryl passed, he mumbled a pitiful "Sorry."

John was floored. "Take care of yourself Daryl." He whispered it.

Garlene motioned and told the paramedic she was right behind him. She turned back to John and Susan. She recognized Susan, and didn't seem to be pleased. She ignored her and looked at John, talking quickly. "Joey and Daryl were messing with that fucking bike and then they went down stairs and listened to music. Daryl said that Joey seemed fine. He told Daryl he was coming up to take a leak and get some beers. After a couple of songs, Daryl wondered what was going on, so he comes up and he can't find Joey. He comes to check with me and about the time he comes into the bedroom, we hear the motor scooter revving up and pulling out of the garage. Daryl lit down the steps and outside, screaming at Joey until he was hoarse. He ran a block or two and then came back. He was already kicking himself for running after him instead of getting in his car and going after him. I told him that there wasn't anything he could do. I told him to come back in and let the little prick get it out of his system. I said it that way, *the little prick.*" Her voice cracked. She looked back toward where her husband and the paramedic had disappeared. "So we stand on the porch and we can hear him. He's winding it out up and down the streets around here. Daryl is hopping mad, jumping up and down. I kept reminding him that about the time he goes after him, he'll be pulling back in, like a little kid who broke the good dinner dishes and hopes you forget because he disappeared for a while. After about five, maybe ten minutes we can hear him tearing down a street, and then we hear the tires screeching, and then a bang, and then a bunch more bangs and metal rattling and scrapping and then nothing. I felt like my skin had come off and every nerve was exposed. We ran to the car and I made Daryl let me drive. He actually hit me once on the shoulder, really hard, I've got a big ass bruise now, but he gave in. We found him pretty fast because there were people up and down the street where he spilled it." Her chest heaved and she forced a huge sigh out. "Jesus, John." She hugged him. "He skimmed the street for six blocks, and then it caught on the car here. Half his face is just white gunk and bone. His arms are all twisted like a broken doll. It's fucking creepy. Daryl tried to pull him out, but he was jammed under the tire so tight he couldn't move him. He was dead anyway." She sounded resigned now, exhausted. "I gotta go." She gave Susan another quick look, but Garlene was tired. There was no threat or anger in her face when she looked at her this time.

John wondered how they knew of or knew each other. "Do you need me to stop by tomorrow?"

"I don't know. Just call." She walked toward home.

Susan took John's hand. "So were they related? How do you know this kid?" Her voice was soft, velvety.

John squeezed her hand. "Let's get out of here." He started shivering again. They worked their way out of the crowd and back to Susan's car without speaking.

Susan started the car. They had been on the rode for a few minutes when John realized that she had asked him questions. " I'm sorry Susan. I didn't mean to ignore you. I met

Daryl at a job maybe five years ago, now. Joey isn't related to any of us. Daryl took Joey under his wing, like a son. Joey came from a pretty messed up family. It messed him up pretty good too." Images of Joey started flashing through John's mind like a sloppy slide show. Here was Joey jumping up and down, smiling, laughing, on the pavement, lifeless with his head ripped open, jerking as the last bit of his boundless energy evaporated out of him like so much alcohol and blood spilled on a hot sidewalk. The wreck reversed and Joey was whole again, screaming backward on his bike like an insane jackal, foam spilling off of his lower lip.

"This is really gonna screw Daryl up."

"They have kids?"

"A girl."

"Does she get this kind of attention?"

A small laugh escaped through John's closed lips. "You know, oddly enough, she doesn't."

Susan was intent on the road. The rain had turned to a mixture of sleet and snow. "Maybe it's a good thing this kid isn't getting that kind of attention."

John put his hand on Susan's leg. "Yeah. You knew he had a kid, didn't you?"

Susan kept her focus on the road. "I guess I did."

John moved his hand up to Susan's crotch. "You are amazing. You have this strong mixture of intuition and smarts, like a mind reader, or a soul reader."

She laughed and put her hand over the top of his and moved it deep into her crotch. He could feel the warm moisture through the jeans. "You're just horny." His brain started firing strong sexual images.

They arrived at Susan's apartment building and went up to her place. She turned off the phone. John made love to Susan with a vigor, a wide eyed sensitivity and energy that he had never conjured before. He felt like he was vitally and intensely alive every minute and the life perpetuating coupling of sex, distilled into an understanding of every smooth feminine inch of her body, like the power of her life and his had come together and magnified far beyond the power of the two of them to make them something close to perfection. They fell asleep in each other's arms as the sun came up.

HOT POODLE PEE & PORTULACAS

John awoke to Susan stroking his legs and as soon as she saw that he had been awakened, she initiated sex. As they coupled, he thought about how over blown his view of their sex had been the night before. The sex in the light of day was intense, but it was just sex. Susan was blessed with a great figure and the firmness of youth. Her dissipating life style and the grind of being poor were going to take their toll, but they hadn't yet. After she had climaxed, which was permission for him to; it was a yard stick that had served him well, he came and they lie side by side staring at the ceiling. "You are good, Johnny boy."

"I try."

"You do. No wonder the girls just *love* you."

For the first time, he noticed the apartment was a mess. There were clothes strewn everywhere. Pizza boxes, carry out Styrofoam, fast food bags were abandoned all over the furniture. There was makeup, blow dryers (three different ones!), and newspapers topping off the chaos. He could look out the door of the bedroom into the bathroom which was as jumbled, and dirty to boot. "Yeah, I'm a pig. Sue me." She said.

John recalled his drunken pronouncement that she could read minds. He looked over at her. She was a brunette, and her skin was a little darker than the average woman's, much more than the blondes he tended toward. Diane was bleach blonde, but her natural hair color was a light caramel. She was very pale. Diane's skin was creamy and John had noted with some fascination, that it actually bordered on translucent at her hair line on the scalp, under her arms, and in her crotch. It was like God had mixed up a very pleasant flesh tone, delicate enough that when he tapered off the spray job (God used a really nice paint sprayer to put the skin color on each of us) near the hair, she became the semi- invisible woman. A few very pale blue veins were even visible under her arms.

The thought that John picked women who were in their early twenties to have passing relationships with, despite his turning thirty soon rose in his consciousness, and he pushed it backout effectively by looking and touching Susan's body again. "Can you read minds?"

Susan looked surprised. "I'd be rich." She stroked his hair. "You're face says a lot about what you're thinking."

It was John's turn to be surprised. "My face? If what I'm thinking is on my face all the time, you are the first woman I know who actually sees it." He had imagined himself as the quiet inscrutable man, the mystery man, the puzzle whom women invariably want to solve. He was a bit embarrassed to realize that he might actually play on that instead of passively observing it. After all the times he had been told he was impenetrable, when did he start believing it? When did he stop thinking it was so much baloney.

Susan continued to stroke him. "You're thinking that you've been found out, and you've been thinking about your girlfriend."

John pulled away from her, uneasy. "Jesus."

She laughed heartily. Her long, gently curling hair fell across her face. She pushed it back and he could see her blush. "I just figured you were probably trying to come up with a story for the fact that it's three in the afternoon and you haven't talked to or seen her for almost an entire day. She's got to be royally pissed."

John sat up and looked around for a clock. He was disoriented. She had just said it was three in the afternoon. She laughed again. "Maybe I was wrong about that." She picked up a little white alarm clock that was next to her on a small cluttered night stand, and showed it to him. "Nope." It was three twenty one in the afternoon. He thought the sunlight seemed to be at a strange angle. Then he recalled that they had been going at it until daybreak and all the booze, and his getting up early that morning, and Joey.

"It'll be ok, John." Her voice had a hypnotic tone to it.

The observation conjured a fit of pique for John. "I'm not worried. You don't seem concerned about Sam."

"I don't live with Sam."

John was embarrassed that he hadn't thought of that, and didn't remember telling her that he lived with Diane. Maybe Annie had told her, but then she didn't know either. Maybe she read his mind. He was beginning to wonder why, in the span of a day, he seemed to have gone from being a hard core skeptic of mysterious, superstitious beliefs to a man who thought he had seen a ghost, a specter and slept with a mind reader. He grimaced. "I don't have to worry about Diane."

"She's well behaved, is she. Puts up with your shit?" Her tone was sharp.

"Hey," he stood, naked next to the bed, "you came on to me, remember?"

"Yeah, and I know what my relationship to my boyfriend is, but I'm not so sure that you know what yours is with your girlfriend, but you were willing to sleep with me anyway."

John was amazed that he could flip feelings toward Susan from admiration, desire, to disdain and anger in a few seconds, and because she was telling him the truth. He started picking through the clothes on the floor for his. He wouldn't speak. His anger wasn't fair to Susan, so he figured he'd keep his mouth shut. He told himself that maybe he was constantly counting to ten.

As he wavered between feeling defensive and sad, he latched on to the feelings he had discarded as ridiculous when he woke up, his feelings about their love making the night before, the romantic images. He held it up in his mind as proof that his heart as well as his cock had been in the right place the night before. He had always marveled at his ability to look at a naked woman he had slept with for the first time and be relatively removed from the newness of the experience and all the extra sexuality that's normally loaded into the moment. It was sex with any woman, but when he looked at Susan lying on the bed, the sheet draped over her hip, her breasts large and firm hanging at a slight angle as she rested on her elbow, he felt a tugging in his chest that, if he had to describe it, was possessiveness and yearning mixed together in a steaming brew.

In fact, he now imagined Susan as a white witch. One of his former girlfriends had fancied herself a good or white witch, as he had learned they were called, but John had always silently ridiculed her. She was just a fool looking for a religion that allowed her to fuck more than one guy at a time, and justify, he suspected, many other things she had had to do growing up in a dirt poor family of seven. John hated her father the first time he met him. He acted like a jealous suitor, and John suspected he probably had slept with all three of his daughters. The guy was probably disappointed when the poor broken wife bore sons the other two times.

As he dressed, Susan silently watching, a feeling that he couldn't allow this to end, burgeoned in him at the same time that a feeling that he had to get away from this woman who seemed to conjure fantastic thoughts in him that he had no familiarity or bearings with grew along side it. The two opposites seemed to mix, in a forced way like oil and water in a blender, making a gray unidentifiable and wholly unappetizing brew.

He sat on the bed to put his shoes on. She sat silently behind him, continuing to look at him, he supposed. He felt that the bitter fluids in his mouth might evaporate if he opened it and said, at least, a few things. He turned toward her. She had lain back down, and closed her eyes. It was like he had already left. It pissed him off. He tried to picture her five years from now, a gut starting to form on her stomach, adipose fat deposits forming up and down her thighs and the upper legs, her arms puffed with the fat on the underside swinging when she lifted a beer, her teeth a mass of black and stench, an injured arm or leg from whatever crap dangerous job she was forced to take to make a joke of a living but it hurt him to see it, it didn't distance him from her like he thought it might. He was becoming very upset that no matter where his thoughts seemed to veer, wherever his emotions lingered, they all started rolling back toward him as an ache, a tenderness he didn't feel he could bear to have in him for long, lest it drive him insane, and a melancholy exhilaration that he was with her now, but it would not be like this again and his brain was working like a frenzied over heated computer trying to calculate it's way out of it's imminent shutdown.

She spoke with her eyes shut, in a tone like she was talking about a new pair of shoes, or the weather. "Anybody ever ask if you were gay?"

His face puckered like he had chewed lemons. "Hell, no." He turned back and put a shoe on. He was glad she said something. "Look," he held the other shoe in his hand, "I never tell women that I have feelings for them."

She continued talking with her eyes shut, her arms crossed over her bare chest. "I'll bet."

He pushed air out of his mouth in exasperation. "I mean, that I don't say it because it wouldn't be true."

177

She kept her back to him, like an executioner with a hood. "You don't want to lie."

"Right." He replied. He was terribly unnerved that she could take the conversation into areas that completely baffled or upset him, and then right back into areas where he felt like he had sure footing and all of his facilities were in place.

"I said that about being gay, because you are more sensitive than most guys I've met. I wondered if somebody, like your daddy thought you were soft."

He laughed. He put his shoe down. "Nobody's called me soft, at least to my face." He was glad he could provide evidence that men tended to fear him.

"Oh, yeah. You're tough." She was sarcastic.

John picked his shoe back up and started putting it on. He didn't want to deal with this any more. "I gotta go. I have to see how Daryl's holding up." She didn't reply. He tied his shoe, stood up and turned toward her again. She lie quiet. "Look, I think you're great Susan."

"A good lay." She replied.

He was exasperated. He turned away. "I gotta go."

He walked over to a corner of the room and picked his coat up off the messy floor. He vaguely remembered the frenzy to remove their clothes, and it started taking his memory through the entire torrid night. He felt he had to speak to break the rerun. He didn't want to see it. "We'll talk soon. I just have to..."

"Do you have feelings for me?" She said "feelings" with the elongated inflections with which he had said it. He wasn't sure if she was being sarcastic, mocking him.

He knew he would say "yes, I have feelings for you" if he opened his mouth again. He put his coat on and left the apartment quickly. He would say it later. He would say it. It distressed him. He wanted to get out of the building and see if she had put a hex on him and if the spell had a radius of effect that he could breach. It occurred to him that he had at least an hour and a half walk to get to Daryl's.

He could catch a bus but he knew that at this time of day, people getting off work would slow the stops down and he would be on the different buses, downtown and back for over two hours, so he decided to walk. He hoped the vigorous pace he kept would help him clear his mind. He considered a bus again. It reminded him of a random encounter he'd had with an old work friend, Freddie Floyd. He always loved thinking about the alliteration. The last time he'd seen Freddie he was waiting on a bus for a job at a call center. It was part time, but it was all he could get. Even recalling the moment when Freddie told him about his new job, John's face grew red with embarrassment on his behalf. He was strong, could punch concrete and win the conflict. Picturing him with a precious little head set on, sitting in an ill fitting office chair was hard to imagine. It made him physically uncomfortable just thinking about it. More importantly, the man had an incredibly heavy accent. John could never quite figure out what sort of accent. There were hard rolling "r's" and a sing song quality in a rubbery enunciation. He thought it might be some deep back wood Kentucky accent. He thought about the countless attempts Freddie would make to sell whatever junk he was called on to peddle and the fruitless end to each as the potential client angrily exclaimed they couldn't understand a word he said. Why was Freddie put in that position? For that matter, why did he have to lay carpet until the knees that allowed him to walk in this world were ruined. He'd never seen a lot that made sense in the work world he'd inhabited to that point.

The sleet from the night before had stopped, leaving little patches of ice on the grass, still
emerald green, stubbornly wearing the color of spring and summer until the cold, slush and ice beat it into the drab brown it would be burdened with throughout winter. The air was very cold, but there was no wind. It was overcast, the gray of the sky being a perfect backdrop for the greens, reds and gold; an overture of autumn.

Even though his coat was inadequate, he kept warm by walking as quickly as possible, working up a sweat at one point. As he approached Daryl's house, he could see that the narrow street was more jammed with cars than usual. He suspected the jam was from people who were at Daryl's. As he walked into the yard, he could see that he was correct. The front door was open like the last time he was there. The storm door was closed, the glass fogged from the warmth of all the people standing in the living room, and the cold condensing it into mist from John's side- outside.

As he stepped onto the porch, he could make out that one of the numerous people standing in the entryway was Garlene. He was amazed to see that she was talking to Pat. Of the hundreds of times he had been around Pat, he had never seen him in a social setting. He had a suit on, and a grim sad look on his face. John briefly felt that he belonged on this side of the door, the cold side, and that he'd be better off there. They could be warm and emotional on the other side. He stopped on the last step, and reached into his coat for a cigarette. As he lit it, Garlene spotted his movements through the foggy glass. She opened the door, leaning out into the cold. She wore a baggy navy blue sweater with new jeans. Her long black hair, usually a flyaway static ridden nest was carefully brushed and gleaming. It was as dressed up as he had ever seen her.

"Get your ass in here, you idiot." She laughed. "You could smoke in the cold, or in a nice warm house. Tough decision."

John grinned as he stepped in. Pat grabbed him and hugged him. It startled John. Pat was in his civvies, behaving like a civilian. "You been drinking Pat?"

He put a mock hurt look on his face. "Well,... a little." He laughed loudly.

Everyone had come to Daryl's house to pay their respects. John wondered what Joey's parents would think of Daryl being treated like he was Joey's father. He was amazed to spot them sitting in the living room. They sat on what John called the dog couch. Normally, it was a lumpy dog hair matted mess of a couch, but Garlene had obviously vacuumed it, and put a dark brown throw over it, with a couple of dark pillows that disguised the lumpier cushions on the back of it. The dogs were probably tied up in the back yard. Joey's parents sat looking like two immigrants who were in the US their first day trying to understand it all. People whom they obviously had never known were walking up to them and telling them how cool Joey was, that they'd felt lucky to know him, and Joey's parents would look at them like they didn't believe that he was dead, that they were hearing these strangers speak English, but they didn't have a grasp of it to fully translate what was being said. It looked like they were on their best behavior too. They looked grudgingly sober.

John turned to Garlene. "Where's Daryl?"

"He's been on the phone all day helping with funeral arrangements. Joey's folks basically handed it over to him."

John looked at them. "Lost both their sons. It's unbelievable."

Pat spoke quietly, "Do they have the money for the funeral?"

Garlene nodded, "yeah, they had a small insurance policy. They're gonna cremate him and instead of a viewing, because the casket would be closed anyway, and it cost more than they have, we'll have the wake here."

John looked around. "Looks like one today."

Garlene smiled. "Yeah, everybody started showing up."

John thought that it was odd that Joey's parents had life insurance policies on their adult kids. He didn't think it was a scam. He felt that maybe they were admitting to themselves what a wrecked life they had given their kids and the only thing they would or could do about it, was make sure it didn't come out of their pockets when it came to it's inevitable conclusion. The tiny premiums, a few dollars a month, would allow them to brag that their boys wouldn't be "stuck in no pauper's graves." John felt depression sweep through him like a mischievous ghost. It passed through his body and moved on to torment someone else. He was suspicious that the ghost had emanated from the evil that probably resided in Joey's parents.

Pat took a sip of a green drink he had. "I'll do the food for the wake tomorrow."

Garlene and John looked at Pat, pleased. "Thanks, Pat."

"He was irritating, but he was just a kid. He didn't deserve to die."

John, in his mind, added, "And he didn't deserve these loser parents, who'll probably have some money left over from the insurance and use to it buy booze." He didn't understand why people were forgiven their cruelties when someone died. They were directly responsible for the death. It seemed, John thought, so *hillbilly*, whatever the hell that was.

Garlene pulled John and Pat in closer. "Daryl wrestled all day with the idea that he might have killed himself. I mean, why'd he get rid of that car? He fought to keep it because it was his brother's. All of a sudden, he sells it and gets that fucking scooter..."

John continued, "and he souped it up and he used the money from his brother's car to get it."

Garlene nodded, "but then Daryl said that Joey didn't seem to have any plans. He just didn't like the speed limit."

Pat cleared his throat. "A death wish."

Garlene nodded again. "Right, but he seemed pretty happy when he didn't think about his brother. I don't know." She reached into her back pocket and pulled out a pack of cigarettes. Her jeans were tight, hewing to her rear end. The pack was flattened. "Shit." She looked at the flattened cigarettes. John quickly pulled one of his out of his pocket and pointed it toward her lips. She glanced at him, and opened her mouth to receive the cigarette. As she threw the misshapen pack on a nearby end table, he pulled out his lighter and had a flame ready when she turned back. She smiled and took the proffered light.

John was confounded by his sudden desire to sleep with Garlene. He had known Daryl and Garlene for years. He knew their marriage wasn't perfect, but it had a strong core that would endure through most or all of the distractions that might crop up. He had two good friends in them. John always enjoyed his easy relationships with women, but it seemed like it was going out of kilter and he didn't know why. He had made mistakes before but it seemed that Diane was a disaster from start to what he supposed was an inevitable end, and it was all on him and he'd had enough women in his life that he wondered what lessons were there that he had ignored, blown off, or could not decode and why. "Is Daryl in the basement?"

She nodded. "Yeah, him and Leon are down there with a couple of the guys."

John did and didn't like Leon. Leon was a ladies man of the first order. He was overt, he voiced how much he loved women, and he always scored. He wasn't tall, but he was built like a middle weight boxer. He was handsome enough that even his ugly mullet haircut didn't impinge on it much, if at all. The effect was like that of teenage girls wearing ridiculous clothes-they were stunning no matter what they wore. Despite it never having happened, John figured in some corner of his mind that Leon might hit on a woman that John had set his sights on, and that made him uncomfortable. He even entertained the idea that Garlene and Leon might have already had a fling.

In all the turmoil, John was comforted by the familiar careful descent down the steep worn steps into Daryl's basement. The fact that there wasn't music blasting at ear bleeding levels was disorienting. It felt so different, light and airy, that he imagined that he could step off any of the steps, and if he willed it, he could continue walking in the air in front of him. He couldn't be sure where he'd go, three or four feet off the ground, but it would be a pleasure going there and amusing to wow friends with the feat.

He moved outside himself to wonder what the hell all of these thoughts of magic, levitation, mind reading and other mumbo jumbo were doing residing in him. He returned to himself as he spotted Daryl.

There was a drone of hushed talking behind the dry wall that separated the stereo and weight lifting equipment from the rest of the unfinished basement. Daryl's eyes were puffy and he was haggard looking. Leon, looked sharp in a nice suit, and two other guys he vaguely knew were in oxford shirts and new jeans. He tried desperately to remember their names.

Luckily, Daryl introduced him to them again, forgetting that he had met them at some point in the past. "John, this is Carl, and this is Eric. They lived with Joey for a while."

John shook hands with them. Daryl reached over to a cooler sitting next to the weight bench and pulled a beer out for John. "So'd you see Pat?"

John took the beer. "Yeah. It's strange seeing him out of that little hole in the wall."

Daryl smiled. It looked like it took an effort to do it. "Yeah. It is weird." He looked at John with pleading eyes. "I have to go to the funeral home again tomorrow. You doing anything?"

"I'm going with you." He raised his beer to Daryl.

Daryl raised his beer. "To Joey." They all repeated the toast, and drank. John could smell Susan's deodorant wafting around him. He looked around startled, but she wasn't in the room. Had she cast a spell on him, pulling on him, calling him back to her. As hysteria started welling up in him, it occurred to him that he had put her deodorant on because it's all he had.

Daryl noticed the change in his expressions. "What's wrong buddy? You look like you saw a ghost?"

John snapped out of his reverie. He wasn't going to talk about Susan. "I thought I smelled something sweet, that reminded me of someone."

Leon gestured with his beer bottle as he spoke. "I saw a TV show where they said that some ghosts you can't see, but you can smell their perfume, or their hair. Shit like that."

All five men looked startled. A tear ran down Daryl's face. " I could smell that blood all night last night, and most of the day today." He looked at John again. He didn't wipe the tear away. "He looked normal on the one side of his face, like he was sleeping, but the other side looked like someone took a planer to it." He choked off a cry, making it a stifled yelp. He took a long drink from his beer.

Someone was coming down the steps. About half way down they stopped. John imagined that they'd figured out the secret of walking in the air, and were working out whether they would be coming in the room three feet off the ground. The person continued down and Garlene walked into the room. "Hey John, Pat says he has to leave, and wondered if you needed a ride?"

He looked at Daryl. He knew he should go home and talk to Diane, or at the least, call her. He didn't think that Daryl would want him staying there tonight, or if he did, he would say so.

Daryl did speak up. "You can stay here tonight if you want." Garlene stood quietly waiting for an answer from John.

John thought about the lust that had been stirring for Garlene these last few days, and thought it would be a bad idea if he stayed the night, yet he knew Daryl would like his company. He also knew Leon would stay if he were asked. "Ok. I'll stay, if you need me here."

Garlene turned to leave. "Ok, well you come up and tell him so he can go, then."

John wondered why she didn't tell Pat herself since she was going back up. He stood. Daryl spoke up again. "Can't you let him know baby?"

She turned, emotionless. "I think he wanted John to help him with something. He needs to go tell him himself." She turned again and left. John stood to go up. "I'll be right back."

He caught up with Garlene as she started up the stairs. "What did he want, do you know?"

Garlene answered without turning around. "He didn't say, but he's gonna do the food for the wake tomorrow. Maybe he wants help with that." John watched her ass as she walked up the steps ahead of him. He tried to look away but was incapable of doing it. Had he been given some sex tonic, a love potion?

Pat was wearing an overcoat that John had never seen before. It was a nice one. "Hey John, do you want a ride home? I'm going now. I have to make arrangements for the wake tomorrow, and I wondered if you were coming along, you could help me bring the service stuff back here?"

John wasn't sure he understood, but he did know that he wouldn't mind helping, and that he would be grateful for a reason to break away from the gathering. There were certain times when he hated not having a car and this was one. He always had to be attached to someone's errands, or convenience or generosity. It rarely had something to do with what he wanted or needed. "So you need to haul something?"

Pat nodded, walking toward the door, like John's decision had already been made. "Right. I've got a bunch of containers and such that we'll stow in the car, then I'll drop you off."

"Ok, I'll be happy to help." John ran down to let Daryl know that Pat needed his help with wake arrangements, so he'd go with him. Daryl gave him an emotional hug and the good-byes were long enough that Pat appeared in the room to find out what had happened to him.

As soon as they were on their way, Pat asked if he could stop by the bar to speak to Paul. John told him whatever he wanted to do was fine. As they rolled up to the bar, John could see that Ralph's car was there. He decided to go in with Pat. As he unbuckled, Pat looked over and stated, "I'll just be a minute." which John took as, "stay put." The same as always, someone else's schedule, someone else's agenda. It reminded him of the hours he spent in dull hallways waiting for someone to run him through a demeaning paperwork gauntlet when he was on unemployment. Diane described far worse when she was on welfare for two years. She said that the building she spent hours and days in was painted from top to bottom with a nauseating green paint. She said they asked deeply personal questions over and over with a consistent indifference that she thought was a joke at first, because it was so thoroughly devoid of emotion or sensitivity. It only took making one joke and getting an icy stare to realize that this robot-like behavior was the norm at the county welfare office. They all made you do what they wanted on their schedule, their way, to get a pittance in assistance, one that you paid for with taxes that were taken out of every single dollar you ever made from the first day you worked. Now, they were going to make you bow down each time you got a dime of your own money back and look at you like a freeloader to boot.

Since he had told Pat he would assist him, it felt a little more like he was in control. He stared out the window at the surrounding neighborhood. Ralph's car was parked in the same place it had been yesterday, at the front of the bar. John was glad to see it. It meant that he had driven it despite his fear of the old lady's ghost.

Pat hopped back in the car with an observation about Ralph. "Good grief, that car might do what couldn't be done. Ralph's drinking his beer slowly. I don't think he's had more than a couple. I might go broke, but his liver will be better off."

It felt weird to hear him talk about one of the patrons outside the bar. It was like John was on the other side of the bar with Pat.

As they drove, it occurred to John that he had never been around Pat like this, and that he'd never seen where he lived. As they headed toward the highway, Pat struck up a conversation about work. "So did the office building finish and this is a new project?" He had recalled where John was working. John didn't think he paid attention to that. This felt a little like the one-on-ones he and Pat occasionally had when he was the first person at the bar in the morning and the two men sat alone talking, but it was outside Pat's place of work, Pat wasn't behind a bar, it wasn't as formal, it was more personal and John wasn't drinking.

"No, I just took off the last couple of days. Kind of a protest. They're cutting me back to three days starting next week."

"Well, they can only give you what work they have." Pat drove fast. It was a bit unnerving to John.

"I understand, but they have too many guys on each job, because they want to be able to cover the work no matter how many people call in. They hire any jerk that comes in the door, so half of 'em don't work, don't show up,..."

"Like you." Pat interjected.

"I work hard for them. I'm the best guy they have, but it doesn't count for anything. I get my hours cut back with the rest of them when jobs get thin."

"Tell 'em how you feel. Explain to them that you're the best thing they have. Maybe they're not aware of it."

"Well, my supervisor is. He's with us every day, all day."

"But your supervisor isn't the boss. He's not the guy running the show."

"I'm not sure that he knows who runs the show, we're so far down the totem pole."

"He knows who his boss is, and probably who his boss' boss is."

John was aggravated that Pat was giving him grief over blowing off a couple of days, but then he realized that he was talking to a guy who was at the bar three hundred and sixty five days a year, never missing a day. It was his bar though, and the money getting made was his money. John would be there three hundred and sixty five days a year too, if that bar were his. It was an easy choice once those conditions were in place.

Pat must have taken John's silence as a sign that he had upset him. "I'm not saying that you're lazy. God knows, you're an industrious guy, John. I'm just saying that you gotta make noise and you'll get more money and better hours. They'll figure you're indifferent until they know otherwise."

"They make it hard not to be indifferent."

"It's their way of getting everything to the lowest common denominator. They don't want to have to worry about whether they're going to get done on time because you don't show up."

John's slow burn turned to exhilaration. He was being shown the other side of the work fence- the bosses side. "But if they always start with the lowest common denominator, that's what they always get, no matter who they have working for them. It's actually hard for me to work as hard as I want to, because I have to rely on everyone around me."

"Maybe you should run the construction company."

Pat was copping out with sarcasm. It pissed John off. "I'd do a better job."

"You'd be broke."

John pulled out his cigarettes. He offered one to Pat. He took one. John lit them both. "I don't normally smoke in the car, but I'm dying for a cig right now for some reason," he explained. He was letting John know that he was breaking the car rules for him.

John wasn't going to let Pat think that he was right. "I just don't think that setting low goals for people is a smart thing in the long run Pat."

"Yeah, well, they aren't the ones setting the low goals. The workers are. The owners are just trying to be sure they can be owners next week and the week after that, and they only have themselves to count on in that case."

John could see that he wasn't going to get anywhere with Pat. He decided that he'd done enough talking. He held out a sop to Pat to end the conversation. "Maybe you're right."

"You bet I am."

Pat shifted in his seat. John decided that he drove like the devil was chasing him. They pulled off the highway. They were in a suburb John was familiar with, but hadn't been through in years. "I'm gonna have my cousin do the food for the wake tomorrow, but I don't want him charging me for the fixtures, and I know he will. I have my own from my catering days and I want to use them to save the money."

"You catered?"

"Oh my wife wanted to get into it. She did it for a couple of years, but she decided it was a lot more about dealing with hard ass customers than making good food, so she stopped." He sighed. "You're not getting married are you?"

John thought it an odd question. He felt that Pat's wife must have the patience of Job to deal with his being at work all the time, never going on vacation, never being there for family functions. "I'm not getting married tomorrow, if that's what you mean." He wouldn't put marriage down. He surprised himself by picturing Susan.

"Yeah, well, it's just another job. You work two jobs." John couldn't tell if he was serious.

They pulled into a driveway in a neighborhood that made John uneasy. It was a very exclusive area, big, older houses, brick and cobblestone streets, with lots of grand trees and hedges perfectly trimmed, the kind of place where, if you drove through in a beater car, you were a good candidate to be pulled over by a suspicious cop for absolutely no reason whatsoever.

As they drove around a circular drive with a fountain and then behind the house, John found himself baffled. This couldn't be Pat's house. It was huge, beautiful. He was in awe.

Pat glanced at him as he turned off the car. "See? She's got rich tastes." John still didn't believe that he was looking at Pat Calhoun's home. This was the dude who sat every day serving shitty beer to poor bastards in a funky old bar in one of the poorer parts of town.

"This is incredible." John looked around like the country yokel arriving on the bus in New York for the first time.

Pat walked toward the six car garage, motioning for him to keep up. "The stuff's in here. I want to put it in the trunk and back seats."

John followed, still looking around him at the beautiful yard, garden and house. "Is there that much money in beer?" He laughed. It felt like a joke had been played on him all his life and the punch line had finally been delivered.

Pat laughed, a bit uneasy. "There's a decent amount, but I told you that this is Marie's idea. Auspicious. You're as successful as your possessions. I think it's bullshit."

191

Pat punched numbers in on an alarm pad on the garage door. They stepped in. It seemed, in John's estimation, that Pat wasn't completely opposed to nice things. There were a number of motorcycles and antique cars in the garage. John was speechless. Pat walked past the vast wealth nonchalantly. He started digging around in numerous stacks of large plastic containers. "Ok, it's this stuff here."

He turned to John, who was still looking around him, stunned. Pat got an odd look on his face. "Don't go talking about this with fuckers like Ralph, or anybody at the bar for that matter." Pat was rich. It was his dirty little secret and he expected John to keep it. He drove the old car, wore the same old clothes for show. It was all a charade. Pat could afford two thousand dollar suits, and fifty dollar cigars. He had just bummed a cigarette off of John. He battled with Ralph over the cost of a vacuum cleaner, worried about spending a dollar or two to repair the cooler at the bar, they were here picking stuff up to save a few bucks on a catering job that a relative of Pat's was going to do, for cost no doubt.

He'd always heard that rich people were the biggest cheapskates in the world, and now he was staring at the proof. As Pat started handing boxes to John, he looked at him in a way that indicated he was sizing him up. "You're the closed mouth sort, John, someone who can keep private issues private. It's nobody's business where I live."

"Or that you're a rich fucker," thought John. He nodded. "I don't spread anybody's business around."

Pat seemed to relax. "I knew I could count on you." As they walked to the car with their arms full, Pat continued on the subject, "I saved every dime I ever made John. I don't waste money. My wife takes care of that." He sounded angry when he mentioned her. I bought this house twenty years ago. I was up to my ass in debt when I did. I just worked that much harder to be sure I kept it. None of this came easy."

"I'm sure." John knew that talking to Pat about this would be like talking to someone from Pluto about the weather on Neptune. He'd just agree to whatever Pat said.

They dumped the boxes in the trunk and went back for more. "I even did things I wasn't proud of to keep it going." He said hesitantly. Pat seemed to sink deep into thought as they made a number of trips to the car, filling the trunk and back seats of the clunker. He finally came out of his revelry, and looked at John as though he had forgotten he was with him and was shocked to see him now. His demeanor changed to what looked like forced amusement. "You can see why I don't like Ralph. If he ever came here, I'd wake up in the morning with my cock in my hand and nothing else."

John thought that Pat and Ralph weren't as different as Pat thought. He wasn't sure that observation was accurate, but it felt like it. Ralph had acquired his car by the force of his will and the savings it provided to him. He probably had done things that weren't on the up and up to accomplish it, like Pat. He would not share that thought with Pat.

John felt like he was sitting on top of the world, gazing down casually on the grimy parts with detachment. Just being here made it hard to understand poverty. Everything around him was so big, certain, substantial, permanent. What did being poor have to do with him?

Pat had given John a glimpse of a world he had never seen before. John liked it, but had no idea how he'd ever get there himself. Then he was amused to note that he was there, to an extent. It stirred memories he had of a summer he worked for a man who had a lawn service and they did a couple of very nice houses. He remembered one house that he thought was pretty big but when he mentioned how impressed he was with the place, he was told that they were doing the guest house. He couldn't get his mind around the fact that the sprawling structure sitting on a hill behind where they worked was the customer's house. Besides being so far out of his frame of reference another reason he couldn't think about it clearly was that his boss had him plant flowers in a sandy part of the garden, where, he realized the owner's poodles urinated. The hot summer sun made the stench thicker and stronger, and John nearly retched when one of the gaggle of little dogs came over and peed near him while he worked his hands down in the sand to the designated depth for the roots.

Today was different. The air was cool and fragrant. He stood with the owner of the magnificent house. John was anxious to see the inside, but Pat got back in the car after they finished loading so his hope of a nickel tour was killed. As they sped down the driveway, Pat spoke with a formal edge in his voice. "Now, like I said, I don't want you talkin' about my house to the customers. First, it's none of their business, and second, I don't want them to think I'm uppity. I'm not."

So it wasn't good for business either. "Count on me, Pat."

When John looked back on his next remark, he was embarrassed to recall it, because he firmly believed he did it to upset Pat, to somehow get back at him for having succeeded. John was unfamiliar with jealousy, so it was an excruciating moment to mull over, but he couldn't come up with any other reason for having said it. It was out of context with anything that he had been thinking about or talking about. He recalled that as they drove onto the cobblestone street and headed back toward the pot holes and chewed up asphalt of his world, that an image of Susan naked on the bed filled his consciousness, then a glimpse of her bad tooth, and then the Romanian talking to Cheryl. All of the images gave him pangs that, while strong as electric jolts, couldn't be pinned to any one emotion. Knowing that Pat hadn't seen him, he asked any way. "Did you see Cheryl with that Romania thug yesterday?"

Pat looked suspiciously at John. "What?"

"I know you always watch people at the bar. I wondered what you thought about that Romanian guy that Cheryl was hanging out with yesterday. I didn't get a good vibe." John looked ahead, out of the windshield, and not over at Pat.

Pat's voice showed a bit of a strain. "You called him a thug. I'd say you already know what you think of him." John knew he was treading in dangerous territory. While he had easily recognized Pat's attraction to Cheryl, no one else had, maybe not even Pat.

"I want your opinion of him."

"I didn't see him. When was he there?"

John realized that his construct was coming apart. Pat had left before he and Cheryl returned, and the Romanian didn't come in with Cheryl when she dropped off the food. "Now that I think of it, you'd already left when we came back. Paul was there."

Pat was obviously upset. "Well, then I couldn't tell you what I think, could I?"

John looked out the window. He was usually comfortable with long stretches of silence during any conversation he was involved in, but this time he strained to think of something to say. "What time is the wake? I didn't find out."

"It's four to eight. I'm going over at three." Pat didn't offer to bring him along.

"You need help?"

"No, but thanks for offering. I'll have Daryl help get the stuff in." Pat's body had tensed during their discussion about Cheryl and the Romanian. He started to relax back into his seat. "If you're at the bar, you can tag along when I go if you like."

"Thanks, I'll probably take you up on that." They pulled on the highway even faster than they had coming over. John was going headlong back to poor town.

SEWING PATTERNS IN RAGS

Pat pulled his car up to the apartment building where John lived with his girlfriend. John was hungry, dirty and tired. It was six o'clock, so Diane had been home for over an hour. He would just as soon have gone back to the bar with Pat and got good and drunk before he came back here, but he figured that if he hesitated now, it would precipitate a conversation with Pat on why he was stalling after he had delivered him on his doorstep. He should have told Pat that he could drop him at the bar, because that's where he was headed anyway. It wouldn't have seemed strange then, but John had been running various versions of his conversation with Diane through his mind, and Pat, who drove like a bat out of hell, got to Diane's before John thought of going to the bar first.

"Might see you later, Pat."

"Later, young man." He gave him a distracted smile.

John walked up the sidewalk and was genuinely relieved that his clothes were not on the lawn, or in the hallway. He fumbled with his keys to unlock the door, only to realize that the door was unlocked.

He stepped in. He heard the shower running. He made a bee's line into the bathroom. He hoped that if he got her naked and vulnerable, she wouldn't be so angry.

He was wrong. It made her more angry that he interrupted her during a quiet relaxing time. When he stepped into the bathroom and pulled the curtain enough to poke his head in she jumped back, nearly falling down. She looked wonderful wet, and slim. The light delicate caramel hair of her crotch made her look like an angel to John. "What the FUCK do you think you're doing! Where the FUCK have you been!" She was in a rage.

He ducked out of the bathroom and walked to the kitchen. He opened the refrigerator to see if there was any beer. There was one left. He opened it and went into the living room, pacing and drinking while she finished her shower. He looked at the room with new eyes, like he'd come in for the first time. It was a tidy room with cheap, but well kept furniture. The carpet was spotted from all the tenants before Diane, but it was clean none the less. She had gone after all of the stains at least twice with a can of spot remover, a brush and a ton of elbow grease. She had found some picture frames at Big Lots and put up a number of family pictures. John was represented in one that someone had taken at a picnic. He held Diane at the waist firmly enough, one of her feet was up a bit to lean into him. He wondered if he saw the room from a fresh perspective because he believed it would be his last time in it.

He could hear Diane hurry through drying off and getting into some clothes. She didn't put her robe on and zip around the apartment. She said she felt that the bathrobe was for morning, bedtime and sick days spent in bed, not the afternoon. John had bought her a pair of pajamas but she had not worn them. It was as if there was no place in her schedule that she could see a proper time to wear them. He thought he'd done a good job because it wasn't sexy lingerie, which he always figured was just a selfish way for the gift giver to say he wanted sex.

She charged out of the bathroom as she pulled a white turtleneck shirt on. He had mentioned that he liked it because it showed off her shape so nicely. John doubted that was the reason that she put it on today. "I'm a decent person, so that's the only reason your stuff isn't on the street right now you piece of shit!" She stood with her hands on her hips, her hair hanging damp almost dripping. She rarely came out of the bathroom until her hair had been combed, styled, dried thoroughly, but today was not such a day. John thought it made her look a little nutty. "I've put it all together in trash bags. It's in the bedroom on the bed. There's six bags. I plan on sleeping on my bed tonight, so they'll be gone or they'll go out with the trash." She stared at him like she wanted to bore a hole through his head with her eyes. He thought if it was Susan, the hole would already be a smoldering reality.

"Diane, I can explain." He spoke softly, deeply.

She sneered at him. "I'm sure you fucking can."

John waited. He thought she'd call him a liar next, but she stood silent, staring at him, biting her bottom lip so hard that he was convinced that blood would start to flow any second. "I, stayed at," he realized that if he was going to use Daryl for an excuse, he probably should have covered it with him before he did, but he had no choice at this point. It was all he could come up with. He was angry with himself for deciding that he would cover for what he'd done with Susan, but he knew that there was no way he'd have any chance with Diane if he didn't, "at Daryl's. Joey killed himself last night."

Diane's face and stance betrayed a profound change of attitude. Her severe snarl disappeared as her mouth opened in disbelief, her hand came off her hips into a stance that John noticed looked like she was going to draw side irons and shoot him. John wasn't sure how much he needed to say, but knew that he wanted to say the least possible. It always served him well. "Daryl is devastated."

Diane put her hands on her hips, but it was without commitment now. "Joey *killed* himself?" Diane knew Joey to the extent that John knew him, seeing him around all the time, but not really sitting and talking or interacting in a meaningful way with him. He was always flitting around like a hummingbird, never lighting anywhere. "Suicide?"

"Well, that's what most of us think. He wrecked his scooter last night."

"Scooter? What happened to his car?"

"He sold it to buy the scooter. When he sold that car, I feel it was like he wasn't going to let his brother's car be, like," he wasn't sure how to put it.

Diane helped. "He didn't want his brother to be responsible for his death."

John felt a chill as they sorted it, "but his brother is the reason he killed himself. I don't think he could take it, the loneliness."

Diane sat down in the chair behind her. She reached over and pulled a cigarette out of a pack on the end table and lit it. She usually offered him one, but didn't this time. He pulled his last cigarette out of his pack and lit it. He remained standing, feeling that his status was still in question, and not wanting her to think he had taken anything for granted. If he was going to be dressed down further, he would stand and take it like a man. She puffed on her cigarette and looked at him through squinting eyes, the smoke burning them a bit. "And you stayed over there. Why didn't you call me?"

John knew that he had a good excuse for last night, but today was tougher. "We were up all night. It was a disaster. Daryl was hysterical. I've never seen him like that. The paramedics gave him something to calm him down. They were going to take him in...""

"Take him in?" She leaned forward, like she had found a flaw in this story that she very much wanted to believe.

"Yeah, shock like, I guess, but he refused. He was a mess. The shot calmed him down but he was a blubbering nut for hours. I sat with him 'til dawn, and then we all fell asleep."

"All?"

"Yeah, Garlene went to bed and Daryl and I fell asleep on the couch. It wasn't long after I woke up that Pat came by. I got a ride with him. He had me go with him to get stuff for the wake tomorrow."

Diane's shoulders slouched. She put her hands in her lap and looked at them. She started crying, hard. " I was so worried."

John continued to stand. He didn't figure it was over yet. "You had good reason to. I'm sorry. It was a fucking mess, though, Diane." He'd space the bad news out, and tell her about Susan in a few days.

She cried quietly, but from her shaking, John could tell she was sobbing. She was one of those women who cried without a lot of noise. He wondered if they stifled it, or it just was the way it worked for them. It didn't seem like a healthy way to cry. Those old Italian women in the movies who wailed at funerals seemed like they were getting the grief out, letting it float away with the dead person's soul.

He stood silently. He knew he had to stand there and take whatever she was prepared to throw at him. He liked staying there, and he liked Diane, and for putting her through what he put her through, he was prepared to take whatever she dished out, even though it was all based on half lies he concocted.

She finally looked up at him. She flipped a long ash from her cigarette into the ash tray. She never missed the tray. He was always impressed by her accuracy. She should have played basketball. "You could have called me, godamn it, and if you hadn't pulled this shit before, I wouldn't have been so freaked out. I just don't seem to trust you, John. Why would that be?" She looked like a cop in the interrogation room. "I trust my girlfriends. I trust my mother, and as fucked up as my dad is, I trust him."

"You trust your dad?" He wondered if he had lost his mind. Why was he lingering on her
father. Underneath his calm façade, her mistrust angered him. He was almost aware of it.

200

She leaned her head to the side, looking at him askew. "What do you mean by that?"

"Nothing." John hoped he could backpedal fast enough. "I mean, what does trusting me have to do with your dad, or anybody else?"

"They've earned my trust, John and you haven't."

John took a long draw on his cigarette. She had brought her dad up. He wanted this out and resolved. It was one of the reasons he had kept his distance. He knew he could be out in the street with his bags in a minute or two, but suddenly he didn't care. "Your dad? Did he ever do anything to you?"

She moved her head like a viper, ready to strike. "What the fuck are you talking about?"
Her voice cracked.

"I mean, you tell me you trust your dad more than me. Did he ever do anything to you? Why would you trust him more than me?" He had said it.

She didn't want to understand him. "What are you saying about my dad?" She stood up, shaking.

"I'm just asking. You have this look on your face sometimes when you mention him. It looks like you're hurt. I never understand why you look hurt when you're talking about your dad." John felt something beginning to well up in him. He couldn't tell if it was fear, anxiety or nausea.

"You fuck." She screamed it.

John felt a burning in the pit of his stomach. He walked over to an ashtray and put his cigarette out. He started walking to the bedroom to get his bags. He'd leave them in the bushes,walk to find Ralph and have him take him to Daryl's. He'd be able to stay there for a few days.

Diane followed him into the bedroom. "You piece of shit. You fuck me, you blow me off, and then you blame it on my father?" She was already losing her voice.

John's sorrow was quickly turning to anger at her insistence on bullshitting herself rather than have a relationship with him, such as it was. He was thrown by the immediate realization of the irony of him being upset with her about withholding thoughts and feelings in the relationship. He was full of crap.

She stood a few feet from him and continued to scream as he picked up four of the six bags and headed toward the door. "You are the lowest fucking piece of mother fucking shit I've ever fucking met!" Her voice disintegrated on the last word. John figured if he didn't get out, the cops would be called, and he did not want to deal with that.

As he walked down the steps to the front door she continued to yell after him. Her voice only worked part of the time. She was crying between the blasts, losing her volume as well, as she gasped. "Fuck you, fuck you, fuck you. Cock sucker, fag. I'll have Tommy beat you to a lump of shit. Fuck you.!" She was talking about her brother.

John felt anger rising in him, and he was glad to walk outside. The door closed behind him dampening her voice, and the air cooled his face, which felt like it was being baked in the heat of anger.

He put the four bags he had grabbed near the edge of the building behind shrubs that lined the front. He started thinking about the fact that everything he owned fit in six bags. He'd sent everything he could to his kid and her mother, and he'd never really thought about what he'd do for money because he figured it would come, but it hadn't and he didn't know why. He couldn't deal with things the way they were. That he did know.

He went back inside to get the other two bags. Diane had thrown them in the hall, and locked the door. He tried to push his copy of the key under the door, but the ring it was on, was jamming it. He stood to take the key off the ring, when the door swung open. Diane stood with a contorted expression. Her face was soaked in tears, her damp hair clung to her face where it was wet. John thought that she looked like some sort of bog creature. He held the key out. She hit his hand and knocked the key into the room somewhere near the wall. He saw her drawing in a deep breath, like a pitcher winding up for the strike out pitch. "Fuck yoooooooou!!!!!" This last scream came out fully formed and piercing.

The scream went through John like an electric charge. The next thing that happened felt like he was watching it from outside of his body. His hands reached her shirt, and yanked it toward him with full force. She flew off her feet. It felt to John like she had no weight at all, increasing the feeling that he wasn't attached to the actions his body took. Her face was within an inch of his. He yelled. "You fuck your dad, and then he fucks me!" He said it with hatred and anger, hissing through his teeth. His face felt like it was on fire. "Keep covering for the low life mother fucker, Diane, but not on my godamn dime."

When he grabbed her, fear flashed on her face, but it disappeared in a harsher sneer than before. "Did you fuck your mommy, you mute fucker?"

John imagined slapping her with the back of his hand, the soft flesh of her face yielding to a frightening degree under the force of the blow. She would fall out of his single handed grip, against the door, her shirt stretched and torn, sliding down the door and onto the floor, her cheek already swollen, red with blood trickling from the lip.

IIe released her from his grip, picked up the other two bags and leaped down the stairs and out the door. He threw the two bags with the others and dashed off. As he ran, part of him knew he was running from the terrifying image of hitting her that had flashed in his head. The exertion began to calm him down. He started seeing the vividly imagined slap over and over again. He continued to run, despite his exhaustion, certain it would help to crowd out his intense feelings.

He was appalled that he was ready to hit her. Remorse coursed through him like adrenaline. He felt burning in his lungs and his legs hurt, his knees stinging like pins were jabbed in them. One extremely sharp pain in his right knee threw him off enough, he nearly fell along the sidewalk like a tumbleweed. He stopped running. His knees ached in waves. He sat down on the curb quickly. The pain subsided, but now the cold seeped into his wisp of a jacket. He could see the cold puffs of his breath as his chest heaved. It had started getting cold again, fast. The pace of his breathing started to slow, and his thoughts turned from what had happened at Diane's to what he was going to do to get out of the cold. He was closer to the bar than Daryl's, so he figured he would head there. Twilight was turning to night quickly, a few colorful golden and orange strains of light poked up from the horizon. The thick gray shadows he had witnessed in the morning had reappeared on the other sides of the same buildings, telling him it's different but the same. He didn't like the message. When it shifted, the air alternated from fresh and crisp to thick with dirty soot from the foundry. John pictured the owner rubbing his hands together in evil glee as he ordered a bedraggled slave to discharge all of the dirt now, when government officials were safely tucked in his lounge chairs at home watching television. Their air monitor devices, gauges and white gloves lying idle at work.

The back of his hand hurt a little. He wondered, surprised, if he had actually hit Diane, and the version where he walked away was the illusion. He pictured her lying unconscious against her door, blood dripping on her white turtle neck. He was mortified. He started to think that he had better go back and see if she was ok, but he figured if she was, she'd just start her tirade all over again, and he'd be in another jam. He decided that he would call her place when he got to Pat's and see if she was ok.

He spotted Ralph's car sitting in the front as he approached the bar. He was glad he was there. When he entered, Ralph looked at him and smiled sloppily. He was fairly drunk. John wondered how far along on his tab he was. He saw Charmain and William sitting in a corner table, heads together, talking quietly. Paul was covering the bar. A number of the old regulars had three tables together. It looked like they had spontaneously started a checkers tournament. John walked over to Paul. He noticed activity in the back office. Pat must still be there. He motioned to Paul that he was going to get behind the bar and go into the office. Paul nodded. He walked in the back to see Pat moving cases of beer around. He noticed the movement and looked up from his task and smiled. "Hey John. Long time, no see."

John had no idea what sort of look he had on his face, but when Pat looked at him, his smile disappeared. "What's wrong?" He stood and walked over and put his arm on him. "What's going on boy? Why are you back so soon?"

John hadn't intended to saddle Pat with his problems. He just wanted to ask to use the phone. "I, uh had a fight with Diane."

Pat chuckled. "Everybody says you're so smooth with the women, John. None of us escapes the big fall, not even you."

He couldn't bring himself to tell Pat about the violent fantasy he'd had. "Can I use your phone and see if she's ok?"

"Sure, son. Go ahead. I'll get out. I just needed to rework the beer. We been going through more Rolling Rock for some reason. All the old guys, like me, been coming in here and drinking it up." He laughed and slapped John on the back. Pat left the room and closed the door behind him. There was a small cooler that opened from the office and from the bar. The safe was in the office. John had never seen Pat leave anyone in the office by themselves because of that, yet here he was alone in the inner sanctum. It boosted his confidence. He must do something right. He dialed Diane's number.

The phone rang six times before she picked it up. Diane spoke, her speech a bit thick. "Hello?"

John didn't know whether he should hang up or speak. "It's me."

She hung up. He called again. The phone rang twenty times. He hung up and waited a minute. He called again. She picked it up again. "Why are you bothering me, you bastard?"

John tried to speak softly and gently, even though he was getting worked up again, bitter regret, sadness and confusion welling up. "I just wanted to see if you were ok."

There was a pause on the other side. " You got a lot of nerve wondering how I'm doing." She sounded like she was happy. It was bizarre to John.

"I didn't have a right to hurt you, Diane. I just, it hurt me. I'm so sorry. I.."

She interrupted. "I called the police."

John felt dizzy. Jail, prison, no, not again. How is this happening. He sat down.

Her voice was intent. "I sent them away when they got here. I thought you'd come back and sock me. I never saw you look the way you did."

John let the receiver fall in his lap. He started to cry. He was relieved. He was ashamed, he was confused and appalled by her sudden warmth. Did she feel more love toward him because he might hurt her? Was she that twisted? He was overwhelmed.

John heard her voice distant and electronically diminished, calling to him from his lap where the headset lie while he cried. He noticed that he cried silently too, except for a rhythmic gulp of air that sounded like a wounded animal gasping between attempts at a howl. He desperately hoped that no one could hear him, because he couldn't stop. He thought he heard a footfall near the door, but then nothing.

He cried himself out quickly. He kept telling himself to pull himself together, that he wasn't doing himself or anybody else any good by crying. It was a waste of time. The misery was replaced by a sour stomach and aches throughout his body. He lifted the phone to his ear. Diane sounded desperate. "John, it's ok. It's ok." Her speech was thick. He could picture the red cheek turning black and blue and yellow, hot to the touch. He pictured the feather soft translucent skin near her scalp contrasting the damaged skin on her face, dressing him down for what he had almost done to a tender, delicate girl. It all had been a second or two away from happening. How did he put himself into a position where that could even cross his mind? Why would he perpetuate things his parents and their generation did? It made no sense. He had bigger issues. He cursed himself for getting in the same kinds of relationships over and over.

He could feel sobs coming over him and he sighed to relieve the pressure. "No it's not ok Diane. I cannot fucking believe that I treat you the way I treat you. You never deserved that. You never will. I'm really fucked up. I'm a fucking joke. I gotta go. I just wanted to be sure I hadn't…" the words caught in his throat, "killed you."

He wanted to hang up, but felt like it would be another slap in her face if he did, so he held the phone to his ear, his mind emptying and refilling with tortured images of Diane and her disfigured face.

"John, I thought you were cheating on me, that's why I was so mad." She didn't say anything about her father. That had been locked back up. "I'm sorry that you had to go through that mess with Daryl. I know they were really close. I'm sure he's bad off. I just didn't know where you were so it freaked me out."

John remained quiet, listening, passive. Diane continued, like a gap in the talk would take things the wrong direction. "I called the bar last night and Paul said he didn't know where you were, but it sounded like a lie." John knew that he wasn't lying, but that he had seen John with Susan and Annie, and that was probably the source of his discomfort.

"He didn't know where I went."

"I know. I know, now, but it sounded like he was bullshitting me, and then you didn't call and I remembered all the girls you've had and I just couldn't bear it. I love you, and...." She still didn't mention her father.

John interrupted. "I'm sorry about your father." He wouldn't say that he was sorry for what he said about her father. He figured she wouldn't notice the difference.

There was silence on the other end. It lasted for twenty seconds. "Thank you." She was quiet and calm.

John had come to believe in the last thirty minutes, through his fragmented sorting and ruminations on the argument and his feelings, that she had become infuriated, not because he had insulted her and her father, but because he had hit a nerve, exposed a dirty little secret that even Diane could not look at, even though it affected her at her core. He would not back down on it, and he firmly believed that it was the end of their relationship because of the loathing it brought up in him, and because of the deficiencies in him, his inability to communicate to deal with those issues directly, and maybe resolve them. It was too big of a breach for the likes of Silent John. He knew that he had baggage, and that every woman he'd been with had their baggage. He just needed to find a woman for whom his baggage wasn't more for her and vice versa. He felt Susan was that woman. He was very confused about his certainty regarding Susan. It was illogical. He'd sort that out later.

"Look, I'll call you in a couple days and we'll talk." John had to tell her he wasn't coming back there.

"Aren't you coming home?"

"I think you'll be safer if I don't." He felt like a coward using the possibility that he might lapse into physical abuse as an excuse to stay away. He knew he wouldn't hit her, no matter what. A fever had broken and it would not return. He was immune now. He thought of his clothes in the bushes. He'd get Ralph to go with him and get them. He wouldn't have her bring them in the apartment because he'd have to see her to get them, and he was sure there would be another scene.

She sounded like she was ready to cry again. "Maybe."

John was appalled that she let him get away with what he did. "I'll call you on Monday. We'll sort out what to do."

"But where will you go?"

"I'll stay at Daryl's."

"You don't have to do that. You can come back." There was a hesitation. "You can sleep on the couch."

"I'll be ok. You rest, and we'll talk when we have our heads screwed on straight. It's the smart thing to do Diane." He hoped it would appeal to her hope of reconciliation enough that she would finally acquiesce.

"You can come home John."

"I know, damn it. Diane." He didn't want to curse, but he had made his mind up.

"You don't have to be mean. Fine. I'll talk to you on Monday."

"It's better for us Diane." He wanted to say something about them together.

"Maybe. Goodbye." She didn't hang up.

"Bye." He did hang up. He was grateful for how long Pat had let him stay in his office to sort things out. It was very generous of him. John was baffled sometimes by why people liked him so much. He wasn't personable, just quiet.

He picked up the phone again and dialed Daryl's number. Garlene answered. "Hi Garlene. It's John."

"You sound like you have a cold."

"Nah, I'm just tired. Can I talk to Daryl." He could hear the stereo in the background, blasting.

"Sure, hold on a minute." He heard a loud banging. He had seen her use a broom stick handle to bang on the floor directly above were Daryl sat listening to his stereo so she wouldn't have to go all the way downstairs. She must have answered the phone in the kitchen. He heard the stereo turn off and Daryl yell something unintelligible. Garlene put her hand over the receiver before she shouted. "Pick up the phone." He heard Daryl say something else. "It's John."

The phone in the basement picked up. "Hey John. What's up?"

John was comforted by the fact that Daryl had chosen to do something normal for him, to listen to blasting music. He half thought he would here funereal organ music swirling around when he called. "What are you listening to?"

"It's Iron Maiden. The new one. Joey loved it."

"That's cool." He paused for a moment.

Daryl spoke up. "Hey, are you ok?"

"Yeah, I uh, had a big fight with Diane. I wonder if I could stay there to..?"

Daryl broke in. "I already asked you to stay here tonight. Get your ass over here. Do you have a way? Where are you at?"

"I'm at Pat's. Pat might bring me." He didn't want to push his luck with Pat. "Or Ralph could bring me over."

Daryl put his hand over the phone. "Hey, babe, I'm gonna go get John over at Pat's." He always thought the tendency Daryl and Garlene had to conduct conversations over distances of entire floors of a house was amusing. He heard Garlene say something unintelligible. "Yeah, ok. I will." He shouted. He got back on the phone with John. "I'll be there in about forty minutes. Hang in there." He hung up before John could say goodbye. Daryl didn't usually say hello or goodbye on the phone, so he didn't seem to expect it out of any one else.

He walked out of the office, and started to close the door behind him. Pat held up his hand, "Whoa, I left my keys in there." John let go of the door.

Pat sidled up to him on his way to get his keys. "Take care of business?"

John didn't want to talk about it, but he didn't want to cut Pat off. "I'm not sure, Pat."

"She's really ticked at you? What did you do?"

"She thinks I'm cheating on her." John wanted to find a way to end the conversation.

"Cheating? Did you tell her you weren't?"

"We talked it over. We've got a lot of issues that are causing problems."

With the possibility that there were a number of things to disclose about the problem with Diane, Pat had to decide whether to continue the conversation or not. He looked at his watch. "Well, if you need to talk, I'm available."

John saw a way out. "I can see you're on a schedule. Let's talk tomorrow or Sunday."

Pat nodded. "Ok, my door is always open. " He laughed. "At least to you, otherwise it's never open." He slapped John on the back and went back into his office.

John walked out into the bar, avoiding eye contact with anyone, and sat down next to Ralph. He could smell the booze, like a pungent poorly conceived cologne. He figured he didn't smell all that great either. He thought of his stuff in the bags behind the shrubs at Diane's.

"Ralph, can we run an errand real quick?"

Ralph looked over at him. "Whazza matter with you, Punjab?"

He was drunker than John had thought. "Diane threw me out. My clothes are sitting in the yard at her apartment and I'd like to go get them before someone takes them.

Ralph laughed like a brain damaged pirate. "She threw you out, huh. Mr. Smooth."

John looked around to see if anyone had heard. It seemed they hadn't. "Godamn it Ralph." He whispered as loud as he could, "I'm telling you this, no one else, just you." He figured he would try to appeal to his sense of exclusivity.

It worked. Ralph leaned over to John, nearly tumbling to the floor. "Oooooh. Sorry, man. What do you care if someone else knows?"

"It's none of their business. I'm telling you because you're my friend." Ralph moved his hand up near his face, nearly poking his eye with one of his fingers. He would not pass a field sobriety test. "Come with me so I can drive your car to Diane's and get my stuff."

Ralph made several attempts to put his hand in his trouser pocket. He finally put his hand on his leg, and moved slowly to the edge of the pocket and slipped his fingers over the edge and into the pocket. He pulled out keys and promptly dropped them on the floor. "I'll get..."

He started leaning toward a trip to the floor. John caught him and righted him. "Man, I think maybe we need to get you home too."

"Muhbe. Coube."

John leaned Ralph against the bar, and got off the stool to retrieve the keys. He looked at the floor to locate them and decided that Val from the restaurant would be very unhappy with the cleanliness of the floor. Packs of dust bunnies skittered around below them, and one had caught on the key chain. He picked it up and knocked the dirt back to the floor. Pat really did need that hokey.

"Coudez" Ralph blubbered.

"Either you just learned French, Ralph, or you are one drunk hillbilly."

Ralph squeezed his eyes shut, and dropped his mouth open. John figured out that he was attempting to laugh but was having a hard time maneuvering his facial muscles and lungs into a coordinated effort. A window rattling burp came out instead, and he laughed with his tongue stuck out making him sound like a deranged whoopee cushion.

John looked at Paul who was staring at Ralph skeptically. John was sure that he wondered if what was going on was going to require the puke clean up kit. He steadied Ralph with one hand, and put the other on the bar. "Does Ralph owe anything? I'm gonna get him home."

Paul shook his head no. "It's on the...you know." He mouthed the word "tab" quietly, obviously having been warned by Pat not to spread around the fact that he had one.

"Ok, we're outta here."

Paul raised his eyebrows. "Good luck."

John had helped Ralph walk home many times, so just getting to the car would be a cakewalk. He shoveled Ralph into the back seat on the driver's side, but as soon as he had got him in and he had straightened up to get a little air and reorient himself before he buckled him in, Ralph put his hand and arm out and followed them out of the car, toppling onto the sidewalk. John broke his fall with his legs, so he didn't crack his head on anything. Ralph got on his hands and knees. "Godda go."

He tipped over, like a drunken dog playing dead, opened his fly, pulled his penis out and started peeing on the sidewalk. Lucky for Ralph, the car blocked any passersby from inadvertently seeing him, and the sidewalk was tilted toward the curb, so the urine ran down and away from him as he let it drain out of him, lying on his side. A little got on the front of his pants and one of his knees, but it could have been far worse. When he finished, he took a while getting his penis back in his pants, and zipped. John would drive him home with it sticking out before he'd help him put it back.

He lifted Ralph up like a giant dog being put in the car to take to the vet. He rearranged him again, holding his breath most of the time. Ralph's slight sour smell was stronger today, and the alcohol vapors mixed with it to make a nauseating cloud that would have John tossing his cookies if he was in close too long.

As he got in the driver's side, he figured that his own shaky hygiene had just been taken down another notch by being in such close proximity to Ralph. He pulled the car from the curb and made a half ass broken U-turn to take them to the boarding house. "Two skunks in the ghostmobile." He shook his head.

Ralph roused at the word ghost mobile. "Saw the ghoz tdy."

"What?" He could usually translate, but John was exhausted so he couldn't focus.

"Goz. Sawid."

John sighed. "Ralph, save it for tomorrow. I cannot tell what you're saying." Ralph responded by letting his head flop forward, his chin touching his chest and snoring loudly.

John pulled the car into the drive, and after much struggling, leveraging, and pushing, he got Ralph up to his room and on his bed. He knew it was a formality because Ralph was out of it, but he said it any way. "Ok, I'm gonna borrow your car and get my stuff. I'll be back in a little bit." Ralph didn't respond, he snored loudly. He looked around the room. It was the same as the last time he had seen it, except that it was far less dusty. Ralph had used the vacuum cleaner after all. There were a couple pictures on the chest of drawers. They were of the boy he'd seen in the other picture on a stack. He knew it was Ralph. The one where he was actually not the focus of the photo, the one where he ran around behind the couple was the only one in which he smiled. He frowned in the two new ones, where he was the actual subject of the pictures. John figured he frowned in one because the sun was directly in his eyes but the other had the sun behind him yet he scowled the same. That one, while in a decent frame, had a large semi circle shaped stain across the body of it. It was almost certainly from a wet glass or beer or pop bottle.

John got in the car and pulled out of the driveway. He was thrilled. He was behind the wheel of a car, by himself and he loved the freedom, the feeling of unlimited horizons. It was intoxicating. He knew he would limit himself to the essential tasks he had to accomplish, but the fact that he had the car and could conceivably do whatever, go where ever, was a delight. He headed toward Diane's. She refused to let him drive her car while they were together. The few times he did, she was with him and complaining about his every move. He had always supposed it had something to do with the car being a gift from her father.

Other girlfriends had let him use their cars on and off as needed. He made a point of not taking advantage. He looked at the opportunities of access to a car as money in the bank against times when he really needed to get somewhere that walking or the bus could not accommodate, and he knew that if he wasn't pushy or a nuisance, it would be easy when he really did need to use a car. It was the same plan he used when figuring how to get his laundry done. He liked banking his favors in all areas. It was the buffer he needed against being filthy, broke and homeless.

He pulled in front of Diane's apartment building and quickly retrieved the six bags, throwing them in the back seat. He noted that the lights in her apartment were off. It was a quarter to eight, but she had already gone to bed. He pictured her curled in a fetal position on his side of the bed, weeping on and off. He was sorry for the way things had gone. He figured he had better get back to the bar before Daryl showed up.

He drove through a neighborhood he hadn't gone through when he walked. He wanted to have a mini-adventure. He drove several blocks slowly, looking at the myriad houses that he hadn't seen before. Seeing house after house with different yards, sizes, colors, cars, made it easy for John to imagine tens of thousands of city blocks with millions of homes in cities all over the world. He was disappointed that he didn't have one of them. He figured time was getting short to get back to the bar before Daryl arrived, and he did not want to miss him, so he turned in the direction he needed to go at the next block. As he rounded the corner, he looked in the rearview mirror and jumped. There was a figure in the back seat, black and looming. His skin tingled as he finished rounding the corner and turned to look in the back seat. He became angry that he had forgotten the black trash bags stacked up in the back seat creating the outline he had seen in the rearview mirror. He was confounded by his second bout with superstition, of allowing himself to believe that Mrs. Emery was with him in the car.

He drove back to the bar and parked the car where Ralph favored, across from the front door. He locked the doors before heading in. He looked around for Daryl's car but didn't see it. He did spot Cheryl's car parked where she had left it the day before. The fact that she hadn't come back to get it yet meant that she was having a serious weekend of dissipation with the Romanian. He put it out of his mind, justifying it by his judgement that Cheryl, more than most of the people he knew, could take care of herself and steer her way clear of real trouble while courting it all along.

He strode into the bar, and hopped on his regular stool. He thought it was amazing that most of the people who came here were aware on some level who's stool or table was who's. Paul put a beer in front of John within a half a minute. He started to sip it, and startled himself by wondering if he had any money left. Diane knew he put his cash in an old cigar box he had got from Pat and then kept that box in the closet under an empty shoe box. He pulled his wallet out, and checked what he had on hand; a ten, some ones and loose change in his pocket. He didn't get paid again until next Friday, and he had just undoubtedly pissed off his boss enough that he would refuse to advance any money, which he had relied on more than once.

He drank his beer quickly, frustrated and distracted. He would have to sort through the six bags to see if his money was in there. He didn't have much because he had taken the bus downtown early in the week and paid Diane's power and phone bill. He hoped because he had done that, she would have mercy on him and leave the money in the box.

He would go through the bags once he got to Daryl's. There wasn't anything he could do about it one way or the other now. The door opened as John took a sip of his second beer. It was Daryl. The phone behind the bar rang at the same time. Daryl strode up to John and took a seat next to him. Paul asked him what he wanted, picking the phone up at the same time. He poured a whiskey for him as he talked on the phone. John could hear someone crying on the other end of the phone. Paul listened, saying one or two words between the gasps coming from the ear piece. He held the phone away and rolled his eyes. Daryl and John were intrigued, even more so when Paul handed the phone to John.

"Me?" John was confused. Paul nodded yes, and grinned. "Hello?" He said tentatively. A sob and some unintelligible words came over the line. It was Cheryl. "What the hell is wrong Cheryl?"

Cheryl said more. John couldn't understand. John spoke quietly, hoping the calm would rub off on her. "Listen, hon. I can't make out what you are saying. You need to slow it down and calm down. We'll make things ok."

He heard her breathing in short spastic spurts. It started slowing down some, and she tried again. "I'm, I am in , in jail. In jai.."

"You're in jail?" John looked at Daryl, a resigned look on his face.

"Ye, ye, yeah."

He wanted to ask for what, but didn't want to deal with the long drawn out explanation. He figured he'd get the bare essentials. "How much to get you out?"

She was breathing faster again. He could tell she was trying to calm down. The pace of her gasps and pants would slow and speed up. She attempted to speak again, but cried out instead. John figured this couldn't be good news.

"Fivehundreddollars." She spit it out in one word between gasps.

John put his hand over the phone. "Shit!" He was unsure what to do. He got back on the phone. "Should I call your sister?"

She howled the answer, "Noooooo."

He wasn't sure what to do next. "Should I call Pat?"

Cheryl barely muttered her response. "Yea, yes."

John was not happy. He didn't want to get in the middle of the mess, but if he let Pat know what was going on, he'd be out of it. "Ok, Cheryl. I'll call him right now." He sighed. "Where are you?"

"Down.. down."

"Downtown jail?"

"Yes."

"Ok Cheryl. I'll call Pat. I need to hang up to do that."

She was calmer, but not much more coherent. "K" The phone hung up.

John handed the phone back to Paul. "That was Cheryl, in jail."

Daryl looked surprised. "Jail, Cheryl, big Cheryl?"

John nodded. "Yep. I can guarantee it has something to do with that dude she started hanging out with yesterday."

"What dude?" Daryl was on it like a pit bull.

"Some Romanian dude that was smoking a cigarette with us at the diner. She went off with him yesterday."

"Romanian? It's got something to do with the fruit place, right?"

John noticed that Daryl always seemed to know what was going on in the neighborhood. He knew where most of the trouble was, who it was, and when it was. He was a gossip, pure and simple.

"Yeah. He works there. I didn't like his looks"

"Why didn't you stop her?"

"I thought she'd have enough sense to stay out of trouble, and who am I to tell Cheryl what to do?"

"You can't let friends get in trouble."

John was getting aggravated. He looked Daryl in the eyes and said quietly, "Sometimes you can't anticipate every bad thing a friend will do." He figured he was taking a chance throwing Joey's demise at him, but he was tired and not in the mood to be criticized.

Daryl hung his head and said, "True," very quietly.

"Paul," John pointed to his beer, which was already half empty, "another, and I need to call Pat." Paul put another beer in front of him and the phone. The cord barely reached the bar. "What's his number?"

Instead of answering, he turned the phone around, dialed the number, and handed it to John. It rang a number of times, but no machine picked up. He couldn't believe that Pat didn't have an answering machine. It rang for a while. Paul killed the connection, and dialed another number. The ring sounded like a cellular phone call. Pat picked up. "Hello, this is Pat."

"Hi Pat. It's John."

There was silence, then "John? What's up?" John figured Pat was trying to remember if he had ever given him his cell phone number.

"Well, Paul called you for me. We just got a call from Cheryl. She's in jail."

Another silence. "Cheryl, in jail? What for?" He sounded distressed.

"I don't know. She was hysterical. I was lucky to get where she was and her bail amount out of her."

Silence again. "How much is her bail?"

"Five hundred."

"Jesus." The response came quickly.

"She wanted me to call you instead of her sister."

"Well, her sister probably doesn't have the money, or she's afraid her sister will kick her out. They haven't been getting along."

"What do you want me to do, Pat?"

Silence again. "Well, I'll get the money. I suspect that they aren't going to let her go tonight."

"They'll only take the bail between ten and three."
John knew this because he had known so many people who had
to be bailed out, for everything from public intoxication, to
check kiting. He didn't have anyone to bail him out when he
went to jail for burglary.

"OK, John. I need another favor from you then. Come
with me tomorrow to get the money, and you pay it and get her
out. I don't want to sign anything."

John figured he didn't want his wife to ever hear that
he had bailed Cheryl out. "I can dothat. I'll be here in the
morning first thing."

"Fine, let me talk to Paul. I'm gonna need him to pull
more time tomorrow."

"OK. See you in the morning Pat."

"Yeah. What a lousy weekend." He sounded
depressed.

"Not all that unusual, really Pat."

"Yeah, maybe so."

John handed the phone back to Paul. Pat and Paul
talked and then argued briefly, and after they hung up Paul
looked peeved, but kept his complaints to himself.

Daryl and John sat drinking. He knew that Daryl
wouldn't want to go directly home. He loved being out as much
as he loved listening to music, or fiddling with his car.
Anything he put time into, he went full tilt with it. He grinned
at John as he drank his beer. "I covered for ya tonight."

John knew exactly what he meant. "Diane called?"

Daryl nodded. "I told her you stayed over. She seemed
pretty upset. Why didn't you let me know ahead of time. I
almost blew it."

John was embarrassed. "I basically got cornered and came up with it off the top of my head."

"Well, be careful. Ol' Daryl can't take care of business if he's not in on it." He took another swig. "She seems like a good girl."

"She's got problems."

"So do you John, my boy." Daryl laughed.

It hurt John's feelings. "Not as bad as hers."

Daryl's laugh subsided. "I guess. So is Pat gonna bail her out?"

"He's gonna give me the money and I have to go do it."

"In the morning?"

"Yeah."

"It's the weekend. I bet they won't take the money."

"Oh, shit. I didn't think of that. I wonder if Pat will."

"Guess you'll find out."

"Yeah."

Daryl took a drink, and made a face like it was bitter. "So, where were you last night?"

John didn't want to discuss his night with Susan. At that point, it had already seemed like a strange dream. "I just slept somewhere else. I needed to get some sleep."

Daryl looked angry now. "Ok, fine. If you don't want to tell me the truth."

John couldn't figure out how to avoid talking about Susan without Daryl getting nosier. Maybe he could change the subject. "I helped Pat haul a bunch of catering stuff to his car today. It's for the wake at your house tomorrow. "

Daryl snapped. "Yeah, Gar told me about it." It didn't look like changing the subject was going to work.

He took another shot at it. "Did the cops or the coroner decide whether Joey had an accident or not?"

"Well, they're incompetent anyway. It's really about what we think." Daryl looked hurt now.

"You said he killed himself? Do you still believe that?"

Daryl's pained expression changed to a thoughtful one. "I think that he didn't necessarily mean to kill himself." He put his glass down with a loud slam. Paul turned and looked at it. It was nearly empty. "I think that maybe he was worked up."

"Was he on something?"

"Oh, yeah. I'm sure, but not any more than usual, I don't think. I think what he was doing was trying to die like his brother. His brother didn't die on purpose, he was just having fun and he drank too much, but he was always doing stuff that was dangerous, too many drugs, driving really drunk, pissing off guys who were twice as big as him, playing with guns like they were toys. It's like one of the less dangerous things killed him because he spent more chances than God was willing to give him. He took him on a lesser mistake." He looked at John wondering if he was making sense. It sounded like this was the first time he was trying out this theory.

John looked at the bar. If Daryl started getting teary eyed, John wanted to give him a little space. "I get it."

Daryl continued, looking away himself. "So here's his bro, just having fun, drinking, carousing with the girls and

223

boys, and it killed him." He held up his whiskey. "This killed him. It wasn't a gun in his face, or thirty pills, or being plastered and driving. " He paused. "I tied Joey up once, when I couldn't figure out how to calm him down."

John looked at him to see if he could read whether he was joking. "Tied him up?"

"Yeah. He was really out of it that day. I don't know what the hell he took. I can't remember. I think he was doing uppers and crank and all kinds of shit. He was out of his fucking mind, and he kept telling me he was gonna go kick this guy's ass. He didn't know the guy from shit, but he was on a fried brain kinda mission. I knew this guy would turn him into hamburger, but he just kept going on and on. So I told him he should do a little lifting to get him pumped, and as soon as he laid down I pinned him and tied him down with a bungee cord, and then I added some rope for insurance. He was crazy. It took a couple hours before he finally started calming down. I thought he was going to have a heart attack. It looked like I tied down the Tasmanian Devil."

"So he wanted to die?"

"He wanted to die like his brother. He got on that fucking scooter and drove around as fast as he could because it was fun, and since he wasn't all that fucked up, he figured he could push it." Daryl finished his drink. Paul had put a fresh one in front of him. He took a gulp from it." I think that's why I didn't figure it out. I could usually figure him out. It was like his head was invisible to me. I could see what he was thinking and keep him from doing something really stupid."

"But he wasn't sure he was trying to kill himself."

"I think he knew it might, but if it didn't, then it wasn't meant to be. I think he would have done something else to do it though. He couldn't deal with his brother dying. He just could not accept it. It hurt him every day like it was the day he died. I think they were like two guys in Vietnam. Bound together by their terrible experiences and fucked up the same way."

"How do you feel?"

Daryl thought about it. "I'm fine. I love life. It won't be as good as it was when he was here, but life's pretty big. It's hard to hack enough out of it to make it useless."

"That's true." John felt a bit guilty distracting Daryl from a discussion about Susan by talking about Joey, but he knew that Daryl wanted to talk out his sadness and it served John's purpose.

"I really appreciate you letting me stay at your place tonight."

"Yeah, what are you going to do now? Is it over, over with Diane?"

"It's over. We can't see eye to eye about eighty percent of the time. I didn't want it to end, but it doesn't make sense."

"Does she see it that way?"

"No, but she's not thinking straight. This isn't any more fun for her than it is for me. I just know that it's not good. I mean, I'm the one without a place to stay. I still think it's the right thing to do."

"You want her to be happy."

"Yeah. I don't know how happy she can be, but yeah I want her to be happy."

Daryl's next remark revealed that he must have been casting around for a girlfriend John could stay with. John didn't feel that it was because Daryl didn't want him around, he just wanted to see if he could find a more permanent solution for John. It's what a friend does. "Talked to Annie, lately?"

John exhaled a short laugh. "Strangely enough. Yeah. Yesterday."

Daryl's eyes widened. "Is that who you slept with?"

John wondered why it hadn't been. "No, I talked to her a long time yesterday though. I don't think we'd pick up in any better place than we were before, but I do want her to break up with fucking Billy. I made that clear."

"Billy Baker?" Daryl knew everyone.

"Yeah. Billy Baker."

"What in the hell is wrong with that girl?"

"I think she's trying to punish me, but I don't think it's working out that way. She's the one that's suffering."

"I'd say so. Billy's a lunatic. You need to break her away from him."

"I already told her that if he so much as touches her, she better call me and I'll dispose of him."

"Kill him?!"

John was surprised. He wondered why Daryl thought he could have murder in him. "No, he'd wish he was dead though."

"I'll take a piece of that if you do it. Let me know."

"I might take you up. He's a crazy fuck. That gives him strength he doesn't have a right to."

The conversation reminded him of his promise to buy a cell phone. "Shit."

"What?"

"I told her I'd get a cell phone today and get her the number."

"Well, let's go to Celland."

"Where's that?"

"It's over in the strip center about five minutes away. They look like they're open all the time."

John was embarrassed. "I'm not sure I have the money now. I haven't looked through my stuff to see if Diane took my money."

"Let me pick this up for you."

John sighed. "I don't have much of a choice. I'm sorry. I don't want to take advantage."

"I'm your friend. That's never what it is. Let's go." Daryl drank his whiskey down. John left his beer. Daryl paid both their tabs. John was relieved. Guilt over his thoughts about Garlene welled up in him, but dissipated quickly. He had heard once a long time ago that he wasn't responsible for what he thought, but for what he did. There were many times when he had to remind himself of that. Being a man who didn't talk much, he thought a lot and those thoughts didn't always head down the right alley.

As they left the bar John pointed to Ralph's car. "I need to get my stuff and drop his car off."

Daryl frowned. "Let's do it after we get the cell phone."

"I promised I'd bring it back."

"Fuck him." Daryl would occasionally put John in a position where he would test his loyalty to Ralph by suggesting that he do something unkind or inconsiderate to him. He always smelled a little jealousy in it.

"It's my promise Daryl. I can't break my promise. It's not about him."

"Fine." He looked like a kid that had been told he couldn't buy a toy he wanted.

They transferred the bags to Daryl's car, and Daryl followed him to Ralph's.

Ralph's key set had one for the back door to the house, so John quietly unlocked it and crept upstairs to the rooms, rapping lightly on Ralph's door before entering. He found him sitting up in his bed, fully clothed, weaving and looking ahead of him at nothing in particular.

John smiled. "You ok Ralph?"

It took Ralph a few seconds to respond. "Hm. Yeah. Jus drunk."

"Here's your keys." He held them in front of him.

Ralph motioned with his eyes. "Put 'em on'a dresser."

John turned and carefully placed the keys near one of the few small framed photos on the top of the chest. John looked at the pictures of Ralph again. He noticed this time that the one with the sun behind him, that along with the frown, there were tears welling in his eyes.

He turned back to Ralph and decided maybe he was drunk enough to talk about his past. "Is that you?"

Ralph turned his head, the move was a little exaggerated. "Hm. Yeah. S Me."

"Why were you gonna cry?"

"Dad was teasin' me bout bein' a baby cause I din wan a picture. Scared me."

"He took it any way?"

Ralph hunched his shoulders for a brief second and moved his arm at the picture. "The picture's there isn't it, Columbo?" He stared at John, glazed and emotionless.

John smiled again. "So why didn't you stick your tongue out?"

Ralph stared at the wall. A tear fell on his cheek. John thought it had come from a leak in the ceiling. It was inconceivable to him that Ralph was on the verge of crying. He had never, ever shown vulnerability around John. "Nothin."

John started to back away. "Hey. Don't worry about it. I just wanted to be sure you had your keys."

John wasn't going to force Ralph to relive the event his father had put him through in the first place. Ralph muttered what sounded like "Slow," and then lie against the wall and closed his eyes. He started snoring within a few seconds.

John backed out of the room, being sure the door was latched to lock when he closed it and crept back down the stairs. He shivered.

As John hopped back in the car Daryl remarked sarcastically, "Nice place."

John stared up at the window of Ralph's room. "At least he has a place to live."

Daryl looked a bit embarrassed on John's behalf. "Let's go." They drove to a strip mall John had never seen. The cell phone guy acted like he could not wait to get back to the magazine he had been looking at when they walked in. There were a lot of choices, so they had to ask him a lot of questions. After about ten minutes of the clerk's aggressive indifference, Daryl rose up and looked him straight in the eye. "Do you care if you sell anything. I'm sorry we bothered your sorry ass."

The clerk looked at him and with the same indifference said, "I don't care if you buy anything or not."

Daryl was undeterred. "I'll bet the owner feels different."

"Yeah, so." He shot back. He picked up his magazine, as if in anticipation of their leaving.

Daryl stepped closer to the counter, within reach of the clerk. "I'll break your fucking arms if you don't start paying attention. It'll be tough to read that magazine with scrawny little bloody stumps." Daryl hissed the words.

The clerk had obviously not anticipated Daryl's response to his attitude. He stood back, putting the magazine down as he did. He furrowed his brow. "Tell me what you want to buy."

Daryl pointed to one in the glass. "That's the one for fifty bucks?"

"Yes."

"I can make do with the thirty dollar one Daryl."

The clerk couldn't seem to help himself. "I'd let big shot buy you what he wants to."

Daryl shot the clerk an icy stare. "I'll take the fifty dollar one."

"We only take cash here." He said it with glee. It was a policy that had blown many sales.

"I don't believe you." Daryl leaned forward.

The clerk pointed to two different signs that said, "cash only."

Daryl looked at John. "I think the owner deserves this pathetic fuck. Cash only. What a joke." He pulled out his wallet and handed the clerk sixty dollars. He rang it up, made a call to the cell phone company, programmed the phone, and wrote a couple of numbers in a little booklet that came with it. Daryl snatched the booklet out of his hands, and opened it to the front page. "Which one is the cell's number?" The clerk grudgingly pointed it out.

Daryl spun around and headed out the door, with John running along behind. "Rotten fucking place. No wonder it has to stay open twenty four hours a day. They'd go out of business if they didn't." He handed the phone to John. "Here you go. The phone number's in the front. Call her."

He took the phone. He had intended to call Susan to give her the number for Annie. He felt uncomfortable making the call now. He wanted to speak to Susan privately. "I'll call when we get to your place."

Daryl looked at him. "Want some privacy?"

John blushed. "Yeah."

"We'll wait 'til we get home."

They drove to Daryl's house in relative quiet. Daryl did go on about a new show on public access where a "dude" played heavy metal videos on a show that he put together. "It's sloppy, but the videos are great. We'll have to see if he's on. They play the shows on public access over and over."

John didn't have a television. He was often out of conversations simply because a lot of them centered around what had been on TV the night before. Sometimes it bothered him, but if he watched a few hours when he did have access, he thought it was so miserable an experience, he decided that it must soften people's brains to the point they don't realize what they are staring at is so bad. He figured it might be like sitting in a room full of shit- you wouldn't smell it after a while.

WITCHES AND BAKERS

Diane had taken all of John's money but twenty dollars. He wasn't mad. The fact that she left him twenty dollars told him that she wasn't so much taking it for spite, but survival. She probably figured if he was cheating on her with another woman, he might cheat her some other way, but she wasn't willing to empty his pockets. In fact, he tried to recall if he had told her that he paid the utilities. He might not have. He couldn't recall where he left the payment receipts. She might have thought she needed to pay them yet. He was angry with himself for not talking to her enough.

Daryl and Garlene had helped take his stuff to the guest room, which was next to their daughter's bedroom. It had a lot of discarded toys in it, but Garlene promised to clear them all out the next day. John told her it wasn't necessary, but she said he wasn't going to live in a storage room. He acquiesced.

They left him alone to get his stuff together, take a shower, change clothes and make his phone calls. He cared a lot about Daryl and Garlene. He tried to compare his intelligence to Daryl, and felt he stacked up about the same, yet he had nothing, was virtually a street person and Daryl, had a house, a car, wife, kid and a job. He knew that Daryl's dad had helped him put a down payment on his house. His father had recently received money from his father's estate when he died. He had lived in Kentucky and died there. The old man had put away more money than anyone had imagined, so by the time his father's two brothers had got their share of the money, his dad still ended up getting over fifty thousand dollars. He gave Daryl half of it for his house. Daryl had freely offered this information to John.

John decided he just wasn't focused enough. He might think a lot, but he must not be thinking enough about the right things. It looked as though Pat was the one that was going to do that for him instead. He sat down in a fresh pair of jeans and a sport shirt. They smelled good. Diane did a good job on laundry. His clothes always smelled better than he could imagine. There were many times when he would pull a part of his shirt to his nose just to smell it. He pulled the cell phone from his pocket and stared at it for a minute. He wanted to start being focused tonight. He had to call Susan and he wasn't sure what to say.

His emotions swirled around his thoughts, chopping and breaking them into pieces that he couldn't hold together long enough to examine. He grew frustrated and put it off to being tired. He knew he had to give Susan the phone number and that it would make Annie safer, so he decided he would start with that, and barring being able to think any more clearly, he'd end the call with that.

He dialed. The phone rang several times without an answer. He was pretty sure he remembered her saying that she would be there. His heart sank and he cursed himself for feeling that way. Just as he pulled the phone away from his ear to press the off button, he heard a little voice in the ear piece. He put it back to his ear quickly. "Hello?"

A man responded. He had a deep gravelly voice. It must be Sam. "Yeah, this is Susan's. Who's this?" John was profoundly unhappy that he was talking to her boyfriend.

"This is John. Is Susan home?"

"Yeah. Hold on." He heard him mumble to her. She was close by. They were in bed.

Susan was on the line. "Hi, John. You got the cell phone?"

John tried to sound unaffected by his short conversation with Sam, whom he realized he saw as his competition. "Yeah. I just got it."

"You're using it, aren't you?"

"Yeah, does it sound different?"

"Yeah, the caller ID said cell phone. I didn't know if I wanted to answer."

"Oh." John tried to focus. He felt like she had him under a spell again. No wonder they wrote songs about love like that. "You have a pencil?"

"I'll just save the number from the call, but I want to write it down too."

She said that for Sam's ears. He heard her walking into the kitchen. He could hear her bare feet on the linoleum. "I broke up with Diane." He was astounded that the words came out of his mouth.

Her response was restrained. "You did? Why?"

He felt hurt that she didn't suppose it had something to do with her, that she didn't immediately suppose it was about them, together. He felt weak and foolish. He choked out a response. "It wasn't going to work."

Her responses continued to be cool and short. "That's too bad."

"Is that Sam there?"

"Of course," she replied in the same matter of fact way. Maybe her demeanor was a show for Sam. "Go ahead."

He gave her the number slowly.

"That's easy to remember." He could hear her writing the number on a dry wipe board he had seen on her refrigerator.

"Yeah." He didn't know what to say next. "I'm really glad we hooked up. You're amazing." He pictured her making sweeping, graceful motions with her arms and hands at the phone, sending a trance through the phone line, drawing the remarks from him like blood through a needle. He had undoubtedly left a few hairs there that she could use for the magic that would benefit him as well as her.

Susan sighed. "I'll give her the number as soon as we hang up. That bastard is probably there so I'll have to bury it in the conversation somewhere to be sure that he doesn't pick up on it."

John wanted to, felt that he needed to know how she felt about him right now. "Are you mad at me?"

She seemed aggravated. "No, I'm not." She paused. "I'm gonna tell Annie to call you when she gets time without him around. I'm sure she won't have to wait long. He's always out fucking someone. I hope she doesn't get anything from him." She had remained in the kitchen. It was far enough away from Sam that she could have whispered something to him, but hadn't.

John felt a giant depression coming over him. Words formed in his head that he didn't want to say, but also wanted to more so.. "You are fabulous. Can we get to know each other better?" He felt so foolish. Normally, he would have been

235

subtler, his desires would have been veiled in more obtuse language. With Susan, he sounded, to his ear, like a high school boy trying to be sophisticated.

"We'll see." She said it in the same normal full voice she had said everything else in. "I have to go now. I should call Annie right away. Billy really worries me."

He realigned his thoughts as best he could. "Yeah. I have a feeling that she'll be needing me soon."

"That's right John. Annie will need you."

He felt that was a remark made that could be juxtaposed to his remark about wanting to get serious with Susan, like she wanted to know where his relationship with Annie was going to go. He knew it was going nowhere, but maybe Annie didn't feel that way, and Susan knew it. While she might not feel loyalty to Sam, she would be loyal to Annie. He wanted to sort these things out. The idea he would have to wait another day to know what felt like the solutions to the mysteries of life was unbearable. "Can you break away and go to Pat's tonight?"

There was a pause. He heard her writing something on her dry marker board again. He felt uncomfortable, so he spoke again. "He's open 'til two thirty tonight. Its' about nine right now."

She continued writing on the board. She must be doodling. "That's a little ways for you
to walk." She was measuring what she said while Sam was there.

"Can you pick me up? I'm at Daryl's."

"Yeah."

"When?" He felt that if she was being careful about what she said, he'd have to say as much as possible so she could answer with yes or no. " Nine forty five?"

"Yeah. That works."

"Ok. I'll look for you then. I'll be on the porch." He paused, feeling like he was hurtling down a steep incline on a roller coaster. "I think I love you Susan." He was out of control. He never said that. What had she done to him?

It sounded like she was smiling. "I'll call Annie, now. Bye." She hung up.

He sat staring at the cell phone, and then the hard wood floor. He hadn't uttered the words "I love you." for a long time. He couldn't remember the last time he had spoken the words, yet he had just blurted them out to a woman he hardly knew. She was very sexual, very enticing, but he had been with women as alluring as her before. He felt his experience had given him a balance when it came to dealing with very attractive women, yet he was blathering like an idiot when he talked to Susan.

He had to explain to Daryl that he was going back to Pat's within the hour with Susan. He figured Daryl would not be put out. As long as Daryl felt like he'd been let in on it, was a part of it, he'd be cool with it. It occurred to John that while Daryl always insisted on his friend's confidences and trust, he had chosen to keep his marital infidelities to himself. John understood why he'd never tell Leon. Daryl knew about Leon. If he had ever confessed to Leon, Leon would make a point of letting it slip to Garlene in hopes of causing a rift that he could take advantage of to try to get her in bed. He wouldn't want anything as earth shattering as their divorce, he'd just like a roll in the hay with his friend's wife, before things went back to normal. Leon was the kind of guy who would stand with other men at a party and complement various physical attributes of the men's girlfriends and wives, in lascivious detail, like it was some kind of huge compliment that the playboy of the hillbilly world thought that their chicks were hot enough for him to want to sleep with them.

John was not as sure why Daryl didn't confess to him accept in circuitous hints. He had never judged anything Daryl had done. Maybe he felt that John was as much a friend to

Garlene as he was to him, and didn't want to put John in a position where he might have to make a judgement call for one or the other of them against the other. That would make sense.

Despite the bizarre schedule and the steady diet of alcohol he'd had the past few days, his shower and change of clothes made him feel like a new man, albeit a new man with throbbing pain in his knees. He wasn't sure what was going to come out of his meeting with Susan, but he was glad that it would happen. He could hear the stereo cranking up in the basement. He could hear a television in their daughter's room. He stepped into the hallway and toward the steps. The door to the bedroom of Daryl and Garlene's daughter Cecilia, was open. He glanced in and saw that she was on her bed typing something on a laptop. There was a colorful pencil drawing and a slew of pencils next to her. The walls of her room were filled with all sorts of drawings and posters. It looked to him like she was trying to draw a new reality around her. He started down the stairs. Garlene was on her way up. They stopped midway. She was wearing a scoop neck blouse that she'd had on under the sweater she wore earlier. It buckled out as she leaned forward, heading up the steps. She was not wearing a bra. Her breasts were fully exposed to John's view. He was stunned. He looked at the top of her head, and awkwardly said, "You're hair is really nice."

She seemed oblivious to the view she was affording him. She did stand up straight, which pulled her blouse back against her and covered her again. "I just messed with it a little. I never mess with it. It's a waste of time." She laughed heartily.

"You have gorgeous hair Garlene."

"Smooth talker." She smiled. She stepped aside to let him through.

As he reached the step below the one she stood on, he turned and said quietly. "I really appreciate you two letting me stay here."

"Well, thank Daryl. I didn't know anything about it."

John was taken aback. "Holy cow, I, if you don't want me to stay, I'll…"

She laughed again. "I didn't say I wasn't glad you were staying, I just meant that I didn't know you were staying. You're welcome here, John Hamilton, you dumb ass." She turned and headed up the steps. John caught a glimpse of her rear end as she ascended. He was convinced some kind of weird hormone or voodoo stew had been injected into him. It was like every woman that came near him was now, in his mind, a prime candidate for sex. He had always been very much detached from that sort of thinking and behavior. He left that kind of thing to the other guys who talked a lot, gawked a lot and bombed a lot. He corrected his observation as she continued her ascent. He was sexually aroused by women he connected with. Maybe it was spill over from his intense attraction to Susan.

"Thanks again," he managed to say as she rounded the corner and proceeded to the landing.

"You're welcome," she replied from the other side.

John went directly to the basement. Daryl was on the bench lifting weights while a metal band John could not identify played. He'd heard them before, he just couldn't remember who they were. Daryl saw him enter but continued lifting. John walked over to the ever present cooler and dug a beer out. Daryl grunted and huffed as he manipulated and leveraged the bar and weights up and down. He said "Dio," loudly as he continued.

Now John knew it was Ronnie James Dio, the little dude who was in Rainbow and Black Sabbath. He was rarely so informed, but Daryl went on and on about him. He nodded his understanding and Daryl continued to lift as John sat drinking his beer. Finally he sat up, swung his feet to the floor and sat huffing and puffing, "Want to lift a little?" He always encouraged John to lift with him.

"No, I just took a shower, and I came down to tell you, I'm gonna go riding with Susan for a little while, if that's ok."

Daryl gave him a blank stare. "Susan?"

John was stunned. Daryl knew everyone. "Susan, black long hair," and he added to his description by making the hour glass shape with his hands. "Hangs with Annie?"

Daryl still looked puzzled. John tried to think of something else he could add to the description. Daryl finally looked like something dawned on him. "That's really weird. I know who she is but I couldn't remember for some weird ass reason. That's stone cold weird. I must be sadder than I thought." He paused, "So that's who you slept with last night?"

John hung his head. "Yeah."

Daryl shrugged his shoulders. "She's hot, but isn't she with Sam?" The Daryl who knew everyone had reasserted itself.

John repositioned himself on the boxes he had sat on. They were shifting a little under his weight. "Well, I think that's what we're gonna talk about."

"Do you know about her?"

John moved around on the boxes again. "What do you mean?"

"She can disappear."

"What do you mean?"

"People say she can become invisible." He laughed. It rolled out from a place deep in his chest.

"People? What people."

"A couple of women I talked to at a party, and some dude at Jackson's."

"She can become invisible?" John felt a shiver run down his back.

"I know." Daryl huffed air out of his nose in a half laugh. "I think she's just sneaky and it makes people nervous."

"Sneaky?" John felt offended. He was already her champion. That didn't normally happen until it was officially an unofficial relationship for him.

"I don't mean in a nasty way. I mean, she watches. She's like me that way. People don't pay attention to other people unless they're right in their face. I think she knows where everybody is and where they're going so she moves through them without anybody noticing, even being as pretty as she is. She'd be a great chess player, or race car driver, always finding the path to push ahead."

John was skeptical that he had meant it as a compliment. "Ok, Daryl." He'd find out what Susan was about himself. He wasn't going to buy the gossipy third hand version of her offered by Daryl.

"It's lame. I know." Daryl laughed. He spun and lay down again, lifting the weights over his head. "When's she coming?" John thought he detected an interest in his voice that was out of place.

"She'll be here in about forty minutes." Thoughts rolled through his mind at an overwhelming pace.

"She probably shouldn't be here too long. Garlene doesn't like her."

"Garlene. Why?"

Daryl grunted a laugh, pushing the bar up and down, "women with bodies like Susan tend to make other women a little nervous."

"Garlene? Bullshit. She's not the jealous type."

"Well, she is. She just hides it a lot better than most women. You might not see it, and Leon might not see it, but man I get it; the cold shoulder in bed, or my dirty clothes pile up for days or she'll leave the garage door open so every crooked sumbitch in the block can see what they can rip off from me."

John didn't mention the garage door incident from two days ago. It indicated that, based on Daryl's explanation, she wasn't thrilled with him at the present time. "Dirty clothes piled up, huh? I'll have to check that when I come over."

Daryl laughed between exhalations. "I'll put a pair of dirty underwear on your head if you do."

"I'll pass then."

"You'll pass out is what you'll do."

John laughed. "She said she was going to pull up and grab me off the porch, so she must've known about Garlene being unhappy with her."

"Women like Susan know how they affect other women."

John figured it was because Garlene was not thrilled specifically with Susan. "Well, I'm gonna go on up and wait on the porch. I'll take my beer if that's ok."

"Sure. I'll put a key under the mat so when you get home you can come on in. Just be sure to lock up."

"I can do that."

"Ok." Daryl continued his workout. John went back up to his room and got his heavier coat, an old leather bomber jacket. He took the last twenty he had and put it in his wallet. He had some condoms in his pocket, but Susan hadn't said anything about protection. John's experience was that women who didn't take birth control always had condoms on hand if it was necessary. He tended to neglect having one with him, usually, he liked to tell himself because he didn't have designs on the women he ended up with in bed.

He went out the front door and sat down on a swinging bench attached to the ceiling of the porch. It made his ass cold. The air had turned winter cold. He wasn't sure if he could sit outside for half an hour. He realized that he didn't have any cigarettes left. He cursed Ralph for all his mooching. He got up and tried the door, but it was locked, and Daryl hadn't come up with the key yet. He sat back down. Just as he settled in, trying to ignore his nicotine craving, the door opened. It was Garlene. "I thought I heard the door. What are you doing out here?"

John stood. "I'm glad you came down. I locked myself out. I need to see if I have any cigarettes."

She waved him in, wanting to get in because of the cold. "Why did you go out to smoke?"

"Oh, I didn't go out to smoke. I was waiting for a ride."

"A ride? To where? Aren't you staying here tonight?"

John motioned to the steps. "Do you want a cig? I'm gonna get a pack out of my bag."

"Sure."

John ran up the stairs, unsure of how he would broach the subject of Susan with Garlene. He wouldn't lie to her. He decided that made it simple. He'd explain what he was doing. The music started blasting from the basement. John wished Daryl would get his ass upstairs and smooth all this out. When he came back down Garlene sat on the couch waiting, looking for all the world to John like a spouse waiting for an errant husband's answers to questions he did not want to be asked.

He gave her a cigarette and lit it. He lit one for himself. He glanced out the door. Susan hadn't arrived. "I'm waiting for a ride to Pat's."

"You're going back there?"

"Yeah, I'm going to talk to Susan."

"Susan? Susan Baker?" Her eyes narrowed. "You were with her the other night."

"Yeah."

"How in the world did you get mixed up with her? She fucked a nigger, you know?"

"Everybody seems to have a problem with her."

"That's because she's a slut."

"She's been really nice to me."

"You don't need the kind of shit that she's gonna shovel out, John."

He looked at his feet. "You could be right."

"There's no "could be" about it. She's not welcome in this house."

"Daryl told me that."

"Oh, he did, did he."

John felt he might have slipped. "I told him, just now, what I was doing."

"What did he say?"

"That she wouldn't be welcome here." He felt himself on the edge of a slippery slope. The music blasting from the basement angered John. He wished his friend would sense his distress and get up there and save him from the grilling.

"Did he say why?"

"He said you don't like her."

"He didn't say anything else." She was furious.

"Not really. I think he was afraid to hurt my feelings."

"Well, he isn't a friend if he doesn't tell you what I told you."

"I'm glad you did, Garlene. I didn't mean to distress anyone. I've only spoken to the woman one other time. She was very nice to me, and she's a friend of Annie's so I thought that.."

"Annie is fucking stupid to have her around. It'll only make her life a bigger mess than it is now."

"She sounds like a nightmare."

"That's about the sum of it." Garlene was righteous, indignant, like she shouldn't have been forced to talk about Susan. John felt even more strongly that Susan played a bigger part in Daryl's and Garlene's life than either admitted.

"Well, I plan on talking to her about Annie tonight." He would keep his own secrets. And would do so by telling the truth with pinpoint precision.

"Tell her to get out of Annie's life." Garlene was still fighting mad.

"Garlene, thanks for the warning. I'll keep that it in mind, but I do want to see what's going on with Annie. She's with this ass hole..."

She interrupted. "Billy, yeah. He met her through Susan."

John was shocked. "Susan fixed Annie up with Billy?"

"That's right."

"Wow. Well, I need to..." John saw headlights move up in front of the house. A car horn honked two times, quick and sharp. He pointed, "I guess I better look into this myself."

"You don't need to, John. You got the scoop from me."

"Garlene, I appreciate what you're saying, but it seems even more clear to me that I have to work to get Annie clear of her mess. I'll update you two when I get back."

Garlene headed back up the stairs. "You'll still go fuck her. Don't bother telling me."

John watched her go up. He was rattled. The things she said were meant to shock and appall him, he knew, and it did a little, but he was even more anxious now to talk to Susan. He dashed out the door, pulling it firmly shut behind him. He ran down to the car and jumped in the already open door. "I'm sorry I kept you waiting."

"That was Garlene going at you, wasn't it?"

John didn't think she could see into the living room from the angle she was at. "How did you know?"

"That's not hard to guess." She smiled at him warmly, even, John thought, possibly, lovingly. "I slept with Daryl once. That means she's not a big fan."

Things quickly fell into place. The jury was tainted. John snorted a laugh. "That would explain the hatred. Why did you sleep with a married guy?"

She pulled the car away from the curb. "Well, he didn't tell me he was married." She paused. "Not that I haven't slept with a married man and known it, but I was a lot younger." John figured she must've been illegal too, if it was much younger.

"It's hard being as pretty as you are, isn't it?"

She took her eyes off the road and glanced up and down John's body. "It's a good thing that Sam had already fucked me when you called. I never would have gotten out of there otherwise."

John was getting angry. In the space of a minute, she had talked about fucking two different guys and neither one of them was him. "I'm sorry to have interrupt..."

She snapped an answer over his remark. "No you're not." She glanced over at him again. "You told me you loved me. It's upsetting to hear me talk about fucking someone else. I told you about Daryl, because God knows what poison Garlene spit at you, and I told you about Sam because I wanted you to know that I worked very hard to get out of there without getting my ass and yours beat by a big 'ol burly grease monkey." She looked at him for a long time, long enough that John wondered if she had eyes in the side of her head. How could she look at him, and drive perfectly while she did. She smiled a sweet smile again. "and don't tell me that you could beat his ass. He turns and lifts wrenches as long as your arm, and he does it all day long."

John felt the truth of what she said swirl around the car and suck into his lungs when he inhaled, and as it got into him, it calmed him and made him trust her more than he trusted some people he had known for years. She seemed, despite the bad press, to be without guile. It seemed lying, he joked to himself, was in opposition to her superpowers. They turned a corner on a street that he guessed headed toward her apartment. "Are we going to your place?"

She pulled over to the curb. "Sam's at the apartment. I got out, but I couldn't talk him out of leaving."

"He's still there?"

"Yeah. I told him I had to go to Annie's, which is true. I did stop over there. I gave her your cell phone number and checked on her. She seems firm on dumping Billy, thanks to your support. I think he figured that I'd go over there and be right back. Let me have your cell phone. "

He gave it to her. She dialed a number. "Sam, I'm gonna stay with Annie tonight. You go on home and I'll talk to you tomorrow." She listened. "No, I want you to go home. Yes, me too. Ok. I'll talk to you tomorrow. Cell phone? Yeah. We got Annie a cell phone too." She winked at John. "Bye."

She sighed after she hung up. "I do not like games. I half lied to him. He saw the caller ID that it was a cell phone. I told him it was Annie's." She leaned over toward him. "I hope you know how to fix cars? Do you? Because," she pecked him on the cheek, "I'm about to lose a mechanic."

John and Susan kissed, embraced, touched each other for several minutes. Finally, Susan pulled away, looking at the windows on the car. They were fogged. "Let's see if Sam has left yet."

She turned on the defrosters full blast and after a minute or two pulled away from the curb. John wanted to talk to her about a million things, but he was speechless, overwhelmed.

She started. "So that was some phone call there fellow." She laughed. "Annie's always said nice things about you, but being squishy and gushy wasn't one of them."

"I, can't explain it."

"We'll go to Pat's and have a drink and give Sam plenty of time to clear out." She turned the car toward the bar. "What can't you explain?"

"I'm usually not so gushy, or forward."

"You let the girl come to you."

John was embarrassed to admit it, but it was part of his approach. He'd put himself out there in ways that gave the women permission to speak to him. He was in the driver's seat from the first moment. He hated having to admit what she said, but as usual, with her, he felt he had no choice. "Yes."

"Why would I be interested in you, John? I'm know I'm pretty. I'm tired of knowing it
sometimes, but I'm grateful. Down here where us po' folk are, it's a major asset. It might get me out of here." She gestured with one hand to the landscape outside the car. "I know my looks are fading fast. I can't afford to go to a dentist. I can't afford to eat like I should, I abuse myself to numb myself to the squalor and ignorance around me, and you might be a part of that, but because you're so quiet, it's hard to tell if you are. I need to know you."

John continued to be overwhelmed. The more Susan talked, the more enamoured he was of her, but oddly, the more insulted he felt. He felt removed from it, looking down at the hurt and warmth and marveling at it. He picked the one piece out of her remarks that he felt he could do something with. "What do you want to know about me?"

She laughed a girlish laugh. "Plenty. We'll have time." She put her hand on his leg. "I do know you're good in bed. It's a great start." He felt pride swell in him. She continued the thought, "and I figure that means you can pay attention to needs, at least on that level, that you aren't always stuck in yourself."

She took her hand off his leg and put it back on the wheel. He was crushed. This roller coaster was unpleasant. Strangely, because of her off handed, non-judgmental matter-of-fact tone, he didn't feel any animosity toward her while she distilled him down to components. All of his feelings seemed to stay centered.

"Man," he finally exhaled. "You sure are messing with my mind."

Susan grew serious. "I'm not trying. I'm just talking to you."

John wanted to put the focus on her for a few minutes, to give him a break. "Daryl told me that some people believe that you can become invisible."

Susan laughed loud and long. Her long black hair fell across her face. She brushed it aside quickly. "You are quiet John, so I know you watch. If a human being is not talking, then they are thinking or listening, so you must be doing that a lot." She looked at him for acknowledgement.

He had to think. Did he listen? Not much really. He thought. "I think more than listen."

"Well, still, haven't you noticed how slow people are?"

"Slow?"

"Right. They're dazed, victims of the environment. People eating shitty government cheese, cans of Chef Boy R Dee, splurging, yes, *treating* themselves, to McDonald's. Sugar and salt and sugar and more salt. No vegetables, no vitamins, no water, nothing really good."

"They could if they wanted to."

"It's pretty hard to when that's all your parents ate, it's all you know, and it's cheap. Vegetables aren't cheap. Ten cans of watered down peas from the food shelter are, but that's about it. Fresh vegetables are hard to find in poor neighborhoods, and harder to transport and keep."

Susan pulled the car over at Pat's, near where Ralph had already made a habit of parking. John understood what she was saying. "So we don't eat so good."

She pointed to her head. "Especially the poor. The brain can't work if it doesn't get the right stuff. Poor people are addled. Let's add that we usually can't sleep comfortably because we can't wash our bed clothes regularly, or any other

250

clothes for that matter. We're all crammed together, so it's noisy all the time. Let's add sleep deprivation to the bad diet."

"I get it." John was impatient. He had known that poor people had it bad. This was nothing new. He didn't like thinking about being a poor person, but he was and this made it clear. He thought about his Achilles Heal, which he laughed to himself, was a couple of feet further up-his knees.

"But do you get it? Disadvantaged is a better word than poor. Take a poor person and put them next to someone who has grown up with even a modicum of money, put them at a table with a book on it, and a plate of good food on it."

John liked this game, but he wanted a beer. "Let's continue inside."

Susan grew impatient. "It'll wait."

John stretched. "Ok, let's add a TV, too."

Susan smiled, "Ok, add a TV set too."

John answered. "The poor person will eat the food and watch TV, and the person with money will eat the food and read the book."

Susan nodded, "but that's stereotyping. You oversimplified what would happen. That's the kind of thing that a rich person would point to and say, "see, they choose to be stupid, but they didn't have much if any choice at all. First of all, the poor person would probably pick the sweetest foods from the plate because they are either hypoglycemic, or diabetic or on the verge. They're bodies are so screwed up, their bodies are telling them the wrong thing. The well fed person doesn't have to deal with this corrupt signal. Their bodies are healthy, balanced. They started with an advantage."

She tapped a finger on the steering wheel. "The book, or the TV. Well I gotta tell you. I think just half the time the well off person will pick the book, which is scary, but only because when you and I think of TV, we don't think of PBS, we think of Married With Children, stupid shit. Really brain rotting stuff."

John spoke up. "I noticed when I don't see TV for a while, it seems incredibly dumb, but if I watch every day, everything seems pretty entertaining."

"Right, right John. It lowers the brain, uh, mind work! So here's a person who has a TV, but not books or magazines or newspapers. They're brains are starved for nutrition, rotted by TV. It scares me. Now, the book isn't even a consideration for the poor person, except," she held up one of the tapping fingers, "for a few aberrations. There are a few disadvantaged people who, just because of genes, and luck, lots of luck, will want to pick up the book first, and eat the food second, and ignore the TV."

"Annie seems to be self destructive. What happened to her? Where does she fit in? Is she some kind of martyr?"

"No, she has friends. Martyrs don't have time for friends."

"So what is it?"

Susan hesitated. "Well, in the big picture, she suffers from lots of the things we suffer from. In the simpler sense, she made a mistake. She's lonely and that makes it easier to goof up by settling. But she has your number, and mine. She's ready to correct her error, get herself out of the unpleasantness."

"Well, we'll get her out of that." John put his hand on Susan's leg. "I'll bet the mechanic didn't want to talk about this?"

She pushed his hand off. "Let's not get off the track. Ok, so the poor person already has a scrambled brain, but even scrambled people know what's unpleasant. In fact, they are intimate with unpleasantness every day, and human beings need goodness in their lives, so when you're around this all the time," she motioned around them, "foul air, foul water, foul homes, they need to escape, so in come the alcohol and drugs."

She pointed to her and then him. "You and I do it all the time. It takes us above it for that brief time we're stoned. We're sitting outside a bar right now."

"So you don't want to go in?"

"I'm not saying that. I'm saying that poor people resort to alcohol and drugs as a survival tool. You can't be miserable twenty four, seven, three hundred and sixty five days a year. The only problem with alcohol and drugs is that..."

John wanted to participate, "They are addictive."

"Yes, and they damage our poor put upon brains. More damage to this already battered mess." She knocked on her head.

"So," John shifted toward Susan, his legs pointing toward hers, "poor people are brain dead."

"Close, zombies is more accurate. They move and react like the movie zombies, not so exaggerated. I see it around me all the time."

"It seems like we're talking like rich people, calling poor people inferior."

Susan laughed heartily. "The rich say that they are that way at the beginning. They pop out of mom as inferiors. We're saying that they are forced into their inferior position by poverty."

John nodded, " but why aren't you that way?"

"Luck, genes probably. I have withstood the beatings to my brain better than most, but I won't be able to take it too much longer. Luck has given me an edge, such an edge." She thought and continued. "Because I've always been pretty, even as a little girl, the teachers favored me, people always smiled and complimented me. I got good grades, good vibes from everyone. I get a lot of things just because of that. I was lucky because I grew up with my aunt, instead of my horrible parents. My dad died from alcoholism, and my mom died from cancer when I was five. My aunt loved me to pieces."

"She's dead?"

"Yeah, cancer. It ate up every dime she saved. Her insurance wouldn't pay for a lot of the bills. She planned on suing them but the cancer made her too sick to function. When she died, she was broke. Of course, she willed everything to me, but I was out on the street at the end of it all. Anyway, I looked up to her. I emulated her in a lot of ways. She was religious about taking her Geritol every day because her mother had, and I was fascinated by the bottle and the smell and I liked it, so I've always taken vitamins. When I couldn't buy toilet paper, I bought vitamins. I was lucky that it was important. I think it's helped me a lot."

"Kept the brain rot away?"

"It helped. I eat better than most, as you can see." She waved her arm over her body.

"You are perfect."

She shrugged. "So what I'm saying is that when I get around, in a room full of people, for example, I watch what everyone is doing, where they are looking, who they are talking to. It's like watching a bullet coming out of a gun in slow motion, it's easy to dodge for me, but not for the guy who sees it coming at him full speed. One night I was at a party, and I was sober. I was getting over a stomach flu. I was bored, there's nothing worse than being stone cold sober in a room full of drunks. To entertain myself, I started standing in certain places in the room, and when someone would talk to me, or my boobs, more likely, then turn their wobbling heads to take a drink or answer someone else, I would step back a foot. Some people would look back and think I was gone, some would see me and wonder if they were staggering that bad, and apparently, a couple of people thought that I was invisible. I did it for half an hour or so, until I got bored with it."

Susan didn't sound egotistical. She sounded like a scientist, observing, expounding. "That's all there is to it?" John wasn't convinced.

"Yes. I heard the rumors a couple days later. Don't forget that some women are jealous of me, and I haven't gotten the impression so far that being invisible is like a feather in my cap. It's like I'm a horror story."

John laughed. "Yeah, it's not an asset." He opened his car door. He wanted a beer, now. Susan followed suit without protest. It was getting cold in the car.

Susan started to skip. "In fact", she turned to John as she bounced along, "Someone asked me if I was a witch once, too."

As they crossed the street John wanted to ask about something else that had kept coming to the forefront. He never would have talked about this to any other woman, but he felt comfortable talking to Susan about it. "You sleep with black guys?" He tried, unsuccessfully, he noted, to sound indifferent. He wanted to tell her about his experience with his freckled aunt.

She furrowed her brow. "Who cares?"

As they got to the door, she put her hand on his shoulder and turned him to face her. She looked at his face. It made him uneasy. "YOU care?"

"My jealousy is color blind." He smiled and shrugged.

She turned and started back toward her car. "I don't think I can deal with this."

John ran after her, "No Jesus, Susan, wait." His mind was racing. His confusion was spiking, making it tough to be as eloquent as he felt he needed to be at that moment. Depression started coating each thought that jumped up and away. He was scared. He felt tears starting to pour out of his eyes. "I don't want to hurt your feelings. I wasn't insinuating…"

She looked at him as she opened her car door. She saw the tears. It shocked her. She closed the door again. "I'm not sure…" She finally seemed at a loss for words.

John didn't know what to say. He grew more upset. The tears had felt like a mechanical reaction to his sadness but now the sorrow and tears seemed to unite in their cause. He started to sob. He was so embarrassed. Susan stood looking at him. "Don't cry."

John looked at her, upset. "You don't want me to bullshit you, yet, here I am showing you exactly how I feel, what I wonder about and you're telling me to fuck off, jumping on me for things that you think I'm saying without even knowing. I'm not a racist!" He was surprised how free he felt to cry. Because of that, it flowed through him and the sadness left quickly, like the old Italian woman at the graveside. Susan stood looking at him a half a minute longer, and then stepped up to him and hugged him, and then lifted his head to kiss him.

"I got all self righteous on your ass, didn't I?"

John gulped down the last of his tears. "Yeah."

She looked at her feet as she spoke. "Prejudice is ignorant hatred."

He looked up at the gray night sky. "Jesus Christ you put me through it."

She laughed. "And you love it."

John's grin showed he agreed. He took her hand and led her to the bar.

THE GRASS IS ALWAYS GREENER ON THE OTHER
SIDE OF THE BAR

As he escorted Susan into the bar, John looked down the street to the main intersection.
He noticed a man walking away from them who wore an overcoat similar to Bob's. He didn't feel a chill this time. It was as if Susan's presence had dispelled the possibility of fear. He gently squeezed Susan's arm and, distracted, asked her to hold on a moment. He called out toward the man. "Bob!"

The man scrunched his head down into his coat. John called out again. "Bob." The man looked around, but he was too far away for John to identify. If it was Bob, why wouldn't he answer? Maybe he was embarrassed, or he didn't recognize John and wasn't about to acknowledge any one he didn't know in this neighborhood at this time of night, or maybe it wasn't Bob and the guy was just turning to see who was so insistent.

The entryway of the bar usually caught wind and magnified it. A cold breeze surged through. John shivered.

"Shit, let's get in." Susan insisted. She reopened the door. "Dead Bob?"

"I'm not sure."

"He doesn't seem interested if it is."

John laughed. "Yeah, true."

As soon as he had a clear view of the length of the bar, John could swear that he saw Cheryl ducking into the office.

Susan had scoped out an empty table in the far corner and was dragging him that way. He didn't resist. After they had removed their coats, she sent him over to get a tequila for her and his beer. John stepped up to the bar where Paul was working quickly. He looked perturbed. "Hey, Paul. What's up?"

Paul pointed toward the office with a jerk of his head in that direction. "What'll you have?" He was aggravated.

He looked over at the office. He distinctly heard Pat, and then Cheryl. He zipped back to the table with the drinks and told Susan the story of Cheryl's arrest and phone call to the bar. She wondered aloud about how she got out of jail on a Friday night.

"Let's find out." John grinned and stood up.

"I'll go invisible." When Susan laughed, a vibration seemed to pulse out into the air and warm John's flesh. It was deep and rich and hung with him. He walked toward the office as Susan crept behind him. She was very light on her feet.

He walked to the office door, while Susan stayed at the corner, within earshot, but completely out of sight. He looked at Paul before he walked in, to let him know he was heading in there. Paul's slight nod was permission.

He looked into the office to see Pat sitting on his desk, his feet on a chair. His imposing bulk was more so, since Cheryl sat in a chair, essentially at his feet. She had obviously been crying. She had black rings under her eyes and dried blood on her nose. She dabbed at it with a wet bar towel. She wiped her face with the other side, and held it limply in her hand at her side. She was wearing the same clothes she had the last time he saw her, and her perpetually white tennis shoes were badly scuffed. She saw John when he gently leaned down and took the spent towel from her hand. She started weeping gently. "Christ, did I fuck up."

Pat's facial expression seemed to sway back and forth from forlorn to disappointed. It depended solely on what Cheryl was saying.

She looked at John. He was glad that Susan was invisible, because Cheryl would have clammed up if she had known she was a few feet away. "Godamn it John. Why did you let me go with that fucker?"

John was taken aback. "I really thought you had the situation under control Cheryl." He didn't feel that was enough. "You always do." It was largely true.

Cheryl became meek. "I don't understand how someone whose just trying to have a little fun, blow off steam ends up jacked so bad." She frowned. "Same thing at work- bust ass, get hurt and then I'm not a productive citizen, I'm a mooch." She looked at the floor.

John thought about what she was saying. "Well," he spoke slowly, "fun is fun. No harm. The company you keep is different. There are a lot of users out there. That can be not so fun." Cheryl sat silently. She glanced at him to acknowledge his observation. "Bosses and employees are always trying to get over on each other and bosses hold most of the cards. There are a lot of users in that world too. It's not easy." Cheryl nodded, almost imperceptibly, but she agreed. John didn't know where some of his observations were coming from. "Also, too much of anything isn't good, and it certainly isn't fun."

He briefly channeled Ralph in his head. "Cheryl ain't no Otis, and this ain't no Mayberry." He put it aside and cursed Ralph for putting the thought in his head somehow.

Pat spoke up. "Damn it girl. You made a mistake. Everybody's allowed to make mistakes." He was very obviously smitten with her.

Cheryl looked at Pat. "Not me, brother. My sister finds out that I went to jail, I'm homeless. It's a guarantee. She has been all over my shit lately."

Pat's shifting expression turned to one of concern.

An awkward silence followed. John spoke up. "How'd you get out so soon Cheryl?" He looked at Pat sheepishly. "I was coming in the morning to get you out."

She laughed. She put her hand on Pat's calf. "This man came down like a white knight and talked them into letting him bail me out. It was a major deal."

John and Susan were very impressed. They had never heard of anything like it.

Pat's expression changed to embarrassment. He blushed. "I know a couple of guys. I serve on committees. You get to know people that way." He sounded modest, but John knew it was more about holding his cards close to his chest. John thought about how intent Pat was on keeping his elevated status from the people in the bar. His secret was safe with him. John wondered if Pat would be able to keep this from his wife. He wondered if Pat was fully capable of burying it, or had he stuck his neck way out for Cheryl?

John spoke softly. "What did the bastard do to you?"

"What most fucking men do, really. Chicken piece of shit. We were at an all night club," she looked up at Pat, "sorry, hon, you were closed," and drinking and having a good time and some guy comes up to Zim," John figured that was a short version of the guy's name she was with, " and he starts giving him shit in some language that I didn't understand, Romanian, but what the hell do I know." She shook her head. "Any way Zim yells something at him and the guy goes away, fast." She looked at John and Pat. "I was impressed. This dude he was talking to was pretty big. Anyway, we keep on drinking blah, blah, he gives me a fist full of pills, and I don't think anything about it. I took a couple and stuck the rest in my pocket. Next thing I know this other dude is having a fist fight with some other guy in the back of the bar. He's hitting this guy pretty good, when all of a sudden, this guy who's on the floor from a fist to the jaw, he pulls a gun and says that it's a raid."

She paused, John thought for effect, but then he saw her draw several breaths. She seemed to be winded. "It was one weird ass raid, let me tell you. There was just this guy, and one other guy who pulled out his gun at the same time. He seemed to be following the other guys lead. Anyway they flashed badges, lined us all up against the wall, and started searching us. They found the pills in my pocket and I figured Zim would be a stand up guy, but then I realized that there was no way that was gonna happen. He didn't have anything on him. He dumped it all on me. I think he knew that there was gonna be a problem and he didn't want to be stuck. Because I was with him, they checked me real careful. They went through until they found a couple other people holding and took me, the other dude that was bugging Zim and a nigger." The word went through John.

"These immigrants," Pat pronounced, "don't have a right to be here."

Cheryl looked at him skeptically. "I think they thought they had someone important and were just falling into it, but Zim was a step ahead of them and made me the patsy."

She looked at John and then the desk across from her. A drink glass sat half full. He picked it up and handed it to her. "Thanks hon. So the one guy is fighting all the way to the car and then the station and he's thrashing around and hits me in the nose, and damn near breaks it, and no one seems to care. Now I've been brought up on drug charges."

"We'll get those dropped." Pat seemed confident.

Cheryl looked at Pat with admiration. "I hope so, dear heart."

John felt awkward. It seemed like a mutual admiration society and he was the odd man out. "Cheryl, I'm really glad you're ok." He looked at Pat. "Do you need me in the morning then?"

Pat thought. He put a finger to his lips. "Well, I guess not. I appreciate it John. I jumped the gun here, so I guess I won't need you." He stood. "I have some other business I need to discuss with you, if you have a minute." He looked at Cheryl. "Will you be ok for a minute?" Cheryl nodded, smiling, sniffling.

Susan had heard Pat and scurried back to her seat anticipating that the two men would come into the bar, but Pat led John to the back and through a door and up a narrow set of stairs. They came up into a large empty room with hardwood floors that were worn but clean and shiny. "What do you think of it?"

John looked around. It was like a lot of older buildings. The base trim and frames around the doors were heavy duty maple and oak. The rooms were off white except for the occasional papered wall. The wallpaper had old flowery patterns, peeling at edges here and there. The ceilings were so high it seemed like they were more of a way to block the sky than to complete the room. "It's nice. Has a lot of possibilities."

Pat slapped him on the back. "Possibilities. Good point." He started walking through the rooms as he spoke. He opened his mouth first without saying more, and then after a moment's hesitation, he began again. "Paul is leaving. He is finishing school and he's got things going on that don't have anything to do with this bar. I don't have kids." He looked at John, searching his face. "You knew that, didn't you?"

John nodded. "You mentioned it before. Couldn't have 'em you said."

"Right". Pat looked away and through the front room windows that opened onto the street where the boarded up house and the field of torn down houses sat. John could see Eta's too. There were three windows crowded on the wall that faced that direction, almost as if the builders had realized that they hadn't put enough windows in the rest of the house and threw an extra couple in here. It provided a great view of a rough area. They were no longer covered in the film Pat had inexplicably adhered to them and John had spotted from the street a few days ago. It looked like the change in weather had chilled the window surfaces and neutralized whatever made them stick. They lie in a dark twisted pile on the floor.

"I've got a wife that is bitching and bitching about all the time I spend here. She says we're not getting any younger, and we should be enjoying our time traveling and all that other shit that she wants to do to spend my money. She says that we can't take it with us, but I keep saying that I don't intend to leave any time soon, so let's go slow." He paused and shook his head while he smiled. "I love running this bar, and she doesn't get that. She didn't work in a shitty white collar job like I did for a big chunk of my adult life. This seems like my time in the sun, but, well, I guess I need to think about what she wants too."

"Stuff like what's goin' on down there." He turned his head back toward the steps briefly,
indicating, John supposed, Cheryl and the more chaotic events of the bar, "It does make me wonder if it's time for me to wrap it up."

He shook his head, like he had water in his ear. "Anyway, I wondered if you'd be interested in working for me, replacing Paul's hours, and maybe a few of mine? It doesn't pay that great, but you know I'll be square with you."

In the back of his mind, John had thought Paul might be leaving soon, but he hadn't conceived of a scenario where Pat would ask him to replace him. He was dumbfounded. He stood silent, thoughts and projections of what it meant swirling through his head.

Pat fidgeted. "Don't be too excited." He said dryly.

John looked at him, startled. "I'm sorry, Pat. I'm just, well, I'm shocked."

"Don't you want to do it?"

John was trying to formulate sentences, responses in the midst of being stunned. "I'm sure. I could I do it though, I mean..."

Pat grew impatient. "Look, son. I certainly have reservations about bringing in someone who isn't family, but I believe you are an honest hard working fellow, ignoring the fact that you blew work off the last few days.."

John interrupted. "I'm loyal and hard working. Some people deserve that, some don't."

Pat gave John a quizzical look. "Well, do I?"

John still had problems forming sentences in his head. "I, sure you do. You're one of the Finest, specimens, er, people I know."

"Specimen?" Pat's eyebrows furrowed. He smiled. "I suppose that's a compliment."

John was still trying to formulate. "Yes, yes. I'm just at a loss, Pat. Your trust in me is, wow."

"Didn't' see this comin', didja son?"

John knew the answer to that question. "No, I didn't"

"Well, do you want to do it? You'll make a living. Plus, you can live up here, if you don't smoke up here." Pat looked at the floor and shook his head like he was in the midst of a major disagreement with someone. "I know that seems harsh, but I cannot risk having my place burn down." He paused and then dropped the next bomb shell. "If it goes good, then we can talk about you taking over ownership."

"I, Pat, may I think about this for a day before I tell you what I want to do?

Pat looked hurt. "You're not sure?"

"No I'm pretty sure. I just, I think you deserve an answer that's well thought out, not a sloppy one."

"What do you have to think about? From what I can see, you're damn near homeless, you hate your job, you carry everything you own, you..."

John got the point. "You're right. I mean, I'm just confused." Every fiber of his being told John to wait another day, but he knew on a gut level that if he thought it over for twenty four hours, nothing he was going to come up with that would make him tell Pat no.

He grinned sheepishly at Pat. "I'd be honored to take the job."

Pat slapped his back again, the concern disappearing from his face immediately, replaced by a huge smile. "Good. Good job."

"What will I make?" His curiosity over rode decorum.

"You'll make a living. We'll discuss it the day after tomorrow. Too much going on tonight, and tomorrow. I want you to start this coming Friday, though. I want you to shadow Paul."

John's head was swimming. "Ok, Pat. I, thank you again, man. I'm knocked out."

Pat reached around behind John, grabbed his shoulders in a sort of sideways hug, and guided him toward the steps they had come up, saying, "It'll be fun. You'll see."

"Yeah." Was all he could say.

"This is between you and me for the time being, John." He tapped John's chest as he said it , emphasizing each word.

As they descended the steps, Pat stopped abruptly. The stairway was narrow, so instead of turning to John, which would have put them belly to belly, he spoke looking at the landing below. "One thing I should mention now though, is, I don't drink on the job, uh, with the rare exception," he smiled thinking of his beer with Ralph and John the previous day, "and Paul doesn't drink, so you understand that you won't either." Pat's tone didn't make it sound like a request or a demand. It was the way it was.

John felt like a giant bird plucked him from the step and took him up high on a short circular flight, returning him to the same spot, but facing the opposite way. He was immediately suspicious that he had made the flight on his own with newly emerged nubs of wings but that his mind had to conjure the bird to ease him into the reality of his new situation. He spoke when he touched down. "I, uh I understand."

Pat nodded as he resumed walking down the steps. "So little or no drinking off hours either." He said it like his thoughts involuntarily became words.

The two men walked back to the office where Cheryl still sat, bedraggled and dazed.

Pat held a finger up. "Do you have your car keys, Cheryl?"

She rooted through her purse. "Yeah, they gave 'em back."

Pat was sorting thoughts. "Ok, fine, I'll follow you home to be sure you get there ok."

John started away, "I'll see you tomorrow then, Pat.." Pat didn't hear him. He was already engrossed in Cheryl. Susan was back, standing where she had been when she eavesdropped on the office conversation.

"I thought you couldn't see me, thought I would screw with you." She giggled.

He leered at her. "I see you alright."

Susan leered back. "I think we need to wrap it up.....here." she teased. John eagerly agreed. "Sex is the poor man's entertainment. Doesn't cost a thing." Susan laughed.

"Funny," John replied as he put his coat on, "I feel like a million dollars."

She waved her hand in front of his face. "Money can't buy me love."

"And I can't afford it."

They enjoyed their semi coherent banter, the intermingling words being the only socially acceptable foreplay they could perform in the bar.

As they headed toward the door, John wondered if Pat had bought himself a huge amount of trouble doing what he'd done for Cheryl. Then he laughed. "Rich people can do anything they want." He said it to himself. He would keep Pat's secrets. He did, however, want to talk to Susan about his new job.

As Susan drove them toward her apartment, John worked his logic, trying to pry out a reason that he could break his promise to Pat about keeping the job to himself, so that he could discuss it with Susan. He told himself that Susan would be his wife soon, so she should be told. He was dizzy from the fact that the thought occurred to him from nowhere yet with so much certainty.

They entered and went upstairs. John snapped out of his revelry for a moment. "Is there any chance Sam is going to come back tonight?"

Susan shook her head. She unlocked the door. "No. He won't be back. He sleeps like the dead. He's at home snoring for all he's worth."

John looked at her. She looked at him. They stood in the doorway. "I'll call him tomorrow and break it off. He's not a bad guy. He won't make a scene." She went in. John followed. He wondered if he had imagined the chaos in her place, but he hadn't. She was sloppy. He didn't care. He recalled the spotless apartment he had left earlier that night and felt a twinge of regret. It was regret that he had gotten into the relationship with Diane at all. It was right to break it off.

John decided he was lucky. The offer Pat had made to him came from the bar owner's observations regarding John's behavior, but it also had to do with his looks, his genes. People liked him because he was easy on the eye. Maybe that played a conscious part in Pat's decision; It wouldn't hurt to have a pleasant looking person behind the bar serving the drinks. While he could accept that he got things because of luck, he didn't want the world to be so cruel and shallow that only the strong survived. How would the meek inherit the earth? How would they even exist? He realized, as he always did when his mind wandered in this direction, that there was little he could do about that. He had to take care of himself and his loved ones. He also realized he was so tired, he didn't have the energy to discuss the job with Susan. Susan had grown quiet. Apparently, they were both talked out. They got in bed and began kissing.

#

The alarm clock radio was absolutely cruel, and unusual. John shot up in bed like he had been hit with a bucket of freezing water. Susan lie sound asleep. He looked over at the little white clock that played some sort of sports wrap up show at what sounded like a thousand decibels. He couldn't believe a sound so loud could be coming from the little white object, but there was no other clock radio in sight. He reached over Susan's prone body and grabbed the offending device and switched it off. It was one o'clock. He was supposed to be at the wake by three, so obviously Susan had set it so that he'd have time to get up and get to Daryl's house. They had been up until nearly four.

He looked at Susan. Her breathing was slow and steady. She had a peaceful look on her face. He was amazed that she looked even more beautiful than she looked awake. He wondered why everyone couldn't look as bliss filled awake as when they were asleep. Susan was so pretty that he decided it hardly mattered in her case. He felt like he was in a fabulous dream when they were together any way.

He had felt romantic when he was around her. It made him uncomfortable, but his happiness effectively countered that. He wanted to change clothes, and then realized that his clothes were at Daryl's so he would have to change there when he arrived. He knew Susan wouldn't go to the wake since Garlene would make things uncomfortable. She didn't really know Joey either, but then, John thought, he didn't really know Joey. No one but Daryl did. He was going to be there for Daryl.

He thought, that if Susan would take him, he'd stop by Pat's first and see if he needed help with anything. He got up and went into the kitchen. There were dirty dishes everywhere. He found some coffee in tea bags. He boiled water and made himself a cup. It tasted like the little bags had been there for a while, but it would do. He started cleaning the dishes and straightening the counters. He would work at it while he waited for Susan to wake up. He finished cleaning the kitchen and went into the bathroom to use the toilet. The bathroom was a disaster of clothes, towels, curlers, makeup, cotton balls, trash and after he splashed his face and went to the restroom, he started straightening that room. He didn't know what to do with her clothes, what was dirty, and what wasn't, so he carefully folded and stacked it all outside the bathroom door in the narrow hall. He'd take it into the bedroom and put it in a laundry basket he found half buried in the corner. While he was picking up, he noticed a couple of check stubs. They were from Target, the department store. That must be where Susan worked. That was undoubtedly where Annie and Susan got some of the clothes they wore. Susan would certainly get a discount. He'd have to ask her what it was like there, what she did.

He had found some spray cleanser under the sink when he straightened the kitchen and went to get it. He looked at the alarm clock. It was now two thirty, but he'd rather be late than wake his sleeping beauty. He got the cleaner and continued his work in the bathroom. He had started scrubbing down the tub with the last of the cleaner when he heard rustling in the bedroom and saw Susan shuffle toward him naked. She got within a few feet of him when she jumped back startled at the sight of him crouching in the tub with his bottle of cleaner.

He admired her body. She crossed her arms over her breasts in what John figured was involuntary modesty. "What the hell are you doing there?" She was curt.

John's feelings were hurt. He figured she would be grateful. "I'm cleaning."

She looked at the window, and around the room, disoriented. "What time is it? Aren't you supposed to be at the wake?"

John's feelings were hurt again. She must have figured he could walk to Daryl's. He answered sheepishly. "I thought maybe I could con you into a ride over there."

Susan looked puzzled. "I, sure, I was going to take you, I mean what time is it?"

"I'm not sure. It was two thirty two the last time I looked at the clock, but that was a while ago."

She looked around again, as if she could glean the time from her surroundings. She walked back into the bedroom. She sprinted back to him, still naked.. "You're late. It's five past three!"

270

"It's ok. I couldn't bear to wake you up."

She looked around the room. It was very tidy. He had cleaned the toilet, sink, floor and was nearly done with the tub. "Jesus, you didn't have to do this."

"I like doing it, for you."

"I'm a slob, John." She laughed, taking one hand from her breasts to cover her mouth as she yawned. "Hell, like you haven't figured that out yet."

"Yeah, I did kinda figure that out. At least you have your shit together enough to have your own place to mess up."

She tilted her head. She walked over and pulled his shirt over his head. "I think we both need to take a shower, and we can save time taking it together."

"That'll probably take longer."

"Oh, no. I'm planning on a real shower." She continued to strip him. "Why don't you have a place of your own? I know you work hard. I know you make money."

John didn't want to talk about his daughter. He felt ashamed. "I haven't been good with money."

She yanked his underwear down around his ankles. "I should just push you over now and you could crack your head." His eyes widened. She looked glum. "Why would you lie to me?"

"Lie?"

"You send most of what you make to your daughter. Annie told me."

"Why'd you test me?" He felt ridiculous having this serious conversation while she playfully twisted his underwear around his feet.

"I wasn't testing you. I thought it would be a way to get you to talk about your kid. Apparently," she turned on the water and closed the shower curtain, "I was wrong." She pulled the stop on the faucet and water blasted out of the shower head onto them. She hadn't been kidding. Despite what John perceived as a moment rife with sexual possibilities, Susan grabbed a wash cloth that was hanging, sniffed it and started to lather it with bar soap. She handed him the bar. "Use it directly on your skin, all manly like." She smiled and started scrubbing herself.

John felt stirring. "I'm gonna have a hard on the whole time."

"I can hang my wash cloth on it." She laughed. "So you're destitute because you've sent everything you make to your daughter. How does that do either of you any good?"

As John mulled the question, he became aware of his erection subsiding. He scrubbed himself while he answered. "Well, I guess it's going to hurt me someday, but I couldn't risk her going without. I just couldn't. Since I'm not in touch with her all the time, I don't know what she needs or wants. I don't know if it's hurt her to be separated from me. The money is insurance that she knows I think about her, care what happens, that..."

"That you love her." She finished the sentence. "But she's how old now?"

"Thirteen."

"What's her name, Darlene, right?"

"Yeah." He didn't remember telling her his daughter's name before. It baffled him.

She was amused. "Don't look so surprised. Annie told me her name."

"But you remembered it."

She looked at him with an ornery expression. "I already had designs on you."

"You did." The look of surprise remained on his face.

She laughed. "Well, to be honest. I'm not sure I did, but I was so impressed with the sacrifices you'd made. I don't think I'd ever known any one who'd done that. You're trying to be sure she doesn't have to come down to Poortown with us."

He nodded. "I guess so."

"Well, John Hamilton." She kissed him, and pressed against his soapy body, "you need to get out of poor town too. It doesn't suit you."

By the time Susan pulled up to Daryl's house to let John out, it was four thirty. "They are gonna be so pissed."

"They'll be thrilled that you're here. I'll pick you up at seven."

"Seven? Better make it ten."

"Ok. Be sure to have your trash bags at the ready."

John felt himself blush. "Susan, you'd let me move in with you? I feel like I'm taking advantage."

"My kitchen and bathroom have never been that clean. Who's taking advantage?"

He laughed. "Well, I've got my cell phone if you change your mind. I have some other things that could change our situation too."

She looked surprised. "Good things?"

"Yes."

"Ok. We'll talk later. I've got a mechanic to break up with."

"I'm sorry."

"Hey, John. Don't flatter yourself. We were both pretty casual about the whole thing."

"I'm pretty serious."

"You're very serious."

"Yeah, I am."

He kissed her, lingering. It made him feel good.

"See you in a bit." He hopped out of the car. Snow flurries had begun to fall. It looked bizarre against the green trees and grass and the few leaves that had changed.

He walked up to the front door. As it had been the last few times he had come there, the front door was open and the glass in the closed storm door was fogged from the heat inside. He opened the door. No one stood in the entryway this time. He stepped in, pulling his coat off as he entered. A number of people he didn't know filled the living room. Nearly all of them looked at him as he came in. He could see some of them searching their memories to decide whether they should know the latest guest to arrive.

A couch that was usually against the wall was gone and replaced by tables full of food.
Pat's spread was very nice, but John didn't see him anywhere. He suspected that he was somewhere with Cheryl.

He knew that Daryl would be holding court in the basement and headed directly through the living room to go there. Garlene was in the kitchen, in a circle with four other women. They were all talking and smoking. The cloud of smoke was thick and swirling from their hand movements and shifting as they laughed and yelled. John was stunned to realize that he hadn't smoked a cigarette for at least fifteen hours. The idea of being under a spell came to him again. If it was, he decided, bring it on. Garlene looked at him with an angry stare. John thought it amusing that the roiling smoke from the cigarettes made them look like a coven of witches without a caldron. He was disappointed in himself that the stereotype came to him so easily, but he admired what he considered the artistry of it, since Garlene had insinuated that Susan was mixed up in bad things. He amused himself with the idea that if Susan was a witch, Garlene had labeled her a black witch, when in reality, she was obviously a white one.

He looked away and made a bee's line for the basement stairs. As he descended, he heard Daryl yelling loudly, "Who's that creeping down my steps? Is it the black sheep come home to roost?" He was drunk.

John walked in smiling. Daryl held up a bottle of whiskey. "It is, it is my black crow." He looked at the bottle he waved around. "Black crow, meet Old Crow." John figured Daryl was wasted enough there wouldn't be serious discussion.

Leon was there. He looked fairly loaded, his narrow eyes narrower than usual. He gave John a look that wasn't too far off the one Garlene had given him. The other two posse members were there and one other guy John had seen around before. "Sorry I'm late Daryl."

"It's ok John." Daryl tried to look serious, but he just looked brain dead. "I know you're trying to sort," he made a pumping motion with his hand. "things out with Susan." He smiled, maniacally.

Leon burped and spoke. "You're banging Susan Baker? Man, I'd love to get a piece of that ass. I'd love to pump it right up her booty."

Daryl looked at Leon, and pushed him sloppily. "You are such a prevert Leon. I suppose you'd like to put it to Garlene too."

Leon looked dazed. He moved side to side, his equilibrium on the leading edge of impairment. "Well, yeah I would Daryl."

Daryl laughed like an evil scientist. "God you are such a fuuck."

Daryl stopped laughing suddenly and leaned forward. John jumped back thinking he was going to vomit. Daryl, Leon and the posse laughed uproariously. "He thought I was gonna spew on him." He leaned back, threatening to topple backward this time. "I'm, well," his face displayed distress. John still wondered if he was preparing to vomit, "I'm gonna lift."

Leon sniggered. "John thought he said "I'm gonna heft." One of the posse laughed, in a loud, short spurt.

Daryl looked at John with an expression that was a mix of knowing something he shouldn't and insanity. He stood up and unbuttoned the white dress shirt he was wearing. "You wanna lift first, John, buddy?" He sounded threatening.

"No. I'm gonna change my clothes and come down and try to catch up on the drinking."

"You don't have to change your clothes. You stink anyway." Daryl wasn't laughing. John knew that Daryl swerved between undying love and death threats to the people around him when he was as drunk and upset, as he was now. Daryl needed to get off the steroids.

"I'm gonna go change my clothes. I'll be right back." He bounded up the stairs and through the kitchen. He felt Garlene's stare burning his back. He half expected to see his trash bags in the snow. It was the second time in two days that he had to worry about it. He stepped into the bedroom. Everything was as he had left it. He rifled the bags and assembled a change of clothes. He found one pack of cigarettes. He slipped them in the shirt he intended to wear and headed into the bathroom. He could hear paper rustle in the kid's room. She had to have drawn enough of a new world that she could step through and away from all of it and all of them.

He looked in the mirror, messed with his hair and tried to straighten the collar on his shirt. He heard his cell phone ringing in the other room. His first thought was that it was Susan, and then he remembered that the reason he had got it in the first place was for Annie to be able to call if she had been assaulted by Billy again. He dashed into the room and dug the phone out of his coat pocket.

"Hello."

"Hi John." It was Annie. She sounded weak.

"Jesus, Annie. Are you ok?"

"He beat me up, John. He's passed out in the other room."

"Annie, I'll be there fast. Call the police."

She started to cry. "I'm afraid to."

John felt his throat constricting. "Annie you have got to call the cops. What if he wakes up again and he, he, you have got to call the cops. Call them now."

She wept quietly, pitifully. "I can't."

"Well, I will."

"Ok" she said.

"I'll be there as fast as I can."

He felt panic. He had supposed that Daryl would be available, or he'd be with Ralph and be able to go quickly, but it was not the case. He called Susan's apartment. A machine picked up. He left a quick message that he was going to Annie's as soon as he could get a ride, and that she had been hurt by Billy again. He asked that she call him as soon as she got the message.

He flashed down the steps and headed toward the basement. Daryl was lying on the bench, his arms prone on the weights that lie on his chest. He was afraid it was choking him, but then realized that he'd propped them against a chair that was sitting nearby. "Hey Daryl, I have to go. Annie's in trouble."

Daryl sat up. He had apparently forgotten he had the weights on his chest, and they flipped off of him, hitting the concrete floor with a loud bang and clang. "I'll drive ya." He could hardly sit up.

Garlene had heard the noise and came down quickly. "What the fuck are you guys doing down here?" She sounded more angry than he had heard her in a long time. She walked in with her hands on her hips, and saw her dazed husband sitting weaving on the bench and the others looking like ten year olds that had been doing something that they shouldn't and that mom had come in and caught them at it.

Daryl spoke with loads of spittle in his mouth. "Annie's in trouble and me and John have to go save her."

She looked at John, more gently. "Is it that fucker Billy?" John nodded.

"And we have to go save her." Daryl said, sounding like he had a half eaten sandwich in his mouth.

Garlene looked at Daryl, and then at John. She laughed, slapping her hand on her leg. "Right." She looked at the other men in the room and immediately decided that none of them were in any condition to drive John.

She took him by the hand and led him upstairs and into the living room. "Is there anyone who can drive my friend John to take care of a family emergency? He needs a ride right away."

"How far?" Garlene looked at the young man with purple hair and piercings all over his face who had answered. "You'll be back in plenty of time to finish eating what's left of the food, and drinking the last of what there is to drink Carl." She spit the words at him like venom.

He didn't look contrite. "Ok, ok. It's just that I didn't eat anything today."

Garlene lunged at him, and pushed him toward the door. "Just take him. I'll make sure you get fed and watered, you idiot."

She spoke to John without looking at him. "Go. Help that poor girl."

John was touched. "Thank you Garlene. I owe you big time."

"Just go and don't get yourself killed by the crazy piece of shit."

John followed the purple punk to his car. It was a rusting hulk of a Volkswagen Beetle. He wondered if the kid knew that the car was for hippies, not punks. They drove in silence. The kid seemed to be content with picturing the plates of food and drink that awaited him when he returned to Daryl and Garlene's. John realized a few moments after they left that he still needed to call the police. He took his cell phone out and dialed nine one one. The phone went to a busy signal immediately. He tried it again several times. The kid looked at him. John explained that he couldn't seem to get through to nine one one. The kid said that he didn't think that you could dial an emergency number on some cell phones. John wondered if that was true or if the phone wasn't working correctly. He felt helpless.

As the kid followed his instructions, John realized that he was directing him on the route he would take it he walked, a zigzag path that took him past Pat's place and past Ralph's. Ralph's car was at home. He wondered if he had left it there because he was drinking, or because he was still worried about the ghost. He doubted that he was home on Saturday. He always drank, often heavily on Saturday. John wouldn't want to be the corn syrup guys relying on him on Mondays.

279

Purple punk dropped John off without a word. He walked up the sidewalk. The snow had stopped, but it was cold. He spotted Annie standing in the hallway. His cell phone rang as he ran to her and she ran out the door. Her face was swollen on the right side. He was mortified to note that it was where he had imagined he would have hit Diane if he had given in to his base urge during their break up argument. She had blood on her ear, and on her chin. The flesh around her right eye was black and blue and swollen enough, that it looked like it might burst open. John was insane with anger. He clutched her and held her like he could subsume her into him by sheer force.

"Is he still up there?" She nodded. Tears were washing the blood to her chin. The phone was still ringing. It had to be Susan. He pulled the phone out, holding Annie firmly with one arm. "Hello, Susan?"

"Yeah. Are you there with Annie?"

"I just got here. Can you call the cops and get them over here? I couldn't get them on this fucking cell phone."

"Is she ok?"

"No, she's been beaten up. Have them bring an ambulance."

"Mother fucker. Ok. I'll call them and I'll be there in a little bit."

"Ok."

John hung up the cell phone. He examined Annie. Some of the blood, thinned from the tears, was drying on her chin. Fresh blood ran down, making a mini goatee of the brown and red caked fluid. "We have to get you in a warm place."

He turned her around toward the apartment. "I don't want to go back in there, John. If he wakes up and doesn't find me right away, he'll kill me when he does."

"We're just going back to the hall where you were. The police are on the way."

She hesitated. "Ok, but if he wakes up. We have to run."

John scoffed. "I'll kill him."

She whimpered. "Don't go near him. I don't want him to hurt you. He's nuts."

"To say the least" John thought.

The two stood in the hallway. Fifteen minutes passed, then twenty. After twenty five minutes, Susan's car pulled up. They walked out to the car. John carefully sat Annie in the back seat, laying her back and sitting next to her. He had removed his jacket and his shirt to clean her face. He had put his coat back on over his bare chest and continued using the shirt to pat her face with clean spots he made by folding and refolding it.

Susan was crying. "That low life bastard!"

John was concerned. "Did you get through to the cops?"

Susan's sadness quickly turned to anger. "Oh, yeah. I did. They are worthless. The dispatch said that they were busy and they'd send someone as soon as possible. I made it sound like he was killing her, and it didn't affect the bitch one bit. Christ, it was a woman and it didn't seem to bother her one way or the other that a woman was getting her brains knocked out."

While Susan was talking, a police car had pulled up behind them. The sirens weren't on. She pointed out the back window. "They finally bothered to stop by and visit."

John moved to get out of the car. "I'll talk to them." He was afraid of what Susan would say to them.

He walked toward the car with his hands in the air. He could see the police officers tense. The one on the passenger side got out quickly, his hand on his gun. "Officer, I'm a friend of the girl who was hurt."

The policeman responded with an order. "Put your hands on the trunk of the car there, and spread your legs wide."

John looked at him and knew this cop figured him for the assailant. John stepped backward slowly, his hands still in the air. "I'm a friend of hers officer. I'll go ahead and let you check me, though."

The officer barked back. "You aren't letting me do anything, godamn it. I'm telling you what you're doing, now spread 'em!"

John moved quickly and put his hands on the trunk and spread his legs. He shivered uncontrollably. The policeman moved toward him slowly, his hand still on his gun. Susan, who had been talking to Annie jumped out of the car and started yelling at the police officer.

"You fucking asshole. The guy who beat my friend up is in the apartment building, in her apartment. This is her friend. We're her friends. Where the fuck is the ambulance?"

The officer drew his gun, but kept it pointed down. He motioned with his free hand. "I want YOU to put your hands on the car too. NOW."

The officer who drove the car opened his door and jumped out. "Ok Minnow, slow down here." He looked at Susan with what looked like a leer. John would have been certain except he couldn't fathom someone ogling a woman at a moment like this.

Susan had seen the first policeman pull his gun out of his holster, and she had put her hands out from her sides. She refused to put them over her head. "My girlfriend is in the back seat here. The fucker who did it is upstairs in her apartment. *I* called you people." She motioned broadly toward the back of the car.

The policeman who drove the car had put his hand on his holster. As he approached Susan slowly, she backed away, continuing to motion to the backseat, insisting that he see Annie. He crept up and peaked in the car. He saw Annie crying, her battered face more swollen now than when John had arrived. He spoke gently. "Are they correct ma'am? Are you the complainant?"

Annie looked at him, confused. "He's in the apartment. Is that what you mean?"

The policeman looked at John, and Susan and apparently made a decision that they were telling the truth. "Minnow, I think she's telling the truth. We need to call for an ambul…"

His remark was cut short by a bellow from the doorway of the apartment building. Billy had awakened and was charging around looking for Annie. He wore a pair of questionable looking jockey briefs. . One of his testicles hung out. He had a silver object in his hand.

Both policemen's attention was jerked toward the apartment building door. The weapons were now trained on Billy. The officer who had driven yelled, "Police! Drop the weapon and hit the ground now!"

Billy was slow to realize that not only had he found Annie but her friends and two nervous policemen. He was over six foot tall, and solid. He lumbered forward a few steps. The policeman known as Minnow, who was much closer to the half naked man screamed this time. "Drop the weapon NOW, and hit the ground, spread eagle. NOW, NOW, NOW, NOW."

He kept yelling the command. It looked like the sound waves of the policeman's blasting voice were slowing Billy down. It didn't look, from Billy's contorted face, that it had sunk in that these were two armed policemen, with their weapons pointed at him, the hammers cocked. John had heard the clicks.

"DROP IT." The second policeman now started yelling his command.

Billy spotted Annie in the back seat of the car. He bolted toward her. As soon as

Billy passed him, Minnow holstered his gun and tackled Billy. A spoon flew out of the enraged boyfriend's hand. It had looked to all of them, like a knife or a small caliber gun. The officer wrestled with Billy. The second policeman called in back up and jumped on top of Billy. Between the two uniforms, they were able to restrain him and cuff his hands and shackle his legs together. After he was bound, chest down on the ground, he started saying that he was just trying to check his girlfriend, that she was hurt by these strangers. The cop who drove the car checked Annie, called an ambulance and had her explain what had happened.

When Susan started complaining, asking why it had taken so long for them to get there, he looked at her with indifference. He only seemed interested when he stared at her chest. "Look lady, domestic calls are just baby sitting gigs. There's a lot more going on than this kind of crap."

Susan intended to explain that she had told the dispatcher that Annie was being seriously injured and they needed to get there right away, but she lost her patience with his staring and got back in the car to check on Annie. One officer crouched at the open car door, talking to the battered woman and John sat in the front watching her. Susan got in on the driver's side and sat down. She spoke to John loud enough that she could be sure the policeman heard her. "Well, if Billy hadn't done us the favor of acting like the nut he is, we would have been going downtown to explain why we beat Annie up."

The officer stopped his questioning long enough to give her a cold stare. The ambulance arrived, and paramedics rushed over, helped her to the vehicle and left for the hospital

after a cursory examination. The lead medic explained that while they didn't think her injuries were serious, they wanted to x-ray and MRI her for concussions, internal bleeding, fractures and other things that they would not find with a visual
examination.

Susan volunteered to give a statement, and the officers essentially told her that it wasn't worth the trouble, that Annie would press charges, then drop them and they'd be left holding the bag. They left but not before the second cop, the slow one, as John thought of him, leered at Susan one more time.

Susan looked at John. "So if they were cops in the nice part of town, they'd be licking our shoes in between every sentence."

John looked at her, thrilled that Susan was, the term occurred to him for the first time in a long time, a pistol.

"So let's follow the ambulance!" She hollered. They jumped in the car, Susan looked at John and they both said. "Shirt!" John got back out of the car, and ran up to Annie's apartment. The door was wide open.

There was a small boy standing near the entry. "Door's open."

John smiled. "Thanks, kid."

He entered the apartment quietly, as if he'd disturb something or someone if he moved quickly. Images of he and Annie in different places and moments in the rooms flashed in his mind's eye. He felt a pleasant nostalgia. He opened the closet in her bedroom and was surprised to be confronted with one of the few nice shirts he ever owned. Annie had bought it for him. She still had it. Was it a souvenir? Was it an oversight? He couldn't remember if he had packed up or she had. He supposed she had and kept the shirt for whatever reason she had. He pulled it on, tucked it in and buttoned it. He felt more civilized. After he fetched Annie's purse, with the apartment keys, he locked the door and pulled it shut. Susan and John easily caught up with and tailed the ambulance all the way to the hospital. No one yielded for ambulances any more.

They parked in the free parking in the emergency area and ran in at the point when they were putting Annie through the gauntlet of paperwork. Because she had no insurance, she sat swollen and aching for over an hour while they assembled the proper forms. Finally, after she had placed her signature on the last form, they sat in the waiting room for another three hours as it filled with coughing, moaning, stinking children, adults and senior citizens. Susan was going to complain about the delay, but she and John, had overheard discussions between police and emergency crews about having to divert some patients to another hospital because they were understaffed and over whelmed. They were, in the strange world they lived in, lucky because Annie had been hurt earlier than others.

John had been amazed that he could resist smoking for so many hours and was now consciously testing the limits of his ability to leave the cigarettes in his last pack. With Susan around, it seemed effortless.

They had avoided telling Annie about the depth of their new relationship and had been able to stifle their inclinations to touch each other, so she would not trouble her mind with this new thing. After she went back into the treatment area, they were relieved. They went to an office that was closed, held hands and kissed, consoling each other that Annie was going to be ok.

They walked outside knowing that they would not be able to see Annie for another hour or two. It would be mid-evening, eight or nine o'clock by then. "So when are we going to tell her about us?"

"I think we should tell her as soon as possible. Tomorrow, if we can. We should probably stay with her and make sure she's gonna be alright." John was thinking ahead over the next few days, and wondering, hoping that Billy would be in jail, but doubting that would happen. It meant another and hopefully final run in with him Monday or Tuesday. He had already decided that he would take Monday off, no longer caring if he had his old job. "I'm gonna stay with her tomorrow and Monday during the day, in case 'ol Billy gets out and comes straight back.

Susan thought for a moment. "Yeah, I'll cover too."

John didn't like that. "I'm worried that we'll make a mistake and spill the beans about us."

She considered it. "We'll tell her about us tomorrow. She needs to get over this fast."

"I want her to know that you and I together mean that I'll be around more to help."

"Can you do that?"

"I can't leave her alone."

Susan smiled. "The white knight speaks."

John blushed. "Yeah, right."

Just as they had supposed, at around eight thirty, a doctor came out looking for them. "She's going to be ok. No fractures or bleeding, just nasty cuts and bruises that should heal up in a normal span of time. We gave her a shot that should reduce the swelling. We'll give her a sheet telling her how to take care of the injuries, and she should see her family physician as soon as possible."

Susan spoke up. "She's going to need pain pills. She can't afford a prescription."

The doctor looked at her suspiciously. "I don't really have anything I can give her to take home."

Susan broke in. "You know she's going to be miserable. Can't you make an exception?"

The doctor looked at the soda machine intently, like it would dispense the correct answer. "I'm sorry to say, I can't give her anything to take home, but because we've checked her and she's in one piece, I should be able to give her a sedative before we release her. It'll help her sleep through the night tonight." He looked at Susan's breasts in what he thought was a surreptitious glance.

"Can't you spare a few pills for her too." The doctor had focused on papers he had in his hand. "I'll see what I can do." He bolted out of the room. When they rolled Annie out in a wheel chair, she had her discharge paperwork along with a small bottle of pills, and a glazed look on her face, which told them that the doctor had administered the shot he had promised.

Susan spun toward John, lifting her foot and curtseying. "These babies pay off sometimes." She motioned to her breasts like they were a new appliance being displayed on a game show.

They put her in the front where they could adjust the seat into a reclining position, and pulled away at a little after 10 PM. As they drove, John asked Susan if they should pick up his clothes at Daryl's. "Sure, we'll do that. Let's stop at Pat's too and see if he'll sell a twelve pack to us."

John nodded. "He will. He never turns down a sale."

Snow showers started again. The flakes were bigger and wet. It required windshield wipers to keep the view clear. They drove silently, listening to Annie's relaxed breathing. Occasionally, her nose, which was still a little swollen, whistled as she breathed in. They both laughed when it whistled a fairly mournful little combination of tones. They drove past Ralph's house. John noticed that the car was on, idling. He was amazed that Ralph had stayed sober enough he felt he could drive. When they arrived at Pat's there were still large numbers of patrons there. Susan waited in the car with Annie while he went in and bought the beer from Paul. He gave John the beer for nothing, saying he had already heard about the rescue of Annie. John thought, "well these people may be addled, but gossip runs through here faster than the speed of light". As he exited, he realized that Ralph hadn't arrived yet. He turned back to Pat. "Hey did Ralph come in today?" He wanted to touch base with him.

Paul shook his head. "Oh, yeah. He was here all right. He took off drunk as a skunk around nine, give or take"

"Thanks," he waved goodbye.

He looked at Annie, who was covered up and had her head resting comfortably on a hospital pillow. She was sound asleep. He whispered to Susan as he settled in. "Can we stop by Ralph's for a minute?"

Susan frowned. "Ok, if we have to."

"I just need to catch him up."

Susan was the first person who seemed to be able to do a complete, uninterrupted U-turn on the narrow street in front of the bar and he was impressed. A man in a trench coat like the one he had seen before, flashed into his field of vision as they swung around. As the lights swept his back, the man turned his head toward them. John was getting tired of seeing Bob in every shadowy figure that wore a trench coat in the neighborhood. He would get together with Pat and find out what had happened to the guy, one way or the other. Maybe that would exorcise him from his consciousness, because, he was, once again, sure that he stared into the face of Bob as the car whipped around and past. Bob had a creepy look on his blanched face.

They drove through what was fast becoming a blinding snow storm. "We need to make this fast John. We need to get Annie home."

"It'll be a minute, two, max." They drove, slowing as John told her that they were getting close. As they pulled up to the house, John could see that the car was still running, which was odd. John noticed that the trunk was partially open. He could see something sticking out of the trunk. He figured it was something Ralph planned to sell and this was the beginning of turning his car into a rolling sales floor. They stopped near the car. John squinted. He couldn't believe that he saw legs sticking out of the trunk. The snow was swirling around the car and everything in sight, as if it were trying desperately to drape it all in a pure, clean white blanket.

"Oh my God!" Susan had figured out what was sticking out of the trunk.

John jumped out of the car. He recognized the shoes. They were Ralph's. He ran up to the idling car. He raised the trunk lid and the strong smell of exhaust fumes rolled out, nearly knocking him over. It was sweet smelling, like there was something in the lining of the trunk that added to, or changed the usual oily smell into a macabre perfume. He had smelled hints of it the two times he was in the car. He tried to push the trunk lid all the way up, but it would not stay in the open position. He held it open with his head and looked inside. The interior trunk light blinked on and off as he struggled to keep the lid above the bulb's trigger position. He noticed a broken dowel rod around four foot long on the right. It was probably what Ralph had tried to use to keep the trunk lid open. Ralph's hat was still on his head, even though he had fallen head first into the trunk. "That hat has got to be glued on." He laughed to himself. The laugh squeezed John's eyes partially shut and tears started to pour out. A pungent smell of alcohol now assaulted him. Paul had said that Ralph was very drunk. He must have come out to run the car, following old man Emery's pattern of keeping it in shape. He was going to put something in or take something out of trunk and passed out when he leaned in. The dowel broke and the lid came down. The fumes from the leak did the rest.

He looked at his face. His eyes were closed, and he had a slightly aggravated look. John noted that there was snow piling up on Ralph's shoes. John unbuttoned Ralph's coat and felt his chest. He couldn't discern breathing. He moved closer to Ralph's face. It was gray. He put his hand on his neck at the carotid artery. There was nothing. He didn't feel cold but John knew he was dead and had been dead long enough, nothing would bring him back.

He lowered the lid gently and walked to the driver's side of Susan's car. She rolled down the window. "Dead." She whispered.

John nodded. His throat was tightening from the fumes and the emotions. "I'll stay here and wait for the police. It's gonna be a long night. You go ahead with Annie. I'll call when it's over."

Susan leaned out the window, a tear rolled down her cheek. She kissed him, and sat back in, and rolled up the window. John walked up to the door at the front and informed Mrs. Weddington that she needed to call the police right away, that Ralph was dead in his car. Her face froze in fear. "The ghost got him!" Ralph must have mentioned the car's history to his landlady.

She turned to make the call, then turned back again. Tears drenched her cheeks. "The ghost wanted company." She turned again and ran off to the phone. John returned to the car. He got in and turned it off. He left the keys in the ignition. He got out, walking slowly and lifted the lid on the trunk again. He took a crow bar he noticed in the back near the tire well where the spare tire was stored. He realized he was disrupting what could be construed a crime scene, putting his fingerprints all over the evidence, but he didn't care. He felt he would be numb to any slings and arrows the half-baked cops might throw. He used the crowbar to jam the trunk open. The little bulb that lit the trunk hung loose from the back of the lid. It shown on Ralph's face.

His flask had slipped out of his back pocket, and sat perched on his lower back. John picked it up, and looked at the inscription, half certain that it would be a meaningless name and proverb, figuring Ralph had bought the flask and lighter at a pawn shop, but he was wrong. The matching items had indeed been a gift to Ralph, from, of all people, his mother. He wondered what sort of mother would give a son a liquor flask and lighter. The blurry image from the photo on Ralph's chest of drawers of Ralph as a child, fed into John's mind. He imagined Ralph was running in dirty shorts with the same familiar gate John had seen many times. He didn't look much different than he did as an adult, barring the constant five o'clock shadow and the pock marked skin. There was a small scar on his chin that he'd told John he got when he'd decided to jump into a bush to hide during a game, and a bramble had torn his soft young skin wide open. He told John that the cut had not hurt much, so he stayed hidden to see if he could win the game of hide and seek while blood had poured all over his shirt, pants and hands. He did win, and got the added bonus of freaking everyone out when he leaped out of the foliage, a dripping bloody mess. He also had laughed, mentioning that when his father had seen his blood stained clothes, he whipped him to within an inch of his life calling him a retard. Ralph laughed that by the time his dad was done with him, there were more blood stains on his clothes and Ralph remembered being grateful that his dad hadn't beaten him further as punishment for daring to bleed even more on his precious clothes. The child John saw in the picture upstairs had a burr hair cut, foreshadowing his hairless pate as an adult, and he imagined the child crying every time he was forced to go to the barber to be subjected to the bright silver tools of the trade. He saw the child, Ralph running again, alone, smiling and laughing, nearly falling over and curling up to allow the sheer joy of play to wrap around him, tickle him and tell him how fast and clever he was, how much fun it all was being with him at that moment.

John remembered the two of them sitting a few years ago, sober because they were very broke, at a bus stop, heading to what Ralph had heard was an all night party where there would be plenty of free booze.

They had sat on the bench waiting, happy they had the two dollars for the fare there and back the next day. They had been quieter than usual, half hung over, no doubt, and full of anticipation of what and how much would greet them at this party. A drug dealer was supposedly throwing it, so the odds were very good what they heard wasn't just the usual bullshit rumors that spread around now and then.

John had quietly asked Ralph if he felt lucky. He was referring to the possibility of scoring with one of the impaired women that usually populated these sorts of gatherings. It had been a brave question on John's part because it was definitely outside the subjects "allowed" by Ralph. He looked at John, a world weary smile on his face, "I got the fifty cents. I'm pretty lucky." The idea he might get a woman wasn't on Ralph's radar, the idea that two quarters in his pocket was the best luck Ralph could conjure for himself made John sad. He was too tired that day to sort out why, but he could understand now, that the boy he pictured had hope in all and everything, while the man he had become felt blessed because his alcohol ravaged body would be assuaged again courtesy of a bus fare and a drug dealer.

John angled the flask in the weak light so he could make out the inscription. It said, "To Ralph, with Love, Mom, "New Wine Must Be Put Into New Bottles." He couldn't tell if she was joking or was serious, but no matter what he guessed, he was sure that something had fired wrong in the woman's brain.

John looked at Ralph's face. There was none of the nervous energy, none of the jokes, none of the dysfunction. The poor man had been trapped by a decrepit car. Poor slow women and men were easy targets for machines, cruelty, drugs, disease, and their quick witted accomplices. The ghost of Mrs. Emery rescued Ralph from the horrid life he lived, but had not only elevated the horror to another dimension, it extended back to the world where John stood looking at Ralph's lifeless body, snow flying madly, still hopelessly trying to cover and cool the sharp edges and gritty air that were just a few of the subtler enemies of the poor slow people. The cold snow blew up the back of his thin ragged jacket and goose pimples rose on John's warm tingling skin. The wind shifted and the angle at which the snow fell changed sharply. It felt like the world was tipping off its axis. John steadied himself.

He put the flask back where he'd found it, put his hand on Ralph's shoe and let it remain there for a while. He had wanted to put a sympathetic hand on his chest or shoulder while he waited for the police but Ralph's coarse life led to a coarse embarrassing death and he would be denied dignity. He was surprised to realize that it looked like there was a haze behind the snowflakes that looked as if it were made of gold

293

dust. There was gray and gold to choose from again. He knew he'd be able to get his daughter good Christmas gifts and felt pride swell in him. He would talk to Susan and together they might conjure whatever good they could in the sunlight of long days pushing the grays into corners nearby. He couldn't believe it kept coming up in his head but he wasn't sure that there was enough room in the bar's second floor living quarters for the guilt he would feel selling alcohol to people like Ralph. He was confused when he realized he was sad that he would not be able to stand on the other side of the bar and give Ralph the occasional beer "on the house." He pictured the thin dark tinted plastic membranes Pat had used to cover the windows while the place was unoccupied. He remembered the three sheets that had come loose and peeled away into a dark tangle on the floor and imagined broken men standing in their midst, men who had lived there, staring out the windows with John, seeing he didn't know what, eyes still not adjusted to the new found light. He took the last pack of cigarettes from his coat pocket and put them beside Ralph. If there was a God, He wouldn't care if Ralph smoked, and if there wasn't, he'd still leave them with Ralph. He didn't want them any more. They slowed him down.

www.ingramcontent.com/pod-product-compliance
Lightning Source LLC
Chambersburg PA
CBHW071301170626
46809CB00001B/316